"Tell me, Nikki, what is it about me they want you to find out?"

His hand reached out and circled her long braid, but instead of pulling it, he slid the length through his closed palm.

Nikki watched as he started to loosen her hair from its barrette. She thought she should say something to stop him, but his expression fascinated her. There was a reverence in the way he handled each thick strand as he unwound the length of it.

"Well?"

"They want to know whether you're safe," she breathed out as he reached the halfway point of her braid. His hands stopped, but only for a moment. He had loosened her hair with the quickness of someone who had done it often.

"Am I?" Rick asked. "Safe?"

He was a master manipulator. He knew the correct question was what was he supposed to be safe *for,* what they were afraid he would do. Instead, he chose to make it personal, using her words against her. Just as they had suspected all along, he wasn't a man who played by the rules. And it seemed as if he didn't care whether they found out.

"No," she whispered as he fanned her hair between his fingers. "You're not safe."

GENNITA LOW

FACING FEAR

AVON BOOKS
An Imprint of HarperCollinsPublishers

This is a work of fiction. Names, characters, places, and incidents are products of the author's imagination or are used fictitiously and are not to be construed as real. Any resemblance to actual events, locales, organizations, or persons, living or dead, is entirely coincidental.

HarperCollins*Publishers*
77-85 Fulham Palace Road
Hammersmith
London W6 8JB

Copyright © 2004 by Jenny Low

ISBN: 0 00 773959 1
www.avonromance.com

This edition published 2005
First Avon Books paperback printing: March 2004

Avon Trademark Reg. U.S. Pat. Off. and in Other Countries, Marca Registrada, Hecho en U.S.A.
HarperCollins® is a registered trademark of HarperCollins Publishers Inc.

Printed and bound in Great Britain by Clays Ltd, St Ives plc

To Mother and Father,
my Stash, who gave me Hard Lessons,
and Mike, my Ranger Buddy, who taught me hard work
Yun Tzi Tcho, Sing Poon Si

———————————————

Acknowledgments

Special thanks to Patti O'Shea, my writing partner; Melissa Copeland, the sidekick who looked between the lines; the sea mammals who helped with special hands-on research; Lynda Mikulski, whose assurances were much needed; Erika Tsang, my helpful editor; and Elizabeth Trupin-Pulli, my wonderful one-of-a-kind agent.

And always, to the Delphi TDD ladies, the best reading BSHes, whose encouragement gave me so much joy— Maria Hammon, Miriam "Mirmie" Caraway, Sandy "the Philosopher" Still, Karen King, Theresa Monsey, Angela Swanson, Shelly Hawthorne, and Teena Weena Smith.

I also want to thank my sister Debbie Low for her website expertise and wonderful creativity.

Much thanks to those who gave me so much research information over the phone. For more information on TIARA, please check http://usmilitary.about.com/library/glossary/t/bldef06205.htm.

Creative license: Some departments and locations have been grouped together or moved closer for plot convenience.

CIA DEPUTY DIRECTOR ARRESTED

Washington, D.C.—Veteran CIA counterintelligence Deputy Director David Philip Gorman was arrested Saturday and charged with committing espionage by selling highly classified national security information and technology secrets, Attorney General John Patrick, CIA Counterintelligence Chief Marcus Landow, and United States Attorney Caroline Starr announced today. Gorman was arrested at sea while negotiating a deal with international arms dealers. His conversation was caught on tape by a TIARA (Tactical Intelligence and Related Activities) operative who worked under him. A search of Gorman's apartment revealed evidence of highly classified information that had been copied.

Chief Landow expressed outrage and sorrow. He said the charges, if proven true, represented "a serious violation of national security, of which the extent of the damage will reverberate for years." In a criminal complaint filed in federal court in Alexandria, Virginia, Gorman was charged with espionage and conspiracy to commit espionage, violations that could carry, under certain circumstances, the death penalty.

A detailed affidavit revealed that Gorman compromised the lives of numerous sources of the U.S. Intelligence Community, dozens of highly classified "Top Secret" and "Secret Codeword" U.S. documents, and covert and field operations of immense value and importance. "Task Force Two, TIARA's elite counterintelligence unit under Gorman, is now tainted and needs to be reevaluated," Landow said. "A special Homeland Security Investigative Committee will be formed to assess the damage and to recommend changes." A report of the findings, Landow assured, will be shared with the Intelligence Committees in Congress.

U.S. Attorney Starr added that "the Department of Justice will devote all its resources to ensure that all persons and parties who will betray their country and the people of the United States are prosecuted and severely punished. I want to express my deep appreciation for the outstanding assistance provided by Internal Investigations, the Internal Security Section of the Criminal Division of the Department of Justice."

The damage is believed to be exceptionally grave. Gorman's alleged criminal activities are believed to trace back at least a dozen years.

Chapter One

A martini at lunch. Preferably alone. Classified files on everyone. Tabs on women he slept with. Dark navy business suit and black tie. A briefcase of papers. And the careful suspicion of everyone working under him.

Ricardo Harden had become what he hated most in life—A bureaucrat. Worse, a bureaucrat who followed the rules, shoved all the right papers, dotted his *i*'s and crossed his *t*'s. He was getting gray from just the drabness of his existence, and if he would just take that final step, he'd stop jogging five miles every other morning and let his body turn into what he was in real life.

And now, despite walking the straight and narrow line of red tape, he had become the object of suspicion. Again. Internal Investigations, the self-governing arm of covert activities in the government, had all but officially put him in the crosshairs. It wasn't stated in the front page article in today's newspaper, but he could read between the lines.

Rick stepped out of the shower, wiped the excess water from his wet body, and threw the towel into the hamper. He strode nude out of the bathroom, picking up the newspaper and small plastic bag on the antique stand. His body ached happily because he had forced another three miles on it this morning. His legs, toned from years of running, felt bulkier and heavier as each group of muscles came into play when he climbed the small staircase that led into his bedroom in the tri-level apartment.

There were two rooms up the short flight of steps. One was the master bedroom. The other was his office, which was always locked. And as he had every day in his life for the past ten years, Rick checked his office door, making sure nothing was touched. Satisfied that the safeguards were still there, untampered with, he turned to his room.

It was still silken dark inside, the other occupant in his bed fast asleep. He walked over to the window and drew the shades open, letting in the morning light. His companion from the night before frowned and turned away from the source, giving him a view of her naked back.

Rick stood over the bed and watched her for a long moment. He must have been in a strange mood last night. He hadn't had sex four times in a night in Lord knew how many years, but he had been hard all night. Hard and wanting, and needing something. His companion had loved it, but he felt empty. Because what he was looking for didn't come with sex.

He blamed it on work. His lips twisted. Well, not work exactly, since he couldn't work with the Big Scandal getting bigger every day. David Gorman, the deputy director of Task Force Two, had been caught selling classified information to the enemy and Rick knew it wouldn't be long before Internal Investigations came after him. He was Gorman's operations chief after all, though no one would have ever guessed that Gorman was his enemy, that he had been living a lie the past ten years.

Last night Rick had gone out to relax, to celebrate having an old enemy finally out of his hair, and who did he spy sitting in the best seats of the opera house but reminders of what a failure he had been. Steve McMillan and Cameron Candeloro, the two heroes of the department, the ones who had taken down Gorman. Rick couldn't help but feel a twinge of envy at the happiness radiating from the two men sitting down with their female companions, so satisfied with life and what it had to offer.

Of course, they had to be attending an opera called *Turandot*, about a cold-hearted princess who schemed to put her men to death. The happy ending was so obviously manufactured that Rick didn't even bother to consider it part of the story. In true life, he knew, Princess Turandot wouldn't have succumbed to love. She would happily send that suitor to his death for being so stupid and generous with his heart.

But he saw Steve McMillan caressing Marlena Maxwell's back as they walked off in the lobby, saw the way she smiled up at him when he pressed a kiss on her forehead. He saw how Cameron danced attendance on his girlfriend. Rick had smiled bitterly. What love could do to a man.

Something dark and needy had risen inside him then. Something forbidden. He had crushed it down with ruthless practice, but knew he needed to give it an outlet.

The pale flesh of the woman on his bed caught his attention. Sex. Hard, calculating sex. The kind that was all taking and not giving.

He had taken his companion here to his place and given in to that part of him that was always locked up. She hadn't protested, and he would have kept going all night long if he hadn't run out of condoms. No, he was more careful than that. Animal desire was one thing. Getting carried away was another. And he never, ever, got carried away. Not anymore.

He sat down on the bed, contemplating whether to wake his sleeping companion. He shrugged, then slid a hand down her bare back, under the covers, and between her legs. She was still sticky wet from the night before.

She moaned and turned around, squinting against the morning light. "Richard?" she murmured sleepily, then smiled. Rick knew she thought it was something to do with her, this sudden insatiable side of him. "Hmm, no more condoms, remember? I can't believe you're ready again."

He didn't bother to tell her that it wasn't she, that after this, he probably wouldn't ask her out again. She knew his reputation when they had started down this road—they all did. To the women, he was Dick Hard-On, and no one could get more from him than sex.

"I bought a new box on the way back from jogging," he said, tossing the plastic bag on the pillow next to her. He spread her legs apart, moving his fingers skillfully, letting her know it was time to wake up, whether she wanted to or not. One thing he had never relinquished from his past training was this—sex on demand. He easily found her weakness— deep inside her—and had her moaning in seconds.

Hard, punishing sex. He closed his eyes and let the sexual animal in him take over. She quivered under him, her sensual urging turning into screams, and then low, breathless moans. His bedsheets turned damp as she helplessly gave him total control of her body. He made sure she lost consciousness at least twice from prolonged pleasure. He was good at that.

It gave him satisfaction that he was in control of the situation during sex, that she couldn't fight him, even if she wanted to. That she didn't, couldn't, wouldn't even think of doing anything while he was doing this to her. That she didn't, couldn't, wouldn't dream of killing him, if that was part of her seduction plans. Because he was doing something to her that no woman could resist. He was giving her total, mind-blowing sexual satisfaction.

She lay there, eyes closed, her breath coming out in hiccups, but he was far from finished. He still wanted. He still needed. And if it took all weekend to stamp out the emptiness inside, he would keep her here in his bedroom. That was why he had bought the biggest box of condoms he had ever seen. Just in case.

She moaned but didn't protest when he slipped a small metal ball inside her, taking a moment to find the spot. He pulled on the attached cord and turned the switch on. Her prone body came alive, and she jerked up with a little scream.

Rick pushed her down as he mounted her. He reached for the box of condoms. The woman scratched his chest violently as she climaxed. He ignored the pain, turning the switch to high. She stopped scratching, lost in her own swirling world. Then, and only then, did Rick thrust into her body to ride the waves. Because he was sure she was out of it, and not a danger to him. His breathing came faster. He moved in tandem with the hum in the room, but was still unable to truly let go.

A whole weekend. Maybe he would tire himself out, and when he returned to work on Monday, he would be himself again.

Dick Hard-On. Sans heart. Sans conscience. And as all his men said behind his back, a total prick.

He escorted her to the elevator on Sunday night. She hadn't brought any of her work clothes and had to leave him. He didn't mind. She was leaving in good spirits, and he was in a generous enough mood not to spoil it with his own dark one. He watched as she sashayed before him, stopping in front of the lift. His silent sigh was self-directed. She was curvy and sexy, and could actually hold an intelligent conversation. Plus she was good in bed. But she wasn't the one either.

The elevator door opened, and there were three occupants inside. Out of habit he checked them out, even as his companion turned and threw her arms around his neck for a goodbye kiss.

"Call me," she murmured in his ear, her voice huskier than normal. "Soon."

He allowed a quirk on his lips. Still looking straight into the lift, he lied, "Yes."

He frowned a little as the door closed with a quiet swish. Two tall men and a short woman he couldn't see standing behind them. At least, until they parted a little to make room for the new arrival. Before the door slid shut, he thought he had seen a ghost peering back at him with gleaming dark eyes.

Washington, D.C., Monday morning
TIARA Task Force Two, Office of Operations Chief

Rick reread the new orders that had come down for TIARA. There was going to be a major revamp of the department. He had expected that. With the Gorman scandal, and without a department director, change at TIARA was imminent. He reread the article from the day's paper and compared the information in his memo and the piece. At least they had one thing in common: Gorman, former deputy director of Tactical Intelligence and Related Activities, was being charged for expanding on the meaning of "related activities" in the most traitorous way.

Rick swallowed down a harsh smile. All these years under the man who had given him a permanent black mark in his records, all this time being held back from any worthwhile promotion because the man's recommendations were always accompanied by this one fatal black mark, and for what? Gorman's downfall only emphasized how far Rick had fallen. He had been so beaten into the bureaucratic mold of conforming to rules and regulations that he had missed the most important thing happening under his nose. That Gorman had deliberately chosen men like him to work in Task Force Two was a bitter pill to swallow.

But swallow he must. He already had to apologize twice to people he didn't even like. Steve McMillan and Marlena Maxwell. He owed them that at least, for not being the team leader he should have been to his men, allowing his personal past to cloud his judgment. Then there was Admiral Jack Madison, Steve's SEAL commander. Rick had to formally apologize for all the leaks that came from TIARA, costing the admiral the lives of his men during covert activities. The admiral depended on TIARA for Intel before instructing his highly covert teams into action, but there was enough evidence of an inside mole that caused the admiral to transfer one of his men inside. No one had suspected that TIARA's own director would turn out to be the rat that sold information to the enemy.

Rick tossed aside the newspaper article. Nothing else had been mentioned, except that the Department of Justice promised an internal overhaul. That one line and this morning's memo cemented his suspicions that Internal Investigations would be after him next.

Why hadn't he seen this coming? There was a SEAL imbedded in his team all that time. Gorman hadn't protested. Rick should have known it was something more important than petty interdepartmental spying. Now he felt responsible, for being so blind to everything but following paperwork and rules. He hadn't thought that his shortsightedness would be a danger to anyone.

"Sir? Bad news, huh?"

Rick looked up, and saw Cameron Candeloro, one of the men directly under him in Task Force Two. "What do you expect, Agent Candeloro? A big party celebrating the fact that TIARA is actually one big flea market for information dealers outside?"

Cam failed to wipe the beginning of a grin. Rick stared at him until the younger man pretended to look serious again. Cam would never make it any higher in his field; he didn't have an ambitious bone in his body.

"Do you find that funny, Agent Candeloro?" Rick asked.

"Yes, sir. I mean, not what happened to our department, sir, but the flea market comment was good."

Rick cocked a brow. "Are you standing here for the rest of the day for some witty repartee or do you have something job-related to do?" ·

"Sir, all our cases are suspended until further notice. I thought maybe the new memo would tell us who the new department director is, and when we can resume our open cases."

There weren't any open cases until every one of them was reviewed. And there wasn't any new department director coming. But Rick didn't have to let anyone know that. Task Force Two was in more trouble than a mere suspension of operations. "Have you finished the report for your last assignment with Agent McMillan before he retransferred?"

It was Cam's body wire that had recorded the evidence needed to charge Gorman. It might be the only thing that would save Task Force Two and, more importantly, Rick's ass.

"Not yet, sir."

"How hard is it to write a report, Agent Candeloro?" Rick looked at Cam sharply. "I expect it on my desk by tomorrow morning."

"Yes, sir."

"Cam." Rick paused until he had the man's fullest attention, and added softly, "Write it like your job depends on it."

He stared thoughtfully at the closed door after Cam left. He hoped Cam realized how important the report was going to be. He had been in this business for a long time. A major scandal like Gorman's selling Intel wasn't going to fade away quickly, and the Department of Justice certainly wasn't going to take all the blame. Rick knew the bureaucratic score. First came the red tape, with paperwork shoving from one department to another, finger-pointing one another as the culprit. Then heads would roll.

The memo made it clear to him that Task Force Two was going to be the first target. After all, it was the tool that Gorman used for a lot of his activities, so all those under him were now prime suspects. Of course, it didn't directly say so, but Rick was an expert in B.S.—bureaucratic shit—and he could read between the lines.

He rubbed the back of his neck, suddenly tired. It didn't take a genius to know who the number one prime suspect would be. Him.

His demotion a long time ago had forced him to swallow a lot of his pride. So when he was shifted from desk duty to being operations chief of Task Force Two as Gorman's hand-picked recommendation, he had taken it without batting an eyelash. Better the devil than total banishment in hell, he had thought then.

So it was time to pay the piper. He wondered what he would look like, and how high the price this time.

Nikki took down the wind chime she had hung on her balcony. The management said there had been complaints about it making a lot of noise. She stood there, observing the sight and sounds of morning traffic as everyone in the neighborhood went about his business.

Noise. They didn't know what real noise was. The wind chime was the wind talking. A quiet melody spread out to bring balance to its surroundings. Even on a blustery day, the noisy chime was what was called the *chuung,* the center, and it took years of listening to catch the perfect pitch underneath the din. That was the center. The peace and harmony sought by many.

She held the wind chime out for a moment, wishing she was back home where there were trees and flowers, wind chimes and fountains. She didn't like her small apartment with its square rooms and tiny windows. It reminded her of things she would rather forget.

It had been years since she was last in Washington, D.C., the old center in her life. She looked out from the balcony, watching the other buildings in the way. Ironic that she was here, completing a circle, but wasn't that expected?

"Beware the center," she said out loud in Chinese, remembering the three prophecies given by her grandmother a long time ago. She didn't heed those warnings until it was too late.

She understood why her agency came and asked her to do this contract for them. She hadn't wanted it. She had retired after serving a productive five years. Wasn't that enough? But she owed them this one last favor. They had saved her from hell when no one would have given her a second thought.

Besides, the money they offered was generous, and she would finally get what she wanted—an apology from the Department of Justice for what they had done to her. All she had to do was this one job, and if she succeeded, it would show those who had forgotten about her what an asset they had lost when they had abandoned her.

Nikki wasn't exactly bitter. It was the nature of her former profession—an asset that no longer held any value was what her kind called a damaged wing. Why use up manpower and man-hours to save what was no longer useful? No, that part she understood. The bitterness came later, after she had discovered that her identity was wiped out *before* she had been taken prisoner. Which meant that she had been sent in with someone knowing full well that she was a sacrifice. The need to find out why had finally won over her reluctance to return to her past.

Drawing away from the balcony, Nikki went back into her apartment. She was here because she was an asset again.

How ironic. This time, though, she had a price. They weren't just going to discard her after she did her job. She had learned from her past, and the agency that saved her had taught her well.

Her past was her price. All those months under torture, she had assumed it had been a misstep that had caused her capture, but she wasn't a damaged wing because of her own mistake, as she had thought. Of course, she hadn't known that at that time. She only found out much later that someone had betrayed her team. This time, she would make them acknowledge this. This time, she would find out the truth.

Nikki shut the sliding glass door and locked it. The wind chime in her hand jingled disharmoniously in protest. She looked down at it as she walked slowly into her bedroom. There would be no balance or harmony until this job was completed. She would then return to her simple life, her center, where the only people who knew her were those who had saved her.

She had been busy writing, a sort of cathartic release, in her retirement, when the call came from her former supervisor, T. When she had realized the exact part she had to play, she had almost refused.

"It's time to face your fears, Nikki," T. had said. "All this time you had requested noninterference, even when we could have contacted the DOJ about you. Now you can go back anonymously. This is your chance to right a wrong done to you."

Facing fears. She had one main one; she wasn't ready for it, not really. But she owed her agency her life and her sanity. She would come out of retirement for one last time to do this for them. And for herself.

Chapter Two

During the days following the memo, Rick opted to go with routine. If he changed his pattern right now, there might be more questions. He had his usual lunch alone, flipping through the files that were now technically useless. He couldn't do anything until he was further instructed, either by the Department of Justice or the new deputy director, if they ever sent one.

He would give them a couple more days. If they were going to let him stew out here for the sake of seeing what he would do, then he would oblige them for forty-eight hours. Paperwork took time, and the clock in the DOJ had always run weeks slower than real time. Sooner or later he would piece together what they were up to.

Rick hadn't heard about Gorman since they took him away. Even the newspapers hadn't dug up more than the fact that a high-ranking agent meant high-level classified information passed on. What was Gorman saying? Rick suspected the man wouldn't talk easily.

Back at TIARA headquarters, he took a moment to check the list of names of Task Force Two operatives in the building. He had to start monitoring their activities, to see if they were doing anything unusual.

"Can you direct all of last month's sign in and out files to my office?" he asked Security.

"No problem, sir. Can you sign the request form?"

"Of course." Paperwork. Endless red tape.

"I will transfer them up to your secretary, sir."

"No, I want the information strictly FMEO."

The woman arched her eyebrows. "For My Eyes Only" was usually meant for very classified files, some encrypted for security reasons. Rick knew the information he had just requested was a far cry from a federal secret. When he didn't give any explanation, she just nodded, although the curiosity in her eyes was obvious. "Yes, sir."

Rick signed the sheets and picked up his briefcase, heading toward the secured area where the elevators led to offices not allowed to the public. Visitors had to go through the cordoned-off area to the right, walk through the metal detectors and security guards, and were allowed access to only certain areas in the federal building.

He was surprised at the long line of visitors for a Monday, and they were all women. Dozens of them, with similar badges on their clothes, meaning they were all in a group together. They were chatting and laughing as their line slowly advanced through the necessary precautions. These days any big group had to have special permission.

Rick cursorily glanced in their direction as he went toward the private elevators. And froze. Way ahead, already past the security guards, was a group of four women just heading out of sight.

Her long hair had caught his attention. It was way past her hips, a rich, gleaming blue-black color that hung down her back. He stopped. He hadn't seen hair that color and that long for years, and still it caused his heart to lurch, still made his hand grip the handle of his briefcase tighter, imagining it wound around and around his fist. The women turned the corner. He stood there indecisively, caught between memory and disbelief.

"Sir? Do you need something?"

Rick blinked. It was one of the security guards. "A lot of visitors today," he said, casually nodding toward the crowd going in the opposite direction from him.

The guard grinned. "Yeah. A writers' group, all wanting a

tour and to meet some real-life agents. Some big brass sponsored it personally."

That was interesting information. Frowning, Rick looked that way again. "Who are the agents in charge of the group?"

"Don't know, sir. Do you want me to find out?"

Rick shook his head. He could do that in a less conspicuous way. "No, thank you. I just wondered, that's all."

He resumed his walk to the private elevators. It had been years since little things stood out in a crowd and caused him to stare. In the old days it was tough, because there were many Asian residents in D.C., but in a way that turned out to be a blessing. After a while the Asian features helped to numb him. Nowadays he was seldom reminded of the past.

But hair that long. And that black. And last night, didn't he think of her again when he saw a pair of dark brown eyes staring solemnly back at him from the lift at his apartment? And why the coincidences now? Maybe it was his guilty conscience making a return because of the Gorman scandal. He had been thinking about his past too much.

In the privacy of his office, he turned on his computer, bypassed a couple of codes, and pulled a printout of all the visitors downstairs that morning. He made a short list of names in his notebook. There weren't that many Asian-sounding names, after all.

Nikki took a deep breath. She wasn't very good with crowds. Something had happened when they'd locked her in that isolation cell. She didn't realize it until much later, that her sensory perception went on overload when she was in a huge crowded place.

Her agency had taught her to use her new talent, so that she wouldn't be overwhelmed. First focus on the space. Then the people. Lastly things.

The building had a headache. That was as close a sensory description of how she felt about it. Call it *feng-shui*, or whatever, but the building was sick.

She would never include these "feelings" in her reports,

of course, especially for this contract. She opened her mouth only if they asked her specifically for this part of her review. Most people wanted a diagnosis they could understand, with a definite solution. If there was a problem with the security, then obviously they needed fixes in that direction. If the problem was too much paperwork, then they would eliminate some red tape. Naturally, they wanted it all in writing so they could pass it around.

Nikki smiled at the thought. Problems weren't always what they seemed. Lax security couldn't be fixed no matter how many surveillance cameras were added, if the people behind it were the problem. Red tape was only part of the communication disaster between the different departments, and telling them in writing wouldn't solve a damn thing, if no one was really listening. Besides, when it was time to implement any changes, the new administration would bring in its new group of people. The problems just continued, and worsened.

This building, in an overall sort of way, emanated impending disaster. She had only walked around in the areas marked for tourists today, and already could see enough problems that needed more than money to fix.

"So what is this romance you're writing?" a male voice asked right next to her.

Nikki blinked. She had been too busy gathering the feel of the building to really pay attention to the tour. The romance authors were just the sort of joke that her agency liked to play on its operatives. Somehow they had gotten her a badge to go in with this group. It was an excellent cover, since almost all of them were women, and she could ask all kinds of questions under the guise of research for her book. But she didn't really need to; she knew this place like the back of her hand.

The man speaking to her was an operative given the responsibility of taking them around and answering their questions. He was young and pleasant, obviously enjoying himself amid a bevy of female attention. He had the cocky air of a young operative. Her guess was he hadn't seen much fieldwork.

"It's a spy suspense," she answered, returning his smile.

She stepped away just a tad. She didn't like men standing too close; her being short was one of the less important reasons.

"Really? Let me guess—a government agent, right? And the heroine is in trouble, right?" he teased.

"Actually, the heroine isn't in trouble. She's the government agent," Nikki answered.

"Oh, of course, it's a women's book. Sorry, I'm used to reading spy novels by male authors. You know, Ian Fleming. James Bond stuff." He shrugged. "But please, if you have any questions about the job, I'll be happy to help you out."

"Thank you." Nikki gave him a reassuring smile. "My heroine isn't quite as lucky as James Bond, though. She doesn't get to escape as easily as he does in the books. And of course, no handsome man to the rescue, either."

"No handsome man?" He shook his head. "Wait a minute now—isn't that usually the rule? My sis reads them and she's always complaining she can't find any tall, dark, and handsome heroes out in the real world. I know that's what she's reading in those books. So don't tell me your hero is overweight and short."

His observation amused her because he was more right than wrong. "No, my hero isn't going to be overweight and short," she agreed.

He arched a brow. "So what kind of hero's going to rescue the poor heroine?"

Nikki smiled slowly. "Tall. Dark. Dangerous. And you're wrong again. She's doing the rescuing."

"Excuse me, Miss . . ." The operative paused to glance at her badge. "Miss Taylor, but the others are signaling me that we're moving on."

"All right."

The group gathered to go down another level. The leader told them that they were going to get a view of different weapons and a question-and-answer session on that topic. Some of the ladies made some comments about agents and guns, and there was loud laughter when one of the operatives happened to overhear and went beet red. Nikki took another deep breath as she followed along.

"You lucky thing," one of the women said to her, gray eyes twinkling. "You got to talk to the cutie-pie. He has his eyes on you. Did you get his name?"

Nikki shook her head. "No, no, I didn't."

"Of course, I'm old enough to be his mother." She sighed. "But a woman can look, can't she?"

"Yes," Nikki agreed, but she wasn't really thinking of the young operative. She could look, but in a roomful of weapons, could she block the terror they brought her?

"Tell me what she looks like," Rick said, studying the young man in his office, mentally recalling his file to mind. Erik Jones, in his second year of field training after laboring for four years in the encryption department. From his demeanor, he had never been summoned for a debriefing before. Rick sank into his leather chair and waited expressionlessly.

"I remember her quite easily, sir, the woman with the long hair. She looked Asian, but her last name is Taylor."

"Taylor." No wonder the list of names sent up that morning didn't have an Asian name. She was probably married.

"Yes, and she is writing a romance." The man flushed as he realized Rick expected more than that. "Some kind of James Bond romance."

"How long did you talk to her?"

"The first time was about five minutes, sir, and then later, maybe fifteen minutes."

"And you started the conversations each time?"

"Yes, sir."

"Why?"

The man flushed again. Rick continued looking at him. The trouble with the young ones these days was their inability to cut off emotions, even when it was a simple interview. How would Erik Jones stand under fire, in front of the enemy, with his life on the line?

"She seemed different, sir."

"How so?"

"Well, the long hair, for instance," Eric said, finally making a helpless gesture. "I mean, that's very noticeable."

"Do you make it a habit to talk to women with very long hair, Agent Jones?" Rick asked politely, noting the flush had darkened and traveled down his neck. "If, let's say, she had very short hair, would you have approached her?" He watched the Adam's apple in Erik's throat move up and down, and added, "Does my line of questioning make you uncomfortable?"

"Yes . . . no, sir."

"If you can't answer simple questions, how are you going to learn to ask them when it's your turn?"

The young man looked down at the floor, then defensively shrugged. "It would be different. Asking is different from answering, sir."

Rick cocked a brow. "Is that so? What did you think I wanted to know from my questions?"

Erik met his eyes for a moment, then looked away again. "You wanted to show me that I shouldn't be talking to anyone without first establishing motive. I have to know why I want to talk to them." His eyes brightened. "And I did question her, find out things about her."

Rick shook his head. "No, Agent Jones. What you do when you're attracted to a woman is your business. However, when you're doing it within the context of your job, it becomes mine. This is a group of writers, and therefore I assume their questions would deal with certain aspects of our work. Did you ask anything that would be of use to you, or did you volunteer information?" The flush returned. Rick bet that all the man could tell him would be about the woman's book, and nothing more. "When your O.C. asks you for information, and you keep opening yourself up the way you did to me, you're just inviting reevaluation. So far you have told me nothing of value, Agent Jones."

Erik cleared his throat again. "No, no, you're right, sir."

"Good. Let's start again, shall we? Tell me what Nikki Taylor said."

"Sir, it might be easier if I give you a report."

It was going to be a long hour for the young man, Rick thought. "I don't think so," he countered softly.

Nikki couldn't stay with the group and lunch at the cafeteria. The building was suffocating her. The coordinator had told them that they had an hour and a half before they resumed the tour. There was a restaurant nearby where she could have a quiet lunch, one of those where the food was expensive and dependent on the local business clientele. She didn't feel like sitting in another touristy place.

The sight of the weapons had taken a toll on her. It had been years since she had seen so many in a room together. They were laid out in cases and hung on the walls, some of them instruments of pain she remembered very well. The walking cane with a secret knife. The short but sharp boot knife that could slash the throat it kicked at. The belt buckle that had sharp spikes on it. She had wanted to reach out and touch them, but of course that wasn't allowed.

At one point amid the writers' chatter, an inner voice had yelled, *You're asking the wrong questions.* But she couldn't ask the ones she wanted. The operative who had talked to her earlier had handed them all official caps for souvenirs. Out of a sense of irony, she had put it on.

The cool air in the restaurant calmed her nerves. She sat at the table she had specifically chosen, looking around her curiously. It wasn't quite what she had expected. The lighting was natural, coming from overhead skylights. It wasn't a place to conduct secret business. People couldn't hide behind potted plants here.

So she was wrong about him again. A dark, secretive man who boldly sat in the open. She knew he had noticed her the moment she walked in, even though he hadn't really looked in her direction. She sat showing him her profile because he was a man who liked mystery, who expected everyone to hide from him. Besides, she didn't think she could meet his eyes as she had the other night and not show recognition. It wasn't time yet.

Fate and timing were strange companions. They bound people together, that was how history was made. Her history, unlike his, had been deleted. He, on the other hand—she peeked at him sitting to her left—wished his would suffer the same fate.

The other night she had wanted to feel his space, to judge him from afar. She didn't trust the words people wrote about him; she preferred to see how and where he lived. She had watched him when he was at the opera with his date, and he had been too distracted to notice the show. His eyes had constantly strayed down to a group of people, one of whom she recognized, and she caught a yearning so strong coming from him that it made her heart ache.

That was the first wrong fact she was given. The man wasn't as cold as the files made him out to be.

Then fate and timing intervened again. Her sources had assured her that his date was with him all weekend, so she had thought Sunday night would be perfect for her stroll in his space. The elevator door had opened on his floor and there he was, looking straight at her. Even with his arms around another woman, his eyes and mind had reached for her. The tingle of connection was instantaneous. She had to block the urge to walk out of the elevator right then.

The sandwich she ordered was delicious. This was the first good meal she had since returning to D.C., and she found her appetite returning. She called for the dessert cart and spent a good five minutes joking with the waiter over what to have.

She was enjoying the last spoonfuls of the fluffiest cheesecake when a tall glass was placed in front of her. She looked up. The waiter smiled and said confidentially, "The gentleman sitting to your left highly recommends that you try our strawberry daiquiri. He sends you his compliments."

Nikki slowly turned to meet those green eyes that glittered back from a hard, proud face. His gaze pierced her, and she felt that jolt again, as if he had touched her. He didn't smile but nodded. She nodded back, searching the expressionless face for . . . something. He was good at blocking, too.

She thanked the waiter and then returned her gaze to the man. His eyes were still on her. Without looking away, she took a long sip from the straw. The cold nectar filled her mouth. She drew back, savored the fruity flavor with the hint of rum, and swallowed. Strawberries—her favorite fruit.

Rick didn't believe in coincidence. Or fate. Or luck. Not that Nikki Taylor cared, one way or another. She sat there seemingly oblivious to everything but the food in front of her.

Her hair was even longer than he had thought. She had twisted a knot in it around waist-length, to keep it in place. She was the second person he had ever seen who wrapped her hair around her neck like a scarf before she sat down. That solved the problem of having it sweep the floor, of course. He blinked, annoyed with himself. Here he was imagining the feel of her hair when he should be watching her closely. He didn't hide his interest. She walked in because he was here. What did she want from him?

Her profile showed small and delicate features, and he wished she had chosen to sit facing him. He wanted to see her without that veil of hair. It distracted him. A woman could possess a man with hair like that. But that was just a faded memory. Just like the lingering dreams that left him unsatisfied this morning.

Nikki Taylor's hair could cover his whole body easily. He wondered what it would be like, with that curtain around them, wrapping his limbs with hers. She could hide her nakedness behind it, and he would part its thickness to reveal her secrets, starting from the top.

Rick's eyes traveled down her body. Small. Delicate. One couldn't trust small or delicate. He knew that from the past. What was Nikki Taylor hiding from him? Why did she ask Agent Jones those questions? And why was she following him?

He kept staring at her, as if his will alone would compel her to turn toward him, but she continued to ignore him, her whole attention on her meal. She was enjoying it with a singular delight that amused even the headwaiter, and Dakkar wasn't an easily impressed man. Still she ignored him, asking for the dessert cart when she was finished. Watching her made him hungry. He wanted to taste her. He wanted to look into her eyes again, as he had the night before.

So he forced her hand, calling the waiter over to send her that daiquiri. Satisfaction welled up inside when she finally gazed at him. Liquid dark eyes. The kind that saw too much. They didn't flare with recognition, didn't show any sign of fear at all. He waited for her to accept his offer, to acknowledge him.

The tip of her tongue teased the corner of her mouth briefly. The merest hint of a smile. Her lips touched the straw. Her hand caressed the chilled glass. And her eyes never left his face as she took her time finishing the whole daiquiri.

Rick didn't open his briefcase to read his notes. His lunch didn't whet his appetite. A man his age shouldn't get a hard-on by watching a woman suck on a straw. She hadn't flirted with him. She drank the daiquiri like she ate her meal—with a sensual intentness that bordered on intimacy. He was still hard when he paid his bill. On the way out, Dakkar quietly handed him the paper bag with the glass in it.

"Love me," she whispered, twining pale sallow arms around his waist. "You promised to love me forever."

His hands were lost in her familiar long hair and he parted it, looking for her face. His heart thundered as if he had been running hard, and his breathing came out harsh and uneven. He started pulling the hair out of the way. Nothing. He couldn't see her.

"Liar!" he screamed out, and he saw that his hands were bloodstained.

"You promised! You promised to love me forever!" her voice accused over and over. "Liar! Traitor!"

He tore at the hair, looking for her. Her arms lifted, and long strands of hair gathered around him, swallowing him in sensual heat. "Love me," she demanded again.

"You're the one who lied to me. You betrayed me." He fought the cold hands that seemed to move all over his

nakedness, his own limbs tangling with hair that snaked around his body lovingly.

"Love me again."

"Never." He pushed off as he made the vow, but her hair imprisoned him to her. He had once loved its dark brown thickness so much. Now she hid from him, and her hair mocked his attempts to get away. And still he couldn't see anything. He roared, "Show yourself!"

Her laughter, as always, was scornful, derisive. He resisted the pull of her arms this time, roughly tugging the hair away from his body. His breathing was as loud as his heartbeat echoing in his head. The more he fought the thickening need to give in, the more he thought he saw her shadowy face. Gathering fistfuls of hair, he strangled her, and her seductive caresses turned to struggles. She continued laughing even as she choked, and finally she stopped.

He looked down. His hands were still bloodstained.

He slowly parted the curtain of hair, expecting to deal with the usual ending. She would be dead and it would be his fault. But this time, it wasn't his traitorous wife.

Nikki Taylor opened her eyes and stared up at him. He drew back onto his haunches in shock, letting go the thick strands of dark hair. She lay there, with a half smile, those dark brown eyes calm and assessing. His heartbeat thudded into a regular rhythm as she raised her hands to him. And her touch was very warm. Tender. She put his bloody finger in her mouth and sucked.

"The daiquiri tasted good," she said, "but now I want to taste you."

Rick jerked up with a start, exhaling a long rush of air from his lungs. His heart was racing madly and he ran a hand across his forehead, wiping off the perspiration. He kicked away the bedsheets so the fan overhead could cool him down.

Crossing his arms behind his head, he broodingly stared at the shadowy moving blades as they went round and round. He would never conquer his ghosts. How long had it been since he had this nightmare? It returned in spurts and faded for long stretches, until he was lulled into forgetting. Then, it would spring out of its dark prison, like a Jack-in-the-box.

Only, this time, it wasn't really a nightmare. It had a different ending. *She* was in it. He stared downward in the darkness. It wasn't fear that had roused him from sleep. A nightmare wouldn't give a man this kind of reaction; he was too old to deal with waking up like a teenager with raging hormones. He turned over onto his front abruptly.

The fan was small relief to his heated body, and he knew he wouldn't be falling back to sleep for a while. He turned to look at the alarm clock. Barely four in the morning. Muttering a sharp expletive, he buried his face in his pillow, trying to block out the image of Nikki Taylor sucking on his finger.

"I want to taste you."

He cursed and turned over again. The semidarkness reminded him of her. The fan caressed like her hair did. The sheets tangled like her legs were around him. He needed relief.

"Nikki Taylor," he said her name out loud. He thought about the way she ate, and the release he sought and received was strangely more satisfying than the past weekend's excess.

Chapter Three

Rick didn't go jogging that morning, and that put him in a bad mood. He didn't like breaking his routine without a good reason. A nightmare and a stranger weren't good enough reasons.

Today he would get the results from that glass at the restaurant and he would have something concrete on Nikki Taylor. She might turn out to be exactly what she claimed, but he doubted it. Those questions she'd asked Erik yesterday were too clever. Besides, the replies she gave intrigued him even more. The vague description of her story, about saving a man in trouble, about disappearing files and political investigations—very general, and yet almost seemingly given to catch his interest. He would like to go a round of questions and answers with the mysterious woman.

When he had one of those nightmares, he had one place to go lick his wounds. His study. He rebuilt Ricardo into Rick Harden there. When he felt the merest hint of a crack exposing any softness, all he needed to do was enter this room and be reminded of what was at stake.

That woman had somehow slipped through and gotten inside his head because not only was he sure he was seeing her everywhere, now he was dreaming of her. He needed a dose of reality. And what he had in his study served as that reminder.

So instead of breathing in fresh air and sunshine at a punishing pace, he spent the extra hours in the shadowy secrecy of his den, with the flickering computer screen the only light in the room. This was his private sanctuary. No one was allowed in here.

This was his reality, what made him as he was today. Things people knew about him and things he knew about them. Facts that he couldn't change, like his past, but the image that he now projected, he had built with the deliberate care of a toddler playing with Legos.

He had learned the hard way that information was power. He now gathered it for his protection as well as use, if necessary. He had been trying to move up the ladder since his personal disaster, but one person had always stood in his way. Gorman. The ex-director of TIARA was his enemy; he was also his teacher, showing him how a mere piece of information could be used repeatedly to destroy one's future. But now Gorman was in jail for selling information to the enemy.

Rick typed in his password to activate his encrypted system. The program started to run after a series of executed commands. There were secret encoded files within his puppet files, things that only he knew about. He had collected a large one on Gorman, but he might as well toss that out. All these years of trying—and failing—to find something tangible to push Gorman out, only to have a hotshot SEAL operative sent into his very team blow the whistle. He didn't feel bitter about that. Just . . . an overwhelming disappointment that revenge wasn't his.

Rick frowned. Of course, with Gorman now incarcerated, there was the problem that Task Force Two was going to be under investigation because they were essentially Gorman's team. Not to mention the fact that Rick himself was the team's operations chief, Gorman's handpicked man. But if he could escape I.I., he could finally move up and regain access to certain archives. With Gorman and his threats out of the way, he would be able to request closed cases to be reopened.

He opened Gorman's file after a series of special coded prompts that disabled several firewalls. Cam's wiretap before Gorman's capture was going to play an important part in Task Force Two's defense, and Rick knew that he had better back up any evidence before politics started to dip its stinking fingers into the mess. Things had a strange way of disappearing when they caused big waves at the Department of Justice, especially if they involved big, important names.

He slipped the tiny silver diskette into place and started data transfer. It took him a long time to learn how to program Shadow files, a new technology that scanned and transferred without trace. Cam's recording at the department might disappear, but if they were going to use him for a sacrificial lamb, Rick wasn't going down without a fight. Backups. Always have backups.

Once the data transfer was completed and encrypted, he emptied the temp file cache and redisplayed the puppet files to cover his tracks. He was now an expert at that. It had become second nature to back up and cover and re-back up and hide. Sometimes he wondered if he peeled off all the layers he had put on, would he still find himself inside. He looked at the blinking cursor for a few seconds. Maybe not. Maybe he wasn't inside there anymore. Maybe that was why he hated himself and his life sometimes. He had buried himself alive.

One last thing before he finished. A new file. Nikki Taylor. He was going to have her in here, in a little box he could fill with data, where he could build her bit by bit so he would see the whole picture, where she couldn't slip in and out of his dreams.

By the time he relocked the study, Rick felt at ease, in charge of the situation. He was Hard-On again, bureaucrat and nobody's victim.

Nikki walked out into the open, making sure she didn't interrupt any joggers. He hadn't shown up this morning. He was, by all reports, a creature of habit. He took this hilly path, a scenic route favored for its hard climb and its direct contrast to the two-lane curvy highway across the chasm with its cars speeding down to Connecticut Avenue. On this side, the cars looked tiny and insignificant, and the winding jogging trail let everyone set his own pace.

She could see its attraction for Rick. She felt sorry that

she had interrupted his one enjoyable thing; his decision not to jog meant that she had jolted him out of his daily routine. He was thinking, and not about rules and regulations. That was what had bothered her when she read those files on him. She wanted to see him behind all those papers and rigid policies.

Two joggers passed her, panting hard. She looked around her, seeing the deep green of the trees, her favorite color. It was the shade she missed most when she was living in darkness, and she would never forget the deep joy she had felt when she had caught sight of the deep dark green of freedom.

She sighed. She would love to walk along here and enjoy every minute of it, but she wasn't here for herself. Ricardo Harden used this path for harmony, and today she had caused him to miss his ritual. The path would miss him. A missing link in the chain weakened harmony, and she didn't think Mr. Harden needed any more discord in his life. In fact, he was probably in a bad mood. She smiled. How was it that she could always make everything end up her fault by sheer argument alone? And about a stranger, at that.

She twirled her braid into a bun and clipped it securely. She couldn't just leave this place; she caused the imbalance and she would fix it. Today she would run for Ricardo Harden, in his place. See what he saw. Breathe the air and feel his need to run. She set out at a trot.

Why would anyone do this disgusting exercise day after day? It disrupted the lungs and it was, she was sure, very bad for the brain to bobble up and down like that. Nikki burst out laughing in mid-stride.

"Hello there! What a surprise. What's so funny that has you laughing all alone?"

Nikki turned to see Erik Jones, the operative from the day before, running up the path in sweat-damped T-shirt and shorts. He caught up with her and stopped.

"Hi, Mr. Jones, I didn't know you jogged here, too," she said.

"Nah, this is my first time. I wanted to check out somebody." Erik winked before wiping his damp forehead with his sleeve.

"Ahhh, doing spy stuff." Nikki smiled, relieved. She needn't run after all; someone was here to bring balance. She sent out a silent prayer of thanks. Maybe the rest of the day would be good.

Rick adjusted his tie. He should have gone jogging. If he had, maybe the day would have gone better. It was lunchtime, and he was reduced to grabbing a sandwich at the cafeteria because he had to wait for an important call to his office. Internal Investigations' email was very specific. There would be an update about status today.

Knowing them, they wouldn't call him on his cell, and in all likelihood they would call the office at lunchtime to say someone was on the way and would arrive at oh-one-hundred hours. If he went to lunch, he wouldn't be back in time, and his secretary would, of course, let any operative from I.I. do anything.

Rick Harden didn't want to come back and see any EYES operatives, as they were called, playing around in his office. Not that there would be anything there to find, just that he didn't trust the person wouldn't "find" something anyway. So he sacrificed his martini and expensive lunch and grabbed takeout while Greta waited for his return. His secretary was one of the few remaining in Task Force Two who actually had some responsibilities left. The man waiting in line at the pay counter turned. Rick almost smiled at the shock on Cam's face. After all, the younger man had been trying to avoid him all morning, and the cafeteria would be the last place to bump into Hard-On.

"Been busy all morning, Agent Candeloro?" he asked politely.

Cam cleared his throat. "Hi, sir. Fancy seeing you here."

"Isn't it?" The line moved forward a few feet. "I had my secretary page you but your pager was off."

"It is?" Cam asked, surprise in his voice as he searched his pockets, then pulled out and looked at the offending gadget. To his credit, he didn't show a smidgen of guilt. "It is! I must have accidentally turned it off, sir. I apologize—it wasn't an urgent matter, I hope, sir?"

Rick studied the other man's face. He wondered, with mild irritation, if the whole of Task Force Two was this good at making work a lot harder than it seemed. After all, Gorman had picked every one of them for a reason. He knew his own weakness, his myopic view of how to run things. Agent Cameron Candeloro was just laid-back enough to not ask the right questions, and Gorman probably chose him for that.

"A late night, Agent Candeloro, doesn't mean a late report," Rick said. "I hope you're bringing it to me sometime in the near future, maybe within the next twenty-four hours?"

"Today, sir, really," Cam answered. "It's almost done, it really is, but I'm not good with writing reports."

"Why?"

"Too many long sentences, man, I mean, sir. I look at the blank page and after twenty minutes of typing, it's only half filled." Cam made a face. "I read the other stuff and mine is like . . . shit, sir. Besides, I didn't know how much to take out about Steve and Marlena, and you did mention to be very specific but I also know that operation was far from kosher."

Rick shook his head. "I'm asking for an account of what you saw and heard the night we caught Gorman. We have a tape of him incriminating himself. How hard is that? Leave out McMillan's romance with Miss Maxwell, just tell how the hostage extraction was done, what happened, and where you were at each point. If that's only half a page long, then it is."

They reached the front of the line and the saleslady rang up what was on Cam's tray. It was a long list. Rick raised his eyebrows but didn't say anything. Cam had always amazed him with what he could stuff in that lean frame of his. Rick wasn't fooled by all the excuses. Cam was trying to protect his friends from in-depth investigation, what with Steve having called in his own SEAL team to do the job without any-one's permission. The absence of his own men would come into question. Another potential black mark to watch out for, Rick privately noted.

After he had paid, Cam stood close by as the saleslady rang up Rick's lunch. "It doesn't read like a report," he ex-plained, and his expression was comically mournful. "It reads like a comic book action essay."

Rick frowned. He was Hard-On, not someone who would shoot the breeze with any operatives in the cafeteria. He needed to get back to his office and had no time to give a lec-ture about writing, but he couldn't help but wonder how they were training operatives these days if they couldn't even write a decent report. "Bring it," he ordered curtly. "Let me read this comic book report."

"Yes, sir. I'll be at your office later, sir." Cam went off with his tray, whistling.

Rick mentally shook his head. If there was a man who didn't worry about anything, that would be Agent Cameron Candeloro. Tucking his lunch bag under his arm, he started to head out of the cafeteria.

"Mr. Harden, sir, can I have a minute with you?"

It was Agent Erik Jones. Wonderful, now it was someone who *liked* writing reports.

Internal Investigations Office

Nikki looked across the conference table at the man sit-ting there quietly reading. Everything in the room was big, meant to intimidate more than impress. Her leather chair was built for large men. The conference table was meant for a group meeting. The temperature in the room was set lower than necessary.

She had been kept waiting alone here for half an hour ear-lier but she didn't bother to walk around. Let them watch and record. There was nothing to see. She had sat down where she was and just waited.

The man finally looked up. He tossed down the black plastic folder carelessly. "You're wasting our time and money," he said.

"I'm sorry you think so," Nikki said quietly.

He paused, clearly expecting more than that from her but she just sat there. Leopards didn't change their spots. It had been a while, but she could still play mind games.

"Is that it? You're sorry? This report is useless. You haven't even assessed any personnel of account. Why did they allow your idea of entering as a visitor when you could have just walked in and looked through everything you wanted?"

"Because that's not what I have been contracted for." Because that was what you would have done, she wanted to say.

The man's expression hardened. "Miss Taylor, you know we don't like outside resources handling our internal affairs. I have been forced to accept your 'job' because of Admiral Madison's pressuring the president, but I don't have to like anything you say or do." He clasped his hands together on the table. "It's nothing personal, you understand. To me, you are just an inconvenience that I have to put up with because some military brass not in the business of counterintelligence wants more pins on his uniform."

Nikki had sat before men with colder eyes and harsher intentions than mere intimidation. His deliberate disdain was a tiny drop of water in hot oil. Saying that it wasn't personal was a lie, anyway. He was taking it very personally, since it was an affront to send in an outsider to make an independent report apart from Internal Investigations.

"You don't have to like me or what I have to say in my reports, Mr. Stadler," she said quietly. "*That* isn't in my contract."

The man threw his hands up in the air, the first hint of frustration. "Miss Taylor, maybe you ought to tell me what is in this contract to which you keep referring. I'm a busy man. There are other more important things happening around the world. We have bomb threats to our embassies by terrorists. We have unrest in the Middle East to deal with. We have planes shot down from the sky. A small laptop sold by a department director is the very least of our worries." He gestured at the folder again. "That tells us nothing. 'You walked around the building and surveyed building safeguards.' What the hell is that?"

"I have only been there for one day," Nikki replied mildly. "Mr. Gorman had been selling information for years. I'm sure the laptop meant very little in the overall picture but it is part of the chain of events underlying the problem of information leakage. The admiral didn't believe that Mr. Gorman worked alone, not without help from higher officers."

Fresh anger glinted in the man's eyes. Nikki knew he had expected defensiveness from her, even arrogance, when he attacked her work. Her answer had only made what was left unsaid very clear—that the admiral didn't trust Internal Investigations, thus, Mr. Stadler's staff, not to muddy up any findings. It was standard knowledge that one just didn't blow the whistle about internal problems. She glanced at the whitened knuckles of Mr. Stadler's clasped hands.

"We know how to deal with our traitors," he said. "The media has blown this thing up so big that everyone from the president down to the admiral is worried there are a thousand rats in our fold. I don't believe it." Nikki kept silent. That only angered him more, and his voice rose a notch. "We're handling our own investigation our way. We have better knowledge of Gorman's men in Task Force Two. We know their activities, and we can find out a lot more than you. You, on the other hand, will only interfere with our work, as you nearly did the other night."

"How so?"

He leaned back, a little smile on his lips. "I did a little research on you, Miss Taylor."

"That's to be expected."

"Yes, but the most interesting thing is, we can't find a thing about you. Why is that? No background, nothing." His eyes narrowed. "Which leads me to wonder, what is it you have done that even our side doesn't want anyone to find out? Would you care to fill me in?"

It was Nikki's turn to smile. "I didn't know I was under investigation," she said. "Why don't you ask the admiral? Or the attorney general?"

Stadler's smile disappeared. "I also know why they picked you. You look quite a bit like Richard Harden's ex-wife."

"His name is Ricardo Harden," Nikki corrected, "and his wife is dead."

"Now that is a man with an interesting file, isn't he? And you just happened to look like the dead wife. Is that whom you're after, Miss Taylor? He is, after all, our most likely suspect, being Gorman's handpicked number one. We don't need you to collect evidence against him."

"It's not in my contract to build a case around Mr. Harden." Far from it. When Stadler started to speak again, she lifted her hand slightly. It was the first time she had moved since this interview began, so she knew it would catch his attention. "I know, it's that contract thing again, and I'm quite sure you've been told what my specific job is. I'm to give an independent report on Task Force Two and a specific recommendation on whether Mr. Harden has the capabilities to take over the reins."

"He doesn't. If you've read his file, you'd know that."

"Obviously the board that is in charge of recommending directorships didn't think this is enough. Since Mr. Gorman had manipulated all the information for so long, an independent review was recommended. Now, as to whether Mr. Harden is qualified or not, I'm sure he is. Whether he is part of Gorman's network, that I don't know."

"And you've been 'contracted' to find out because they know he'd notice you," Stadler said, his lips twisting cynically as he made the quotation marks with his fingers. "As if we couldn't send in our own pillow companion."

Ah, she understood now about his reference to the other night. Sending in a pillow companion was the oldest form of intelligence-gathering. "That woman with him outside the elevator. You sent her to him."

"Agent Denise Lorens."

Apparently it was a signal. The door opened and the

woman from the other night walked into the conference room. Nikki studied her. She looked very low-key compared to how she was dressed at the opera, but the dark conservative outfit didn't hide her sensual voluptuousness.

Nikki could still recall the look in Denise Lorens's sleepy blue eyes when she had sauntered into the elevator, barely glancing at the occupants before turning her back on them. She had blown a kiss at Rick as the door closed, then leaned sideways against the elevator wall.

Rick Harden liked dating women, Nikki had known that. The woman in the elevator had told another story. They liked dating Rick Harden. Nikki had seen a very different Denise in that lift. Softer. And extremely sated.

"Denise, please tell Miss Taylor about Richard Harden's likes and dislikes."

Nikki shook her head. "No."

Stadler lifted his brows. "Why not? It'll save you time, knowing how to get him close to you. Or, if you like, you can have Agent Lorens report back to you each time so you can have the information she has extracted. You can call it your supplemental independent report. Go ahead, Agent Lorens."

"Yes, sir. Mr. Harden's profile is nonstandard. He doesn't do the romantic very well, changing his moods often, from quiet to silence altogether. So far he hasn't talked about his work but this was just our first weekend together." She turned to Nikki. "He likes submissive women and he enjoys sex. A lot. He can be made to talk. Give me a few more weekends and I'll know for sure whether he has anything in his personal computer. And I'm quite sure he's tied to Gorman. I can build a good case to nail him. It's really not a good idea if you interrupt my time with him now."

Nikki wanted to say no but she didn't have a good reason to give. What I.I. did was their business, not hers. "I can give you those weekends you want," she said, "but he won't call you again, Agent Lorens."

Denise Lorens blinked. She gave her superior a quick glance then turned her attention back to Nikki. "I'm good at what I do. I left him supremely satisfied."

Rick Harden wasn't looking for satisfaction. He was looking for balance. But that kind of answer would just prolong this conversation, and Nikki suddenly wanted to get out of there. She felt dirty, somehow. "I'm sure you're good at what you do, but you won't be hearing from him. You see, I'm quite sure he already knows all he has to know about you, Agent Lorens. If you had checked with file request logs, you would know that your file had been requested by him a while back."

"Not the full file," Denise Lorens told her smugly.

"I'm afraid so. You forget, Agent Harden was sometimes assigned as a pillow companion a long time ago, and unfortunately he still has security clearance codes. I've already checked—he regularly updates everything that goes on around here."

"That's impossible," Stadler said, disbelief on his face. "It's been years. He no longer works here."

"You really should contract me for an independent study on security holes in your department," Nikki couldn't resist telling him.

She turned to the female agent standing there. Denise Lorens was trying very hard not to show her disappointment and anger. It was obvious she wanted to see Rick Harden again, and it was also very obvious that she now understood he had used her. Vanity was hard to swallow down. She had thought he had liked her a lot more than a mere one night stand. After all, he had kept her for a whole weekend.

"He still might call you," Nikki told her, "but you now know that he knows. You're likely to betray this fact and trigger his suspicion."

She crossed her fingers under the table. She would pay for the little deception with meditation later, she promised. She had just manipulated Agent Lorens out of the picture.

"You may go now, Agent Lorens."

"Yes, sir." The woman quietly left.

Nikki looked at Mr. Stadler levelly. She had made a point. She would not be told how to do her job. "Mr. Stadler, you collect data to support your conclusions. Right now you want a scapegoat for this mess. You have Gorman in custody, but no missing laptop, and you need to point a finger at one or two more people to wrap up your case because, as you put it, you have more important things to do." She leaned forward and clasped her hands, just as he had done earlier. "My independent report won't be about finding a scapegoat, Mr. Stadler. It will be a complete analysis of security measures needed to be taken, and whether Agent Harden will do his job, in spite of what his files say."

She paused to let the words sink in, then added, "You see, I don't have to like what you say or do, either."

They were going to hang him out to dry. Rick had gone through this routine before. Internal Investigations. Suspension. Then evidence of inappropriateness. It all depended on how much the media was pushing for answers. The more noise, the more people would come down. Not that the answers would be the truth. It was never the whole truth. The Justice Department had its own take on the meaning of that word.

Rick didn't care what they were planning to do. He had sunk years into rebuilding himself and wasn't going to let history repeat itself. Let them find another sacrificial lamb.

Internal Investigations could move around as it pleased, so he was going to have very little room to maneuver. They wouldn't like an uncooperative party and wouldn't hesitate to cause all kinds of problems.

There was only one department I.I. couldn't touch, and that was the General Accounting Office, which checked and balanced the Justice Department. Too bad he didn't have any connections with the GAO to find out what was happening to Gorman, so he would have an idea what I.I. was trying to pin on him. He needed outside help. But he was all alone.

Right now they were just starting to tighten the noose around his neck. The presence of an EYES officer was only the beginning. Even his attitude and questions were heading Rick toward a foregone conclusion.

"You were Gorman's O.C. We need all the files in your office turned over to us."

The man, in his early forties, spoke in imperative terms, as if every sentence he said was a formal order. Rick knew it came with years of being the Justice Department's velvet glove. "You have my full cooperation, Mr. Harpring," Rick told him. "It would be faster if you'd tell what you're looking for."

Not much hope of that happening. Internal Investigations would never make it that easy. Part of the whole package was to create dissension among the staff and an inability to communicate. Then, when it came to one-on-one interviews later, distrust and chaos would already have weakened departmental loyalty. That was when the scapegoat would be let out for the public to see. And, Rick mocked in silent recrimination, his head would be offered to the masses.

Harpring opened his briefcase and handed him a sheaf of papers. "Here's all you need to know about the investigation. We'll begin from top to bottom starting tomorrow, so be prepared to answer any questions about the cases Gorman ordered Task Force Two to undertake."

"Of course." Rick took the papers without glancing down at them.

Harpring studied him for a moment before continuing in his monotone, "You realize that you might have to answer questions that could incriminate you. I suggest that you retain legal counsel before an interview. Every paper not signed will be put under a microscope."

"Every paper connected to me has been signed and copied."

The man gave him a questioning gaze. "Agent Harden, I've been doing this for two decades. I have never found a government department under investigation with all its paperwork intact. And, with your record, you do know that the first thing our people will do is go after your paper trail. You were, after all, Gorman's number one man."

Rick opened his desk drawer and put the papers on top of the increasing pile of folders. Harpring watched him close it. "Everything that has to do with my job will be here," Harden told him quietly. "All signed and with multiple copies."

The older man drummed his fingers on the desk. "How many copies?" he asked.

Rick smiled. "Enough," was all he said.

Half an hour later, after Harpring had left, his intercom buzzed. "Send him in," Rick said tersely to his secretary.

The door opened and Rick turned away from the window. "You said at the cafeteria you were out jogging and bumped into Miss Taylor this morning, Agent Jones. Tell me about the meeting."

It was time to turn the tables on Nikki Taylor.

Chapter Four

Unclean.

Nikki stood under the shower with her eyes closed for a long time, letting the hard spray beat against her face. With her long hair, she preferred taking a bath. It was one of her favorite times of the day, when she took the time to concentrate on herself. For her, bathing wasn't just a daily chore of soap and water. It was a luxury, a way to set her mind free.

Sometimes, when she sat very quietly in the scented bath, listening to the soft popping of bursting bubbles, with the lapping water caressing her like a lover, she could hear herself sing with the universe. There was nothing like that moment of contentment when she achieved that state; she could escape even her memories then.

Today, however, she didn't feel she could bear sitting still. She didn't have the patience to wait for the colorful vibrations that bloomed like kaleidoscopic flowers behind her closed lids.

That interview had been more than a fencing of words. She didn't like men like Hal Stadler. He was the sort of person she tried to stay away from, and she had retired from the business because there was no way to keep from seeing too many of his sort. Stadler and his kind generated negative feelings that she would rather not have. Once upon a time, she had plenty of that, churning out hate and anguish until life seemed hopeless.

Hate was a strong word. She understood hatred like the back of her hand.

Unclean. There were many ways to make a woman feel dirty and helpless inside. One didn't break a human being down with physical pain. That would be too easy. And a woman's self-identity could be dismantled piece by piece, if she didn't learn to disassociate from what was happening to her.

With an ease that came from years of training, Nikki deliberately blanked her mind of the invading memories. She turned the water off, her eyes still closed. The unbidden image of Rick Harden appeared out of nowhere. Funny how she knew what he looked like when she had never been within two feet of the man.

His eyes were a piercing green, with an uncompromising spirit that reminded her of the rocky mountains of Tibet. His face had the same strength of will that bordered on ruthlessness, and the proud tilt of his head challenged as well as distanced anyone who came too near. She could almost taste his lips, as if she had touched them before. They belonged to a man who rarely smiled, with a cynical curl that edged the corners. It was a jaded mouth, meant to punish as well as give pleasure.

Rick Harden with all his unfathomable complexities burst like a sudden revelation into a simple truth. He was a man standing still, waiting. For what?

She shivered at her own thoughts. Pushing open the shower door, she grabbed the towel hanging from the hook and wrapped it around her. Her stomach was roiling with panic at the unexpected insight that had jumped into her consciousness. She walked quickly to the sink to look into the mirror, her breathing uneven, because she was hearing her grandmother's warning from years ago and her mind was now making connections she had been too blind to see before.

Beware of the center. It will betray you.

Release the frozen heart. It will burn you.

Nikki stared into her reflected dark eyes, wide with shock. For years she had thought she was the frozen one, unable to move forward. That she couldn't ever get over her fear of men to love like a normal person. But meeting Rick Harden had changed something in her because she had responded to his gaze, and yes, his eyes seared her like fire each time.

She picked up the hair dryer and turned it on, deep in thought as she ran a comb through her hair. *Release the frozen heart*. The man might look like he was trying to climb up the career ladder, away from his past, but he was frozen. His heart was frozen.

Her hair was too long to dry completely and she gave it a quick towel-off. She usually braided it before going to bed. She opened the bathroom door, clicking off the lights. Her hand was still on the inside wall of her bathroom when another hand grasped that arm from the outside, jamming it and making her gasp. She hadn't seen or heard anything. She pushed off with her free hand, going for the solar plexus. Not quick enough.

It was over in a few seconds, and she found herself trapped against the side doorframe, her hands behind her back. Her towel had loosened, hanging on precariously. The stranger tugged at her hair, forcing her head up.

He was dressed all in black and the backlight from her bedroom put his face in the shadows. He looked like the devil she had conjured up in her mind. And he was much too close. Closer than she had allowed any man in years.

"I heard you were researching an agent who runs a lot. I'm here for the interview."

Rick knew he shouldn't be there. It was rare for him to follow impulse, but he couldn't seem to help himself. There was something going on here, more than the suspicious nature of Nikki Taylor's sudden appearance in his life. What, he hadn't figured out yet, but he was determined to get to the bottom of it. For some reason, she challenged him, just by the sheer fact that she hadn't come to him. He wanted to see her face-to-face, test her strength. He wanted to understand why she invaded his dreams.

She was smaller than he had thought. On her bare feet, the top of her head cleared his shoulders by only a couple of inches. Yet everything about her overwhelmed his senses. He had grabbed her to see how she would react. Someone trained wouldn't have been so easy to trap. This close, her damp hair smelled of flowers and vanilla. Her body exuded an elusive scent—a mixture of woman and something else, and it filled his lungs and invaded every pore in him as his body became aware of her state of undress.

Good. He wanted her vulnerable, just as he felt vulnerable in his dreams, incapable of escape. She couldn't run with a towel on. He tangled his hand in her hair, forcing her face up toward the bedroom light. Her eyes were large, doelike, and her mouth was parted, and it suddenly dawned on him that what he smelled was the combination of heat and fear. The woman's eyes were terrified. He gazed into them, and briefly felt shame and revulsion at putting that look there.

He should let her go. The woman was no danger to him.

Without planning to, he pushed his body against her soft one. That scent surrounded him, the thick, sweet smell of clean woman and fear. But she hadn't made another sound after the initial gasp. Her tongue flicked out, nervously wetting her upper lip. His gaze lowered and studied the pearly glow of her tempting flesh above her towel, heaving nervously and slipping slowly out of its protection. No, he wasn't going to let her go yet.

Nikki watched as Rick's nostrils flared. Something dark and unfathomable entered his green eyes, and without warning he trapped her body with his own, arching her up against him by putting pressure to her locked arms behind her.

Her heart roared in her head as panic bubbled up. She had reacted out of instinct to defend herself with the first move, but the moment he had touched her, the moment her brain had started to assimilate the fact that a man was holding her, all thought had fled. In its place was just the knowledge that she was powerless. Her speeding heart made her faint, and she tried to slow down her breathing. This was Rick Harden. It wasn't . . . them.

Before she could think of something to say, he did the unthinkable. The lower half of his tall, hard body pinned her against the corner of the wall and doorframe, and the hand imprisoning hers behind her back was like manacles, yanking her to her toes.

She was helpless in this position. She couldn't fight back without exposing her nakedness. There were things she had been trained to do but it had been so long, and she had never allowed anyone close enough to harm her before. She resisted by digging down on her heels and gasped again when he inserted his leg between hers and lifted her off the floor, bracing his knee against the doorframe.

She felt every tense and contracting muscle in his thigh. The heat from his body blanketed her. For a strange moment, she caught herself imagining him running in his shorts, those muscles moving and flexing with each step. Be careful what one wished for. She had wanted to see him run, had gone looking for him today; instead *he* had come looking for her.

His hot skin against hers. She didn't know why she was imagining that. She should loathe what he was doing to her but her naked body wasn't pulling away from his clothed one. What she was feeling wasn't revulsion. She didn't like what Rick Harden was doing to her. Her mind rebelled at the thought of giving in.

Her eyes met his. Pleading. Desperate. But of course he would never understand. He was a man. And she was in his power.

"Let me go," she finally managed a whisper. She had to escape before her body betrayed her further.

"Not yet," Rick told her very softly, his lips inches from hers.

"Let me down, then."

His green eyes mocked hers. There was anger in them, and that other dark element she couldn't put a finger on that was frightening her. In answer, he adjusted his position and slid her along his thigh toward him. She felt her towel parting further, and the friction of his black pants against her nakedness pressed home the point that she was in no position to bargain.

"All in good time. After you've answered a few questions." Rick frowned as her dark hair fell forward and covered his hand, a soft caress that distracted him from his goal of intimidating the woman. He wanted to run his fingers through it as it dried. He fought the urge to lift and bury his face in it. He scowled. Diversion.

"Who sent you?" When she shook her head, he persisted. "Who? You've been asking questions about me."

Her gaze lifted. "Really? And you haven't been doing the same about me?"

This time her voice was steady, and although her eyes were still making him feel like a bastard, there was a challenging tilt to her chin now. For some reason, he couldn't stop looking at her mouth and thinking of strawberry daiquiri, and how her lips had pursed around that straw.

Nikki forced herself to meet his eyes. There was no place to run, and she knew, in her heart, that Rick Harden wasn't here to cause her the kind of harm she feared. He wouldn't know—would he?

"You have no background, besides the fake one you've conjured up for the last ten years. It was you in my elevator that night, wasn't it?" He tugged at her hair again. "Wasn't it?"

She didn't see any reason to deny it. "Yes."

"And you were with a group of touring writers the other day. And lunch. You knew I would be there. Didn't you?" He spoke softly, his breath warming her in hot puffs.

"Yes."

"You went jogging, looking for me. And all that talk about your novel, it was about me. Why did you tell Agent Jones those things if you hadn't meant to bait me?"

His eyes demanded answers that she wasn't ready to give. She hadn't really thought about Agent Jones as a connection to Rick until he had shown up on the trail that morning. She had answered his questions because it had been painfully obvious that the young operative was trying hard to get some sort of information on her, and she had felt sorry for him.

"I . . . didn't mean to bait you," she told Rick, trying not to breathe too hard, or her towel would surely fall open. "He did me a favor, and I was returning it."

Rick frowned. "What favor?"

He was a runner, with legs strengthened from years of endurance. He would not get tired of this position for a while, and she was beginning to be aware of too many things about him, things that she had no right to notice. The heat of his body. The curling brown hair above the collar of his black shirt. The easy strength of his body as he bore her entire weight. The way his fingers were half caressing and half pulling her hair, as if he couldn't decide what to do with her.

"What favor?" he repeated, his arctic voice a direct contrast to his body heat.

She closed her eyes. She decided to give him the truth because that seemed to be the only thing he couldn't see, but she had a feeling he wouldn't appreciate it. "I interrupted your routine and was attempting to balance your not being in your usual . . . place. However, Agent Jones ran your miles for me instead. I owed him that, so I answered his questions." Which brought Rick into her space. All debts were paid in full.

The silence was drawn out to a screaming pitch. "Look at me," he finally ordered, his voice dangerously quiet. She did so, openly defiant now, but her heart still thudding too loudly. His green eyes studied her intently, then he asked, "What do you do besides write?"

Nikki jerked at his sudden change of subject. She had expected mocking recriminations, sarcastic disbelief. Rick Harden had succeeded in surprising her again. She licked her lips, drawing his attention to them. "I observe what is out of balance and suggest corrections."

"Is that another way of telling me that Internal Investigations wants to get dirt on me?" Rick sneered.

Oh no. She would not be linked to that kind of underhanded work. Her chin tilted higher. "I'm *not* Denise Lorens."

This time she succeeded in surprising him into releasing his viselike hold of her wrists. Unable to keep her balance, perched as she was, she grabbed at the nearest thing. That happened to be Rick Harden. At that moment her towel loosened completely and she went for the ends too, falling forward, sideways, rocking and stumbling, her long hair tangling with everything. Panic filled her. And desperate anger. Why couldn't she do what she had been trained to do?

Rick was struck with the familiarity of it all—yet, she was just too . . . soft. Her hair, her body, her smile. Even her struggles. There wasn't any hard edge to her. He knew, without a doubt, that she had been sent to mess with his mind, but whoever was behind this didn't know his wife very well.

He gathered the falling woman into his arms, her hands trapped against his chest. She had been willing to land on the floor rather than expose herself. That alone told him more than she had in the last five minutes. The woman was no Denise Lorens. Or any of the types I.I. would engage to send.

She was trembling but she didn't protest when he stepped away from the bathroom door, with her in his arms. Her eyes shone, even in the semidarkness, and he slowly slid her down the length of his body, feeling her knuckles running down his chest and stomach. She didn't move away when he put her down, her face buried against his breastbone.

He had not held a trembling woman in his arms since forever. It made him ache inside, and he didn't like it. It felt like a hairline crack was appearing where he bottled up all his emotions. He smoothed his hand down her long hair and steadied her with gentle arms. His eyes narrowed. No, she was more dangerous than Denise Lorens.

"Go put something on," he said abruptly. "I don't hurt injured birds, and you tremble like one."

Nikki stiffened at his harsh words. For a few moments there, she had been lost in his heat, and his arms around her had made her feel . . . she took a few steps away from him. She was about to say "safe." The man attacked her, and she felt safe?

How was that possible? She didn't like people touching her, and this man had his arms wrapped around her. Her body had slid against his heat and wasn't repelled at all. And he hadn't let her embarrass herself when he could have easily just let her fall, just to humiliate her.

He cocked a golden brow. Those green eyes glinted dangerously, as if he were about to change his mind. She blinked hard and swiftly made her escape into the bathroom.

Before the door closed, she heard him say, in that silky velvet voice that reminded her of an arrogant warrior who understood the sharpness of a new blade, "Don't take too long, Nikki. I don't like waiting."

Chapter Five

She wasn't the soft one. *He* was. He had her where he wanted her, but instead had let her go. All because of a pair of pleading eyes and a mouth that he wanted to kiss.

Rick wiped his own with the back of his hand. Where the hell was his control? Nikki Taylor wasn't what she seemed to be. If she was an I.I. operative, she certainly hadn't been coached on how to react to men. As she said, she wasn't Denise Lorens.

He understood women like Denise. Even after he pulled out her classified files and knew what she was up to, he hadn't backed away from her advances. It was, after all, better to let them see what they wanted to see. And his Task Force Two job was so dishwater dull that he actually enjoyed the danger of the risks he was taking. Why not? A female operative couldn't be trusted anyhow, and if she wanted to be used that way, he was only too happy to oblige. As long as he was in control of the situation, of course.

This Nikki Taylor with the fake history had gotten under his skin. Whoever had sent her was very good. He realized now that her casual distance from him was all deliberate, meant to elicit his attention. He should have just stayed away and waited for her to come to him. Instead he had allowed her looks to bring back feelings that he had closed off, and even with his suspicion of what she was, he couldn't stop himself. He couldn't wait.

He clenched one hand as he looked around her bedroom

with its cool white and green colors. The blankets on the bed were folded back, ready for its occupant. He walked toward it, taking in the books stacked by on the nightstand. He picked one up. And another. Fiction.

There was a notepad next to the books. He opened it. He was too used to reading private things to feel any twinge of guilt. What he could find out could help save his skin. His lips twisted derisively. Miss Taylor wasn't as innocent as she appeared, anyhow. His name was written in there, circled several times. He didn't think he was the hero of her story.

Nikki pulled on the only thing she had in the bathroom, besides what she had worn that day. The large cotton bathrobe covered every inch from her neck to her ankles. She couldn't put those clothes back on. *Unclean.* She shook her head.

Her hair was a mess. Her eyes were too large. She hurriedly pulled back her hair, braiding it with absentminded ease as her mind raced over what had happened and how to face the man outside.

She had expected anger. Even attraction of some sort. Rick Harden, after all, was a sexual man. All reports pointed to his libido. She even understood that was his weapon. His aura of unavailability made him a challenge to women around him. She had watched him long enough to see it at work. An aloof man with a sexual reputation was hard to ignore.

But she hadn't expected her own response. She tightened the sash around her waist. Five years out of the business had removed that protective layer between emotion and reaction. She had allowed fear to take over the situation, and then to make it worse, she had actually felt something else. She dared not form the word in her mind. That would be admitting something for which she wasn't ready.

A deep calming breath. She put on some lipstick. She still felt naked somehow. Then, before she started to think too much, she turned around and opened the door.

Rick Harden looked good in black. It highlighted his golden coloring and added toughness to his athletic built—

tall and sleek, with powerful arms and, she recalled from experience, equally powerful quadriceps. She pushed away the memory of the feel of his thigh muscles tightening against her, as she emerged slowly from the dark into the lit bedroom.

Gone was the bureaucrat in conservative suit and tie. She had sensed that was just a façade, anyway. She had deliberately stayed away to observe, so she could catch the real Rick Harden. And here he was, in her bedroom, studying her, touching her things. The invaded had become the invader.

He was standing next to where she had hung her wind chime by the bed, and turned when he heard her approach. The significance wasn't lost to her, that in order to understand this man, she would have to listen very, very closely, to hear his *chuung*. It would not be an easy task to know Ricardo Harden. His center was buried very deep.

She was drawn to those eyes. They looked greener somehow, reminding her of the nights in the dark when she had yearned for that color. They had glittered with suppressed emotion when he was holding her in his arms. She wanted to stare into those green depths and seek out all his secret pain.

"Why do you keep looking at me like that?" Rick interrupted her thoughts. She cocked her head, not sure what he meant. He snapped his fingers, and she blinked. "Like that. You look at me transfixed."

She didn't know that. She would have to think about it. "I didn't mean to make you uncomfortable," she said out loud.

He turned back to her wind chime and flicked a finger against one of the hanging wands. It swayed inward, clinking the middle wand softly. The room echoed with the melodic notes. "So what do you see?" he asked, his eyes still on her chime. "With those writer's eyes?"

A skilled operative always asked the right questions. Nikki never doubted Rick's ability to get to the truth. He had refined this skill to perfection for years, just to protect himself from being cornered. She had never intended to hide everything from him, anyway. After all, she needed his full cooperation to complete her contract.

She was glad he stood across the room. The distance took

away some of the tension between them that was so palpable when he was close. With his finger, he stilled the swaying wands of the chime, stopping the musical clanging, but she could still feel the room humming with the vibrations.

He touched her things. She explored his secrets. He asked indirect questions. She looked for hidden answers. Balance.

"I see details no one else does," she answered.

"And do you use these details in your books?"

"Some."

Abruptly he moved away from her chime and gave her his fullest attention. The bed between them, folded back in invitation. Her chimes and the center of the universe. Nikki held her breath and hoped it was only she who saw these details and not the man who affected her so strangely. Sometimes she couldn't decide if it was her wild imagination that brought up these things that seemed to fit together.

"You piece together these details," Rick continued as he walked slowly around the bed, "and what was it you said you do? Oh yes, you suggest 'corrections to what is out of balance.' And this is all connected with your *stories*."

He put the emphasis on the last word, a touch of mockery in his voice. Nikki could deal with that. Mockery was easily deflected, unlike her attraction to him.

"It is my job description," she said gravely.

He stopped about five feet away, close enough for her to see the distrust in his eyes, and far enough for her to feel safe. "Tell me more," he invited, in a deceptively soft voice. "After all, I seem to be a subject of interest in your research. What was it you said to Agent Jones, that you're trying to figure out a man who is always running from his past? Tell me, what are the details you were trying to pick up on that jogging trail this morning? Or is that part of your balance act?"

She had poked at the embers to spark a flame, so she shouldn't be afraid of getting burned now. "Mr. Harden," she began, and his brows lifted slightly at the formality. "My method of research is considered controversial, at best, and 'out there,' at worst. Believe me, I can take any insults you're going to hurl in my direction because I've heard them all before."

"I haven't started hurling anything yet. Why don't you tell me exactly what you're trying to research and who you're after." He smiled for the first time, a humorless curve of those uncompromising lips that brought a startling change to his face. He appeared younger, the lines bracketing his mouth relaxing his usual rigidly controlled facial expression. "Just in case I have it all wrong, of course, but a romance writer shouldn't be so knowledgeable about TIARA and how it works."

"If I tell you that you will know soon, would you leave it at that?"

Her query was followed by a pause. "It depends." He took several steps toward her.

Nikki dug her hands into her bathrobe pockets, willing herself not to retreat. She knew now that he was testing her, seeing what made her tick. He was just as interested in digging deeper as she was. "On?" she asked instead, forced to throw back her head to look up at him.

"On why you're doing this research." His hand reached out and circled her long braid, but instead of pulling it, he slid the length through his closed palm. "Tell me, Nikki, what is it about me they want you to find out?"

Nikki watched as he started to loosen her hair from its barrette. She should say something to stop him but his expression fascinated her. There was a reverence in the way he handled each thick strand as he unwound the length of it.

He looked up, hands still busy. "Well?"

"They want to know whether you're safe," she breathed out as he reached the halfway point of her braid. His hands stopped, but only for a moment. He had loosened her hair with the quickness of someone who had done it often. An unskilled pair of hands would have tangled the long hair by now. He resumed this strangely new, yet familiar, action, as if they weren't two strangers in the middle of a verbal altercation.

Her hair, a little damp still, came free, already wavy from being twisted. "Am I?" he asked. "Safe?"

He was a master manipulator. He knew the correct question was what he was supposed to be safe for, what they were afraid he would do. Instead he chose to make it personal, using her words against her. Just as they had suspected all along, he wasn't that man who played by the rules, choosing his options with dull conservatism by focusing all his energy toward following regulation. It now seemed as if he didn't care anymore whether they found out.

"No," she whispered back as he fanned her hair between his fingers. "You're not safe."

"So what do you suggest to correct this?" Rick taunted. "And how would that help your romance writing? Or am I supposed to help you with that part of your research?"

So they had sent her to find out whether he was safe, had they? Rick wanted to laugh but he bitterly swallowed the urge. He had spent a decade being safe, and now because of Gorman's betrayal, they wanted their dullest man declared a danger.

He looked at Nikki Taylor with her long hair and knowing eyes. Fine. He was tired of playing it their way, anyhow. He would go along with this and in the process expose them for what they were. She was a tool for them, and he would use her as his.

Why not? He reached out, unable to resist touching her long braid. It was thick and soft, and he knew when it was dry and hanging loose, it would blanket her entire body. She hadn't moved or objected when he pulled the barrette off.

For some masochistic reason, he wanted to torture himself. They had sent Nikki Taylor as temptation, and he wasn't even fighting it. Everything about her was a lure, and he went for the thing that had caught his attention, time and time again. He wanted to see her hair unsecured. He wanted to feel the heavy curtain spilling over his shoulders as he made love to her against that bathroom wall. He wanted to find out if it would slide over his naked back, like cool Chinese silk, as he slowly brought her to a climax on that green and white bed behind him.

Would she be trained to please him? He looked up from the undone hair in his hands into her raised face and caught that expression in her eyes that kept bothering him. Her fear of him was very real. He had tested it. When he stood across the room, she was able to fence with him. He had moved within five feet of her, and even though she stood her ground and challenged him, her eyes were wary. When he finally came close enough to touch her, her hands had disappeared into her pockets, as if she was trying not to show her nervousness.

She was right. He wasn't safe. Not to her. Or to himself.

"When can we start?"

Her question jerked him out of his revelry. His eyes narrowed as he tried to determine her frame of mind. Nikki Taylor didn't strike him as a flirt, but of course, that could be part of her act. Her dark brown eyes looked back at him steadily although her hands were still buried in her pockets. It intrigued him, this combination of fear and courage. She might have the strength to take him on after all.

"As soon as I set the rules," he said, waiting for her to bristle at his words.

He should have known better by now. The woman didn't even glare or challenge him. "Of course," she agreed, as if that seemed fair, not knowing that she had handed him the keys to take her where he wanted her.

Rick frowned. Too easy. "And how will you benefit?"

"I need you to answer my questions in an interview format," she said simply. "You will also help my research because you can give me access. Don't worry, I'm not asking you to do anything illegal. My first request is to be inserted into the recruitment classes."

He cocked his head. "And that will help you to decide whether I'm safe?" He made a mental note to look for personnel inspection reviews. Maybe Internal Investigations had more than him in mind.

"My interview and research start from the general to

specifics. The peripheral stuff is usually the weakest and the most dangerous. It tells a lot about the center and the one in charge."

"I'm not in charge of recruitment," Rick said. "I.I. hasn't been filling you in very well."

"I told you, the way I do things is different. With your help, I can finish my assignment a lot faster."

She was sounding more confident now, more like the kind of operative I.I. sent out. Rick felt disappointed. And angry. He didn't understand the clashing emotions, but then he didn't understand what was driving him on with this game either. It was suicide, and he knew it. She was going to troll for information for her handlers, and he was going to help her.

Out to hang him, as he had started the day thinking. He had thought they were going to hang him but it was clear now that was way too suspicious. No, he wasn't going to be given the opportunity to be seen as a sacrificial lamb. Instead they were going to let him hang himself.

He stared at the beautiful hair he still held in his hands. Hell, they had even supplied him with the rope. He released her and turned toward the open sliding door that led out to the balcony. He could feel her eyes following him as he headed for the exit.

He gazed into the dark evening. "Rule number one," he began. "When you interview me, you'll always have your hair loose. You'll not wear it in a braid."

"I . . ." He turned to face her when she paused. She clutched a thick strand of her hair against her bosom. "It's very difficult to walk about outside with my hair untied."

Rick gave her the barest of smiles. "We won't be outside. I'll meet you here. Or you'll come to me at my apartment. A personal interview should have personal space, don't you agree? As a matter of balance?"

How badly did she want to do her job? Her fear or her assignment?

"All right," she whispered.

He nodded briskly. "Come to my office tomorrow and I'll take you to the recruitment center." He turned to go, then counted to a beat of three before pivoting around. "I should have rule number two by then."

Chapter Six

"*Release the frozen heart. It will burn you.*"

"*Grandmother, what do you mean by that?*"

"*Your life will be ruled by three centers, my child, and so three important prophecies to remember.*"

"*But you said the first center will betray me. And how is a frozen heart a center?*"

"*Prophecies don't tell you what to do. They just show you your lessons. See, the first is a lesson in judgment. The center, the sacred place, isn't where you think it is. As for the heart, that is the center of all living things, isn't it? Those who are good-hearted, who are loyal and dedicated to a cause, who are on the side of God, we call* chuung-sum—*the heart that is centered. In the movies, the good guys are all* chuung, *no?*"

"*So why would my* chuung *betray me? And why would my heart burn me?*"

"*Because life isn't like the movies, little Jade Tree. We all see something we want and go after it, but the center is an illusive place. It has many meanings. Our motherland is* chuung-quo, *the Middle Kingdom, but is it truly in the middle?*"

"*So Grandmother, the center is where I believe it is?*"

"*My child, you are old beyond your years.*"

Nikki missed her grandmother. Their conversations ran the gamut from old wives' tales, to historical epics from ancient China, to prophecies using the ancient Chinese calendar-almanac, the *Tuung-sing*, literally, the Book of

Knowledge. Her grandmother had her memorize many of the old poems from this book by the age of five. Even now Nikki could still recite most of them. They were what kept her sane in those dark days when they had put her in isolation. She had found out that one valued the oddest things when the soul was lonely.

She recalled how her grandmother's stories became a kind of strength builder. She spent those hours in the dark remembering the *Tuung-sing*, that wondrous book that told the past and the future, that gave the lunar dates to farm and to make babies. It taught all the Chinese traditional beliefs of palmistry, physiology, and astronomy. It held the secrets to the universe because her grandmother told her everything she knew came from that ancient text, with its updated almanac every year.

Tomorrow she would go down to Chinatown and buy herself this year's text. She wanted to leaf through its pages and see whether it still held any secrets for her.

"*Yun Tzi Tcho, Sing Poon Si.*" Nikki whispered in Cantonese those first two lines of the poem all Chinese-educated kids knew by heart. A new life is innocent, like an empty page, ready for the hard lessons ahead.

Easing the car into an empty parking spot, she turned off the engine, then leaned forward to check her face in the rearview mirror. She had put on a little more makeup today. Again, she hadn't wanted to dwell on the reason. The building loomed behind her reflection, already busy with visitors. She remembered how suffocated she had felt when she was in there. What was wrong with the building?

She opened the car door and stepped out, stopping for a moment to smooth away the wrinkles in her skirt. Notepad. Purse. ID. She was ready.

The building looked back at her, as if it were waiting for something. She shook the thoughts away and started to walk toward it, studying the front side with all its reflective windows. There was a lesson waiting for her in there. She felt it intuitively, the way she always did about certain things.

Her grandmother had talked of illusions. Nikki smiled with gentle acceptance. Her whole life now was an illusion. Her hardest lesson was to accept that and live it, and in the process she had learned to use it as a talent for her agency. Which, in turn, had guided her back here, to the beginning, where she was once an innocent, like an empty page.

She climbed the steps, making her way with the throng of visitors toward the entrance. Her thoughts turned to Rick Harden. A master illusionist. One who had cloaked himself so well, she didn't even think he knew where his center was. He held the key to her quest for the truth, but in order to find it she must break him apart, piece-by-piece.

However, last night he had been the one pulling her apart. She understood how she seemed to him, with her long hair and similar bearing to his old love; she had even been ready for it. But she had been totally unprepared for her response to his touch. Her stomach fluttered from the memory of the heat in his eyes and the sure touch of his hands holding her, caressing her hair. There was a moment when she had believed that she felt tenderness from him, but that instant fragmented quickly enough as his desire turned into anger. She had wanted to call him back when he let her go and walked away.

Illusions, she told herself. All illusions. She reached the security desk and gave the guard her ID to call up to Mr. Harden's office to verify her appointment.

"Miss Taylor, Mr. Harden said someone will be down in a few minutes to take you up," the woman told her.

He had kept his part of the bargain. "Thank you."

Nikki walked under the electronic security beam and sat down where the guard indicated. She looked at the other line, where she had been in a few days earlier, that led to the public-access offices. Those floors had the weakest illusions because there were so many hidden doorways out of the public eye, so many cameras zooming in on the visitors, so many people giving out the false impression that there were no secrets in this place of secrets.

Now she was about to go up another level. She sat, waiting. He had kept his word. She thought about his condition, his rule number one. Again, that strange sensation inside her, a slow curling heat. His rules were going to cost her. A lot.

"But Grandmother, why release a frozen heart that will burn me? That sounds like a painful lesson."

"Don't be so literal, silly girl. A lesson is always hard, but not necessarily painful."

Nikki glanced up. A woman smiled down at her.

"Miss Taylor? Won't you follow me? Mr. Harden is expecting you."

She returned her smile and stood up to follow the woman. She hoped her grandmother was right.

Rick put down the file he had been reading and looked up at Agent Candeloro, who was waiting for his response to his draft report. Cam was his detail coordinator in Task Force Two, in charge of making sure every element was in its place in each operation. He had never had any problems with Cam's work, but then Task Force Two had never been given really big fish to fry. Their department director, Gorman, had seen to that.

But fate had a strange way of playing games. Their last assignment, an operation to monitor an assassin, had snowballed into Gorman's current legal problems. It had also left Task Force Two without a department director, and perhaps facing elimination. Cam's key role in putting Gorman away was very important to Rick and Task Force Two. He had taken care of all the little things, from tracking down the assassin to getting the electronic surveillance set up, from day one.

How could such a good detail man be so bad at writing reports? It was a mystery Rick would rather not discuss right now. For one thing, Internal Investigations wouldn't give him the time to retrain bad habits, just to get his men to look less like Gorman's clowns, and more like an intel-gathering team.

Cam apologized before Rick said anything. "Sorry, sir. I told you I'm terrible at it."

"You have your own notes, your recollection of the events that led to that night on the boat, as well as the wiretap tapes.

How could you possibly mangle that kind of information into"—Rick tapped on the report with his finger—"this?"

"I don't know, sir," Cam answered.

"Tell me, do you want to continue in Task Force Two?"

Cam glanced up sharply. "Is that a threat, sir?" His voice was mild, but there was a combative light in his brown eyes.

Harden studied Cam for a moment. "I'm not in any position to carry out a threat," he finally answered, "but let's just say that you have a choice to your future, Agent Candeloro. You can return to Encryptions or Data, or apply for a new job somewhere else, but at the rate we're going, it definitely looks like neither of us will be continuing in Task Force Two."

Cam's eyes turned thoughtful. "You, too, sir?"

"Yes, me, too. Not that I'm using that piece of gossip to persuade you to write a better report," Rick said wryly. "Obviously, that's not going to turn you into a poet laureate."

Rick waited with vague amusement as his detail man choked back the shock of hearing his O.C. make a joke. Of course, these days he could afford the gallows humor, since there was a noose around his neck. Nobody knew this yet, least of all his men. He wasn't even sure why he told this tidbit to Cam, who would be sure to pass it along to the others. Perhaps it was time to see some panic around here.

"I like my job, sir, and I do it well. I can plan any operation to the last detail, no problem. When a yellow Boxter was needed overnight, I took care of it easily. When we need to track down locations, that's my forte. But somehow when I sit and write, the wires get crossed up."

"I can't help you with this, Agent Candeloro," Rick said as he handed the draft report back to Cam. "As O.C., with EYES sniffing around every day, I would be suspected of tampering. I want you to pick somebody who is relevant with data and records and have him go through your files with you. I trust you know someone who could piece data together?"

Cam's frown lasted all of one second. "Yes, sir. Patty Ostler from Records is very familiar with this case and has helped me coordinate part of the assignment. With your permission, sir, I'll get her as my personal help."

Great. Not only was Rick after a supposed romance writer, he was coordinating his own man's romance life for him. All to save his job, no less.

Nikki mentally reviewed her notes. Rick Harden was operation chief of TIARA's Task Force Two. Directly under the deputy director, he was the main strategist of any operations implemented under his care. Therefore, if the deputy director was crooked, it followed that the O.C. should be thoroughly investigated as well, especially if the former was using intel gathered by the latter to pass along to enemies.

Nikki understood why Internal Investigations would zero in on this man and hoped to close the case quickly. After all, Gorman was yet another embarrassing scandal for the Department of Justice, hit by so many lately. This time, however, it couldn't just sweep everything quietly under the rug because TIARA happened to be partners with navy SEAL commander Admiral Madison's special operations teams. TIARA gathered the intel Admiral Madison's men used for covert action. When leaking information put his men's lives in jeopardy, someone as tough as Admiral Madison wasn't going to just let that go.

She had never met the admiral but was impressed with his tenacity to get to the truth. When she was briefed about the Gorman case, she was told that the traitor would never have been caught without the admiral's wily infiltration of Task Force Two.

Admiral Madison had the reputation of doing things his way. Nikki liked his style. By sending in Steve McMillan, a SEAL operative from one of his teams, the admiral was able to study firsthand where his leaks were coming from. The operation had taken over a year, but Admiral Madison wasn't called Mad Dog without a reason. No one, Nikki was told, liked to get The Dog mad. She had smiled at her handler when he said that, imagining a man being called Mad Dog Madison. Oh, to have him on her side when she had been a prisoner. He wouldn't have left her in that hellhole, wouldn't have conveniently forgotten her because she was no longer an asset.

She had agreed to this contract based on what this man did for those under him. She had never met him, but just knowing that he would go to bat for any man under his care was enough for her. Besides, he, too, had been briefed on her background, and she felt that they knew each other very well already.

The admiral's plan had netted Gorman, but it wasn't enough. In the world of red tape and politics, deals were made to cause the least amount of pain for the people in power. Gorman was a veteran, someone who knew how to play the game, and he was holding out as long as he could while his lawyers worked out a deal.

Nikki looked at the name plaque outside Rick's door. Gorman was important. Rick Harden wasn't. Just as she hadn't been a long time ago, hung out to dry while someone else got away scot-free.

The door opened. A younger man walked out, a smug smile on his face when he glanced up to see her studying him.

"Good morning, ma'am," he greeted cheerfully. He turned to the secretary and added, "Later, Greta."

"Well, what changed that sour look into such joy?" the secretary asked.

"Unexpected luck, my dear, that will bring the love of my life closer to me than ever," the man said, and his face broke into a big smile again as he walked out of the office.

Greta shook her head. "That Cam is the only one who comes out of that office smiling."

Nikki was about to ask why when the intercom buzzed and Rick's voice came through crisply, "Send Miss Taylor in, Greta."

"Yes, sir." Greta turned to Nikki. "That was just a little joke, dear. I'm always talking to myself. Go on in, he won't bite."

Nikki nodded. She opened the door and stepped inside. Across the expanse of the inner office, the man sitting behind a massive dark oak desk stared intently at her. There was a gleam in his green eyes as he waited for her to come closer. Rick Harden was going to eat her alive.

Rick had the same dream last night again. It had started like all his old nightmares, but twice now, Nikki Taylor had appeared at the end. This time she wore that damn towel.

It had been Nikki's curves that pressed against his length as he pushed the hair away from her face. He wasn't surprised by her presence this time, and the dream had given him the freedom to explore a little longer, as she lay beneath him quietly.

He knew now how tiny her waist was and his subconscious had called back each detail of her near-nakedness. Her head was thrown back, revealing the graceful curve of her neck, riveting his attention to the half-exposed breasts above the unknotted towel. Her quick, shallow breathing had loosened the terry cloth even more, and just when he had reached out to pull it away, he came awake.

A man knew when he was being jerked around by his dick. Rick remembered it well—it had been his downfall, after all. He had always hated this recurring nightmare, but now, he wanted it back.

His gaze drifted back to the petite, and seemingly unthreatening woman in his office. With high cheekbones that made those solemn dark eyes tilt up slightly, she echoed another woman in his past who had come to him with a wicked grin. But that wasn't what was appealing about Nikki Taylor because she certainly hadn't shown the same attitude his wife had. He couldn't decide if the calm reserve she exuded was real, or if somehow she knew he wouldn't have gone for a flirt with bold hands.

No, they knew this new act would intrigue him even more. Quiet, with a hint of nervousness. Waiting for him instead of making the first move. Keeping him guessing about what she was after. And despite his misgivings, here she was, in his office, ostensibly doing what he wanted. All an illusion, of course. There were layers she was hiding from him and he was the one doing things her way. One dangerous package.

"Have a seat." There were three chairs on the other side of his desk. She chose the one in the middle, directly across from him. There were shadows under her eyes. "Did you have a good night?"

The tip of her tongue flicked out, moistening her upper lip. "Yes."

"Liar," he mocked. Maybe she had dreams, too.

Her brown eyes were smiling. "You didn't ask whether I had a restful night. I did have a good night." Her own mockery was gentle, as if her amusement was self-directed.

"I see I have to be very specific with you," Rick drawled, and watched her cheeks tinge pink. "Are you ready for our interview tonight? The personal one we agreed on."

The tip of her tongue appeared again. "Yes."

She was a woman of few words. So was he. He wondered how she was going to get him to talk. "This recruiting class—what do you want me to do once I get you in there? Do you want them to pick you for testing? Or is there a specific department you want to test into?"

His quick change of direction was meant to keep her out of balance, but she wasn't at all fazed. "I just want to attend as an observer for now. No special preferences. I know they'll run the usual background checks and I don't want to draw any attention to myself."

"That's why you need me," Rick said, cocking a brow, "to smooth things over, just in case they look too closely and find out that your fingerprints don't bring up anything."

She looked up, eyes steady. "The daiquiri glass," she murmured. When he didn't say anything, she nodded to herself.

"What are you thinking?" he asked, needing to know everything on her mind.

"It was a delicious daiquiri," she said. "I hope next time you will get me one without having to pay for the glass too. It can get very expensive, me and food."

He remembered how much she ate. And how much he enjoyed watching her. "It'll be my pleasure," he said, softly, "to feed you."

But first things first. He rose, pocketing his beeper and cell phone. Today I.I. had given him a stack of questions and demands for files. He knew that was just the beginning. It had occurred to him that with Nikki there, they might be trying a two-edge attack. Perhaps they thought he would be distracted.

She stood up, waited for him, then stepped back just as he reached her. She didn't want him too close. It was a small, almost undetectable gesture, but it annoyed him. Was she just afraid of him or was it done on purpose?

"That's what I intend to do, you know," he said as he opened the door for her. When she met his eyes inquiringly, he continued, "I intend to feed you tonight."

Chapter Seven

Rick was watching her from somewhere. Nikki could feel his lingering gaze as she went through the doors into the recruiting conference room. She also had the speculative attention of the agents taking attendance. That was expected since she didn't have the proper papers and appointment.

There were about forty applicants in the room, all in their mid- to late-twenties, dressed conservatively. A couple looked to be in their thirties. She sat in the back, listening to the introductions, remembering when she had gone through Career Training Program.

She had been eager to learn the ins and outs of intelligence and counterintelligence, going through the mandatory testing, and after being accepted, she was put into training based on her tests. She was here because she wanted to see the whole starting phase with new eyes. Now that she understood the weeding out process, and how each applicant was valued as a potential asset, everything had a new meaning. Under the right conditions, someone high up could pick out who would go out on the field and who would be left behind.

The first agent introduced was Robert Sutton, in standard dark blue suit and gray tie. "First, there are different directorates," he began. "I work for the Directorate of Operations, which recruits people."

Assets, Nikki corrected. Assets. She knew what they were looking for. One who could live a lie, pretending to be someone he or she wasn't, and sometimes, break the laws of the country. Not a job for everyone.

The intellectual ones went into planning. Those with street-smarts were trained in certain covert programs. She listened as each agent stood up to give a short lesson on his respective directorate. She recognized two of them as Agent Erik Jones and Agent Denise Lorens. Nikki looked at the woman. And there were other kinds of assets.

Agent Jones was his usual disarming self. "I just transferred into the Directorate of Administration," he told them, with a grin, "because I was told I'm good at details. We basically take care of the other directorates—shipments, any kind of travel arrangements, paperwork. We support the different agencies by supplying computers, security, necessities. So nobody gets a pencil without my approval. Now that's power."

That last line earned him some laughs from the applicants. He sat down, and it was Agent Lorens's turn. She was a striking woman—tall and sophisticated, with beautiful classic features. She was, Nikki noted, everyone in the room's concept of what a spy would look like. Her voice was low and confident as she introduced herself.

"The Directorate of Intelligence," she explained, "analyzes information gathered by the others. It takes a lot of practice to be good at analysis because there is so much information to process. It takes a sharp eye to see the most important thing and it also takes an experienced operative to make sense of it for her superiors."

She looked up, and her eyes met Nikki's for an instant. Nikki had expected retaliation for what she had done to the woman the other day. She wasn't at all surprised at the combative vibes she was getting from across the room. Denise Lorens didn't seem like a person who liked her plans upended.

"We bring together information from all sources," Denise continued, "such as satellites, human spies, foreign broadcasts, computer bulletin boards, to name a few, and we present a coherent picture of the data. Basically, if you are recruited, everything you find out will be given to me. I'll then make conclusions about what your information means and pass it along to different intel task forces."

Such as TIARA's Task Force Two, Nikki mused. All Gorman had needed was an ally in that department to facilitate certain leaks. An asset who had been chosen to manipulate instead of compile information could easily hide the leaks until it was too late. Such a person could be culled from a Career Training group such as this, someone who fit the background and scores they had in mind. Nikki didn't blink as Denise continued challenging her silently even after she returned to her seat.

The last representative was from the Directorate of Science and Technology, which determined military capabilities through satellites and radars. The supplier of James Bond equipment of the spy trade, as her agency jokingly called it. She should know how important it was; this was where she had started as an operative, where she had studied the armament race and had been part of different teams sent out with the newest gadgets. And—she shifted her gaze back to the woman in the front of the room—a total opposite of Agent Lorens's job. Her type of analysis did not include certain kinds of sacrifices.

"So," Robert Sutton said, after the initial overture, "what do you want to know about gathering intel for the government of the United States? We're here to answer any questions, so don't be shy."

"I see you everywhere. You're not following me, are you?" Agent Jones asked after the recruiting class.

Nikki smiled. "I'm doing a bad job, then. You're not supposed to know you're being followed."

"What brings you here? Are you interested in working for us?"

He was trying so hard. "It's for my book," she told him. "I need to know what a recruit feels like. This way I get a basic course, too."

"So, was it interesting? Is your heroine going to apply for a job here and then head on to one of the directorates?" He pointed to himself. "She should go into Administration. That way, she'd know exactly where everything is going and what everyone is doing. She discovers a discrepancy, then falls into the enemy's trap because she has something they want."

Nikki laughed. "It sounds like you have a story to tell yourself, Agent Jones. Perhaps you should write it."

Laughter gleamed in his eyes. "Call me Erik. And I have a better idea. Why don't I tell you this plot and you write it? I know all sorts of stories from my department. That way we can share the profits and I don't get into trouble for writing what I know. It would be easy for you, too—less research."

A woman's voice interrupted them. "Getting all the information you need for your book, Miss Taylor?"

Nikki turned to face Agent Lorens; she had been waiting for the other woman. It was to be expected. It was always bad karma to stand between a woman and the object of her desire.

"More than I expected," Nikki answered.

"You needn't research the basic recruiting procedures. I'd have been glad to help you with any questions about intelligence gathering," Agent Lorens said, with a smile that didn't reach her eyes. "That's my specialty. Career Training Programs don't really cover everything that we do. You're looking at the wrong places."

Nikki smiled back. She didn't want to fight, she really didn't. "That's my specialty. I find those are the most interesting places for my stories." She looked around the conference room. "A different angle shows different perspectives."

"Oh sure, there are different styles, but good operatives would come to the same conclusions, wouldn't they, no matter which angle they are coming from? So it's a matter of how efficient they are at their job, and how good they are at supporting their conclusions with research. Don't you agree?"

She was being told that she was wasting time, that her conclusions would be the same as Denise's. The gleam in the other woman's eyes was supercilious, confident that she would be proven right.

"Agent Lorens, I have barely even started my research,"

Nikki pointed out. "Besides, from what I have learned today, isn't Intel about observations and not conclusions? That you can draw a certain trend from the observations but the conclusion is best left for the task forces?"

She shouldn't have quoted back verbatim what was said in the recruiting conference. It was like adding fuel to hot coal, which was kind of funny, since the room temperature seemed to have dropped down to freezing. She felt Denise's anger at her and wondered at its intensity. There was more to this than being bested.

"Is that where you would be researching next, the task forces? And would you be going over all of them, or just specifically one? Perhaps I can fill you in with what you need to know."

There were times when noise was just noise, and there was no sense to it. Nikki didn't understand the anger but she could dissipate it. She had done it many times when she was interrogated. Round and round they went until the victim gave in and said whatever needed to be said. Sometimes she told them what they wanted to hear, just to gain strength for another day. As always, in tense situations, she gave herself a gentle reminder. She was a free woman now, and no one was going to hurt her.

She looked up at the taller woman and nodded. "If you like," she said simply.

As she expected, there was nothing left for Denise Lorens to say to that. Like those others who wanted something, she would be back another day, and maybe by then she would have some time to think about this underlying anger.

Watching others. Catching them watching others. Finding out what they are looking for. And making sure he was the one with the information first.

It wasn't even a challenge anymore. Rick glanced away from the television screen in one of the many viewing rooms reserved for observation and checked the time. He had instructed Greta to buzz him when Harpring from I.I. arrived at his office, and it shouldn't be too long now. He should be making preparations for the grilling that was sure to come, and not wasting time here monitoring Nikki Taylor. He had purposely brought those three together—Nikki, Denise, and Jones—so he could see for himself how they interacted.

His lips curled up derisively. He supposed someone else in his shoes would enjoy the power of having the security clearance to see whatever he wanted. It would be so easy to succumb to it. Knowledge was power, and power in the wrong hands could manipulate lives.

He had seen what that had done for Gorman before he became too greedy. Strange that he never envied the man, just hated him for it. Yet Rick didn't live under the illusion that he was the better guy. In many ways he was just as dangerous as his former deputy director. After all, he had stood by and let all this happen, hadn't he? And what did that make him? He didn't like what he had become but there was no going back.

Unless it was of the highest national security, there was a camera looking in on most of the conference rooms. It was a way of life everyone in the building didn't even think much about. There was not much privacy around but those who worked there long enough knew where the safest places were.

At his level, there weren't many things Rick couldn't find out. This was his domain, even though no one saw it that way. In the last decade Gorman had taken credit for the successes, and Rick hadn't cared. Instead he concentrated on rebuilding his file. In those days, after his demotion, no one had wanted Rick in his department, and his only option was Gorman's offer.

Looking back, he should have walked away. Instead he had shaken hands with his enemy, knowing full well that he would be used and tossed away. He had been arrogant and foolhardy, believing that he could just prove to everyone that he was a changed person, that he could transfer out when people saw him as a yes-man, someone with whom they could work. And so Hard On emerged from the ashes of his dead-end career. Bureaucrat instead of operative. Paper Intel instead of field cowboy.

That thought filled him with self-disgust. His gaze returned to the screen to watch Nikki with Agent Jones and Denise. He had used that power to manipulate the three of them together. There was a connection between them somehow, and he meant to find out what it was.

Watching Denise suddenly stalk off, he wondered what Nikki had said to cause the woman to betray herself with her body language so easily. After all, she was a trained operative, and not easily flustered by words. Even in the throes of passionate sex, she hadn't given away her cover. Nikki had gotten a reaction without even raising her voice.

Power. Rick pondered the word as he studied the small figure on the screen. There was a woman who pretended to watch but had made enough moves to put someone like Denise to shame. In the last week Nikki Taylor, had gotten closer to him than any of these other agents I.I. had thrown at him. She hadn't taken him for granted, hadn't bought into his yes-man image, and certainly hadn't been predictable.

He drew the cell phone from his pocket and punched the numbers without taking his eyes off the screen. A few seconds later he watched Nikki pull a cell phone from her purse, a small frown on her face.

He was tired of watching. Once upon a time, he had been a doer, a man of action. This investigation might be his final battle, but he would not go down as a damn bureaucrat. Nikki Taylor was the key. Her fear of him was the key. And he would push her into giving him what he wanted.

"Hello?" Her voice was clear and had a calming effect on his raging emptiness.

"You know you look like her, don't you?" he said to the woman in the screen, and enjoyed the small start she gave at the sound of his voice. When she didn't answer, he continued, "You're going to ask me questions about her, aren't you?"

"Yes," she said.

"Rule number two. I get to ask you personal questions afterward. Since you are into balance, I should have a right to your private space too. And since I'm helping with your research your way, you have to answer my questions my way."

Her expression didn't change. "And if I refuse?"

"But you wouldn't." Just like him, she was after something, too. "I take it the silence means yes?"

"Yes," she said, so softly he could barely make out the word.

The way she said it tugged at something inside him, causing him to give her one chance to escape. "You have talked with Agent Denise Lorens, Nikki. I expect she told you what kind of man I am, that I enjoy certain things. Here is your chance to back out. There will be no turning back once this starts." He lowered his voice. "Nikki, are you still coming to my place?"

He held his breath. For her sake, he wanted her to refuse. Yet the darkest part of him urged her on silently, tempted to capture this elusive butterfly.

"Yes."

He exhaled. So be it. "Good. Tonight, come to me and bring with you something to tie you with. I'll leave the choice of material in your hands." He disconnected without waiting for her answer.

On the TV, she stood still for a moment before putting away her cell phone. Rick mentally shrugged away the urge to call her back. He shouldn't give a lick about her fear. He wanted her to be afraid of him; she was too much in control of this game they were playing.

He didn't know where he was going with this but if she was willing to come to him in fear, then what she was after must be very, very important. Since it had to do with his dead wife, then it had to do with Gorman, because it was only Gorman who knew the truth. Was I.I. trying to get him to confess to Nikki, and if so, how would that tie in with their plans to use him as a scapegoat for the Gorman scandal?

He watched Nikki walk out of the room, her long braid swaying gently behind her. Tonight she would come to him with her hair down. His loins clenched at the memory of how she looked and felt in his arms. He still couldn't decide if what he felt was real or was just some twisted psychological reaction to his past.

Focus, Harden, focus. He stepped out of the room and nodded to the security guard outside. Focus on what she was hiding from him. So far, she had revealed two things. They had sent her to find out about his dead wife. And to learn whether he was a security risk.

His decision to act must have reactivated his dead brain cells. He stopped in his tracks as if a lightning bolt had struck him. The similar looks. Questions to bring back his memories. Seduction. Would she then betray him, like a replay of the past?

His beeper cut into his thoughts, reminding him of Harpring and paper trails. Rick flexed his hands, then looked at them. He had gone crazy the last time someone close to him was killed. Who was deliberately bringing back those memories?

Chapter Eight

Nikki didn't need Denise Lorens to tell her what kind of man Ricardo Harden was. She didn't think that woman even saw beyond the lies that made up the operations chief of Task Force Two. That wasn't the real Rick. Besides, Denise's agenda was very different from hers. She wouldn't care whether she had the truth, as long as she proved I.I.'s conclusions.

Nikki suspected her own image of Rick Harden would be a far cry from Denise's. Of course, she didn't have the same experiences that Denise undoubtedly enjoyed. Unfamiliar warmth flooded in the pit of her stomach at the images that came with that thought.

His request for a rope was meant to bring up those images. He was playing on her fear of him. Well, not exactly of him, she corrected. What she feared were ghosts that could no longer hurt her. What she feared were the strange emotions he made her feel. He wanted control of her, and instead of fighting him, she found that she had to fight herself. She couldn't say no to him. The insight into her own sudden emotional flurry was unsettling.

It was only natural to start comparing herself with Denise Lorens, even though there was nothing in the world that would make her wish to be like that woman. However, it would be nice to lose her cowardice. Denise didn't fear her own body's reaction to a man, didn't even think twice about giving in to her own needs while stealing a man's soul, for it was Rick's shell she had been after, and not what was inside. To take pleasure that way was stealing. And wrong.

Nikki wished, though, that she didn't fear what Rick Harden was making her feel. Her body responded in subtle ways even when he hadn't touched her since those first minutes outside her bathroom. When he had tapped on her chime that night, standing there by her bed, dominating her private space, she had had a sudden vision of him naked.

And that had been the most unsettling thought of all. She had stood there staring until he had mocked her, asking her why she looked at him that way—transfixed, he said. How was she to explain that a few minutes earlier, in the shower, she had suddenly understood her grandmother's second prophecy, and it had to do with him? That he was part of her quest to find her *chuung*? That he was the first man she had undressed mentally in a long, long time?

How ironic that he had shown up, and then played with the very instrument that influenced her life. A person was like a chime, making its own music. She remembered the haunting melody that had invaded her cell every now and then. It was the only sign of life in her darkness. One day, she had asked her interrogator what it was. For once he had answered a question, instead of demanding an answer.

A wind chime, he had said, and had cruelly added, "When the wind played with it, did it make you think of life outside?" He had said it to fill her with despair, but she had listened to that chime and it had brought her hope.

When Jed McNeil, a commando from the group who had saved her life, released her from the cell, he hadn't thought her crazy when she told him she wanted her chime. Jed had smiled and risked his life a second time to retrieve something that meant nothing to him. That man—Nikki smiled fondly at the memory—would fit her grandmother's good guy in the movies—the ones who were good-hearted, loyal and dedicated to a cause, who were *chuung-sum*. Jed would always have a special place in her heart.

"Come on up. My door is unlocked." Rick's voice came through the buzzer. There was a loud click and the secured doors that led into the bright lobby opened. Nikki took a deep breath and stepped inside. The security guard smiled at her. She returned his greeting.

Rick. She mouthed his name softly. She had never said his name to him. She didn't know how to say it without betraying herself. So strange. It was just a name, but it embodied all her wants and fears. She pressed the elevator button to his floor.

Every man owned a dark and a light side. And the *chu-ung*, his center, balanced the two. But only if the man learned to listen to himself because, like a chime, he had to synchronize and balance the noise. That was the moment when he could hear the *chuung*. It wasn't easy to sit and talk to one's own soul.

She got off the elevator and slowly made her way to the apartment on the right. She stared at the door, then lifted her hand and unclipped her loosely bound knot. Her hair tumbled down past her waist.

It was important to take each lesson and give it its proper sound. She would not let fear make any noise in her *chuung*.

The apartment door opened. And Rick Harden stood before her, without a smile, without a greeting. Her lesson had begun.

Rick was wearing a dark green shirt and slacks. Nikki's eyes met his glittering ones for a long moment before he took a step back. She walked in, but he didn't move aside. He pushed the door closed with one hand. His other hand swooped under her cascading hair, closed around her waist, and drew her in. The last time he had her near a doorway, he had attacked and trapped her. This time, the hand on her lower back didn't hurry as he pulled her inexorably closer.

Nikki couldn't resist. If he had used force, she might have. But his green eyes caught hers, and the look in them took away her breath. Her heart quickened. She wet her lips.

"This is your last chance," he said softly, his gaze on her moistened mouth.

He was right. He wasn't forcing her. Nonetheless, she felt his hand firmly persuading her forward.

"You can still fly away, little bird."

She should. *Release the frozen heart. It would burn you.* She should. Instead she found herself shaking her head.

"So be it," he whispered. And his lips seared hers.

They said the cosmos began with intense heat at a single point and a big explosion. Brilliant white heat. Dark fire. Raging chaos. His tongue stole into her mouth, and she sagged against him even as her whole body exploded into this sudden awareness. It was like waking up abruptly from dreaming. Like coming up for air after being trapped under water.

Before, if anyone came close to kissing her, she would be engulfed by sheer blind panic. Somehow, Rick's kiss was overriding her fears. Her whole being vibrated, starting from where their lips met, rushing inward, washing away her old apprehensions like toppled sandcastles and storming past her defenses into her inner sanctum. He swallowed her gasp.

He didn't kiss her gently. Far from it. He stalked every corner of her mind, taking over any thought of protest. His tongue roamed in lazy exploration as his hand moved to her backside and pulled her even closer, letting her know in no uncertain terms that as far as his body was concerned, she wasn't going anywhere.

Rick wanted. He had to taste her. That sensation from the other weekend was back, in double dose. That dark and needy hunger, that forbidden search for satisfaction, grew into a maelstrom. Part of him wanted her out of his life. A tiny, negligible part. But all of him wanted to just devour this woman.

She was petite and fragile, a shivering female way over her head where his desires were concerned. But the feelings she invoked weren't fragile at all. They overwhelmed every protective layer he had, making him throw caution to the wind, to merge all of himself with her. His male into her female. His deep need into her soft surrender.

How could the taste of one so delicate be so powerfully heady? Her soft tongue hesitated and yielded, driving him crazy the way only a woman could. She responded with an eagerness that surprised him, with a passion that he had known was lurking under that calm exterior. He wanted her to taste him. He sucked on her tongue. Almost there. Almost . . . she hesitated. Didn't she know that only drove him wilder? He curved one hand around her soft bottom, and pulled her against him as he thrust forward. He ached to have her.

Rick's aroused state shocked Nikki back to her senses, and she started to push him away. Her shoulder bag fell to the floor, the notepad in the side pocket making a loud slapping protest. He released her lips but still held her tightly against him.

His eyes blazed down into hers. "You weren't afraid a moment ago. Why now?" he asked, his voice a low rumble.

Breathing hard, Nikki couldn't tell him. She had embraced his kiss with mindless abandon. It felt so good to let go and let his heat fill her. He could have continued forever and she wouldn't have been aware of the time, but now the old fears came tumbling back into her and she couldn't tell him why.

"Is this part of your game?"

She shook her head and pushed against his hard, unyielding chest. He didn't budge. "Let me take a step back," she said, trying to keep her voice level. "I just need a few minutes."

Rick frowned, and she saw realization creeping into his eyes. He slid his hand up into the hollow of her back and allowed a few inches between them. She released a sigh, then gulped a big breath. She looked up and saw anger replacing the taut desire in his expression.

"How are you going to do this if you're afraid of it?" he taunted. "That's what you're afraid of, isn't it? Sex."

She tilted her chin up at the challenge in his tone. "I'm here, aren't I?"

"Yes, very brave indeed," he mocked. His hand moved up her back, lingering for an instant to sweep her hair away from her shoulder, as if reluctant to let her go. He stepped back. "Go home, little bird. You're afraid of a man's body. I'm hard, and for some reason, your fear makes me harder. You're afraid I'll touch you, and after that kiss, I'm going to do more than touch you. So go now. Don't play with me. Your fear won't stop me from taking what I want."

His words hurt. She hated her fear, hated the way it controlled her life. Rick Harden might have a reputation of being a bastard but he had attempted to let her go three times now, and that told her more about him than all these words he had tossed to warn her off. She would not let fear make any noise in her *chuung*, she repeated adamantly.

Slowly, succinctly, she declared, "I. Am. Not. Afraid."

Slowly, deliberately, she reached out and placed her hands where she feared most, on the front of his pants, where he had been hard, where he was still hard. She squelched the urge to turn and run. Without thinking, she ran her hands down the length of him, and his immediate response brought her gaze back down. Not just hard. He was hot. And big. Absolutely big. Her eyes widened at the thought, and she wanted to turn and run again.

I. Am. Not. Afraid. She grasped him determinedly and felt him stiffen. She looked up and caught him trying to hide his surprise, and unexpected elation rose. She repeated, "I'm not afraid. You're the one who's afraid. You don't want *me* to touch *you*."

"Lady, you're playing with fire."

The damn woman was challenging him. Why was she so afraid? She was scared shitless, but evidently that wasn't going to stop her from accomplishing whatever it was she wanted. Fine. He was through offering her chances. He covered both her hands with his and pressed down. He wasn't lying about playing with fire. He was burning up. He moved her hands up and down, and with hooded eyes, watched the emotions fleeting across her face. Panic, then determination. Fear, then fascination. Then, to his amazement, he discovered that she was doing the rubbing all on her own; he had forgotten to keep moving his hand as he grew more aroused by her touch.

He quelled the need for simple seduction. She issued a challenge, didn't she? "Did you bring it?"

Her hands stopped. He almost changed his mind, just to get her to continue. Ah, the power of a woman to make a man beg. He had learned his lesson from that. No, her fear was important. As long as she had that fear, he was in control of her.

His apartment had the air of a self-absorbed man, grown used to privacy. The living room was starkly furnished in black leather and brass-gold. Throw rugs provided the only bright colors on the oak shellac floor. There were no decorations on the wall, except for a large ornate clock with external moving parts. No pictures. No flowers or lace curtains. All man.

Nikki walked past the long sofa to the fireplace with a large tricolored animal skin lying on the hearth. There was a pile of books nearby, one still open. A couple of throw pillows. Here, she thought, was the center of the room. She stood there for a moment, looking into the quiet fireplace, then slowly turned to look at Rick.

Hands resting on the back of the black sofa, he stood with deceptive boredom as the green fire in his eyes consumed her every move. He was waiting. Slowly, she reached into her shoulder bag and pulled out a silk purse. It felt cool and soft, quite different from its content. He watched as she approached. Somehow she felt safer with the sofa between them as she held up the silk purse.

He took it. Weighed it in his hand. She watched his face as he appeared to consider opening the colorful bag with its chrysanthemum needlework. Standing this close, she could see how long his black eyelashes were. She glanced away quickly, feeling foolish. That she would be drawn to these little things about him, when he was so tough and unyielding, was bewildering.

She couldn't quite believe what she had done. Her hands still tingled at the memory of touching him . . . there. Never in her wildest imaginations would she have come up with that ever happening. He had been right when he taunted her about being afraid of sex. Before she'd met Rick, touching any man would bring on panic attacks.

There was no denying it any longer. She had pushed aside what she had known ever since the day when she'd drunk down that glass of frozen daiquiri with Rick Harden's gaze on her. He was the first man she was attracted to in a long, long time. She wanted—

"Have you eaten?"

She blinked and shook her head. She had been too nervous to eat anything.

"We'll eat first, then get to your business." He didn't say anything about afterward. He lifted a strand of her long hair and twirled it around one finger.

"All right." It was quite clear the man wanted, too. But he caressed her hair like a fond memory. Nikki inhaled. She must remember that. He wanted, but not her.

The kitchen and dining area was down another level, with a small atrium between it and the living room. She peered down at the view of the private courtyard below. She had walked in there that first night, had enjoyed the quiet privacy, but hadn't known its beauty could also be shared from above.

"Does it meet with your approval?" He waited for her at the bottom of the stairs.

"It's not what I expected. The architect knew what he was doing," she said, making sure there were a few feet between them.

"Yes, he was into balance." There was a light mockery in his voice, and his eyes told her he knew.

"Yes, he was," she agreed, as she went down the last few steps. He didn't move out of the way. "He made everything count, gave thought to every square foot of living space, and he had beauty as his goal."

"That's quite a conclusion from taking a short walk from the living room into my kitchen," Rick said. She couldn't tell what he was thinking as he watched her like a cat out on a hunt. He paused a few seconds, then moved. He pulled out the chair from the dining table and she sat down. "Tell me more while I get you a balanced meal."

She wondered whether he knew his dry sense of humor didn't add up to his image as Hard-On. Like the apartment, the internal makeup of Rick Harden was interesting and different from the outside image. She suspected that this was a view that very few people were allowed to see. Her gaze settled on the silk purse; he had set it beside his plate. She swallowed.

"I don't know—it's just how I feel about things. Maybe another time." She looked down at her own plate, forcing her eyes away from the purse. "I . . . didn't know you were going to feed me."

He sat down across from her and picked up the bottle of wine. "I liked watching you eat." His reference to their meeting at the restaurant brought back her earlier thoughts. Of why she was here. Of what he was thinking of as he watched her. Her gaze helplessly returned to the silk purse. She knew the slow rising heat on her face didn't escape his notice. "You seem to sense so much in so little, Nikki. I wonder whether you see what others see in you. Do others know how you feel inside?"

She was grateful for the cold tartness of the wine. "I thought I was supposed to do my interview first," she said.

He refilled her glass. "By all means."

She stared into his green eyes. He wasn't going to make this easy for her. His hand rested by the purse, cradling the wineglass. He hadn't touched it. Hadn't opened it. Hadn't even looked at it. She picked up her own flute, drank from it again.

"After you feed me," she told him. Food was fortifying. Food was reprieve.

Rick had never sat back and watched a woman eat as a prelude to sex before. This was the second time he had gotten aroused while looking at Nikki Taylor enjoy a meal. It was hard to explain it. Maybe because she always presented herself in such a minimalist, calm, and quiet manner, he hadn't expected her to have such an appetite for food.

The contrast was amazingly sensual. At least it had that effect on his libido. He had the sudden fantasy of tying her in his bed for the weekend and feeding her himself. Hell, he was hungry, too, had been since he met her. And not for food.

From the corner of his eye, he caught the bright yellow chrysanthemums of the silk purse lying close to his hand. He had placed it there to make her nervous, of course. She refused to look at it, but he knew she was very aware of its presence. He wondered lazily whether she was going to run out on him. Whether he would let her. Or whether she was really going to let him open that purse and use whatever it was she had chosen.

He didn't care to analyze why he had set her up this way. Something inside had urged him to. He wanted her in his home; he'd fantasized her in his bed. Now she was here, skittish as a wild bird. But she had come to him anyway.

He wasn't going to rush it. He planned to stir her up, get to understand what made her the way she was. It was obvious she didn't like what she felt for him—yet. But he could make her want him. He knew for a painful fact that he wanted her in every way imaginable. Maybe taking her to bed would stop those nightly dreams of her.

The easiest way was to answer her questions, of course. What was one more bad report on him? She wouldn't find out anything he didn't choose to give away.

For some reason, he didn't want her to make it too easy for him. He didn't intend to have Nikki Taylor on her back, compliant, just because she was doing her job. He wanted her to know sex with him would mean giving him all of the parts of her she was hiding from him, that he was going to fuck her till that serene façade fell away to show the food-loving, sensual creature inside. Till all her calm defenses disappeared. And just maybe, he would stop then.

Rick narrowed his eyes as he watched and waited. The woman wanted him, but feared sex. That itself would make any man a little crazy from wanting to go after her, but he was also very aware that she had a handler who understood what she could do to a man like him. He had never hidden his sexual appetite from those he dated, and the fact that his training had never been a secret brought along many eager women who wanted to try Hard-On. And there were the Denise Lorenses.

So many women since . . . the wine tasted bitter in his mouth. There were a few whose names he still remembered. Maria, who was now living near Chicago, married to a postman. Mel, an operative who had transferred to Paris. None had been able to fill the void inside. He had become so dissipated that he would use fear to get what he wanted. He looked at Nikki, quietly enjoying her filet mignon, totally unaware of his plans for her. Well, perhaps not totally, he acknowledged with a touch of cynicism. She only seemed able to put it out of her mind when there was food around.

It clicked in his head that there was a connection here somewhere, but he wasn't interested in delving into it tonight. He watched her wash down the last of the steak, enjoyed her sigh of satisfaction. Then he pounced.

"Let me show you the rest of the apartment. Maybe you can tell me what is out of balance. Suggest some improvements."

It occurred to Nikki that he remembered everything she had told him. He hadn't laughed at her yet. His voice still held that lazy drawl he had adopted since the beginning of dinner.

"You have an excellent memory," she said as she put the dishes into the sink. "Most people can't repeat my job description back to me."

"Since you tell so little about yourself, Nikki, it's easy to remember. Besides, who could forget the way we met?"

It might be the wine, but she felt warm. She averted her face as she walked past him, glad to have her hair as a veil. His touch at her elbow stopped her in mid-step. His fingers burned through the sleeves of her thin blouse. It was just a light touch, but her whole body honed in on him with an eager, energetic rush. It was inexplicable. He was like a drug.

He tipped her chin up and she had to meet his eyes. "There's a bit of gravy on your lips."

She wiped one side of her mouth with her hand, but he shook his head. Tilting her chin higher, he bent down and gently licked the other corner of her mouth. A shiver ran up her spine, and her lips parted tremulously. He didn't let her go.

"It tastes better from your lips," he murmured. He dipped

down, kissed her full on the lips this time, then lifted his head a few inches. She could see the black that circled the green of his eyes. "Even better."

Nikki wanted his lips on her again, wanted him to kiss her the way he had done earlier, but he just continued the butterfly kisses until she couldn't stand it any longer, till she finally reached up by standing on her toes. Instead of taking advantage, Rick straightened, eyes gleaming.

Comprehension dawned. "You're doing this on purpose," she accused.

"Doing what, little bird?" When she didn't reply, he squeezed her chin gently. "Say it. Doing what on purpose?"

He seemed determined to use that against her. She couldn't utter the word. "You're teasing me," she finally said.

"No, say the right word, the one you're thinking of," he mocked. "It's seduction, Nikki. I'm seducing you, even when you're fighting it."

"Why?" It had to do with her similarity to a certain someone, of course. She hadn't made any sexual advances toward him at all.

His lips lowered to a mere breath above hers. The scent of wine and man was seductive. The promise in his eyes was seductive. With a few kisses, he had opened a hole inside her that needed filling.

"Because I want you willing," he said. "I want you thinking about me when you least expect it. It'll make that interview more interesting because I know you're getting wet and needy while you try to pry my secrets from me."

She blinked at his words, shocked that she was doing exactly what he was priming her to experience. She felt the wetness. Felt the warm need that bunched in her loins.

"I thought I'd be fair one last time—let you know what's happening, what's going to happen," he continued in that lazy, knowing drawl. His fingers holding her chin were still gentle, but the look in his eyes had turned predatory. "Each time you come to me, you'll get what you want—the information for your report . . . book . . . but it won't be just that. I'll have you coming back for me. You'll give me what I want—the truth—and I'll give pleasure, Nikki. Fear or no fear, you will come to me for pleasure."

He kissed her hard this time, then released her. Nikki stared at him. Why did she still want him to kiss her after what he said? But she did.

He was the only man who had ever brought up her fear as a challenge to her. Of course, she had never been part of a seduction before. There was a certain irony in the exchange. She needed him to tell her his darkest secret, to extract the truth of what had happened in his past. In return, he would take her where she most feared to go, and perhaps expose her own past to him. *Balance, wasn't it?* A part of her mocked her.

And she had never fought balance as much as she did now. "Kiss me," she said.

"Later. Think of what we could be doing while you ask your damn questions," he said.

Rick gave her some breathing room. He let her go back up to the living room alone while he made some coffee. He had the amenities in the small bar upstairs, but he understood how a little tension could go a long way when it came to seduction. So he told her where the rest room was, if she needed it, and he dallied a few minutes in the kitchen, torturing himself with thoughts of her making an escape.

It wouldn't surprise him at all if she were gone by now. After all, he had done his damnedest to scare her away. He couldn't even explain it. He had her where he wanted, and then he released her; he had her again, and then chose to give her another reprieve. *What's the matter, Harden? Lost your touch?*

When he returned to the living room, he was prepared for the worst but that didn't stop his heart from skipping a beat at the sight of the empty leather sofa. She was gone. He swept into the room, carelessly holding the tray with the coffeepot and cups, about to curse out loud. Then he stopped.

Nikki was on the rug by the fireplace, examining his pile of books. Relief gushed through his system, and he had to take a deep breath to gather himself. She was here. That meant she wanted him to continue. She glanced up as he approached, and his heart skipped another beat at the smile she gave. It reminded him of—

"You look funny with that tray," she said, still smiling.

"Careful, it's hot," he said, but she took it away from him. "You think it's funny for me to serve my own coffee?"

She placed the tray on the low table by the fireplace and knelt down before it. Her hair pooled around her like a gleaming cape. He caught his breath and fought the urge to slip behind her and feel that hair against his face.

Unaware of her own precarious situation, she poured hot liquid into the two cups. "Ricardo Harden, cook. Ricardo Harden, balancing a tray, serving coffee. What next? Scrubbing the floors? Cleaning the toilets?"

She laughed at her own teasing words, a joyous sound without feminine wiles. It had been years since someone had dared to tease him to his face. And longer still since a woman had served him a cup of his own coffee. Taking the cup, he sat down on the nearby armchair. Nikki settled back on the rug, tucking her legs sideways under her.

She cocked her head to one side as she looked up at him. "I want to make it very clear before we start that I have nothing to do with Internal Investigations, that I'm not another Denise Lorens sent by them." Her voice was soft, modulated.

"I intend to find out about everything," Rick told her.

She nodded. "I don't expect any less from you."

"Who will ask you questions about me?"

She smiled and shook her head. "You agreed to me asking the questions first, remember? I'm assuming you will cooperate after I have done everything you've told me to do?"

Cynicism returned regarding the woman sitting so close to him. "Pardon me, but you sound like someone from EYES." The look of distaste on her face almost made him believe her. She also was very familiar with the fact that EYES was departmental lingo for I.I. "If you're not from them, then you're from somewhere else. Which department?"

"You won't find me in any departmental files."

"Is that a challenge?"

"No." She ran an absentminded hand over the fur rug, smoothing it one way, then the other. "Rick—"

It startled him to hear his name on her lips. He couldn't remember if she had ever done that before, but it sounded unbearably intimate in this setting, with her on his favorite rug, at his favorite reading spot, at his feet.

"Rick, at least hear me out. You can always refuse to answer. I'm not forcing you to answer anything you don't want. I haven't even threatened to tie you up." She paused. "Yet."

He stared at her for a moment, then threw back his head and laughed. Oh, she was good at this. He was intrigued. When his laughter subsided, he took a sip from his coffee as she waited expectantly.

Long, flowing hair. Same height and build. The similarities weren't coincidental. They went to too much trouble looking for an Asian woman to just conduct an investigation or do a report. There was a reason she had been sent to him, and even if she was telling the truth, that it wasn't an I.I. ruse to get at him, this interview had to do with his past. A secret he had buried with a wife he had loved. Why was this coming back now?

She made him laugh. Point to Nikki Taylor. He leaned back into his armchair, stretched his legs, and looked down at her. Oh, she was very good indeed. She knew exactly where in this room to sit, how exactly to get his interest. He wanted to see more of this talent. "Start."

His agreeable state didn't fool Nikki. She had gone into the tiger's cage and pulled his tail, not once, but several times. So far, no bite marks. For some reason the tiger had given her a lot of freedom, but it was because he was still curious, still playing with her.

That was fine, as long as she didn't get too close. She had come upstairs and picked this spot by the fireplace because it felt right to probe a man's center here. She sensed that he was comfortable where she sat—on this rug, surrounded by the books and throw pillows. The big rug was thick and soft. She could imagine him lying here at night, looking into the fire.

His laughter was like a warm caress, and his eyes glinted with amusement. Hands folded behind his head, he was the picture of indolence. "I'm waiting," he invited, but the watchfulness was back in his eyes.

She wanted him to trust her, but how? There was no way to let him know without tainting her report. She was an independent contractor, given a lot of leeway to do as she pleased with the way she chose to investigate, but the submitted report must still be viewed as a professional conclusion, without any evidence of tampering. And for him to trust her, she must submit herself in a way that would test her very courage. She discreetly studied him eyeing her hair, with that distant look in his eyes, and it saddened her that some woman had given him such pain.

She shook it off quickly. It was not her job to find out about the pain but to use it to find out what he hadn't told anyone. The admiral had been very specific about this. Could Rick Harden be trusted to continue as part of TIARA, because his SEAL team depended on Task Force Two's Intel. And to be sure, she was to find out what exactly happened ten years ago that tied Gorman and Rick Harden together. Was Harden a tool, or did he know more than he said? And was Internal Investigations right in targeting this man?

Direct questions never led to direct answers. She should know. She was an expert in interrogation techniques. No, it was better her way. Circle the tiger carefully. "My book," she began, pausing for the expected sneer. None came. A quick glance. His face was blank, eyes hooded. "My book has a government agent. I need a lot of background information and being allowed to go through the different levels of recruiting helped, but it's not enough. That's where you come in."

His lips quirked. "I don't think I'm very good hero material."

"Why?"

"Doesn't a hero save the heroine and they live happily ever after? Especially in a romance?" he asked, hands still cradling his head.

"Yes."

"This hero of yours, does he do that?"

"I'm still researching him," she replied, leaning back on her hands and stretching out her legs. Her feet were almost touching his. "He likes to run a lot. Doesn't seem to get him anywhere, though. I feel there is something holding him back, but I don't know what exactly."

There was a stillness in him that told her she was pulling the tiger's tail again. She picked up her cup of coffee and took a careful sip.

"Is there a question in there somewhere?" he finally asked, in a bored voice.

"What changed him? My hero was a man of action, with an A-Status record, on the up and up," she went on. "Then something changed him."

"Maybe he did something really unheroic," he drawled back, "like commit murder."

Nikki looked at him intently. "Did he? Murder somebody?"

His green eyes flashed and then became dull. It hurt to see him in pain. "Well, you can't be found guilty of murder and work for the government, now can you?" he pointed out coldly.

She noted that he used second person as a reference, and something else—"You mean, perhaps my hero covered one up?"

The silence was razor-sharp. Maybe she had pulled the tiger's tail a bit too hard.

"That wouldn't make it a romance anymore, would it?" he countered softly, suddenly dropping his lazy pose. "And I think we can save the rest of your research for our second interview."

He transformed from languid interviewee to crouched hunter in a flash, leaping forward, like a cat. Nikki scooted back, but her outstretched legs slowed her down. He was before her, straddling her thighs, leaning over her as she put her weight on her elbows.

"My turn," Rick said to her, baring a not-so-relaxed smile.

Tiger unleashed, Nikki thought.

Rick didn't like where Nikki was going with her questions. He was familiar with the technique, of course. The CIA had variations of it. A select group of agents were trained and used as contract agents for the CIA as well as other covert agencies. They called it NOPAIN. Nonphysical persuasion and innovative negotiation. His last brush with a NOPAIN operative was during his interrogation of the alleged assassin Marlena Maxwell.

He stared down at Nikki. Her dark eyes were wide, her lips parted. A NOPAIN operative, huh? That tied her with the troublesome Marlena. Not his most favorite person in the world. She had made quite a fool of him by exposing Gorman, his own boss, as a traitor. And a tie to Marlena meant a tie with the admiral. Things were getting a bit clearer.

There were things he should ask now, make her tell him. After all, his ass was on the line. This report she was putting together—did it have to do with Gorman? Rick had grown to hate that name. That man still controlled his life, even from his jail cell.

"Rick?" She sounded tentative.

He now knew she did certain things when she was nervous. His wait was rewarded when her tongue flicked out to wet her parted lips. The sensual gesture was effective, and suddenly nothing else was more important than the fact that for the first time in a long time, Rick felt more than lust for a woman. He wanted to know her inside and out, not just for the secrets she was keeping. He was mad that she hid herself from him. He was mad at himself for needing to know.

Rick had a thousand questions. But looking down at those lips, he just wanted to kiss her senseless and forget the slow, invading memories her probing had brought back. That had worked before—sex and more of it. As long as he controlled the situation, he didn't have to worry about being weakened by a woman again. For a while he could replace the emptiness inside with nothing but sheer feeling. His gaze hardened. A NOPAIN operative should know a lot about the power of sex.

He reached out. Her hair beckoned like the lyrics of an old favorite song, with words that bring back emotions that were half-forgotten. NOPAIN. Nonphysical persuasion.

"I love your hair," he said, "but then I have this attraction for long, long hair on a woman. It's a testament of a woman's focus on herself. There is nothing like watching her wash and dry it, then comb the length out with the care that it needs. Do you know that?"

"No." Her voice was husky.

Rick slid the strands through his fingers, closing his eyes for a moment to savor the texture. "It takes time to care for hair this long," he murmured. "It tells me more about you than any questions I ask you."

"It does?"

He opened his eyes. She hadn't moved at all. The black pupils in her eyes were large, almost covering the brown irises. His wife had black, black eyes. "Yes," he answered. "You can evade any questions with those strange Oriental mystic terms you use, but . . ."

He let his words trail away as his fingers did the same down as far as they could go, forming ribbonlike strands as he fanned outward. His wife's hair was coarser, tangling easily when he played with it. He pulled the strands to his face.

She moved and gasped at the contact of her hips with his lower body. Her eyes widened as she slowly sank back down onto the rug, carefully keeping from touching him.

She was a paradox, a combination of fear and desire. He released her hair, watching it fall down, contrasting its black with the snowy whiteness of his rug. "Tell me what scares you so, little bird? Is it me?"

He didn't move, even though he could easily push her on her back and follow his fantasies. He sat astride her, yet not touching, letting her get used to his dominant position. He frowned. Where had that thought come from?

"No. Not you."

"Liar."

"Not you," she repeated.

He bent forward, keeping those inches away from her

body, till his face was just above hers. "Must be this then," he said, and as her tongue flicked out nervously again, he swooped, lightning-fast, to taste it. Her body stiffened, but her mouth opened up like a flowering bud.

He kissed her gently, like tasting vintage eight-hundred-dollar 1984 Chateau Margaux. Heady stuff. A man could easily forget that she was a NOPAIN operative. Unless, of course, he had learned a lesson like that before.

She didn't kiss like his wife had. He broke away, licking his lips. Damn it, she was nothing like his wife. Nothing. He wanted her to be, so he could fight this attraction and just use her. But he couldn't. Not with him needing her so badly. She would have him exactly where she wanted him.

No, he would have to send her away for now, and he would still be in control. He must fight to retain the upper hand here. In this case, fear was his only weapon against her soft appeal. He reached for his back pocket and pulled out the silk purse she had brought, watched the wariness return to her eyes. He bounced it on his palm.

"It's very light," he mused. "Let me guess. Do you use this for your hair?"

"Yes." She watched the purse up and down in the air, then added with a stubborn tilt of her chin. "You said anything to tie."

"So I did. Are you ready for rule number three?"

Her tongue flicked out again and Rick almost threw the purse onto the floor and went for her. "What is it?" she asked.

"I'm keeping this. Next interview, bring a bottle of your shampoo and conditioner." She was still staring up at him after he got off his knees. He quirked a brow. "Time to go home to your nest, little bird."

He would play on her fear and see where that would lead them.

Chapter Nine

Jogging wasn't for everyone. It was, Rick had to admit, the dumbest form of exercise, pounding one's feet as a form of punishment. It was the idea of self-inflicted pain that had drawn him to this sport. When he'd first started running, the monotony was exactly what he needed. Something to dull the mind. And he could finish his mornings without even remembering running.

After a decade, he jogged out of sheer habit. The monotony was still there but he had grown to think of it as a contrast to the desk job to which he had been exiled. He remembered that just the other day, he had considered giving it up, just wasting his body away like he had wasted everything else.

Then *she* turned up. Calling up memories she shouldn't. Poking at old wounds that had scabbed over. Making monotony less appealing than ever.

And she had dared to challenge him last night. Her words about her fictional hero returned to mock him. *He likes to run a lot. Doesn't seem to get him anywhere, though. I feel there is something holding him back, but I don't know what exactly.*

Rick stopped, still with a mile to go in his routine. Why couldn't he stop obsessing about Nikki? Last night, after she had left, he had spent a few hours on his computer, looking for clues about the admiral. What he had come up with didn't quiet his suspicions. He knew he had something; he just didn't understand why his past was so damn important to the admiral.

He took a deep breath, looked at his surroundings. He had never stopped in the middle of a run before. Funny how everything looked different once he paused. The trees and grass were greener when he wasn't in motion. And he could smell the morning air. He sniffed. God, now he was starting to spout mystical stuff.

"Sir! Sir!"

Rick turned. It was Agent Jones running down the trail. The younger man stopped to mop the sweat pouring down his face with a towel draped around his neck.

"Agent Jones, planning on taping someone this morning?" Rick asked. The young man was a curious mix of ambition and naivete. "Or are you just exercising?"

"Well, I'd hoped to catch Nikki Taylor here again today," Erik said, still breathing hard, "but no luck. Then fortunately, I looked up and thought you looked familiar, and figured I'd catch up to see if it was really you, sir."

"Well, lucky me," Rick commented dryly. "Is there a reason for your stalking Nikki Taylor? The last time you taped her because you wanted to prove to me that you could do covert questioning. What is it this time?"

"I think she's after something."

"Is that right?"

"She shows up at the recruiting center—"

"With me," interrupted Rick.

Erik paused, as if he hadn't considered that part yet. "Yes, with you, sir. I mean, don't you find it suspicious? She was with a touring group of writers, and then next thing I know, she's sitting there taking notes about our programs."

Rick considered going back to jogging, but the idea of talking to Erik while bouncing his brain cells around wasn't very appealing. The young operative needed his superior to take him under his wing, show him the ropes. This running around proving his usefulness in the oddest of ways wasn't cutting it. He changed direction, taking the other beaten path that joggers used to head back. Erik followed like a puppy dog.

"She has language skills," Rick said, smoothly feeding the lies as if he hadn't just now made them up. "She wanted to research her book and asked to go through training recruitment to get some firsthand knowledge. The tour didn't provide enough information, and I don't have the time to answer her questions, nor can I assign anyone right now, so I suggested the recruiting class. You were there. How did it go?"

"It went fine, as always, sir."

"So what is the problem? Those recruiting programs aren't national secrets, Jones."

"I know that. But I have this feeling, that's all. Sir, they tell me you were one of the best before . . . I mean, shit . . ."

Open mouth. Insert foot. Rick's lips quirked at his own joke. "Before?" he prompted politely, glancing briefly at the flustered man. Agent Jones wanted something but was going at it in a roundabout fashion. Rick supposed he could save some time by asking outright, but hell, he had plenty of dead time on his hands these days. All his cases were in limbo. And it was getting to be a hobby bumping into Agent Erik Bond Jones.

Erik swallowed, then tried again, blurting out, "I want to be part of Task Force Two."

Rick's brows lifted. The young man actually took the direct way. "And your following Miss Taylor is supposed to buy you into the task force?" He supposed that would be a good way to catch someone's eye, and since Gorman wasn't around, of course, Erik would think Rick was the next best thing. "You're suspicious of Miss Taylor, so you tailed her. Tell me, did you expect to bring an entire operation to Task Force Two and demand an assignment?"

The look on Erik's face was telling. He had actually thought that someone would listen to a young rookie storming into the O.C.'s office telling about a mysterious woman he'd noticed. Rick mentally shook his head and continued walking, as if the conversation were over.

"Sir? Why would an author want to go through all that training if all she is doing is writing a romance? I mean, I've leafed through some of those books and . . ." He trailed off when Rick stopped to stare at him.

"You're spending time reading romance novels, Agent

Jones?" Rick asked coolly. "What is this really about? Do you have the hots for Nikki Taylor?"

Erik's face flamed up. "I just wanted to impress you, sir," he mumbled.

Rick nodded. "You're impressing me, all right. Why are you doing what you're doing and then coming to tell me about it? Go on, tell me the truth, man."

"I want to be as good as you were. I want to interview the women and get their secrets. Get promoted out of my directorate. Get into Task Force Two, and then be sent off to . . ." he paused again.

"To seduce women?" Rick asked helpfully. "And you plan to seduce Nikki Taylor?"

Erik nodded, face redder than when he was jogging. "Yes."

Interesting. An operative who wanted to be like Ricardo Harden. Wanted to seduce Nikki Taylor. Rick didn't know whether to be angry or amused. No, maybe he was stunned. Which fate did he want? To be hung out to dry by I.I. or to see a tragicomedy of Erik Jones parodying Hard-On. Or God help him, to have the young man think he was in a pissing contest with him over another woman.

The phone rang. Nikki woke up, startled out of her dreams. A quick glance at the clock told her she had overslept.

"Hello?"

"Miss Taylor?" A woman's voice.

"Yes?"

"I'm Admiral Madison's secretary. Please hold while I transfer you."

"All right." Nikki ran a quick self-conscious hand through her hair, then smiled. Silly woman. She wasn't meeting the admiral in person.

"Miss Taylor, this is Jack Madison," a low masculine voice came on. "This is a secured line, so feel free to talk."

"Good morning, sir."

"Call me Jack. This is an informal call. I want to talk to

you in private because Internal Investigations will insist on being there when you're in front of the committee."

"Then you can call me Nikki." She liked him already. His voice had that firm, commanding quality of a man used to taking charge. He didn't sound the type to just sit and read reports, either. A very rare quality in D.C., where paper pushers made a living.

She could hear the smile in his voice. "Nikki," he agreed. "Is I.I. giving you any trouble? I know they protested very adamantly against an outside contract to the committee. Knowing them, they can cause a lot of problems for someone they don't want around."

"I've only had one meeting so far, and yes, it was obvious they would prefer me out of the picture. They are gathering their own report, of course, and I tried to assure them that I'll do my best not to be in their way."

Admiral Madison chuckled. "I like that. Not being in their way isn't exactly out of the picture, is it? I had wanted T. for this job, as you know—she's a good friend—and was disappointed that she couldn't take this on. This is the first time I've known T. to take a vacation over work." His laughter rang out heartily. Nikki smiled, liking the admiral more. "Anyway, with her gone, I wasn't sure whether I could take on an outside contractor I haven't personally interviewed. T., though, has never failed me, and after hearing about you from her, I understand why she chose you. I know I won't have a chance to discuss it in private until after you've submitted your report, but I wanted you to know that I'm very angry about your situation. T. gave me a detailed account of your past before she left. I'll do my best to help."

"Thank you, sir. That's all I'm asking," Nikki said softly. "And I'll deliver the report in time for the meeting."

"Good. Finding out about Rick Harden is important. We don't want another Gorman. What with that bast—that rat—incriminating so many people connected to him, I've a feeling we might end up with a Salem witch trial, and muddy everything up even more."

"I understand."

"The most important thing is to find out about his past with Gorman. How close are they? And does Harden have those missing disks? Those disks, if they are out there, will give us all we need to put Gorman away for a very long time. None of these damn negotiation sessions over how much and how long. I don't want to give that man a chance to see daylight." His sigh was audible. "Your position is a difficult one, trying to convince the different sections of the committee, but I wanted to make it clear that I won't back away from supporting you."

"That means a lot, thank you."

"If there is anything you need, don't hesitate to call me here. Do you have a pen handy?"

Nikki wrote down the number, then hesitated a second. "As a matter of fact, you might be able to help me with one more thing, sir—Jack. I would like to look at the official files on Agent Rick Harden's wife and the circumstances surrounding her death. I can go through I.I. but I'd prefer not to."

There was a pause. "No problem. Personally, I don't think that incident should be used against him."

"It will be brought up by someone in the committee."

"Yes, I know. Some of them don't like Harden and obviously want to make this an excuse to get rid of him. I've worked with Task Force Two long enough to know he's capable. That's why I want to get to the bottom of this, so there wouldn't be this dark cloud hanging over the man from now on." The admiral laughed. "Not that I think he'd appreciate it. I think the man is a tough nut to crack, with a boulder-sized chip on his shoulder. I hope he's not scaring you off."

Nikki thought about Rick's kisses. His hard body pressed against hers as he held on to her hair. She thought of him with her shampoo. A shiver ran up and down her spine like an electrical current. "No, not at all," she replied quietly, plucking the corner of her pillow.

Scared wasn't quite the right word to describe her feelings where Rick Harden was concerned. He was everything she was afraid of—a sexual man who liked to be in control, who wanted to dominate her. Yet when he touched her, the fear changed into something else—something simmering hot that threatened to boil over. And it made her afraid in another way.

Worse, he knew what he was doing to her. She could see it in his green eyes, like that lazy tiger she had been conjuring up every time she thought of him. She could turn and run, and he would pounce.

"Is that all you need?" Admiral Madison interrupted Nikki's thoughts.

"Yes."

After the phone call, Nikki didn't immediately jump out of bed to get ready. She stared up at the ceiling, absentmindedly studying the paneling. She had to know more about Rick's past. Was he just reacting to her because of her resemblance to his wife? Unexpected anger reared up rebelliously at that thought. Then shock.

Nikki sank deeper into her pillow as she allowed the truth to seep through her consciousness. After all these years, she wanted a man. Rick Harden was going to be her lover. Her body flushed with warmth at the thought of him naked in her bed. It was astonishing that she could call up his image so naturally. She found herself trembling and pulled the sheets up higher.

She didn't want to get out of bed. Didn't want to finish her grandmother's prophecies. She especially didn't want a man on top of her. Holding her down. Parting her legs. And . . .

She closed her eyes. No. She wouldn't allow those images to take hold or she would scream and go mad. Already she felt hot tears escaping the corner of her tightly squeezed eyes.

She was pathetic. How was she going to let Rick Harden touch her? Because touch her, he would. She crossed her legs under the blankets. But that didn't stop the sudden sensation of weight on her lower body. Her breathing turned to pants.

Nikki forced herself to turn to the side, curling her knees to her chest. She squeezed her eyes tightly. She wasn't going to cry.

* * *

Rick supposed he ought to feel important. After all, he seemed to be of special interest to some of the biggest departments in the U.S. government. Not only was the Justice Department's Internal Investigations going through his files with a fine-toothed comb, but from what he could gather, so was the General Accounting Office, the National Security Agency, and hell, why not, even the Pentagon. By the sound of things, he, Rick Harden, was going to be quite the fall guy.

He signed the few pieces of paper in front of him, giving authorization to access his security codes, and pulled back so the assistant to the EYES investigator could take them away. He then nodded to Greta. His secretary came forward and handed over a bunch of keys and computer disks, along with a list of access codes. Harpring sat across the table, studying him, waiting for the first sign of panic.

However, Rick had never felt more cold or calm. He had been preparing for such a day for quite a while now although he had never thought it would be something quite so big. Of course, Gorman was behind this. That man had never done things small. His current incarceration had only served to show how much damage one man could do to the security of a government. There was panic all right, all over D.C., as everyone tried to remember and trace his dealings with Gorman the last couple of decades.

No one could believe one man could wreak so much damage without help. And that was where Rick came in. I.I. was certainly damn sure about his guilt. He could see it in the way they were treating him. Giving them his permission to access his personal codes and files was just a formality, part of the game. Declining to sign would be futile, much like refusing to allow a police officer to search one's car while his K-9 dog was sniffing around it.

Except for one thing. Rick knew any evidence they brought up would not be anything left by him. If they meant to set him up as the fall guy, he had better find out what exactly they were looking for.

"You seem far away, Agent Harden. Shouldn't you be

somewhat interested in what we're doing?" Harpring's question was cutting, meant to put him on the defensive.

"I'm very aware of what you're doing," Rick answered, as he clipped his gold pen back into his breast pocket.

How could he not, when Harpring was going about things the way a good bureaucrat would. Like the EYES officer, Rick was an expert in regulations and paperwork. It was a world where things slowed down to a snail's pace, purely to demonstrate how important being a cog of the wheel was. Never mind the wheel was falling off. That was somebody else's problem. Harpring was here to do one thing, and one thing only, and anything else wasn't of interest.

"And what are we doing?"

"You're doing your job." And that was all. Rick could understand that mentality because, hell, a month ago, he had been going through the same motions, ignoring the warning bells in his head telling him things were falling apart. As a result, he had almost caused Marlena Maxwell to die at Gorman's hands because he hadn't wanted to listen to others. He met the investigator's eyes across the table and added calmly, "And I'm doing mine."

When he had found out the truth, seen how blind he had been, Rick had been shaken to the core. He had almost repeated history by the sheer perversity of trying to avoid trouble. If Gorman had killed Marlena, Rick would have resigned. There was no way he could live through the knowledge that he had blood on his hands again.

"What do you do to keep busy nowadays, Agent Harden, now that most of your cases are suspended? What about the other men in your task force?"

In other words, were they busy shredding paper and hiding things? Rick allowed a small smile. "I'm sure you and other EYES officers have been documenting my moves around the department. I have been busy finishing up the paperwork for the last assignment so that everything will be in order for the next deputy director. Most of my men have been reassigned to the other task force teams for now, with maybe two or three who are either on leave or have some current work to do. I'm sure you checked my routine—every hour is accounted for. I do have several private secured meetings coming up that I can't disclose, so you will have to get special permission from someone higher up to locate me then."

Harpring looked surprised that Rick had brought up the meetings. "You're very sure of yourself," he commented. "Do you think they will let you be part of any private secured meeting when they know you're under investigation?"

"Again, you will have to discuss that with someone higher up than me," Rick replied. "I'm just following orders. They want me at the meetings still, as far as I know. Unless, of course, you have privileged information?"

"Of course not," Harpring said, his thin lips pursed disapprovingly. "I think it would have been best not to jeopardize security even further. In my opinion, they should suspend you while you're under investigation, Agent Harden."

"Maybe they mean to tell me that then." Rick arched an eyebrow. "Or maybe they are all colluding with me, to keep me quiet about things I might bring up by accident."

Harpring's gaze sharpened. "Don't say things you don't mean, Agent Harden."

Rick smiled again. He must be getting perverse in his old age, getting himself deeper in trouble than necessary. "Scary, isn't it? I could bring a whole department down with me. Or two."

"Threats won't help you."

"Why not? It sure is giving Gorman a lot of rope to play with."

"We're not negotiating with Gorman."

"No? Then what are you looking for? Telling me might help expedite your search."

Harpring looked startled, finally realizing that he had been led through an interview, instead of vice-versa. His mouth snapped into a grim line as he stared at Rick. "Do you expect me to believe that you know nothing about what we're looking for?"

Every convict in prison always said he was innocent. Rick didn't blame the man for not believing him. He shrugged. He would just have to do things his way, that was all. Harpring certainly wasn't going to help him. "I know some things," he said, then instinctively hazarded a guess. "For example, I know EYES is hot under the collar because there is an independent investigation of Gorman's activities and I think maybe you're under pressure to be the first to get to the finish line. How far off am I?"

Rick watched Harpring sit back on his seat abruptly. He smiled cynically. Bingo. He wondered whether Nikki would tell him everything before or after he had her naked under him.

Nikki watched from the front row as Rick Harden approached the podium. The operations chief of Task Force Two was making a special appearance to give a talk to the new trainees. Agent Erik Jones had given the introduction, a look of hero worship on his face, smugly telling the group that he had gotten the O.C. to agree to do this.

From where she was, she easily made eye contact. Or maybe he had been watching her with those cool green eyes, waiting for her to look up. He looked down at her directly as he greeted the crowd. Her heartbeat began to drum pleasantly.

Someone asked about information and access to it. Rick didn't glance at the questioner as he replied. "There are small libraries in each directorate, but the main one is the CIA library, which has one hundred and forty-six thousand volumes, including twenty-five thousand books on Intel gathering. There are also close to twenty thousand newspapers and periodicals for those who are looking for more centralized sources." He paused. "But of course, that kind of minute Intel gathering is meant as training ground. The hardest part is direct Intel, human intelligence, the kind where you have to get up close with your target, so you get your information firsthand."

Nikki didn't look away as Rick continued looking down at her. She knew he wasn't here to introduce new recruits to the wonders of the CIA library. This was part of what was happening between him and her. They spoke in a secret language that only they seemed aware of and she found it strangely erotic, as if he were touching her mind.

"What is the main test that recruits have to pass before they go to a different level?" someone asked.

"How to answer questions correctly."

"Well, the Career Training Program takes a year," the same person continued, "so I'd expect by that time, after having done stints in different directorates, I'd be able to answer questions correctly."

"Is that a question?" Rick asked, glancing further back from Nikki to look at the man. Nikki could see the others turning around to follow Rick's gaze.

"No, sir. I was merely stating what I was thinking."

"Why would you need to repeat to me what I know when I'm available to answer anything you don't know?" Rick's voice was soft, but carried all the way back. Nikki didn't have to turn around to know that the young man sitting behind her knew he was in a hole. After a small silence, Rick continued, "That, Mr. Bernstein, is a question that you have to learn how to answer correctly."

Nikki wasn't surprised that he called the man by his name. Rick would know everyone in a room because he would make it his job to know. That was how he was. Also, by being thorough and letting these recruits see it, he would show the good ones something that couldn't be taught about Intel gathering—that it was a never-ending process, that it was a state of mind.

There was always someone to challenge the one who had all the answers. "How would you answer that question then, sir?"

Rick Harden's didn't even bother to look in that direction. His gaze returned to Nikki, warm and intimate. "Ask me that in a year," he said. The class laughed.

"Any other questions?"

She knew a challenge when she heard it. After all, she was there to gather certain information, and he was deliberately daring her.

She licked her lower lip. "I have one."

"Yes?"

"Are there rules about how much to reveal or hide from spouses?"

She watched him closely, but catching Rick Harden by surprise was an impossible quest worthy of Hercules. The man was in control of himself at all times. There was no change of expression or edge to his voice. Mesmerized, she watched him pull out a slim gold pen from his breast pocket. He wrote down something on his notepad, tore the page out, folded it, and handed it to Erik Jones to pass to her.

Nikki took the piece of note but didn't open it, mesmerized by the dark green of his gaze. She always had a weakness for that color, she thought vaguely, as she held on to the paper.

"In that note is what I choose to share with you," Rick Harden said to the hushed class. "How much you choose to reveal or hide becomes your responsibility. Would you want your spouse to be accountable for your job? It also depends on your spouse. Choose carefully."

The woman sitting next to her nudged her. "What's in that note?" she asked, curiosity getting the better of her.

Nikki shook her head and slipped the paper into her folder. She could feel everyone's attention on her. "It's the O.C.'s answer," she said calmly.

"Yes, but what is it? Aren't you going to share?" the woman persisted.

"Yes, aren't you going to tell them, Miss Taylor?" Rick Harden didn't break into a smile but his glittering eyes continued to challenge her.

"Your passing me a note is telling enough, sir."

"But what about the note?"

When she shook her head again, he asked, "Why not?"

"I don't share Intel," she said.

She continued looking at Rick as the recruits around her reacted to the situation, clapping and laughing. Their communication was secretive, like that between old lovers with intimate gestures. She didn't need to open the note to know what was in it.

Afterward, she read it when she reached the sanctuary of her car. His masculine hand was bold and unpretentious, like his message. There was an underlying sensuality in the way he wrote his R, in the old-fashioned cursive way, two loops on each top corner.

Rule number four. Come without underwear.

Chapter Ten

"Always go with your first instinct," Nikki's grandmother had told her. "Once you understand your center and how to listen to yourself, your choices will be clear, like the view from the mountain."

It had been easier to listen to that advice when she was a child, with a young girl's fancy. As time went by it was her second, and sometimes her third, option that became part of her life. How could she have known then that listening to her first instinct was impossible when she had to deal with men and agencies that controlled her fate? Compromise was an insidious thing, and before she knew it, ignoring her *chuung* had become a way of life. Until that fateful day when she was captured. Until she was alone, imprisoned in a dark cell, with too much silence.

Then Nikki had heard that wind chime. And thought of her grandmother.

She had been alone ever since. Even after her rescue, and her subsequent work with a different agency that controlled her lifestyle, she had held herself apart. She no longer compromised and had been known to defy orders. Fortunately for her, the program that had adopted her had a very convenient system for loners—it gave them lone assignments.

So here she was, called upon for one last lone assignment. All she had to do was listen to her first instinct and go with the flow. Finish the job. Complete the circle. Then maybe she would find some peace of mind.

But her grandmother had never met Rick Harden. She could not possibly have understood the way a look from this man would send her granddaughter's center into a rush of pounding heartbeat and confused, excited thoughts. She could not have envisaged that his touch would burn right through, until center and being were meaningless, until all Nikki could think of was his hands on her body, his lips on hers, that there would only be heat and mindless need. No first instinct. And certainly no sound from her *chuung*.

Hence, Nikki was back to options. She could choose to stop this any time. Not go. Not get any closer to the fire. Not allow Rick to take her down this path. She knew he was playing on her fears. He meant to see how far he could push her before she gave up and ran off. Yet he already knew that she wouldn't do that, so why was he doing this?

She shivered and tried to forget the fact that she wasn't wearing anything underneath her dress. There was only one reason that he continued to test her, even when he knew she wouldn't back off, and that was—he wanted her. No matter how much he didn't trust her, he still wanted her, and through these rules, he was punishing her for how he was feeling.

Nikki understood what he was planning to do. Each rule was a way to strip her of her defenses. She didn't need her fertile imagination to show her how. He had planted those sexual images in her head for some reason. Part of it had to do with his past with his wife.

That was why she had asked, bringing up the subject of spouse to see his reaction. But he was unbeatable, throwing the ball back in her court. By doing what he did, he had, she realized with sudden consternation, put her in the role of his spouse. She braked hard, bringing the car to a stop.

She stared at the traffic, then accelerated when the light changed. It was troubling to think that Rick might be responding to the memory of his wife, and not her. There were so many things she wanted to know about the woman that had *nothing* to do with her assignment. All very private things that brought heat to her cheeks.

When she reached her destination, she got out of the car,

breathing in the evening darkness, trying to calm herself by walking slowly. Letting a man come into her space was hard enough, but letting him touch her . . .

She couldn't believe that she was here at all. She was very aware of the soft material of her dress teasing her. She stared ahead as she approached the building. She paused in front of the first flight of concrete steps. There wasn't much between her and the tiger upstairs. A thin piece of clothing. And then . . . he would see her naked.

Her heart rose into her throat, and she tripped slightly. Nervously she checked the clip in her hair, wondering how she was going to take it off when her mind was on the bottle of shampoo in her bag. She swallowed the lump in her throat.

Staring upward, she studied the lit windows of the apartment building. She counted the floors. Right there. If she took one more step forward, she was going to faint from fright. She wasn't ready for Rick Harden to see her naked. And what was he planning to do with the shampoo? The thought of him using it on her sent odd little trills of mixed emotions through her.

Nikki turned away from the building. She couldn't do this. She would panic and everything would go wrong. She couldn't bear to let him see her in a state of terror, it was better she get away while she could. Her instinct told her to believe in herself. She chose not to listen.

Unlocking the car, she slid inside and strapped on the seat belt. Breathing a sigh of relief, she rested her head back against the seat.

"Coward."

Nikki let out a small gasp and whirled around. She would never know how he managed to get into her car, or how he knew she would change her mind. His shadow lounged back against the middle of the seat, as if he had been there all this time, just waiting.

"Why do you keep doing that?" she asked, stalling for time to calm herself.

His teeth gleamed in the shadows. He was enjoying this victory, second-guessing her moves and catching her by surprise. "Doing what, little bird?"

"Scaring me in the dark." Irritation replaced shock. "And stop calling me that name."

"Are you only afraid of me in the dark?" he mocked, and she saw the white flash of his teeth again as he softly repeated, "little bird."

She snapped back around and put her hands on the steering wheel. "What am I supposed to do now, go back in there with you?" She was going to refuse. She would go home and work up the courage to do it another night.

"You don't have to." She heard him moving and eyed the rearview mirror, trying to see what he was up to. He leaned forward and his voice was velvet smooth. "We can do it right here."

She stiffened. "Do it?" The car suddenly didn't have enough air.

"Conduct your interview." His hand wrapped around between the two front seats and touched her hair, unerringly reaching for the big clip that held it up. "But first you have to follow the rules."

Nikki's hair tumbled down and he caught it in one handful, pulling her head back toward the seat. She didn't resist.

"I like this kind of car," he remarked, as he leaned even closer. His cologne and unique scent tantalized her.

"You . . . do?" She concentrated on his movements, trying to decipher what he was doing. He held her hair with one hand. Where was the other . . . "Oh!"

Her seat dropped back and she was suddenly staring up at Rick. "I do. The seat adjusting lever is on the side, very reachable." One hand still tangled in her hair, he reached into her bag on the other seat. "Those bottles must be for me. And were you brave enough to follow rule number four, I wonder?"

Nikki held her breath as his face drew closer, the dark outline of his masculine features sending her pulse back into orbit. His breath was hot and she caught sight of his smile again. His free hand caressed her jaw, then moved slowly downward. He lingered on the fluttering pulse on her neck, then continued lower. His fingers teased the soft round neckline and crept just under the clothing, tracing the circle from one collarbone to the other. She closed her eyes.

"No. Look at me." She obeyed. His eyes glittered back in the darkness. Pulling on her seat belt, he taunted softly, "Got you tied."

Nikki immediately went for the release button, but his hand was in the way.

"I thought you said you weren't afraid of me."

"I'm not."

"Prove it."

He kept saying that, challenging her. She wasn't going to let him win. It was difficult to think clearly when her heart seemed to have relocated and was pounding in her head. He was a complicated man, used to doing things his way. Control was essential to him, and she knew if she were ever to unlock his secrets, she had to gather her own courage and let go of a part of herself. It wasn't him she was afraid of . . . it was her fear of losing control, that part of her that had always held her together through the darkest times. *But this isn't the past and he isn't them.* She had to find a way to stop her fear.

She followed instinct, reaching up with her right hand to trace the side of his face. He felt smooth. He leaned down a little more, so her other hand could explore too. His clean male scent invited her to be bolder. She followed the arch of his eyebrows, felt his eyelashes against her fingertips. His cheekbones. The strong line of his jaw. And miraculously, her fear diminished because this was Rick. Not a faceless enemy, not someone to whom she had to close her eyes because she didn't want to acknowledge him.

This time it was different. She would look at him. Touch his face. Know it was Rick.

He turned, scraping his mouth against her palm. She gasped as the tip of his tongue teased a wet path and he bit the sensitive pad under her thumb. His hand moved under the collar of her dress. She stopped her restless exploration, her hands tightening.

"Don't stop now." He nipped the flesh between her thumb

and forefinger. "I'm just making sure you followed all the rules. Did you?"

Her reply was a whisper. "Yes." She bit her lip as his hand moved lower, sliding over the top of her left breast.

"Such a brave girl," he whispered back. "It's too late to back down now. I told you, you couldn't change your mind anymore."

"And you won't change your mind about answering my questions?" she countered. His hand stopped just above her nipple, and she held her breath for a long moment. She adopted his taunting tone of voice, "Or are you going to back down?"

She knew she had surprised him; he had thought to stop her queries by making a move first. Her body tingled with an electric need, responding to his slow touch, and if she hadn't gathered her thoughts in time, she would have allowed him to take the lead.

"I wasn't the one running away, was I?" he retorted. He slowly withdrew his hand, but the heat from his caress remained. She released a long breath, only to suck in hard again as she felt his hand skim her rib cage, playing with the seat belt, tightening it. There was no escape from the rules, she realized that now. He leaned down further, brushing her lips with his. His breath tantalized her mouth, he was so close. "First things first, little bird. Let me slow that heartbeat down a little, then you can ask your questions."

He wasn't doing that at all as she felt his hand slide down the length of her right thigh. She discovered that she couldn't cross her legs when she was strapped down. Besides, the steering wheel was in the way. She didn't think her pulse could go any faster, but it did. Her skirt was being pulled higher, baring her knees, then her thighs. His knuckles lingered on the warm interior of her legs. The cool night air brushed against her and she shivered, but her thoughts were filled with heated images of his slowly moving hand and where it was heading.

"I'm going to touch you all over. Make your body know my hand." He covered her bared knee and she gripped his face tightly. "First my hands. Then my mouth. After that—"

He paused. He caressed the inside of her thigh, his trailing fingers inexorably moving upward.

"Rick," she breathed. She had to say his name, to remind herself that it was he. She felt feverish, not sure about anything anymore, as she waited for his inevitable touch. She restlessly gripped his head, wanting him to go higher.

Something new was happening. She wasn't even afraid of being tied. Her hands were free and she liked the feel of his face. His kisses were soft and seductive as if he knew how to soothe her. Her nightmares consisted of clawing hands and the smell of sweat. She hadn't been able to get clean enough afterward. This was a sensuous journey that she had not thought possible again. A man's hands could actually be persuasive. Tender. Patient. And his words weren't leering threats, but silken promises.

"After that—we can talk." His voice became intimately lower. He took his time. She bit her lip and looked into his eyes. She gave a choked little cry when his finger explored the crease between her thigh and hip. "Hmm. No underwear."

She thought her heart was going to burst, and for an uncontrolled moment, she lost focus and panic returned. No, she silently screamed. No, no, no. "Don't touch me," she said urgently. If he did, she was sure those dark memories would come back to torture her, like every time before. Surely this time would be no different.

"Why?" To her relief, he didn't find her sudden change of heart a turnoff. Instead he lazily stroked the soft crease that was so intimately close, seeming fascinated by the feel of her skin. "I'm already touching you."

His finger dipped down, ever closer still, until she couldn't bear it. Slivers of lightning streaked through her system, and she choked back the burning emotions building inside her. "Don't. Not there."

"Why are you afraid, Nikki?"

"Because it will hurt." There. She had said it. And it stopped his marching fingers. Every time she had tried to get over her fear of intimacy, it had hurt. Every man who had wanted her had given up. She didn't want Rick to turn away like the others, but of course he would. No man wanted a hysterical woman who had no passion left.

"Hurt?" Again, she didn't hear any surprise in his voice. She waited for his questions. They all always demanded answers. Instead, he gently asked, "Am I hurting you now?"

Not yet. "No. It's not you." Unable to go on, she let go of his face and reached out to unfasten the seat belt. He stopped her, covering her hand with his. "Rick, please—"

"Let me decide when to free you, little bird. The interview hasn't even started yet." His other hand moved and she choked back another cry when he touched her, his fingers tickling her curls. A coiled ball of need inside her burst and her head fell back heavily against the seat as she tried to focus on his words. "This hero you're writing—does he hurt women?"

Nikki closed her eyes, breathing unevenly. He was being so gentle but he didn't understand. The memories she was trying to push away weren't of heroes. It wasn't going to work. "No. He doesn't hurt women."

"Does he hurt the heroine?"

"I . . . I . . . Rick . . ." She couldn't concentrate at all, not with those fingernails lightly raking all the way down, reaching the vee between her thighs. She jerked her legs up to cross them, forgetting that the steering wheel was in the way. That was the opening he was waiting for, and his hand slid between her parted thighs and completely cupped her. She gasped at his intimate possession. Her heart thundering wildly, she turned sideways from him, but there was no escape from his hand. Not when the steering wheel locked her legs up. He curled his fingers inward and suddenly her whole world was centered right where he held her.

Colors swirled behind her closed eyelids. She couldn't breathe. Or maybe she was just holding her breath. She didn't know. Something hot and alive was burning her from the inside. All she could feel was the slow gliding of his exploring fingers as they touched her intimately, opening her, and—

Nikki stiffened, gripping the top of the seat belt button where her hand was still imprisoned under his, waiting for the blast of pain that would follow. It always hurt when they put their fingers in there. Always.

"Breathe, little bird."

He slipped his fingers intimately between her folds and she gave a soft cry, squirming away when he made contact. There was no pain. She felt as his long finger probed and slid inside in one slow stroke. No pain.

She was wet.

For the first time in years, she hadn't felt the screaming psychological pain that tortured her body whenever a man touched her there. Another cry escaped as she felt his fingers pushing in deeply, opening her wider.

"Are you hurting?"

She shook her head as she took in the intense feeling of pressure between her legs. Oh God, no, he wasn't hurting her. The mounting need gushing out of her had nothing to do with pain. She was too shocked to utter a word. She was wet. His slippery fingers told her so.

"Nikki, turn back around if you aren't in pain." His voice was soft but firm. "If you want it, turn around and look at me, damn it."

She did, although she really couldn't see him. All she could do was feel what he was doing to her. She gasped when a finger pressed against the sensitive part of her. A power surge. A burst of sensation. Her entire body jerked up, but was restrained by the seat belt. She reached out with her free hand and grabbed hold of the front of his shirt. "Rick!"

Her body was a bundle of nerves as his fingers moved, sliding in and out. His thumb circled lazily in between strokes, teasing her, getting closer and moving away, and pleasure grew like a sunrise over a dark horizon. He was driving her crazy in her own car, taking his time, using his skills to take over her control. He hummed with approval at the first spasm of pleasure.

She had never felt this way before, as if she was melting from the inside. His fingers teased with such slow torture, pinpointing where her pleasure center was and returning to stroke it over and over until she couldn't bear it any longer, and her hips started to undulate. But every time she jerked, the seat belt tightened even more, restraining her while he explored every tender part of her. She moaned. She couldn't move. In and out. Over. Around. It was unbearable pleasure.

"Please—" she finally managed. She couldn't take much more.

His mouth covered hers. "Open," he ordered, his tongue dipping in, his fingers doing the same, the heel of his hand rubbing her damp need with the slightest pressure. "Open for me."

It was so easy to connect with Rick. Nikki knew what he wanted. He wanted her to give him what she hadn't been able to do for anyone else. And in that instant she let go. She opened her legs. Opened her mouth. Opened her heart. And screamed throatily as she started coming.

Rick couldn't remember when a woman's passion had made him ache like this. He couldn't get enough of her, and he hadn't even started making love to her yet. A few weeks ago, while listening to an opera about a man who loved too much, he had looked down from his seat, and felt an emptiness inside. He had been searching for something since, even in his sleep.

Like a miracle, a woman had shown up literally at his doorstep. She had deliberately sought him out and even though she had an ulterior motive, he didn't particularly care at this moment. Right now she was definitely what he had been hungering for. And he meant to devour her.

The more he tasted, the more Rick wanted. Like the fine wine he had compared her to, Nikki's flavor seeped into him, a slow, sure, fiery desire that was sweeping away his own control.

For some reason she was afraid of sex. It wasn't an act, he was sure of it. And it pleased him to know that she wasn't afraid of his touch now.

He had tasted passion before but not quite like this. There was a desperate sweetness in the way she tangled her tongue with his, as if she couldn't get enough. She was still coming, juicy and slippery all over his hand, and her throaty cries excited him. He pushed his fingers into her as deeply as he could and the fluttering contractions squeezed him so tightly, the thought of climbing on top of her naked body and being held so possessively inside her made him break out in a sweat. Despite her damp evidence soaking his hand, she was still incredibly tight. He wondered how long it had been since she'd had a lover and was surprised that he felt so possessively triumphant at the certainty that it had been a while.

He had wanted her like this ever since he had seen her eating at the restaurant. He had known her passion for food hid a sensual nature. Now she ate at his tongue with such wild abandon, he wanted to keep her coming. And he could, if he wanted to. A woman with a prolonged orgasm would be more relaxed and could take someone his size more easily. And he meant to be inside Nikki Taylor tonight.

Not yet, though. Right now, her pleasure was enticing. Her hands running up and down his chest, caressing his neck and face, made him wish he could feel them on his bare skin. Her legs opened wider. Her hips arched higher. She murmured against his lips and her taste and scent had his seething need straining heavily against the front of his pants.

Rick released a ragged sigh. Her uncontrolled response was like a powerful aphrodisiac, mainly because he had wanted to break that calm exterior and see how far he could go with her. And she still had a long way to go.

She clawed at his collar, moaning. He lifted his mouth a little, still unwilling to stop. He liked seeing her this way, liked knowing she belonged to him mind and body. "More," he breathed. "Give me more."

Inside her, he curled his fingers along the lining beneath her pubic bone, sought the internal pleasure spot. At the same time, he pressed down firmly with the heel of his hand. Her hips arched and shook as she released again. The seat belt did its part, keeping her still as he pleasured her, drawing each stroke out until her orgasm became one long contraction, then another, like a slow heartbeat. Her breath blew against his lips in halted gasps, until he was able to adjust every rolling wave of her orgasm so precisely that she couldn't surface.

He was good at that, making a woman die from pleasure. He had perfected it through the years because it gave him control over sex. But tonight, with Nikki, was different. He was having a difficult time resisting the urge to climb on top of her and take her in that little car. He wasn't sure whether she would still be fearful when he took her back to his apartment.

His own raging senses were urging him to do so soon. Her scent tempted him to taste her but he resisted. A few more minutes, he promised himself. Then she couldn't say no to him anymore. He didn't feel like letting her go tonight.

"Rick . . ." Her voice was a low murmur. Her eyes were closed. Her hand still gripped his collar.

"Hmm?" He kissed her eyes, nose, lips. He stroked her again, heard her inhale sharply, and waited for her to return to him. Her breathing hiccupped.

"Rick . . . don't . . ." He frowned. She had better not ask him to stop. "Don't . . . think . . . I'm finished with . . . the interview."

Rick stopped, then backed away a few inches to stare at her in silent amazement. The woman couldn't lie to his fingers. She was still convulsing, still coming. Her hips were moving feverishly. She was having one huge orgasm.

Nikki Taylor might be afraid of sex, but she was indeed a NOPAIN operative. Even in the throes of being pleasured, she didn't forget that she had a job to do. Rick had to smile. He couldn't help but admire her. A small package of contradictions, indeed. He liked a challenge.

"Finished?" he countered, as he slowly teased her, eliciting another moan. "I've just begun, little bird."

He pulled up her skirt even more and trailed wet fingers down her thighs. He slipped under her right knee and pulled her leg higher. She let him do so without protest, lethargically avoiding the steering wheel, which had aided him to keep her from crossing her legs. He leaned in and kissed her knee and scraped his teeth down her damp thigh. Then deftly he draped her leg over the partition between the front seats and used the gearshift to lock her in place. Now he had wide access.

"Rick?" She shifted restlessly, still tightly held by the belt. Ignoring the restraint, her body eagerly followed his prodding, as if it knew better than she what it wanted.

The husky passion of her voice sent a wave of desire through him, liquefying whatever was left of his ironclad control. He examined her face, and sensing no fear, he said slowly, "Your body knows my touch. Now I want it to know my kiss. I can't wait any longer, Nikki. I have to taste you."

Just a bit. Just enough to carry over to his apartment. He needed to put his tongue on her, gather her scent and taste in his mouth, give in to this need to possess her. He rose and pushed his body forward, reaching for her.

She held on to his shirt tightly and he heard the popping of buttons. "Can't." She was barely audible.

He paused and returned his gaze to her face. "Can't?" He cupped her and she quivered under his hand. "Can't?" he asked again. "Or more?"

There was a strangled cry. "Y-yes."

"Good," he whispered, and didn't give her a chance to say anything else. He put his head between her open legs. And tasted.

He rolled his tongue slowly over her, savoring her. Her cry was muffled against his body as she tore at his shirt even more. She buried her face somewhere against him—he couldn't tell—he was immersed in her. He licked slowly, inhaling her scent. When her right leg jerked up he held it down firmly. Not yet.

He dipped between the silky flesh and prodded her opening. He moved his mouth and because he couldn't stop himself, he started to do the things he knew he shouldn't do. Not when she was so sensitive already. He tasted and swallowed every drop of her, sliding his tongue over and over that spot to make her wetter still, so he could have more. She reared up, but his lower body prevented her from hurting herself. She was moaning into his stomach, half-pleading and half-demanding, mindlessly tearing at his clothes.

Suddenly Nikki's scrabbling hand rubbed over his erection, and it felt so good, Rick almost spilled into his pants. She started to stroke him too, following his tongue, as if he were the maestro and she was playing some instrument. His instrument, as a matter of fact. Her hand imitated his tongue's rhythm. Faster. She went faster. Slower. She didn't like that. She continued to stroke him at a fierce pace, not even aware that she was demanding that he follow her lead.

Rick smiled, half amused and so damn aroused, he knew he had to stop soon. He held on to her hand, stopping her teasing, and at the same time pushed his tongue into her, punishing her for almost making him lose control.

"Oh."

Nikki halted all movement, her body tensing at his invasion. She groaned as he slowly withdrew and rolled his tongue around that little nub, sucking it.

He tongued her like he was kissing her, openmouthed, pushing in, pulling out. Over and over, he licked and tasted, finally just concentrating where it pleasured her most. Her body tensed tighter and tighter under him, straining against his questing lips. She was silent now, almost there. With his lips still holding her prisoner, he made love to her with his fingers, still amazed that she was so tight. He sucked and thrust in deep.

"Rick!" And he wallowed in her sweetness as she released into his mouth, rubbing his face as he licked her like a cat.

Rick reluctantly straightened up. He had meant to just have a sample but somehow had gone crazy at the first taste of her. Her quiet breathing told him Nikki had lost consciousness from the last orgasm. He brushed back her hair gently and kissed her lips softly. She moaned.

He undid the seat belt with a quick click of the release button. Got out of the car and went around to Nikki's side. He made sure to lock the doors and pocket the keys. Her shoulder bag—couldn't forget those bottles of shampoo. It took only another minute to negotiate her small weight into his arms. She lifted her head and opened her eyes.

"Rick?"

"You okay?"

"Make sure my skirt is covering me," she said, then lay her head against his shoulder, her lips searing his neck.

Rick gave a quiet laugh. He was learning much about Nikki Taylor tonight, and he didn't think he would get enough of her for a long, long time. His steps were light as he walked with ease toward the building, heading for the private side entrance. He didn't think she would appreciate being carried through the front lobby with the security guards.

His heart was pounding in anticipation. In fact, his whole body was more alive than at any time he remembered. When he reached the private entrance, he shifted Nikki's weight so he could key in the security codes.

The high beam of a car spotlighted on them. Without thinking, Rick turned his back to the light, his first thought to protect the woman in his arms. Her locked hands around his neck tightened, telling him that she was aware that something was wrong.

The car light went off. A few seconds later the engine stopped, and Rick heard the sound of the car door opening and closing. One door. One occupant.

"Put me down, Rick," Nikki whispered.

"Not yet," he said as he turned to face the intruder.

He was trained to always notice the smallest things, and the sound of the footsteps was familiar. He cursed softly. He watched with narrowed eyes as the person approached, then stopped a few feet away from them. There was a pause.

"Nice to see you again, Rick."

"I can't say the same, Denise." Rick returned coolly. He felt Nikki's fingers digging into his neck as she too turned her head.

Whatever Denise was planning, Nikki was off limits. If she hurt a single hair on Nikki's head, he was going to kill her.

Chapter Eleven

Denise Lorens was alone, dressed in seductive red, her blond hair piled in a sophisticated style on top of her head. The building lights silhouetted her svelte figure against the evening shadows as she posed with lazy indolence. She couldn't deceive Rick, though. He sensed her tension and the growing anger behind it. He saw the flicker of fury in her eyes as she took in the scene of Nikki in his arms.

"I don't like being used."

Ahhh. He hadn't returned her calls. She had come to salvage her pride. "And of course I was just there for your convenience," Rick said, keeping his voice bored. He calculated the minutes this was going to waste, thought of which direction to take from here.

"You knew who I was and still took me to your bed. Was it the challenge?" Denise stepped closer, her eyes glittering. She wasn't paying Nikki any attention. "And you kept me with you all weekend, even though you knew why I was there. You wanted me to stay despite the danger of having me there. It was very good, wasn't it?"

Denise didn't hide the need in her voice, but Rick didn't want to have this conversation with Nikki there. First, it was in bad taste. Second, he didn't need to explain himself to anyone. He held Nikki closer against him and eyed the other woman coldly. "It was no challenge, Denise." She flinched at his words. "Let it go."

"No, you owe me an explanation."

"I don't owe you anything."

"Perhaps you will, after you hear what I have to tell you."

Denise looked at Nikki with such malice that Rick suddenly came to a decision. This would end right here. If he sent the scorned woman away without knowing what she was up to, she was bound to cause more trouble than it was worth. "And that is?" he asked.

"Send her away, Rick," Denise ordered. She lowered her voice seductively. "She's also using you, can't you see that? Sex with her would just give her an advantage. At least with me, you know where you stand, and I can help you get out of the mess you're in. And it would be just as good as that weekend."

Nikki had stiffened in his arms as she listened to the exchange in silence. Rick didn't know what she was thinking, probably nothing good. Denise's obvious threats to expose Nikki meant nothing, he had already figured out for himself what she was. But perhaps she could enlighten him about Nikki's role in this trap Internal Investigations was setting up.

He felt a soft touch at the nape of his neck, a gentle nudge. He understood. Nikki was reminding him of what she had said some nights ago, that she wasn't Denise Lorens. After what had happened in the car, he knew she was telling the truth. Nikki wouldn't use sex as a weapon the way the woman standing in front of them would.

But he could also tell that Denise Lorens, in spite of that sexy outfit, was here on business. Clearly she had taken a dislike to Nikki and was out to get her. This was very unprofessional for an operative, of course, which revealed the instability of the woman's mind right now.

The hunter in him surfaced. She was unhinged. Perfect for the picking. He could get some answers tonight and make some moves ahead.

Since the death of his wife, Rick had never allowed emotions, especially sexual desire, to overwhelm his logic. But now his whole body protested at the calculated thought that had just surfaced. To send Nikki Taylor away was tantamount to being insane. To put off going to bed with her was serious bodily harm.

"If you don't want the information, I'm sure tomorrow will be as good a day as any to say bye-bye to your career." Denise's smile was overbright, confident of her victory. The yellow of the outside lights made the red of her lips strangely garish. She nodded toward Nikki. "Also, she might as well pack and leave town. She won't be needed for her assignment anymore since you would be going down, Rick. You need me tonight. Better decide soon."

Nikki's soft caress behind his neck didn't stop. Her voice was steady when she broke her silence. "Put me down, Rick."

Rick did so reluctantly. Part of him recognized Nikki's pride in not wanting to conduct an argument while ensconced in a man's arms, but the big part of him just wanted to ignore the bitch interrupting his night and throw caution to the wind. It was tempting to turn around, punch the code in, and leave Denise out here. He could deal with it all tomorrow, his body urged. His common sense, he acknowledged with rueful amazement, had finally deserted him.

Denise looked down at Nikki, her lips thinning in dislike. "Tough to be on the other side, isn't it?" A corner of her mouth lifted into a sneer. "You thought it amusing to show me up in front of my superior, telling him I'm wasting time. How does it feel to have your own time wasted? What will your superior think, I wonder, when your report is just as flawed as mine? Because after tonight, he is going to know exactly what you're after."

Rick ran a hand down Nikki's back, hoping that was enough to reassure her. She reached back with her hand and he grasped it. "I never meant to show you up, Denise," Nikki said quietly. "You did what you were assigned to do. All I pointed out was why you didn't need to continue. It was unnecessary because Rick had always known who you are. That is my job, to point out holes."

"Oh, shut up," Denise said sharply. "You sit there pointing

out little unimportant flaws in the system and pat yourself on the back for it. Do you think I don't know your kind? You want the accolades more than I do. And I see you aren't averse to using sex to get what you want either. So the shoe's on the other foot, little Miss Independent Contract. When Rick hears what I have to say, he'll dump you too."

Rick listened, mulling over the information the two women were giving him. Denise wasn't being as careful as Nikki and he was beginning to see more pieces of the puzzle.

"And you'll get accolades for his dumping me?" Nikki countered calmly, still holding his hand.

Denise shrugged. "I don't like being informed by my superiors that I'm losing my touch. You and your so-called expertise put me in a bad light and they took me off my assignment before I was ready. Well, I've made up my mind to let Rick in on some information. He is—" She glanced up mockingly at him. "So sorry to talk about you like this, darling—he's something special in bed, and I want him. What I have will hold him to me for a while. My plans don't include you, Nikki, so you might as well go write your little report and leave. The review board tomorrow is going to be disappointed with what you have to say so far. As for Rick, don't worry, I'll take care of him tonight, and tomorrow."

"So sure of that, Denise?" Rick spoke up, his voice still bored.

Denise arched a brow. "You don't want to be accused of being a traitor along with Gorman, do you, sweetie? I know their plans. You need me to help you out of this."

"In exchange for sex," Rick flatly pointed out.

Denise moued. "You've done it before," she retorted, and smiled coldly. "Why, I believe your whole file said you did so regularly enough, and of course, there is the matter of your wife."

Rick had had enough. "Do you think you can threaten me?"

Denise stepped closer. "It doesn't have to be that way," she said, her eyes sweeping the length of him intimately. "With a little persuasion, I can offer you so much more . . . than she can. What does she know about you, anyway? There is no danger or excitement to her at all. With me, you will gain more power, more control of your destiny. You can get Gorman out of your life, finally."

"Really?" Rick had to admit that Denise was good. She knew what would tempt him most. He turned to look down at Nikki, who didn't seem as weak as she had looked in his arms. Fierce need coursed through him, and he had to tamp down the urge to go with primitive desire. He couldn't just take Nikki upstairs and forget about what was happening down here. He had to deal with Denise Lorens now. "Nikki?"

She looked up, a wealth of understanding in her eyes. "You owe me," she said, referring to the interview. She had given him access to an intimate part of her and was reminding him that he, too, had a price to pay. Her smile was slow and gentle. She looked so beautiful, she seemed to glow from the inside. Rick almost—almost—changed his mind again.

"I know I do," he said, and ignoring Denise, added, "Let me walk you back to your car."

"Okay. Good night, Denise."

"Oh, I intend to have one," Denise mocked and leaned against the lit wall. The dislike in her eyes was even more palpable as she noted Rick's tender exchange with Nikki. Her lips straightened disdainfully. "That's the difference between you and me, Nikki. You're all words, with nothing to back you up. Don't keep me waiting too long if you want to save his career."

Nikki paused, studying Denise for a long moment until the other woman shifted defiantly. She nodded. "I'm glad you finally got it right about the difference between us, Denise. You see, I do still intend to save the department, and perhaps a career or two, but you're bent on destroying everything, including yourself. And know this. I can't save you."

She didn't wait for Denise's reply, turning away and walking off. Not taking any chances, Rick put himself between the women as he followed Nikki closely. He had been listening with increasing interest and admiration for Nikki. She handled herself so calmly, totally unaffected by Denise's venom. Very few women would walk away without a cat-fight. He wanted to know Nikki's strength, understand where it came from. He also wanted to ask her about what she meant by saving the department. He cursed Denise silently again. If it were any information other than Gorman that was dangled in front of him . . .

He unlocked the car door for her, then handed Nikki the keys. "Drive carefully." She smiled, sending a jolt of desire where he was already hurting, and bent down to get into her car. Unwilling to let her go, he stopped her, pulled her into his arms. "Save me, huh?"

Her eyes were secretive. "Yes, and if you give Denise what she wants, I'm sure you'll find out everything after tonight, won't you?"

Rick gently tilted her chin up. "Do you think I can," he asked, "when I still taste you in my mouth, when your scent still lingers all over me?"

She looked away, the darkness probably covering a blush, and he pinched her chin so that she returned her gaze to him. "Nikki, I want you. Now. But I can't just let her play this game with me, or with you. There's too much at stake."

"She isn't going to tell you the truth," Nikki told him. "She has the same aura the building has."

"What building? You mean my office?"

She nodded. "The whole building. She isn't healthy, Rick, and no, I won't bore you with my strange notions right now, but please be careful."

He had to smile at her. She should be angry with him, instead of trying to keep him safe. "I will, little bird. And I know I owe you the interview next." He leaned forward and kissed her. She opened her mouth willingly, and her warmth seeped into him again. He was going to regret letting her go tonight. Straightening up, he dropped his hands, watched her climb into the car. To put her at ease, he mocked, "Be ready for rule number five tomorrow."

She blinked. "There's more?" she asked, eyes widening a little.

His smile was totally masculine. "So much more," he promised. "Now put on the seat belt like I taught you."

He grinned wickedly at her, knowing without actually seeing the heat on her cheeks. To prove he was right, he leaned in and caressed her face with the back of his hand. She wouldn't look at him as she buckled up. He watched with regret as she drove away. Then he turned around to deal with Denise Lorens.

Nikki drove down the stretch of road, turned the corner, timed the red light to change twice, then made a U-turn. She parked her car in a spot close to the apartment building. She sat staring across the street into the parking lot. The image of Rick with Denise Lorens twisted her gut. This, she thought with wonder, was jealousy. She didn't want another woman touching Rick Harden, especially that one.

She looked up at the building. She had cased the place, knew where the lights were coming from. She saw Rick's bedroom lights come on, and took a deep breath.

Rick leaned against the small bar at the side of the room, watching Denise Lorens taking off her clothes in a seductive striptease a few yards away. Her eyes met his boldly, her lips half open, red and wet. She had all this planned out. Her dress had front buttons, and she undid those slowly, revealing her body inch by inch. She knew how to do it just right, shimmying out of her dress in one fluid motion, bending forward to show her ample bosom to advantage.

He kept his eyes on her like a man watching a cobra sway back and forth, just in case venom came spewing in his direction. After touching and tasting Nikki, he wasn't moved at all by the blatant sexual display in front of him. He still smelled Nikki's scent; he still tasted her on his lips. He was still hard from needing her.

Denise came toward him in red lace underwear, wearing only her heels. The strong scent of her perfume reached him first. She was a beautiful woman, one who knew what pleased a man, but he didn't want her. He looked at her body from top to toe, looking for wires. She wasn't here just for entertainment.

She smiled at his perusal. "I have been thinking of you, Rick," she breathed, stepping in between the vee of his legs. "You have this extraordinary effect on me in bed. No one had ever done me like you did."

"And you want more," Rick mocked.

Her eyes were hot and hungry. "Oh yes," she said, licking her lips.

Rick thought about Nikki doing that whenever she was nervous. He doubted Denise was nervous at the moment. In fact, she would probably fly into a rage if she knew he was sitting there comparing her unfavorably to Nikki. He wanted Nikki here, with her soft sensuality and quivering need. Not this.

He sat still when Denise leaned forward and touched him. She purred at his semiarousal, licking her lips again. "Oh yes," she said again, looking up triumphantly, "and I can feel how I turn you on. I knew you couldn't resist what we had together. You were unstoppable for a whole weekend, Rick. That was how much you wanted me."

Rick remembered. He had wanted to forget the emptiness in his life, had done so with his companion with the kind of concentration that was meant to wipe out his own misery. He remembered he wanted to give up everything that weekend because life had become unimportant. Everything was meaningless. But like a miracle, on that very weekend, he had seen Nikki in the elevator for the first time. Something inside him had stirred.

He didn't blink as Denise unzipped his pants slowly. She hummed her approval. "Why aren't you taking me to bed, Rick?" she whispered.

"What do you have for me?" he asked flatly. Her grip on him tightened, and her eyes glittered warningly. He didn't react.

"Don't you like what you see?"

He smiled. "Take everything off and let me see you naked, Denise." He wanted to make sure she wasn't wired. Then he would take her to the bedroom, just in case the underwire of her bra was electronically enhanced.

Denise laughed, then stepped back. Looking down at him, she slowly took off her bra, then pushed her panties down her hips. She stepped out of her heels. Her nipples were hard from excitement. Her eyes had a fevered sexual glimmer. There was a needy expression in them as she stared at him. "See, Rick? I'm naked before you. Now take me."

"In the bedroom," Rick said softly. "You know my toys are in there."

"Oh yes," she said and moved in that direction. Rick looked at her bare back, all the way down, and frowned. She was totally clean. Why had she come here alone, unwired? Was she doing this on her own?

"Oh, I've been thinking about this room." Denise sighed as she carelessly sprawled onto the bed. She looked up at Rick standing in the doorway and slowly opened her legs. "See how much I want you?"

Rick took a step forward. "How much?"

"Enough to be here when I don't need to be," she teased.

"So much," Rick stated, taking another step. "I guess I should feel conceited to have you here, risking your job. Why tonight, though, Denise?"

"Rick, surely you know the answer to that. I don't want her to have any part of you." Denise pouted. "She's already causing the department trouble, with her safety evaluations bullshit, and she thinks she has free rein over everything just because the admiral backs her right now. Everything hinges on her damn report, and I'm going to take her down a peg or two, that's all. An independent review board to investigate about our safety? Our security? Bullshit. What does she know about our kind, Rick? She's an independent. She's just evaluating you, you know. Afterward she will report you as a security risk, and what would you say to the review board?"

Rick took another step. "I see. You're saying that since you weren't evaluating me last weekend, that should make me feel better. You were"—he cocked his head to one side—"just trying to get something on me, and Nikki wasn't." A strange code by which to live, he thought.

"Of course she wasn't," Denise said, pushing up with her

elbows. "I told you, she's writing reports for Admiral Madison, the very same one who dealt with Gorman. He probably dislikes you and wants to make sure about you and Task Force Two. Perhaps get you out so he can replace you with someone he can control."

"There's nothing wrong with that," Rick pointed out. He wanted to hear more. He reached the edge of his bed and looked down at the naked woman, hiding his distaste. "I should have known Gorman needed someone from the Directorate of Intelligence to help him with his schemes. And of course he would choose a beautiful woman like you. What have you got on me, Denise?"

Her eyes glittered. "Give me what I want first." She sat up and looked at the front of his pants. "I promise you, what I have will save your career."

Rick reached for the top button of his pants. "And Gorman?"

"Yes." Her eyes grew hungrier. "Everything on Gorman will be yours."

He unbuttoned and she licked her red lips. "Remember how long you lasted, Denise?"

"Oh yes," she moaned, leaning closer.

"I can make you last longer." Rick watched dispassionately as she reached greedily for him. "But I can't perform with Gorman and tomorrow on my mind. Set my mind at ease. Tell me what you've got." When she paused, he taunted, "Surely your plan isn't so easy to foil."

Denise laughed, then ran her red fingernails down the dark material of his pants. She considered for a moment, then shrugged. "Oh well, it doesn't make a difference." She put one hand on him, crooning at the feel of him. "I only want this." She looked up. "You're right. I'm Gorman's mole from the Directorate of Intel. I pass along everything collected that's of interest to him, sending via disks for his eyes only. After his arrest I went to his place and retrieved them. Gorman, you see, covered his tracks very well. He knew I would take care of things."

It was easy to put two and two together now. Gorman was

negotiating in jail over those disks, but without them, he needed to dangle some names. Rick Harden would be one of those names. He would be the coordinator of every treachery Gorman orchestrated. He was also sure that Denise was keeping something back, enough to stop Gorman from sacrificing her, anyway.

"I have downloaded everything onto one of your computers. EYES will get to it tomorrow, and I'll help them with the very complicated encryption program. By the way, I've manipulated the information to just reveal your name. Don't worry, the real ones have been secured somewhere safe."

"So there are others," Rick said slowly, as he watched her hand stroke him. She didn't seem to sense his growing anger, or maybe she didn't care. She was totally absorbed in her power over him.

"Only I can stop this, dear darling Rick. So satisfy me, and tomorrow none of this needs to happen. I'll take care of it."

"How long? Till the next time you want sex from me?"

She shrugged again. "Power is everything. Gorman used you as a front. So can I. We can continue what he started, with me in my position and you as the new deputy director. Gorman can just rot in there. Hmm, you are so . . . big. Make love to me now, Rick."

She bent forward, opening her mouth to take him in. Rick circled her neck with one hand. "I think not."

Her eyes widened in anger. "You dare refuse me?"

"Yes."

"Then you'll be nothing tomorrow. I'm the one in charge now, you see. Your career is in my hands, darling."

Actually Rick didn't think so. Someone had sent Denise to seduce him, and she was too intent to follow it through. The woman wouldn't risk her cover for sex. She was either obeying orders or she was desperate. She took his hesitation as capitulation. Flashing a victorious smile, she bent forward again. Rick tightened his hold enough that for the first time apprehension entered her eyes.

His eyes were cold as he examined her beautifully made-up face. He felt nothing but contempt. "My career," he told her, in a flat voice, "can go to hell. And so can you."

Denise Lorens's face registered her shock for a mere instant, as she realized that she had been had. With idle curiosity, Rick finally allowed his real emotions to show on his face. Apparently she didn't like being humiliated. Without warning she lunged forward, pushing against his hold on her throat. Her hands clawed out as she screeched her fury.

Much later, back at her apartment, sitting at her desk, Nikki read the faxed report, pushing emotions out of the way as she analyzed the data. It was difficult. This was Rick she was reading about. She looked up and touched the wind chime dangling close by. The sound echoed gently through the room as the truth rummaged through the layers of her mind out into the open.

Truth. This was the emotional connection she felt with this man, so hardened by his past. They were both seeking the truth. Like him, she was still trying to understand about a betrayal in the past. They had both been used and discarded.

Nikki understood the pain of being abandoned. In her own way, she wanted closure with her past. So did Rick. Their lives came together here because of their need to expose the truth. His truth for hers. Could she give him that?

She had known when she accepted this contract that this bargain wouldn't be easy. Her looks were meant to trigger him into action. She looked at the faxed sheets of paper again. So much pain ahead. Right now she wasn't sure about wanting the truth to come out.

She was falling in love with Rick. But could she save him?

Chapter Twelve

Was there ever a bigger fool than he? Rick wondered as he strode up the building steps, watching the morning visitors make their lines. As he had a thousand different mornings, he showed his electronic ID and walked past the cameras to the private elevators. As he had a thousand different times, he punched the button and while waiting to go up to his office, he mentally mapped out the rest of the day so he could have no other thoughts but work.

He had done this day in and day out and rotted slowly away inside. He hadn't cared enough about Gorman's motives when he was picked as his Task Force Two operations chief. He hadn't questioned too deeply because he had decided that he was going to be good at one thing only, and that was doing his job to perfection. After all, his career hinged on his record, and his marred one needed repairing.

So in his own foolish way, he paid penance for his sins. He was exactly how Gorman had shaped him—a pathetic bureaucrat who never went beyond the boundaries. What he once was, he now mocked. How far he had moved from those days when he had thought to save the world with one big swoop from the sword of justice. Until, of course, he had found out that the one nearest and dearest to him had betrayed everything he believed in.

Last night only served as a reminder of how his passive choices hadn't chased away his past, but only served to emphasize it. Denise had misunderstood him, but that was because he had chosen to be seen in that light. It struck him as odd that the only person who seemed to be trying to find out the truth about him was Nikki Taylor, an independent contractor. The rest were just willing to believe a traitor, Gorman.

The elevator arrived and he stepped in with the few people waiting with him. Rick nodded at them, noting their similar dark suits and ties and nondescript briefcases. Bureaucrats one and all. His brothers-at-arms.

He thought of EYES pulling all his careful compilation of bureaucratic red tape out of his files and cabinets upstairs. He imagined how many were sifting through every folder right now, looking at each case for some kind of proof. The computers were probably being confiscated as of this moment.

There was one thing about his determination to excel as a paper pusher, though. He had backups of backups. He had detailed everything with disks and photos and hidden them away. Last night he had removed the hard drive from his computer and replaced it with another. If nothing else, he was a pathetic but careful bureaucrat.

He laughed out loud, startling the other occupants in the elevator. What a night. He was probably the only man who had sent two women away in one night so he could play with his computer hard drive. He wondered how Nikki had spent her night, whether he occupied her thoughts as much as she did his.

The elevator door slid open, and he stepped out onto his floor. He looked down the hall and saw the stacks of boxes outside his wing of offices. Some of his men stood nearby watching the commotion with guarded expressions. He strode toward them, and a few avoided meeting his eyes. Cam turned and, seeing his arrival, approached him. Four others fell in step.

"Sir," Cam said, for once without his usual easy laughter in his eyes, "they unplugged all the computers for Task Force Two."

Rick nodded. "I hope you saved the report that you've been working on because I still have to submit it."

"Oh yes, sir. Patty copies everything. It's ready for you."

Patty copied everything. "Isn't it Patty's responsibility to process all requests for information, especially back and forth for our sector?"

"Yes, sir."

"Get her for me, Cam. Tell her I want to know what was the last request that had to do with Task Force Two, and tell her I also need to know which computer was used for that request. Would that be hard to find out?"

Cam shrugged. "Should be easy. I'll get her right now."

"Good. In your office, Cam."

"Yes, sir."

Rick gave brief instructions to his other men, then walked past the cardboard boxes into his strangely messy office. Poor Greta. His secretary was standing in the middle looking confused. She had been around for so long, she was the only one who knew where everything was. She was probably lost without her neatly stacked files and folders. He would have to give her a great reference if they cut Task Force Two.

A few agents were pulling the rest of the files out of the cabinets. Harpring looked up from Greta's desk and met his eyes.

"Morning, Agent Harden," he said. "We'll be here for a while."

"Morning. I won't be in much today, anyway." Not that he had anything to do here. Everything had been frozen.

"Ah, yes, the review board," Harpring said. "I'm sure they will have quite a few questions for you. I'm impressed, I must say—you documented everything very well."

Rick smiled briefly. He knew a fishing trip when he heard one. Why not take the bait? "Thank you. I believe in a very simple system. A to Z, with backups."

"These backups," the other man said, casually closing one of the cabinet drawers, "how would you prove they are copies of the original?"

Rick's hand paused on the door handle leading into his office. "Like I said, I keep it really simple. My secretary documented everything and sent the files to Gorman and each deputy director in TIARA. If I have to update or change a certain set of documents, I have to do the same for all the other sets as well. I'm sure if you check every set I had sent out, you'll find everything is updated on the same date."

"In that case, any files found that don't correlate with the other files' information or date would mean they are hidden data, not shared with the other deputy directors."

"It means that I didn't put that file there," Rick corrected. Some baiting he would take.

"It can also mean they might be the ones you and Gorman kept just for each other."

Rick knew that was coming but he wanted to hear it from the man himself. "I'm sure Deputy Director Gorman had access to many more classified materials than I did," he said smoothly as he opened the door, "but I would only be too happy to help with any questions about such files that you find."

"I'm sure you would," Harpring said, his voice laced with sarcasm. "So tell me about the Marlena Maxwell files. Why were certain copies suddenly requested by Gorman and then deleted by him? What was in those files?"

Marlena Maxwell. The very same case that got Gorman caught. Unbeknownst to Rick, the deputy director had been using Task Force Two to keep her under surveillance for his nefarious purposes. In fact, Rick had only recently discovered how he and his men had been used in numerous ways by Gorman to spy on others to get information for the traitor's own use.

Marlena Maxwell was a sore point with Rick. His report was riddled with holes because he had chosen to protect her secret identity. Perhaps that would be his downfall now.

"I have no idea what was in those files," Rick answered. "Gorman requested them and later deleted them. Unless he sent me the information, I wouldn't know."

"So you just released a suspect and closed the operations without any information at all?" The sarcasm was even sharper now.

Rick met Harpring's eyes across the room. "I still have to give a final report on that assignment," Rick said quietly. "I'm sure you'll find all the necessary details in it. You see, without setting Miss Maxwell free I wouldn't have been able to catch Gorman. And I wouldn't have been able to send my own man after them with a wire. Everything that transpired was recorded. And lastly, without that tape, you wouldn't have Gorman behind bars now, wouldn't you agree? So you see, my system really works. Excuse me, I have several things to do. Greta, you can take the rest of the morning off."

Rick gently closed the door to the big mess outside. Well, his day had begun.

"Feed the ghosts. They will trap you."

"But Grandmother, I don't want to talk about the dead."

The older woman grasped her granddaughter by the hand and pulled her to the ancestors' altar. There, pictures of dead relatives stared down solemnly.

"They are dead"—her grandmother pointed to the pictures—"because we make peace with them. We have the Festival for the Hungry Dead to make them full and happy, keep them away."

"Grandmother—" She tried never to interrupt when the old lady was in the mood to tell the future, but so far, all she had been told were the dangers ahead. Where was her happiness, her dreams?

"You think things no longer here are gone, just like that. You have to make peace, then they go. If not, they haunt you for the rest of your life."

"Grandmother, how do you make peace with the dead?"

"You tell them the truth and show them they are no longer needed."

She stared at her grandmother, trying to understand. What had the truth and the dead to do with her center and her heart?

"I don't follow, Grandmother," she finally said.

"Of course not. All of you is still alive. Wait till you've lost your center. Wait till the fire melts the frozen heart. Then you will find many ghosts to appease. And not necessarily human ghosts, my girl. You have the future now. Wait till you have some past. Lots of ghosts in the past. The bad ones can be very hungry."

Nikki studied the picture of her grandmother, one of the few things she really treasured. If her grandmother had become a ghost, then she should haunt her granddaughter for not remembering her lessons well.

It had been easy to "forget" the prophecies when she was busy with life. Her grandmother wasn't one who nagged or scolded often. Her goal was simple—to leave a legacy of her beliefs to someone. Nikki's parents were already too old to listen to her, so she had chosen to educate the little granddaughter.

Well, she was older and wiser now. She was always one step behind, though. In that sense, she had failed her grandmother. What good were warnings when they were ignored till it was too late?

Beware the center. It will betray you.
Release the frozen heart. It will burn you.
Feed the hungry ghosts. They will trap you.

She cocked her head, staring unseeing into space. It all had to do with truth. She had understood it in herself, but it took being in a cell in pitch darkness for that to happen. She thought of Rick. And blushed. She wondered if she could ever think of him again without blushing. Even in the midst of serious research, his name brought back memories of his kisses. She would never forget last night, how he had . . . She felt her face heat up even more.

"It was done in darkness, too," she whispered. Her association with the dark had always to do with imprisonment and isolation. Rick had given her a new link, one that released some of the pain she held inside.

She sat up, blinking. *He had given her a new memory to banish the ghosts.* Was that what her grandmother meant by feeding the ghosts?

If that was so, how would that correlate with releasing the frozen heart? How would feeding the ghosts release it? And whose heart did her grandmother mean? Hers? Or, as she now believed, Rick Harden's? Because the more she found out about him, the more she realized how static he had made his life. He had stopped his growth, blocked his *chuung*, ever since the death of his wife.

His center was silent, and Nikki grieved for him. Pain of that sort ate one alive, leaving one in darkness, and she wanted to reach out to him and take away that ache. She didn't know how he felt about her, but last night he had been gentle, and when Denise had shown up, he had also been protective. Theirs was a strange bond, she thought, with their frozen hearts and the dark holes inside them.

She rubbed her heart area unconsciously. It had burned when he kissed her, the kind of white heat that wiped out all thought and memory. All she had been able to do was feel him, and only him. She chewed on her lower lip. Was she supposed to do that to him, too?

Just the thought sent multiple shivers through her. She closed her eyes. Touching him . . . kissing his body . . . doing the same thing he did to hers. Twice she had touched him intimately, and each time he had felt incredible, his heat pulsing fiercely against her palms. It must look—she gave a purely female smile—huge.

It had been a long time since she'd had sexy thoughts about men. It was exciting. It made her feel almost whole again. The fear was still there, but somehow she had lost the distaste for being touched. She wanted Rick as she had never wanted anyone—it was a constant burning need inside. Was that what Denise Lorens felt? No—more, she corrected with a touch of jealousy. That woman had had sex with Rick for a whole weekend. And look how he affected her.

For a rare instant, Nikki's jealousy of Denise turned into anger. She didn't need to be inside Rick's apartment last night to know what that woman had planned. Again, that feeling of unease she had around Denise flared as a warning. She had spent months at the mercy of men who had treated her exactly the same way that Denise used Rick—as a thing, a toy.

Just like that, Nikki's anger and jealousy washed away. Denise had never had Rick, and never would, and to waste her energy on the other times Rick had been with the woman would sully her own growing feelings. She didn't see him in the same light as Denise. She also knew, with certainty, that Rick would never treat her the same way he had treated Denise last night.

The pen she was holding dropped onto the table, shaking her out of her reverie. She sighed. She had gotten clearance to use one of the classified libraries. Here she was daydreaming when she should be working on this report. Rick's future was in her hands, and all she could think about was his body. Surely she was getting a little crazy. She looked down at the page in front of her. She had written a few paragraphs, and then she had stopped when Rick's name came up.

That was what had brought on those sexual thoughts of him. She smiled, wondering if the board would be amused by her description of his sexual prowess and what she wanted to do with him, instead of a cut-and-dried opinion of his ability to function under duress.

"What are you thinking of, smiling like that, Nikki?"

Surprised, she looked up at Agent Erik Jones. She shook her head and shrugged. "Daydreaming." She didn't think her mystical ideas would make sense to anyone but herself. And she certainly wasn't going to share her *other* thoughts.

"Who wouldn't around these tomes?" Erik looked at the pile of books and documents before her on the desk. "What are you researching? Can I help?"

Nikki shook her head again. "No, not really."

Erik pulled up a chair and sat by her. "Is this for the recruit program or your story?" He grinned back when she smiled at him. "Hey, I'm not that stupid, you know. You're mostly going through this for your research, right? And you somehow jumped over some huge hurdles with the help of Task Force Two's O.C."

There was a curious light in his eyes, inviting her to explain. "What are you saying?" she asked, keeping her voice light.

"Can I ask you something?"

"All right."

"Are you an agent after Harden?"

Nikki picked up her pen. "Is that a theory or a suspicion?" she asked, giving him a sideways glance.

"It would make a good plot, don't you think?" Erik asked casually.

"Yes, it would."

"So is your heroine after the hero, then?"

Nikki hid her smile. The young operative sounded like her conversations with Rick. "I thought I told you my heroine was going to save the hero, remember?"

Erik rubbed his jaw thoughtfully. "Yeah, I remember now." He propped a hand under his chin. "Do you remember your first day in the recruitment program?"

"Yes." She knew he was digging for information, but she didn't mind. He was an eager and impatient young man, wanting to excel. "You were telling us your new job. You said you just transferred into the Directorate of Administration."

"Well, actually I wanted to transfer to the Directorate of Intelligence but they told me they wanted me with administration."

"Because you're good with details," Nikki said, recalling his introduction from that day.

"Yes, but I would rather work with data than supplies. Like your hero, for instance. You wouldn't want him in administration, would you? You would want him in Intel, in charge of covert secrets and all the exciting stuff."

"I think every directorate is important in itself," Nikki replied, trying to see what he was up to. "Intel is nothing without administrative work."

"Oh yeah, it's so great to be the one who sends out the micro-eyes and the secret gadgets," Erik retorted wryly. "You really need a brain to make sure each department gets the type of computers they requested, or that the shipment of arms go to the right agency. I thought working in encryption was pretty bad, but where I am now is worse."

Nikki looked down at her unfinished report, then back at Erik. "What do you want to do, Erik? You can still transfer to Intel."

He shook his head. "I've been trying to get on Agent Harden's good side because I want to transfer to Task Force Two, or at least be considered for it." He glanced down at the paperwork and added, "I know something is going down because being in administration, I see all the stuff being shuttled back and forth. Today, for instance, is a big day, isn't it? Some sort of review board is going to meet later this afternoon, and it has to do with Harden and Task Force Two."

Nikki smiled. "Are you looking to me for clues? You seem to be able to find a lot on your own already, Erik."

"But you want material to save your hero, right? In the romance, I mean." His eyes were alert and bright, an eager smile on his lips. His fingers drummed the table impatiently.

"Why don't you talk to the right people about this?" Nikki asked, studying the younger man closely. "There must be a dozen more important people than me."

Erik shrugged. "I can't reach Agent Harden, not with EYES all over the place on him and his offices. I sent an urgent message to him but maybe his secretary lost it in the mess. I can't tell Denise, who dated him for a while, because she won't answer my calls, either. My superiors think I don't have enough experience. I can help Agent Harden but no one wants it."

"So you come to me?"

He shrugged again. His fingers beat a rhythm while he spoke, as if he were seeing some sequence of events in his mind. "Okay, so I got tired of other people having fun. I read everything that passed through, just for the hell of it. Then I found files Intel and some other departments have been requesting about you. It's easy to read the files when you're delivering them, you know.

"They've been busy checking you out, Nikki, so I know you aren't just a writer. You're an outside contractor hired by Admiral Madison, and no one in here is happy with your presence. I know they're looking for some stuff to use against you but your background before the last ten years comes back empty. I said to myself, that is weird, things don't come up blank in a thorough data search unless they've been delib-

erately wiped out." He paused his busy fingers and scruti-
nized Nikki. "How am I doing with the heroine so far?"

Nikki returned his gaze calmly. He was quite good at connecting data. "Perhaps Intel suits you better."

Erik grinned. "Wish you would tell somebody for me.
Denise said she might consider me as her trainee but I think
she'll tire me out."

The implication was fairly obvious and she arched a brow
at him. With his head propped nonchalantly and that open
smile, he didn't seem Denise's type. She gave him a critical
all-over examination, noting the clear blue eyes, the straight
nose, and the stubborn jaw. He was a potentially good asset,
a bit young, but with more pluses than minuses.

"You don't approve," Erik remarked, and he sounded a little surprised.

"I don't disapprove or approve. I don't even know you,
Erik," Nikki pointed out.

"But the look you gave me—"

"I was breaking you down piece by piece in my head, pic-
turing you as an asset, the way Intel would see you. You
won't be a person, Erik, but an asset, and I was merely seeing
how best to use your talents." He frowned at her as she continued gently, "We both know there are many different levels
of Intel work. You seemed to have decided to go with either
Agent Harden's section or Agent Lorens's and they are both
useful to the department. Are you sure, at your age, you're
thinking with your head when you're . . . training with
Denise Lorens?"

He straightened defensively. "Agent Harden started the
same way."

She was seeing patterns of hero worship in Erik for
Harden. She understood Rick's background would be a
tempting lure for young men who thought that kind of life
easy. Rick's past record of commitment before his demotion
had been exemplary.

"I don't think . . ." Nikki paused to choose her words
carefully, "that the heroine would approve of that kind of
hero."

"Oh come on, James Bond slept around."

She had to smile at that. "Erik, I can't stop you if you want to live like James Bond. Why come tell me this, if you're already so sure that's going to be your life—hundreds of women and gadgets left and right?" She supposed that was what all young men wanted. She wondered whether that was how Rick was and her mirth died a little. No, he did love one woman. "So you've decided to use sex to get information."

Erik lowered his voice. "I know there are moles in the agency. I can find out Gorman's contacts at both the Directorates of Intel and Administration. It's easy for me to pull out the files to check the dates and different orders of equipment, but I don't have the time to look at everything on my own. This is big, Nikki, and you're the one who can do something—give me the time to break the encryption and prove that I can really do this."

She could tell he really believed he had found evidence. His motive was to make a big splash for himself. Erik Jones was an ambitious young operative indeed. "How do you know your info is correct and will be where you're looking?"

"I didn't sleep with Denise Lorens and not learn some things," he scolded mildly.

Nikki didn't really want to know what Denise had or hadn't taught Erik Jones. The young man needed a strong guiding hand, and without it, he would run rampant chasing dreams. "I can't promise you anything, Erik," she said. "I'll be watching the whole thing from another room before they call on me. I can't move in and stop the proceedings. I don't have the authority. My role as an independent contractor is merely to observe and draw conclusions in my report on these observations. I know EYES think I'm investigating them and Agent Harden, as well as the whole agency, but that is just their paranoia."

Erik Jones looked a little deflated. "Shit. Nothing is ever as it seems."

She patted him on the shoulder. She couldn't help feeling sorry for him. "It never is, in Intel. Tell me something, Erik.

Why do you try so hard to emulate Agent Harden's past? You don't have to be like him to be successful."

He shifted in his seat, no longer as cocky as before. "I don't know. It's sort of cool to do everything he did, and be good at it." He pointed at her paperwork again. "You're good, too, or the department would have found a way to get rid of you immediately. What do you do exactly, Nikki? When you're not writing romances, of course."

She thought of all the work she had put into finding out Rick's past. The deal she had with the admiral about her own. She thought of Gorman's threats hanging over her man. So much hung in the balance because of the past. "I look for hungry ghosts," she answered quietly. "I feed them and put them to rest."

At Erik's puzzled expression, she explained, "As you said, nothing is ever as it seems, but the truth will surface if we look hard enough. Now, what have you got for me, Agent Jones?"

Chapter Thirteen

Nikki went through the next course in the recruitment program, observing the different ways recruits were targeted for various departments, once they passed the relevant tests. The first time she had gone through this, she was part of the race for a position. Fresh and untrained, she had been molded into what they wanted. Now she could see how someone like Gorman or a person working for him would pick the "right" person for his agenda. After a while, a whole task force would be made up of key people with certain personalities.

She thought of all the files she had gleaned of those working in Task Force Two. Cameron Candeloro, easygoing slacker, good at taking orders, excellent at weapons but seemed to prefer a desk job. Cole Armstrong, consistent but not persistent, nine-to-five, good at taking orders, two censures in his report, trained in electronics. The rest of the team shared certain similarities. They all had censures in their reports that made them eager to follow orders. They all had a certain mentality about their job—good at it but not aggressive in their ambition. They were all smart, with different talents. Gorman would, of course, identify these qualities if there were any questions about his choices.

The only person who didn't quite fit the order was Ricardo Harden. He was a driven, goal-oriented operative before his demotion, and then languished for several years behind a desk. How that must have hurt him. Yet he had molded himself into what he was today, and Gorman had picked him to be his O.C. Why? There was a link here, she was sure of it. She wondered what Gorman had on Rick.

She knew things looked bad for Rick. First, Gorman and Rick's relationship went back more than ten years. While Rick was demoted and stuck where he was, Gorman had steadily gone up the bureau ladder until he became director of Task Force Two. His appointment of Rick was seen as a friend helping out an old friend. Now Gorman was in jail and determined to make a deal with the DOD by giving the names of his co-conspirators. Internal Investigations was determined to find this list before anything went public.

She moved down the hallway, deep in thought. The moment she turned the corner, she already knew she was being followed. She didn't need to turn around to see who it was.

There were people moving in and out of the offices, and some of them greeted the man following her. She turned another corner, hoping for an interruption. There were things she couldn't say, and she was afraid they would spill out unbidden. He had that kind of effect on her.

She heard him answer some questions, but his voice was getting nearer as if he was lengthening his strides. There would be no interruptions.

She stepped into the emergency stairway. He came through the doors a few seconds later. Tall. Brooding. She licked her lips nervously. His green eyes settled on her mouth.

"You shouldn't be talking to me," she said softly. There wasn't much room on the landing, not with him standing in front of her. Disliking the disadvantage of his height, she backed up a few steps of the staircase behind until she stood a few inches taller, looking down at him. Much better.

His lips quirked and amusement flickered across his face. He placed one hand on the banister, blocking her with his body. Another hand reached out, slipping under the heavy knot of hair. He massaged her neck as he drew her face down.

"We don't have to talk," he murmured.

His lips met hers so softly that she instinctively leaned into him. He stayed where he was, barely touching her, teasing with the warmth of his body. She opened her mouth for him, but he didn't kiss her back.

Standing passively, his hand massaging her neck, he seemed contented with the light contact. She caught her breath when his tongue flicked at her upper lip. She waited for more, aching for his possession. His hand slid around her neck and his thumb caressed the quickening pulse there. She leaned even closer, wanting his arms around her, needing to fill her mouth with the taste of him.

"Rick," she said against his lips, finally unable to stand his silent teasing.

"Hmm?"

Realizing that he wasn't going to give her what she wanted, she tugged on his lapels, pushing his lips apart with hers. He took a step back and she gasped, the move catching her by surprise. Falling forward, she hung on to him, and he supported her weight as he opened his mouth for her, the hand caressing her neck holding her securely.

It became clear that Rick would only let her feel safe momentarily before he took charge again. He had allowed her to stand taller to make her point, but it was she who was leaning on his solid frame now. She didn't care. In the back of her mind, she understood it had to do with trust, that he needed to be in control.

Tentatively she entered his mouth, her tongue touching his shyly. He tasted hot and sweet, addictive. She wanted more. Feeling bolder, she delved deeper. His tongue lazily danced with hers, slowly seducing. She liked kissing him. He made her forget everything except the tangling of their tongues, and he continued to tease her, allowing her to be the aggressor as she probed and tasted, reveling in her new role.

Feeling the zipper at the back of the dress slowly sliding down, she broke off. Breathless, she realized how far she had leaned forward, his glittering green eyes inches from her own. The heat in them echoed the fever burning her up. How could one kiss do this?

"Rick," she protested, in a whisper.

His hand slid into her dress, played with her bra strap. "I

need to feel you. I was thinking about you last night," he said softly. "I wanted to undress you, put you in my bed. You wouldn't be wearing a bra to your conferences today. Or—"

"Rick," she interrupted, flushing at his words, "you were busy last night, anyway."

The heat in his eyes cooled but his hand inside her dress caressed her bare back. "I didn't sleep with her, Nikki."

"I know."

His eyes searched hers. "We will have to compare notes someday." His voice was dry, with a tinge of amusement. "What we know, and what we don't, about each other. Right now, it seems like everyone knows more about me than I myself."

"Did Denise really carry out her threat?" Nikki asked, her mind racing at the possibilities of what could happen.

"Don't look so worried, little bird," he said, slowly zipping her dress back up.

"Was her bargain with you very important?"

"Shouldn't you leave all the probing to EYES and the review board later? Would you be sitting there writing notes or passing information, Nikki?"

He sounded more curious than angry, one steely arm circling her waist holding her securely as if he would never let her go. It made her feel safe and wanted. This was where she had wanted to be last night, too. Would he still have wanted her today?

"You aren't answering me," he chided.

She blinked, focusing on his question. The review board. "I'll be there. Admiral Madison hired me to add balance to all the information." Which wasn't going to be easy, she added silently. "Denise Lorens will probably be there, too. We'll be waiting in the same room."

"Don't sit next to her. Don't talk to her." Rick placed a kiss on her forehead, then lifted her off the steps to set her back onto the landing. "She won't be in a good mood, and I don't want her anywhere near you."

"I can take care of myself, Rick," she said, looking up. "It's you who's in trouble."

He smiled. "Tell me something I don't know." She wished she could tell him, but it wasn't the right time. Something must have shown in her expression, because he tipped her face up and warned her again, "Don't say anything to Denise. I don't know what she's up to, but if she could hurt you, too, she would, Nikki."

"She's following orders because someone higher up promised her something," Nikki said, watching the frown appearing on Rick's forehead, "and if she could stop me from making full disclosure of what I have found out, so much the better."

"She wants to use you against me," Rick guessed.

Nikki nodded. "And you against me. If I don't want her to continue to threaten your career, I will do as she says."

"And since I refused her last night, she will definitely go after me. Don't let her stop you from your job." He rubbed her chin with his thumb. "One sacrificial lamb is enough."

But Nikki had been one a long time ago. She had no intention of letting Rick be one today.

"Rule number five," she said, taking a deep breath to calm her nerves. He arched a brow as he waited. "I don't want lamb on my menu tonight. I want something with strawberry in it. Make it through the review board so I can have what I want."

Her heart thumped at the sensuous heat in his gaze. "You're sure?" He wasn't referring to whether he would survive the review board.

This was harder than she had thought. Trusting a man again. Opening old wounds. But this was her chance to prove that she was no longer driven by fear.

"Yes," she said quietly. "Yes, I'm sure."

If fate decreed that she were to feed hungry ghosts, she had better feed the ones that had been haunting her, too.

Later that day, Rick finished what was supposed to be coffee in the employee lounge. He dropped the plastic cup into the trash and looked around. The sofa looked about the same nondescript tan color as the one that was here the last time he took his breaks in this room. That was—he tried to remember—God, maybe seven years ago. The wide-screen television was new; they didn't have such a nice set down here back in those days.

His stomach growled a protest and he gave a wry smile. Too many years a bureaucrat. Too many years drinking martinis at lunch. He was getting soft in his old age—his digestive system couldn't take the abuse of that black sludge and machine-packaged food.

The door swung open and Cam strode in, followed by Patty Ostler from records. Rick liked the way she had handled things when he had talked to them earlier. She was efficient, asking the few questions needed to understand the situation. She had weighed the problem for a few seconds, and had thrown her hat into the ring to help Rick.

Being from records, she was able to track all requests for classified data, when they were taken out and returned or destroyed. Unfortunately, Denise worked within the Directorate of Intelligence, which logged a fair amount of classified data daily. The process of finding Denise's false information was going to take some time, something Rick knew he didn't have, but he wasn't going down without a fight.

They had agreed to resume down here after a short meeting at Cam's small office. Too many distractions upstairs. Of course, anyone but I.I. operatives would know there was something wrong if they were to walk in here and see Task Force Two's operations chief taking a break. Everyone knew Hard-On didn't care for small talk with his team or anyone else.

"Hi, sir." Cam headed straight for the coffee and poured himself a cup. Patty shook her head, making a face, when he glanced her way. She opened her purse and brought out a small can of instant coffee. Rick recognized it as one of those gourmet brands.

"I don't blame you," Rick said to her. "That stuff is poison."

"The trick," Cam explained, as he poured a concoction of sugar and cream into his large cup, "is to put a little coffee into your cream. You stir it, like this, and then you add a little more, then you stir it, and then you add a little more."

He carefully tasted the hot liquid and nodded in satisfaction. "Ahhhhh. Perfect."

"Why not just drink the cream and sugar?" Patty asked, shaking her head again when he offered her a taste. Rick hid a smile as she carefully wiped the plastic cup and utensil with a napkin before spooning her own coffee mix into it.

"What? And not get my daily dosage of government-approved health food?" Cam mocked and gave her a wink. He turned to Rick. "Sir, they wanted to take apart my office. I said to them, 'Go ahead. I need the space, anyway.'"

"They are going to need a shovel," Rick countered sardonically. He had just been there and had seen firsthand what Cam's office looked like. The small space was meant for just two desks and a few shelves. Cam had shared it with Steve McMillan before the latter had left Task Force Two. He could tell which half of the office belonged to Steve because Cam's side was . . . He was at a loss for the word to describe the state of Cam's organized chaos.

"They are going to need several shovels," Patty corrected.

"It isn't that messy, princess," Cam said, pulling out a chair for her. "Everything is where I know it is, just like you and your stuff."

Patty coughed, holding a napkin against her mouth. Cam patted her back helpfully. "Like me?" she squeaked.

"Yeah."

She straightened up in her chair indignantly. "Cam, your office is not just messy—it's . . . it's a disaster zone. Are you saying I'm messy like that?"

Cam grinned, clearly enjoying baiting Patty Ostler. Rick watched as he "borrowed" her napkin and wiped his spoon with an exaggerated flourish before giving it to her. "Have a piece of this chocolate cake, princess. It'll sweeten you back." His grin widened as she glared up at him. "Now, see, you don't pay attention. I said, 'Everything is where I know it is, just like you and your stuff.' I didn't say you're messy. I meant I know where everything I want is, see?"

Rick heard the male possessiveness in Cam's voice as he watched the byplay. Patty Ostler didn't know it yet but she was a targeted woman. Seeing them so absorbed with each other, he felt that old emptiness creeping back inside.

Just then, Cam tried to steal a piece of the cake from Patty's plate, and she smacked his knuckles with her spoon, then glanced at Rick's direction, horrified at her display of bad manners. Giving Cam a last threatening glare, she turned her back to him. "Leave my chocolate cake alone. We're down here to work," she said in a determined voice, and growled when Cam reached over her shoulder and disturbed her plate.

In spite of how he was feeling, Rick laughed. The two of them were so focused on each other, the heat of their attraction so tangible, that for a moment he had forgotten the reason they were down there.

Apparently no one had ever heard Hard-On's laughter because Cam's and Patty's expressions mirrored both shock and fascination. It had been so long since Rick had experienced that kind of camaraderie with another woman. There was that twinge of envy again.

He sighed inwardly. He had lost that ability to even relax with anyone. Nikki. His gut tightened at the memory of her last kiss. He glanced at the chocolate cake on the snack table. She wanted strawberry. There were many ways to feed strawberries to a woman.

He glanced up again and realized the other two were still staring at him. He cocked his head. "Something the matter?"

Cam coughed. "No. Ummm. Right. Sorry about joking around, sir. We know how serious the situation is."

Rick loosened his tie and sat down on the sofa. "It's serious, but if they happen to nix Task Force Two, most of you will get transferred to other departments without any problems. I'll make sure of it. TIARA will have something for you, I'm sure."

"What about you, sir?" Cam asked, serious now.

Rick leaned back and looked around the room. "They're after me, you know," he told them quietly. "Gorman's list must have some big names for them to need a scapegoat in exchange. Since Denise is part of Intel as well as EYES, you know someone in EYES is involved up to their eyebrows. This person doesn't want Gorman's list found."

"This someone ordered Agent Lorens to plant the evidence," Patty said, her brow furrowing as she tried to analyze the mystery, "and when you're charged and arrested, Gorman gets his deal and EYES gets to keep the list quiet. Whether or not the real list is found, it doesn't matter, does it? All Gorman wants is his deal."

"Gorman is too big to get a deal for freedom, but he could avoid the death penalty for treason," Cam added. He rubbed his chin. "So we have to get to the real file with the names. Finding the doctored ones won't help you at all, sir."

"Denise knows where they are and told me last night that they are encrypted in a secured file," Rick said. "It's like finding a needle in a haystack and I don't hold out much hope for it, given the time we have, but it would at least be good to find the fake ones she planted. That might yield a clue to the man directing Denise. It might buy me some time."

"Us, sir," Cam corrected soberly. "Buy us some time. This is about us, Task Force Two. They hang you, they will be pointing their fingers at us next."

Rick met Cam's brown eyes across the room. "It's me they want," he assured them. "Actually, it's me Gorman wants."

Cam looked at him sharply. "You know something. Why don't you sink him, sir?"

Rick shook his head. "That's it. I can't."

He couldn't because his past was catching up with him. He couldn't because if he did, the truth about Leah would come out. He studied the couple before him impassively. They were lucky. They didn't have any past holding them back. He realized suddenly that he could never be like them with Nikki. He had too many secrets, and so did she. And if she ever found out the things that haunted him, she might not want him.

* * *

Nikki liked Admiral Jack Madison very much. He exuded authority and quiet strength, and despite his decorated uniform, he didn't have the pompous style of some military brass. Most of all, she liked his eyes. Old soul. The kind that peered right into someone's heart and saw the truth. Jack Madison was a natural leader—taller than most men, good-looking, with the bearing of a warlord. He had studied her as closely as she did him, and she hoped he saw something good. She had a feeling no one liked to cross swords with Admiral Madison. She had heard that they called him Mad Dog in his active SEAL days.

They were having a light lunch so they could meet and discuss informally. He had asked a few friendly questions at first, getting the feel for her. She didn't mind. Technically, he was her boss, even though she came recommended by T. As if he read her mind, the admiral said, "I talked to T. yesterday."

"How is she?" She was surprised that T. had contacted the admiral instead of her. Her chief had disappeared without a warning, and although most GEM operatives were used to T.'s sudden departures, Nikki had a feeling something was wrong the last time she talked to T. over the phone. Later, after she had arrived in D.C., there was a message for her not to discuss anything about T. with anyone except Admiral Madison. A strange order, but then, T.'s orders were always a bit cryptic.

"I can't tell. You know how she is. But I've talked to my man Steve McMillan. If you remember, he's the one I sent in to work in Task Force Two under Harden. He told me an agent from your side was looking for T., someone called Diamond—do you know him?"

Alex Diamond. He had been stubbornly "missing" when GEM had started working with his agency. Oh yes, Nikki had heard of the infamous COS commando who had been lured by T. to come back in from the cold. This explained quite a lot.

"I know about him," Nikki said with care. "Did she tell you where she might be?"

T. was one of the most elusive women Nikki had ever

met, a mistress of disguises, with enough identities and accents to make up the United Nations, which, incidentally, was her base. If she didn't want to be found, especially by Alex Diamond—well, Nikki couldn't decide whether to call him a lucky man, or not. T. was going to run rings around the poor man.

"No, she was just her sardonic self." Admiral Madison laughed. "Still as manipulative as ever."

Nikki nodded. "She doesn't make a move without a reason. Why did she call you, sir, besides catching up on what's happening, of course." The fact that T. hadn't even contacted her was telling enough. She had a message for Nikki from the admiral.

"I thought we agreed to be informal. It's Jack." The admiral put down his cup of coffee, clasping it between his big hands. "Anyway, she already knew about Gorman's dealings. I don't know how, but she's also up-to-date about Task Force Two and how Agent Ricardo Harden is going to have a tough time at the review board."

"I understand she talked with Rick on the phone before, when Agent McMillan was being held at the hospital."

"Yes, at that time Harden was playing hardball with McMillan. He never liked the fact that McMillan was reporting back to me, so he preferred to suspect my man of being a traitor." Admiral Madison's lips twisted humorlessly. "Never mind that McMillan was knocked senseless in the accident. Agent Harden was quite easily manipulated by Gorman. That's why I need to know whether he can lead Task Force Two. I want to work with a man with whom I can trust my men's lives. God forbid we have another Gorman. I won't allow any more information leaks about my teams' covert activities."

The admiral led a special SEAL team, one of those black operations units that depended on good intelligence before going into terrorist strongholds. Nikki understood his concern. There were too many lives at stake to just let things go on the way they were. Men like Gorman had invaded the government Intel network, selling information to any buyers without any qualms and ignoring the danger put on young fighting warriors. After one too many botched operations, the admiral had inserted one of his own, Steve McMillan, into Task Force Two for a year before discovering its deputy director, Gorman, had been the traitor all along.

T. had told this to Nikki when she presented her with this last contract. Of course, T. never did anything without a reason. She had known Nikki would be drawn to certain elements—the presence of a leader who would not let his men be sacrificed, as well as the chance to return to her past workplace to find her missing files. Lastly, she had dangled Rick Harden in front of her. Rick, she had said, would be the sacrifice to cover up other people's mistakes and greed. Just as Nikki had been sacrificed, and left to die, because no one would do a thing about a few operatives who were betrayed.

Nikki had easily seen through T.—she was her student, after all—but she hadn't been able to resist her manipulation. The idea of someone innocent being tossed to the wolves sickened her, and she had wanted to reach out to help.

"After what I've shown you, don't you think you can trust Rick Harden?" she asked.

"I can only throw in my support, Nikki. The review board doesn't have the evidence we have. I also have my ace, McMillan. He can testify, but I have a feeling some on the board will use his information against Harden, but we shall see how this thing proceeds. We have lots of avenues. You and I have agreed to hang on to this for a while longer." Admiral Madison glanced at the package beside him. "We let this out of the bag now, the real rat will know we're onto him, and will run."

Nikki sighed. He was right. She could help Rick now, but then she wouldn't be able to finish her contract, and without that, she wouldn't be able to get what she wanted—to find out the reason she and a few others had been betrayed and abandoned so long ago. Her ghosts, she thought, closing her hand tightly around her glass of water. She needed the truth to lay her ghosts to rest.

"I suppose T. agreed, too," she said, trying to stop the pain spreading inside. She felt helpless, as if she was one of those betraying Rick.

Jack Madison reached over and startled Nikki by tapping her lightly on her hand. She looked up, meeting the piercing blue of his eyes. There was an open sincerity in them. "T. said to tell you that the past doesn't go away, that everyone has a past that links them to answers today. She also added that saving Rick Harden is really in your hands. Now"—he smiled as he sat back in his seat—"knowing T. and her mind games, she had probably planted some seed in our very pliable heads. God, that woman is dangerous."

Nikki stared back at the admiral, already turning T.'s words round and round in her head. She thought about Alex Diamond's past affecting T. so much that she, the strongest woman Nikki knew, was actually on the run. *The past doesn't go away.* Poor T. She had her own ghosts. Just like that, Nikki came to a decision.

"I have to save him," she said. It was simple as that. She couldn't abandon him.

"The review board isn't going to like it if he refuses to answer certain questions. Is saving him important to you, Nikki?" Admiral Madison's voice was unexpectedly gentle, as if her opinion mattered to him.

"He is important to me," she admitted.

The admiral nodded thoughtfully. "Then we'll do what we can. I have a feeling Harden has his own game plan, but he is one man. You have my full backing in however you want to present your evidence, Nikki. T. has given me the utmost confidence in your abilities."

"Thank you, Jack." Relief flowed through Nikki. She knew that giving up the evidence so soon might bring on new problems, but at least the main thing that mattered would be taken care of. She gave the admiral a grateful smile.

"What you have shown me will blow everything out in the open," he warned. "After this, it's up to you to persuade Harden to work with us, to tell us what he knows. He must know something we can use to trace Gorman's network."

"It has to do with his past. Something happened between

them." She drew in a breath. She thought of Rick's dead wife. Carefully, she added, "I'll have to go back and reread their operations together."

"Speaking of past, Nikki. Once your identity is revealed, there will be a big fight over reopening the files connected to you. There's always resistance to more scandal in this town." The admiral frowned. "I won't let you down, I promise, but politics can get dirty."

Nikki nodded. She was willing to sacrifice something important if it meant she would save Rick from a similar fate.

"I'm willing to compromise. Like you said, lots of avenues, Jack."

Her past didn't matter. Her future did. And she wanted Rick in it.

Chapter Fourteen

Nikki hadn't moved from her seat in the waiting room since the proceedings began hours ago. There was a large screen set up in the front, and every eye in the room was fixed on the lone figure sitting behind a long table. Empty seats lined up in a row on each side of him.

She hadn't been able to tear her eyes away. A review session was usually the most boring thing to watch, with its usual humdrum routine of one side answering the questions that showed the dire need for the department to have the funds for the subject at hand, and the other side hemming and hawing over the costs as well as the necessity.

However, this review session was far from normal. For one thing, the deputy director of Task Force Two was in prison for selling information, which meant that the whole team was also suspect. No one had suggested anything in that direction, but few review sessions included I.I. tearing up the task force's offices. The other TIARA deputy directors were treating the matter like a lit stick of dynamite, keeping their operations separate, so they wouldn't be pulled into the investigation.

It didn't surprise Nikki that everyone just swept what they didn't want to see under the carpet. After all, her files were among that dirt, she reflected with a trace of bitterness.

Everything appeared to be normal when it wasn't. Task Force Two's activities had been suspended. Most of the team had been given temporary reassignments. Yet, except for a few, none had really worked up a sweat about what was truly going on. No wonder it took an outsider, a SEAL operative chosen by the admiral, to expose the truth.

She watched as Rick took a sip from his glass before answering another question. As operations chief, he was the man immediately under Gorman, taking directives from the traitor for all these years. That fact alone could hang him. The questions were full of innuendoes. How could he be in Gorman's confidence for so long and not be part of his schemes? And if he really hadn't known, then what did that say about his effectiveness as an operative? How could he not even suspect when he was in charge of each assignment? It was a catch twenty-two. Either way condemned Rick Harden.

And there was nothing she could do to stop the direction of the questions. One by one they inched toward personal inquiry into Rick's past. The representative from EYES was particularly aggressive, giving the impression that he had already decided Rick's guilt.

Beware the center. Release the frozen heart. Feed the hungry ghosts.

Her grandmother's prophecies might as well have been for Rick. He was the man at the center of a controversy, and he had gone in front of the review board without legal counsel or any aide to help answer the questions thrown at him, hence the empty seats. Few men would have been so bold. Foolhardy, even. But Nikki understood him. She had done the same when she had been grilled. Never put oneself on the defensive before the eyes of the enemy. Afterward, her interrogators had to use . . . other ways to try to break her. She blinked away the memory, brushing it off before the pain and shame settled in.

Rick's quiet voice helped to push it away. "I'm honored to be the sole person the review board is counting on to tighten our national security, and as Director Gorman's former operations chief, I can see how many hold the suspicion that I knew of his dealings. That is an assumption that I hope to dispel." He was looking at the panel, his gaze sweeping from left to right, as he leaned forward, giving emphasis, as he added, "Without legal advice."

Nikki's grip on her pen tightened. He looked so alone out there. A jug of ice water and a glass to one side of him. A microphone in front. A small pile of files and a notepad. That was all he had as he faced a board that held the power to cut off Task Force Two from TIARA.

She supposed nobody understood how crucial support for the O.C. was. A review board came up once every few years anyway, but this one was different. There was the matter of Gorman, who had tainted the whole department. There was an inquiry for national security because of leakage. Yet Rick had weathered the whole investigation alone, using himself as the main target. She sighed. Gorman had picked his team very well. None had come forward or made any effort to understand the gravity of the situation.

The camera zoomed in on him whenever he gave an answer. He was remote, his voice calm, his green eyes cool. Nothing about him suggested the storm she knew was going on inside him. His integrity was being challenged. His capabilities as a leader put into question. Yet he hadn't defended himself beyond a few sentences, words that told the review board nothing. And sitting here—watching, waiting, hoping—Nikki ached for him.

"My record as Task Force Two operations chief speaks for itself," she heard him say. "Our operations deal with Intel, and Intel is passed on by the director to other directors at TIARA. Other than not sharing any classified data at all, which is not possible in our work, I don't see how I could have known that what I reported to my superiors would be used against our own government."

"In other words, you didn't know Deputy Director Gorman was a traitor and you never saw anything suspicious in your years at TIARA. Agent Harden, do you at least know what TIARA stands for and what your job entails?" The question was laced with heavy sarcasm.

Rick's gaze was direct. "TIARA stands for Tactical Intelligence and Related Activities, sir. I wasn't in any position to question the activities of my superiors unless there was direct proof. My job is to gather counterterrorist intel, especially to do with arms dealing, for Admiral Jack Madison's teams."

"If Task Force Two was so indispensable, why did the admiral send in his own man to find a rat in your department?"

The camera hadn't shown the admiral before, since he hadn't asked anything, but he interrupted now for the first time. "I believe that question should be given to me, Senator. The moment Task Force Two O.C. Rick Harden suspected something was wrong, he had sent in a team with my man. He had the foresight to wire one of his own so he could monitor and record any illegal activity. We managed to get Gorman talking and that tape Rick Harden made, Senator, is what put Gorman behind bars. Now, I think that would show a man capable of leading. As for Task Force Two and TIARA, I depend on good Intel to advise my covert teams. Without that, my teams operate without a safety net. If you want to discuss national security, please do not forget the young lives of our military men who depend on Intel. The system isn't perfect—nothing is—but you can't fight a war without good soldiers. We need good men, both in Intel and in the jungle, don't you agree?"

Nikki had to smile. The admiral put a stop to that line of questioning quickly. No one would dare challenge Admiral Mad Dog, a war hero. He wasn't just one of the most decorated veterans in the military; he also had the ear of the president. There were rumors he might be asked to take over as secretary of state. Things like that always silenced the bureaucrats.

"One more thing to consider then. Please take a look at Copy II Classified File B. If Agent Harden were to replace Gorman as deputy director, then we have to consider his past. I believe he should explain certain things in his files, things he had refused to reveal to his superiors. This ties in with his inability to disseminate important data, and from his file, that had led to the death of his wife, Leah Harden, one of our best operatives."

There was a flurry of movement as everyone sheaved through his folders and opened the relevant files. Even from where she was, Nikki could feel the gathering tension in Rick. He was pouring himself another glass of water as he waited. She watched him slowly drink half of it down, following the movement of his throat as he swallowed. His actions were measured as he opened his own notepad. Her heart bled for him when the camera panned back to show the panel, every member reading intently. She knew what was in those files. She had read them.

A fierce protectiveness grew inside her. He shouldn't be out there alone. She thought of the package in her purse. That was the ace. She hadn't planned to use it until necessary. It would just muddy everything if she stepped in there but she had to do something with this. She looked at the screen. There was a resignation Rick's face as he sat there waiting, as if he knew I.I. was just starting.

T.'s message through the admiral whispered in her mind. *The past doesn't go away . . . Everyone has a past that links them to answers today . . . Saving Rick Harden is really in your hands.* Nikki grimly opened her purse. If he wouldn't defend himself, she would.

She reached for her cell phone and spoke quietly to the admiral's aide to pass on a request. Then she punched in another number.

"Erik," she said. "This is Nikki."

Rick knew what hell was. Hell was where something he had become loomed clear and ugly in front of him to pass judgment. For ten years he had fashioned himself to be the perfect bureaucrat, the kind who peered from the safety of mountains of paper, the kind who pretended to understand the real world from mere words that gave accounts of other people's actions. No one would see him behind all those papers, so he could safely, carefully dissect and document every available source, hoping to see beyond the pain and get at the truth.

It was now ten years later and he understood every nuance of being a bureaucrat—how their minds worked and how they compartmentalized things. It was easy to ignore a lot when one kept churning papers and passing them to somebody else. He had the whole act down pat. Unfortunately, he had also been swallowed by the very same system he had abhorred, and now he could see them in his mirror every morning when he brushed his teeth.

He knew what was going on in their minds right now. How to extricate themselves from the problem of being exposed as incompetent. How to use this situation to bring the matter to a close as quickly as possible so no one dug any deeper. How to get Rick Harden out of their hair.

His file. His lips thinned out in self-disgust before he composed his expression again. Ten years hadn't eliminated the wound in his heart. It was still raw, still fresh.

"I understand some events are still classified, but can you explain why you refused to answer questions ten years ago?"

Rick quietly replied "No, I cannot, sir."

There was a shuffling of papers. "Well, Mr. Harden, without your cooperation, all I have is a file saying you were demoted after being given the harshest reprimand for unintentional release of information. Everything else had been redacted. The parts that aren't inked out read really badly against you, Mr. Harden. The part that touches on the death of your wife, do you know how this departmental censure makes her demise sound?"

The coldness of spirit always returned when he thought of his wife's death. He felt it spreading inside him, like a widening fog that blinded all other senses. He looked at the men on the panel, fingering his past and judging him between those blacked-out lines. He knew what the black marker covered up, and he would never tell.

"The fact that you acted alone then, and the fact that you sit alone today showed a certain inability to lead, in my opinion. You needed people speaking for you, and you brought none. You need counsel, and you chose not to have any. Gorman had an agenda that you blindly followed. Who would then attest to your leadership?"

What was he to say? That he deliberately isolated himself for ten years so he could get close to Gorman? That he had been a bureaucrat so he could see what lay underneath all that scheming, so he could reach the level where he could make peace with his past? Who would believe him? Not the bureaucrats. Not the men he worked with.

Before he could answer, the seats to his left and right were taken up. He turned to find his men from Task Force Two. Somehow they had received clearance to join him. Cam sat on his right and gave him a nod. He wasn't alone any longer.

Admiral Madison spoke from the end of the panel. "I gave permission for Task Force Two team members to enter. I believe these men will attest to their operation chief's leadership and character."

The EYES representative grunted. "Their backing is moot. They are part of the problem, part of the investigation. Of course they will say good things to keep their team going. Agent Harden won't even defend himself. We need someone outside who can give fresh insight to the problem."

"Ah. I'm glad you brought that up," the admiral said softly, "since I.I. put up such a fight over my independent contractor. I believe now is the perfect time to call her up."

Rick didn't need to turn around to know Nikki had entered the room. He just knew. Everyone's attention was on her approach. The hair at the back of his neck stood up when she passed behind him. She took a seat at the far end, five seats down from where he was. It took an effort not to turn to stare in her direction.

"We don't need her up here yet. We're not discussing her contract to outline the safety holes in our system. What's more, she isn't qualified to attest to Agent Harden's character. She hasn't known him long enough." The last sentence was spoken with emphasis.

"Of course I can speak for Agent Harden's character. He

is the most loyal of men, willing to sacrifice himself for those he cares about. He is qualified to lead Task Force Two or any team the government puts under him," Nikki stated into the microphone. Rick couldn't help it. He turned to look down the length of the table. This was the first time he had ever seen her profile, with her hair clipped up on the sides, revealing the slender curve of her neck.

"And how would you know that? Would you care to tell us how close you and Agent Harden are?" Rick heard the hint of a sneer behind the question.

There was a slight pause and Rick watched her lick her lips in that familiar nervous way of hers. His gut tightened.

"I know because I am Leah Harden, whose remains my husband has been trying to get the United States government to retrieve for ten years, and who had been abandoned by the same government during an undercover siege." She paused again, then added, "And please call me Nikki. Leah Harden, according to the government, is dead, unexpectedly killed during an operation ten years ago. And for all purposes, that is true. You see, my jailors had very effective methods of persuasion; they destroyed Leah Harden's mind as effectively as they'd destroyed her face. I am, in effect, no longer that woman."

It was so silent, as if the whole building inhaled in shock. The very center of Nikki's being resonated with the tension. She released her breath slowly, trying to calm the erratic beat of her pulse. She hadn't wanted it to be this way, but she hadn't been able to stand it any longer. She might not have all her memory, but she had enough information to piece most of the truth together. And what the truth revealed was not how these men perceived Rick Harden to be.

She loved him. All these years without him, no man had been able to take down her defenses, but a part of her responded instinctively to Rick. She might not be able to remember, but her body did. Her heart did. It was just her mind that was a little damaged.

She felt his eyes. Burning. Willing her to turn and look back. But she dared not. She didn't know whether she could take the anger or rejection that might be there. Right now, the most important thing was to concentrate on this.

Grandmother, help me feed the hungry ghosts. She sent out the silent prayer, knowing how the world around her was going to come crashing down.

She spoke up again. "Agent Harden, my husband, is bound by his oath in office not to reveal classified information. The operation that brought about his demotion is one of those cases that no one could dig up unless they knew where the bodies are buried." She glared directly at the panel. "I happen to be one of those buried bodies. Since I'm officially dead, I guess I can break the code of secrecy and reveal as much classified information as I want."

"How could you be alive and your own husband not know you?"

"Sir, if you look at my picture in that file, you will see that I don't exactly look like Leah Harden. And ten years do change a woman's youthful features, I'm sad to admit." She took another breath. "After my capture, along with others, we were interrogated. I was tortured and raped repeatedly, and later, when it was obvious my government wasn't acknowledging any of us or would come to save us, I was administered mind-altering drugs to try to make me talk."

She closed her eyes for a second, then softly added, "They wiped out everything, including hope. It's hard to hold on to memory when your body isn't your own, and every day they dehumanize some part of your body." Pain and fear. Darkness. Mindlessness. How could one convey to them what that was like? She opened her eyes again. She kept her voice as steady as she could. "I was in captivity for over a year before a special group of commandos broke in and saved the few of us who had survived. I was barely alive. Or sane. It took some time, but the people who saved me pieced together who I was through their own channels. I was told that my fellow operatives and I had been abandoned because it was no longer feasible to negotiate with my captors.

"I have brought a file about the operation I took part in ten years ago and would like to submit it to the committee to read. You will find names, dates, and places of the operation, the agents involved and the top secret project we were working on at that time.

"But I also want to put a human side to the file. I, Leah Harden, am the only survivor of that mission. When I was rescued, my face and mind had been too injured to accept the facts my current agency gave me about who I was. It took a long time to heal." Nikki breathed out. "A long time."

Rick had read that when an explosive detonated at close range, the first thing one noticed was disorientation of the senses. Loss of hearing. Dizziness. Random thoughts that made no sense. Time slowed down and sped up.

At that last moment, when he had caught sight of Nikki's neck, the oddest thought had crossed his mind, that if he kissed her there, he would find a small black mole just under the left earlobe. He wondered whether plastic surgery had taken that away too.

That was right before she started speaking. He had stared hard at her, looking for that mole. Then the world exploded inside his head.

There was a buzzing in the background as he tried to focus on the words being exchanged. He barely caught the questions, like a monsoon wind beating against a window. But he heard her. Every word.

He listened as she related how she was abused after being singled out as an agent. Sleep deprivation. Hunger. Then the inevitable.

A roar howled in him. The pain and anger built as he sat there, holding the glass in his hand like a lifeline. Her voice was soft, but it was concert decibel to him.

"I was raped. Repeatedly. Often. When I was still silent, they started scarring my face and body. The face you see now has undergone five different reconstructive surgeries. After my rescue, it took years for me to adjust to my new 'reality,' to build myself back into a civilized person. I hope you understand why I prefer to be known as Nikki."

A loud crash and murmurs of concern brought Rick back.

He looked at his hand as if it wasn't his. There was blood oozing out in slow motion. Vaguely he noted that he must have crushed the glass he was holding and cut himself.

Nikki rushed out of her chair. There were some shouts for medical help. People parted to let her through. Rick sat there, ignoring his men asking him whether he was all right.

The blood was bright red, a stark contrast to the gray and blue suits and the sober earth tones. She leaned over and swept away the glass shards on the table.

"Rick?" He looked pale, lines etched deeply around his mouth. His jaw flexed as he turned to her. His eyes seemed the only thing alive, a startling intense forest green against his pallor, and every emotion he was suppressing glowed back at her and imprinted her soul. She wasn't sure whether he was aware he had injured himself. "You're bleeding badly."

He turned his bloody palm upward and studied it emotionlessly. "So I am," he agreed. Somebody thrust a handkerchief onto the wound. He calmly wiped away at the gash. "So I am."

Another person came with a first-aid kit and Nikki stepped aside to let him take care of the injury. All the while his wound was being cleaned up, Rick sat there looking up at her, his eyes traveling over her face, as if he was searching for something.

She stared back, wondering what he saw. The woman he loved was dead, long gone. She never doubted he loved that woman, but what were his feelings toward Nikki? She wasn't Leah; she didn't even know which part of her was Leah. Everything she knew about Leah's life was gathered from files and Intel sources. Everything she was today was rebuilt, from the inside out. She wasn't that woman in the files. She was Nikki. And just like that, her center shook with another flash of memory.

The Rick she had loved had been a cocky, passionate man, who never deliberated longer than ten minutes. He had laughed a lot back then, and ignored the bureaucrats who hindered his job, barely able to keep up with the paperwork and reports of his assignments, and had often stepped on a few toes to get things done his way. The man sitting there devouring her with his eyes was no longer the man she had married, either. He, too, had rebuilt himself, from the inside out.

Her head hurt from the sudden bursts of images. Rick and Leah holding hands. Rick and *her*, she amended. Both of them rolling down a bank of snow after tobogganing down. She had ended up under him, screaming from the joyride and the "accidental" rollout. He had snow in his hair, eyebrows, lashes. And the love in his eyes had taken her breath away. She remembered thinking that she would always love the color green because his eyes were so alive with joy and tenderness. He had leaned down, his lips a mere breath from hers.

"Kiss me, Lee, kiss me like you would never let me go."

She had hooked her arm around his neck. Tugged. And had given in to the taste of him and snow and fresh air. And love.

The image fuzzed in slow motion, faded, and Nikki's head pounded like a sledgehammer. She gave in to the pain, and everything went black.

Rick didn't care whether he bled to death. The gash was nothing compared to what he was feeling inside. Nothing compared to what Leah had gone through. Nikki, he corrected mentally. She was Nikki now.

He recalled his first sight of her in the elevator, how he had felt that a ghost had just appeared, but his past had haunted him the last ten years, so his mind had readily dismissed it. His suspicion had grown but there was no way to explain the inexplicable—here was a woman who reminded him of his dead wife but everything about her was different. Her facial expressions. The way she talked. Her fear of being touched.

Yet he had tried to force the issue on her, over and over, hoping to uncover something. Exactly what, he had no idea—but he had known he couldn't resist her, even if she had some agenda against him. Did she remember him at all? She was responsive but her fear was palpable. No wonder he had found that strangely erotic. Something in him had known it was Leah. And something in her had recognized him.

Nikki's dark eyes were gleaming behind a sheen of tears. She looked fragile, as if she would break apart any second, but he knew that she had the inner strength of a dozen men. No one could have gone through what she did and turned out so serene, so beautiful inside and out.

Rick watched her eyes lose focus, and as she slumped forward he shoved aside the person taking care of his hand to keep her from falling onto the floor. There were more concerned voices—questions, suggestions, exclamations. He just wanted them to stop.

With Nikki in his arms, he turned around to face the panel. Some of them were just sitting there taking in the whole drama. Fucking bureaucrats. Couldn't do a thing without a piece of paper to save their lives. His eyes caught Admiral Madison, who was on the way off the small podium.

"Move. Let her have some air," he ordered.

"I'm going," Rick stated quietly. "Indict me, replace me, fire me—I don't give a damn."

"No one's getting indicted or replaced or fired," the admiral retorted. Rick noted that he didn't appear surprised by Nikki's revelation. "The review board can't go on. I'm sure there are many questions we need Nikki to answer. I'll take a motion to suspend the meeting for the day and will have someone let you know when we'll resume."

"Agent Harden can't just leave before the vote. He might be a security risk. He might be gone by tomorrow."

Admiral Madison regarded the EYES representative for a moment. "Would it calm your fears if I personally vouch for Agent Harden and Miss Taylor?" he pleasantly asked. "I assure you, my word is considered quite good around this small town."

The man swallowed, blinked, then shrugged. "Sure. Adjourn the meeting." Then he added defiantly, "but we will be questioning Agent Harden tomorrow concerning certain unauthorized files pulled with his access code. One of my agents will be testifying, and what I've seen so far is incriminating enough for me to give fair warning that you, Admiral, should be wary of your trust in Agent Harden. He'd better bring legal counsel."

Admiral Madison's smile was not much warmer than the glacier blue of his eyes. Rick admired the ease with which he could intimidate a man with a mere look. "I'm sure Agent Harden will do what he thinks is best," he said. He turned to Rick. "Go, and expect my call."

Rick nodded, holding Nikki close. The admiral had already returned his attention to the panel, addressing the members quickly. Cam opened the door for Rick.

"Where are you going, Agent Harden? We need this information," the clerk taking notes called out.

He paused, then answered. "I'm taking my wife home."

Chapter Fifteen

*S*he was going to die in this darkness. She was hungry, hungry all the time. She tried to remember all her favorite foods. Butter pound cake marbled with chocolate. Something with chicken and almonds—she could not recall the name of the dish. She panicked. She had to remember the name of the dish.

Nothing. She spent a long time trying to remember. What was that dish? Chicken with almonds . . . She knew she loved it because she could recite the recipe like a favorite song. A pinch of basil. Two teaspoons of honey. Ground white pepper. Yet the name of the recipe eluded her.

And strawberries. She loved strawberries—she could almost smell the delicious sweetness of the fruit. She wondered whether it was the season for strawberries right now, whether they were fat and juicy this year, or . . . when was the last time she had a taste of it?

She frowned. Someone had fed them to her. She stared into the darkness, hugging her shoulders as she tried to catch some missing picture in her mind. It was a man. She was quite sure it was a man, and he smelled like strawberries. He fed her strawberries with his mouth.

She shuddered, and scurried back against the wall behind her. No. No. She was mixing things up. Furiously, she scrubbed her mouth with her hand, squeezing her eyes tightly. They were touching her all over. Oh God, stop. Don't scream. Don't.

Food. Her breathing was raspy, coming out in animal grunts. The echoes beat at her, a reminder that she was there alone in the darkness. She was going to die here. No food, she thought. The hunger pangs gnawed at her insides.

Strawberry shortcake. Strawberry milkshake. Strawberry daiquiri. Her fear was winning as she heard herself hyperventilating. She mustn't make a sound. They wanted her to scream in this quiet darkness.

Please, please, please let it be soon. Please, please, please. It had to be right now.

Then she heard it. The chime out there somewhere. The most beautiful sound in the world, coming in through the walls, caressing her soul, calming everything. She zeroed in on it, hearing its familiar tones as the chime called to her.

Grandmother, she whispered.

A long time later, she was pulled outside, pushed, prodded, pinched. She was calm. Nothing was going to break through.

"So, what is on my menu today?" she asked.

"Do you have anything to tell us?"

"Yes, I love strawberry daiquiris."

"Cut off her hair."

Nikki opened her eyes. She screamed. And screamed. An opening with daylight. Oh God. She rolled out of the bed and started crawling toward it. Someone pulled her to her feet. His arms felt strong as they held her prisoner. She struggled, screaming, kicking.

"No! Don't! Don't!"

"Nikki!" Rick held her tightly, sitting down on the bed as he tried to calm her down. He had just come out of the bathroom when he heard her screams and had run back up to the room. She was incoherent, gasping out garbled sentences. He frowned, trying to understand her from the few words he could make out—"food," "recipe," "my hair."

"Your hair?" he asked. Going by instinct, he pulled her braid over her shoulder. "Baby, your hair?"

She was sobbing into his shoulder. "Don't cut my hair."

He sat there, thunderstruck. He had thought his heart was

already broken when he became a widower, but pain pierced through him as he realized the cause of Nikki's nightmare. "It's all right," he soothed. "I'm not going to cut your hair. It's beautiful. No one will cut it, I promise. Nikki, wake up, baby. It's a nightmare. You're safe."

His scent reassured her. It wasn't the sickly sweaty smell of . . . She fought against those demons, desperately clawing her way back into sanity. It was Rick's arms around her. His scent. His voice. Those nightmares often came back when her defenses were down. From practice, she willed her heartbeat to slow down, burying her face in Rick's shoulder, inhaling him as she breathed, needing him inside her as his arms held her securely. He crooned against the top of her head, running his hand down the length of her braid. She shuddered again, pushing away the memory of tufts of shredded hair.

"I'm not afraid of the dark," she said aloud. Her voice was hoarse.

Rick fought against hugging her tightly. She just had a nightmare, and he was having one right now imagining what it was that had frightened her so much. He could deal with the anger growing like an avalanche inside him. He could handle the chaos that was his career right now. But he was unprepared for the pain slicing him in tiny pieces as he put the truth together. The truth was far, far more intolerable. He had thought himself punished enough. He now knew he was irredeemable. Unforgivable.

"Rick?"

"Yes?"

"I'm okay."

He almost laughed out loud as bitterness swelled up his throat. Even now, she was trying to reassure him. He wanted to shake her. Wanted to yell at her. He didn't say anything.

"It's just one of those nightmares. They don't come often anymore, and this one just caught me by surprise."

"Nightmares tend to do that," he agreed bitterly. "Tell me about it."

"No."

"Tell me, Nikki," he said. "I have to know."

Nikki shook her head, burrowing deeper into his chest. Not yet. She wasn't ready to tell him the details. There was a catch in his voice, and without looking at him, she knew he wasn't ready to hear everything. The truth had to be told but it must be done when they were both in control of their emotions, in daylight when she was comfortable, in a time when they could trust each other fully.

Right now, she felt dirty, off-kilter. She needed to climb back into her skin. She wished her wind chime were close by. "Are we at your apartment?"

"Yes. What do you need, baby?"

"I want a bath."

There was a short pause. "I'll get one ready for you. Will you be all right now?"

She wanted him to kiss her but he settled her back into the bed before getting up slowly. The loss of his body warmth made her wish she hadn't asked for a bath. "Yes," she said.

"I'll be back soon," he told her. His hand touched her cheek and caressed her braid, his knuckles brushing her body tenderly. He left the bedroom door open and she was grateful for the light illuminating his strong lean body as he left. The light caught part of his face and body as he gave a backward glance. He looked detached, unfathomable. Nikki looked at the empty doorway, feeling alone and needing him back with her.

Rick turned on the water in his big spa tub. He had never felt so drained. He sat down on the commode and looked around. He had put in the best state-of-the-art luxuries in this bathroom. Leah had wanted one of those fancy bathrooms featured in expensive magazines and he hadn't cared how much it cost; he would create it. He didn't care that she wasn't around to enjoy it. This was for her. At that time, he needed to do it.

He had spent hours on the project, paying more money to get the plumbing done his way and renovating the whole place. There was a whirlpool. A detachable showerhead was put in at easy reaching distance. The shower-steam room had strategically placed fixtures that could be used individually or all together. He had put in everything he could think of, from marble tub to heated towel racks to special imported tiles that he had installed himself.

Rick sat there listening to the running water, the sound reverberating in the bathroom that he had dedicated to his dead wife. He had kept his whole life stark and simple ever since his loss, and anyone who had seen this place was shocked by the luxury. They hadn't understood, of course. This was his shrine for his wife.

He ran a weary hand through his hair. Except for one thing. His wife was alive. And this . . . bathroom . . . would mean nothing to her at all. It held the deepest significance to him but what good was that now? He had expended all his love in here, tucked it away under the tile and grout, commemorating it every time he came in here, and all along, the person to whom he had dedicated it had been suffering somewhere. He had given up on her being alive too easily and she had suffered for it. Guilt gnawed ravenously at his conscience.

Rick bowed his head, the deafening roar in his head shutting out the water splashing into the tub. Nikki had observed that her hero had been running and going nowhere. She was right. He had been a fucking coward.

"Rick?" Nikki called out softly from the doorway.

She couldn't stand being alone, so after a few minutes, had followed him. Emotion squeezed at her heart when she saw him so wretched, sitting there amid the beautiful bathroom, repeatedly raking a hand through his thick hair.

His head came up and she caught her breath at the anguish in his eyes. "Rick?" she repeated uncertainly.

"I have nothing to give you." His voice was a strangled echo over the running water. "I failed you. All I did was—this."

He disgustedly gestured around him. Nikki frowned, unsure of what he meant. The bathroom was something out of a magazine, hinting at the hidden passion underneath the cool gaze of the man who owned it. It was a big contrast to the rest of the apartment. She paused, really paying attention to the surroundings.

Bathing and the bath area had always been very private to her. It was part of civilization, a reminder of humanity. Once taken away, a person—a woman—was easily reduced to an animal. She had seen it with her own eyes, when some of her friends had exchanged their bodies for the small comfort of clean water.

This bathroom, with its lavishness, quieted her ravaged soul. Her nightmare receded into the background as she took it all in. The water to clean. The beauty to take away the bad dreams. The luxury to chase away the memories. And some instinct within her told her that this place meant something to the man she loved.

She walked tentatively toward him as he got up to turn off the water. The noise became a soft lazy slapping of currents.

"The bath is ready," Rick announced woodenly, as he methodically pulled out some bottles from a rack nearby. She recognized them as the ones she had brought the night before. "Take your time. I'll be outside if you need me."

He was standing only a few feet away but the day's events had put a gulf between them. He was treating her very carefully, so unlike the Rick Harden who had sensed something familiar about, and had gone after, her. Now, she realized, he was going to keep that distance.

Her chin came up a fraction. He was afraid to touch her because he didn't know who she was. She was Leah and Nikki. Maybe he didn't know which of the two he wanted. Maybe he still didn't believe. It couldn't be easy to reconcile all his past feelings with how he felt now, especially when she was nothing like he remembered.

But she knew one thing. She wanted him. And she wanted him to desire her for what she had become. There was only one way to convince him to find out and that was to go to him, to show him that she was real.

She took the few steps. He didn't move away. So untouchable. So unrelentingly hard. She laid one hand on his chest and felt the muscle jump.

"I . . ." She licked her lips, trying not to rush the words. "I need you now, Rick. In here. Inside me."

Heat flared, deepening the green of his eyes, and receded. "You're afraid of me."

"I'm afraid of men," she told him, "and I'm getting tired of repeating myself. I'm not afraid of you."

Rick gritted his teeth. It would be so easy to give in and just take. These past ten years, he had taken whenever he felt the need to bury the growing darkness inside him. He understood his own sexuality too well. For him, it was a weapon as well as a way to hide. He wasn't going to do that to Nikki, even though every molecule in him was screaming for her.

Both her hands came up, and she started to unbutton his shirt. His jaw clamped together as he resisted the urge to gather her in his arms and take her back into the bedroom. Her dark brown eyes were large, filled with fear and determination, as she finished her task. He understood how tough this was. She must hate the sight of a man's body. He was about to stop her torment when she touched his bare chest. He went very still.

Her hands glided downward, cool and trembling slightly, exploring his nipples, his ribs, his stomach. Softly. Gently. Her fingers trailed up the furrow in the middle of his torso, and he almost groaned as she took that final step, replacing her hands with her lips. His head snapped back and he closed his eyes at the first wet touch of her tongue. She placed kisses across his chest. Her mouth closed around one nipple.

He grasped the back of her head, fighting the urge to haul her closer. "Nikki," he rasped, opening his eyes to look down at her. Her teeth grazed the sensitive skin and he couldn't help it. He pulled her closer. "Nikki, you have to stop, or I won't be able to help myself."

She released his nipple, nuzzling her nose in his chest hair for a few seconds. "That's what I want," she murmured.

Stepping back, she reached back to unzip her dress and pulled it down her shoulders. Rick sucked in his breath as she unhooked her bra. Her breasts spilled out. He quickly glanced up, and she met his eyes steadily. Fear still lurked back there but she continued anyway.

"You'd better decide soon. The water is going to be cold," she whispered.

"It stays heated," he whispered back.

"Oh."

She was down to her panties now, and his body reacted fiercely to her nudity. Her hands hesitated on the waistband. He waited for her to retreat, as she would have done the last few times they were together, if he had let her. He waited, not even aware he was holding his breath, as she hooked her thumbs inside the small article of clothing and slowly revealed herself to him, inch by torturous inch.

This wasn't any planned striptease. Her skin had a rosy flush and her breathing had quickened. She kept her eyes averted, bending forward to finish her task.

Rick stopped her, crouching down before her. "Let me," he said.

Nikki held on to his broad shoulders as his hands went around her hips. Fever engulfed her whole body, and the feel of his sure hands against her thighs made her knees weak. She was naked. She was really standing naked in front of a man.

He caressed the backs of her knees and slid her panties lower, till they fell onto the floor. He was looking at her intimately, his eyes so intense that she quivered from the heated possessiveness reflected in them. She gripped his shoulders harder. His hands stroked the sensitive skin on the back of her calves and thighs as they traveled up, and then he cupped her buttocks and moved closer.

She closed her eyes. His kiss was soft, reverent. Then his tongue probed her gently. She gasped at the exquisite pleasure of his mouth, so hot and wet, his tongue a sliding sensation as he readied her. Oh, she had never felt like this with another man. He stopped at her soft moan, looking up at her in concern.

"I'm not hurting," she assured him. "Surely you know I'm not hurting."

She pushed his loose shirt off his shoulders and he shrugged out of it. The muscles on his arms and chest were pumped, betraying the control he was placing on himself. She had to smile a little. She couldn't believe that she, Nikki Taylor, was the one trying to convince Rick Harden to take off his clothes and make love to her.

"Do you remember anything at all?" he asked, and his voice was edgy. "What we did, how we were, when we made love?"

She kneaded the tense muscles of his neck and his shoulders. "I have flashes of memory," she admitted, "mostly scenes. I guess that's why I write romance as a hobby in between assignments. I have these wonderful visions that come and go, and I try to capture them in my writing."

She didn't add that for a long time, a part of her hadn't wanted to admit that they might be memory of her past. That would mean she had to go back and face things on which she had decided to turn her back. The moment she acknowledged them, she knew she couldn't go on without finding out about the truth, without facing her fears. And then opportunity knocked in the guise of a contract . . .

Rick stood up. He looked incredibly masculine in just his pants, a thin sheen of sweat on his body. "But you don't remember how we made love, do you? That's why you're always afraid. You can only remember—" He stopped, unable to go on. "Are you sure, Nikki? I don't think I can stop once these pants come off, and your fear feeds my greed somehow, I don't know why. I'm afraid you'll be afraid, and I'll ignore you."

"Rick, you were going to seduce me the other night."

"Yes."

"And if I had said no, what would you have done?"

There was a pause. "I wouldn't have paid attention. I would have just kept you coming till you gave yourself to me."

She smiled and reached down to release the top button of his pants. She brushed the thick ridge. Understood why he didn't want to continue until he was sure. "I want to see you," she said, pulling on the zipper. "And if I'm afraid, teach me not to be."

His hot erection popped out and she stared down at it, mesmerized. How could she have forgotten *that*?

Chapter Sixteen

Rick released a shuddering breath when her hands stroked the length of him. She was filled with a sense of wonder, and a little trepidation, as she gazed down at his arousal.

"I . . . you . . ." She licked her lips.

A frustrated sound came from Rick. Without letting him go, she looked up, and the blatant heat in his eyes made her blush again. His erection pushed against her hand—demanding her attention—hot and fierce, powerfully erotic. She was mesmerized by its smooth strength, the veins protruding slightly as they pumped up the already engorged penis. A tiny drop of moisture beaded on the top and she dabbed at it with her forefinger. Slowly, she brought her finger to her lips for a taste.

The last vestiges of Rick's control broke into a million fragments. Her hands were soft as silk. The sight of her licking his seed brought out the primitive side in him. A strangled growl escaped his lips as he jerked her to him. She came willingly, her feminine curves melting against his rough-hewn body. She was his dream, his eternal fantasy. Rick forgot himself. Forgot about being patient. Forgot about being gentle.

He just had to have her *now*. She was his wife, come home to him. He had been empty, filled with darkness, and he needed her as he needed no one else. He knew this as an absolute truth. For ten years he had searched for a substitute, and had found no one. No one. She was his life. Without her, all he had become was a shell of himself.

The surroundings receded. It was just Nikki and Rick, and nothing else mattered at this moment. He stepped out of his pants impatiently. Kicked them somewhere. He lifted her small frame with fluid strength, using the tiled bathroom wall for balance as he nestled between her legs. She was eye-level, her gaze widening as he prodded her soft entrance. One determined thrust up. She gasped his name and pushed against his shoulders as her supple flesh fought his invasion. He simply held her as she wriggled and jerked, his eyes staring deeply into hers. He thrust up one more time. She gasped his name again. Little by little she sank down, sliding against the wall, taking him inch by excruciating inch.

Sizzling bursts of pleasure ricocheted through Rick's whole being. She was so hot. Tight. And more than anything, she was Nikki.

"All of me, baby. Take all of me," he said—*begged*—grinding his hips harder, wanting in, in, in. Needing to feel all of her around him.

Nikki couldn't reply, her breaths coming out in small pants as he stretched her, and *stretched* her. It had been so long and a part of her was fighting this assault on her body and senses. Her heart was beating so loudly she could barely hear his words. She arched away, straining against the cool wall and moaned softly as she inexorably sank lower still, impaling herself.

She trembled with his possession. He felt huge and hard, and just as she thought she couldn't possibly stretch for him any more, his hand reached between their bodies and very, very gently, his thumb began another kind of assault. A sweet and incredibly effective sneak attack, the kind that melted every resisting muscle in her body. She cried out as waves of electric sensation bashed her consciousness. Her whole body exploded into action and, slippery wet, she slid all the way down.

She was impaled. There was nowhere else to go. Helpless, and feeling her femininity as never before, she laid her head on Rick's shoulder. She was his. And already his thumb was moving again, lazy circles waking every nerve, stimulating every drop of desire from her body, and suddenly sharp scenes floated in her pleasure-induced state even as her insides flexed and milked him, contracting in spasms as he strummed and stroked.

"Not fair! I can't do anything in this position. I can't move." Her shrieks of protests were ignored as her husband pushed her higher. She giggled as she tried to picture the precarious position she was in.

"Baby," Rick's voice was deep and amused, "what do you mean you can't do anything? You're coming and coming in this position."

As if to demonstrate the truth of it, he braced a muscular arm under one of her legs and shifted her position against the wall. With one leg wrapped around his waist and the other draped like that, she was wide open—helpless, totally unprotected from his sexual manipulation. A wicked quirk leaped to his lips as he cocked a brow at her. She pretended to glare at him, but couldn't suppress a moan when the assault began. Slowly, deliberately, he began to grind his pelvic bone repeatedly against her clitoris.

"See?" he whispered in her ear, his breath hot and sexy, "You don't have to move and don't you know, you're definitely doing something. I can feel you, you know."

His tongue scalded her ear and she gurgled out a half groan as he teased the sensitive creases. Her whole being melted into a quivering mass of need and pleasure as his groin sharply imitated each plunge of his tongue. Her wet soapy behind was sliding down the tiled wall, and out of preservation, she blindly grabbed at the nearest thing. The showerhead fell off the hook and hit Rick's head with a thud.

"Rick! Are you all right?"

"This damn room is too small."

She giggled again at his grumbling tone. "It's our shower stall, love. We're supposed to shower in it, not do gymnastics."

"I'm showering you with love and attention, aren't I?"

He continued undulating against her, totally unconcerned that he might slip. "Must I do everything around here?"

"The soap, honey. We're going to break our necks in a minute."

Rick sighed exaggeratedly. He turned on the shower. "Well, we'd better wash off the soap then, hmm?"

She screamed as soon as she realized his intentions. "You wouldn't. No, you wouldn't!"

"We're showering, baby," he crooned, and turned the shower spray right where they were connected.

Hot water pressure thrummed against her clitoris. He pushed inside her all the way, and the fullness of him pushed her over the edge. She let go. She could fall and break her neck for all she cared.

"Tighter. Yeah, like that. Squeeze me, baby."

Her pelvis gyrated mindlessly as he continued to use the showerhead, moving it higher and lower, up and down, building her tension to unbearable heights. Her orgasm was a crescendo of color and sound. All she could do was tumble through it, and all along, she knew she was safe in Rick's arms.

"Ungh . . ." she finally moaned and flopped forward.

The sound of water turning off. Rick was still hard inside her, still owned her soul. "You moved. A lot. You happy now?"

"I want a bigger bathroom," she moaned.

Nikki buried her face in Rick's neck and kissed him. "This bathroom," she said into his ear. "It's for me, isn't it?"

Immersed in the feel of her, Rick opened his eyes at her question, focusing outward with difficulty. She must be reading his mind. "You remembered?" he asked.

"Yes." Her voice was muffled, her caressing lips giving little stings of heat. "I remember you promising me a new bathroom the next time we move. I like the way you taste."

Those words sent him into overdrive. He arched up, pushing into her, pinning her against the wall again. "I like the way you feel," he told her.

Bracing his feet, he cupped the underside of her thighs

and opened them wider. He withdrew, inhaling sharply, as her inner walls held on to him possessively. He closed his eyes, savoring her wet heat. Just before he was totally out, he pushed in again. Deep. He could barely breathe; she was clenching him, tight as a fist.

Not enough. He needed more of her. He withdrew, pushed in, using the combined strength of his calves and thighs. Her little throaty cries drove him to the edge. Her hands raked his hair restlessly. Flesh slapped into flesh, slick and sensuous, and still it wasn't enough.

"I like the way you take me inside you so tightly," he rasped out. "Take more of me, Nikki."

He pushed her thighs even higher, farther apart. She moaned as the tip of his sex pressed into her womb. Not enough. Not enough. Perspiration beaded his brow as he hurried the tempo, gliding out, slamming in, sliding out, his intent at one with his desire. He would make her remember this. She couldn't have forgotten this.

He gritted his teeth. Pulled out of her wet silkiness, and throwing back his head, thrust. Hard. Nikki gasped out his name, scratching his shoulders, her head lolling back and forth. He swiveled his hips upward, half closing his eyes in anticipation. A tiny resistance, like virgin lips puckered tightly for a kiss—he tilted her a certain angle, and he was in. Fierce joy forced his eyes closed as the feeling of completion overwhelmed everything. He held on to his control for one instant longer. Then he let go.

He poured everything he had into her—his lost dreams, his hopes, everything he had been keeping inside him all these years. His world exploded and reformed. He couldn't stop coming, his release a long pulsing stream of heat until he thought he was going to die from the pleasure.

This was his place. This was home.

Nikki could only hang on. Emotion swelled in her heart as Rick gave a deep groan and started shuddering against her. He was buried deeply within her. Every time he flexed, she felt him rubbing the very sensitive tip inside, like an internal kiss. It was a possessive kiss. A mark of ownership. And it felt so good.

How could she have forgotten this man? He was bigger than life, imprinted in her soul and very being. Yet her mind had refused to acknowledge his existence. Why? A twinge of guilt twisted her conscience. It seemed so impossible that she could remember some things, and not him. She had regained memory of her grandmother. Favorite foods, even. Why not Rick? Why did she need other people's information to fill the gap? Something was wrong with her.

Her body knew his touch, though. And he certainly knew hers. Every intimate touch, every caress, pulled a response that was earth-shattering, taking her to heights that she never knew existed. Well, she did, she vaguely corrected, but she just couldn't remember! It bothered her. Why couldn't she remember such a glorious experience?

She wrapped her arms and legs around him, hugging him close, as he took her love and returned it in full measure. His breathing was still uneven as he rained kisses on her face. She made a sound of protest when he started to disengage their fused bodies, lowering her back onto the floor. She wanted to stay like that, with him inside her, forever.

"Did I hurt you?" He rubbed her back, a look of concern replacing the hard stamp of male satisfaction on his face.

She was a little sore but there was no pain. She shook her head. He was looking down, studying her body, and the intensity of his gaze made her suddenly aware of her nudity. Heat suffused her from head to toe. Self-consciousness returned, and she looked around for something to cover up.

"No." He stopped her fidgeting, one finger under her chin. "Don't hide from me, Nikki. Not anymore."

She stood very still as he pulled her long braid to the front and started to loosen it, shivering a little as his knuckles caressed her breasts when he followed the length of the hair. "Remember the rules? I want your hair loose." It fell like a heavy curtain, and he gathered a handful, lifting it to his face.

"I remember. You always loved my hair loose, wouldn't let me tie it up at home." Another flash in her mind. "Those rules. Rick, they have some connection with our past."

His eyes were a brilliant green. "Yes."

She tried to ignore his hands cupping her breasts, rubbing her nipples with his thumbs. "You . . . you knew?"

He shook his head. Then he nodded. "Something inside me knew you, but my mind refused to accept it. How could I?" He caressed her sensitive peaks till the now familiar heat began to build again. "I would have known, though, once I had you in bed with me. I would know your body, Nikki."

She touched her cheek briefly. "My face . . ." she began.

He cupped her face, his hands tangled with her hair. He looked into her eyes, as if he could see something in them. "It's still you."

"But I've forgotten so much."

He shocked her with a slow crooked smile. "You seem to remember more every time I touch you down there. Let's make love about a dozen times, then we'll talk about what you can remember."

She laughed. Rick was teasing her. She looked down at the telltale sign. Was he? Surely he wasn't serious? She glanced up at him, and the sexy quirk of his lips that told her that he wasn't done with her yet.

"A dozen?" she echoed. She hadn't allowed any man near her for years. A dozen times was unimaginable. She looked down at him again, so ready for *her.* She bit her lower lip nervously. "A dozen?"

There was so much to learn again about this man and she didn't mean from the files. Her husband. Yet, from her flashbacks, he really wasn't the same man of her memories. He was harder. In many ways, stronger. And, she suspected, infinitely patient. He was determined about something, and making love to her was part of it, but she couldn't figure out what was going on in his head, not when he was already starting to explore her body again. Her legs parted without any urging. Again she was filled with a need beyond anything she had ever experienced. She was half amazed, half shocked at how easily he aroused her.

"Tonight, let's just continue where we left off last night. You were coming up to my apartment. You had questions for me. And . . . I had rules . . . remember?"

Of course she remembered. He had her half-conscious from wanting him, not unlike now. She could only nod as his hand coaxed between her legs. Part of her wanted to ask him what he was up to, but all of her just wanted him.

He turned her gently toward the big spa tub. Taking a bath used to be peaceful for her, a private sanctuary. She had a feeling that Rick was going to take over that place now.

Rick couldn't tell her what this bathroom was to him. There were no words to explain how he felt whenever he sat alone in this tub. In the early days, in the darkest despair, this was the only place to escape his nightmares. As time went by, this was the one place where he felt a semblance of peace.

He had never wanted to share a bath with anyone again until he met Nikki. He wanted to seduce her then, had even wondered briefly whether she could replace Leah. He had even played with this fantasy, setting up the seduction that would take her to this place. He had thought to pleasure her until she gave him all her secrets and took away his pain.

Little did he know how real a turn his fantasy would take! Here she was, in the bathroom he had created for Leah. He helped Nikki into the spa tub, watching her gleaming body slide into the water. She was his wife, and yet, she wasn't. *Nikki, meet Leah. Leah, meet Nikki.* He meant the silent introduction to be mocking, but the irony of it didn't escape him. Last night he had planned to bring a live woman to replace a dead one. Tonight the dead woman was alive. His eyes narrowed as he took in her wet breasts and long, long hair floating invitingly. His body responded to both women.

He joined her, the water lulling hot and sensual, as it lapped their bodies, maneuvering her to sit between his parted legs. She didn't resist, although he could tell she was nervous again. That tiny flick of her tongue tempted him to kiss her, which he intended to do. Later.

Right now, he wished to make her want him as badly as he wanted her. He desperately wished her to remember him, too. She had locked away some part of them—she and he—in her mind, and he wanted her to release those memories. It was important.

He opened the bottle of shampoo she had brought the night before. He poured some into his hand and worked it into her hair, slowly massaging her scalp. It had been a lifetime ago when he had done this. She sighed softly again, relaxing against his chest.

"You started this," he whispered. "You came back to me. I want to keep making love to you, just to make sure you're real. A dozen times. A dozen dozen times. I'll never get enough of you, Nikki."

She leaned into his chest, angling her head. He didn't give her a chance to say anything. He took slow, thorough possession of her mouth. Deeply, because she tempted him so. Insidiously, because he was selfish. Did she remember this, he wondered, as he explored her sweetness, loving the taste of her.

Without lifting his lips, he reached for the washcloth from the stack of towels nearby and dipped it into the water. Rubbed it down her exposed neck. Glided it down the velvety soft skin of her bosom. Her tongue quivered as he played with the small swells of her breasts, teasing her nipples till he felt them harden through the material. He moved the cloth between the valley of her breasts, and she groaned into his mouth as he went lower. Did she remember this?

When she tried to spin around, he tightened his arms around her, keeping her still. He allowed her to break off. The washcloth closed in on the underwater target. Her words came out in a rush as he teased her, using the pull-push of the water to elicit the response he wanted. Did she remember this?

"I . . . can't . . . become her . . . again, Rick," she gasped out. She had managed to surprise him. He paused. Her understanding of his inner struggle amazed him. "Don't make me."

Make her remember. He had to. He shifted his knees un-

der hers, and very gently drew his legs up, parting her wide
for the washcloth. For her sake, she had to remember.

"Rick!"

Nikki wasn't even sure whether she was protesting or
pleading. The old shadow of terror loomed close, threatening
to take over. Every time he pushed her over the edge, her
mind shut down, and although she was elated at the memories that had zipped in and out, the fear had also returned,
each time more constricting than before. Her subconscious
wasn't used to this stimulation—too fast, too uncontrollable.
Something was warning her to stop, or face the consequences. But she couldn't stop Rick. He was insistent, as if
he didn't want her to think, just respond. He drew up his legs.
She found her own draped over his, and she was wide open.
His hand was heavy, the washcloth barely any protection
from his fingers.

"Hmm, no underwear," he murmured against her ear, a
sexually satisfied voice. "Do you remember when you told me
you weren't wearing any panties right before we went into
conference? It was just before you went away on assignment."

Nikki couldn't recall. Her mind was screaming a protest.
A warning of some sort. "No," she replied. And for some reason, she didn't want to.

"You drove me wild crossing and uncrossing your legs
while I stood in front of the map, trying to make sense of all
the locations in my head that I was supposed to pinpoint. You
had me in a sweat and were loving every minute of it, sitting
there so innocently with the rest of the team, with that half
smile on your lips. And I punished you like this afterward
and almost made you late for your departure."

She quivered with reaction as he slipped his fingers
deeply into her curls. Punished her like this . . . punished her
like this . . .

*With scented oil on a rug. An alpaca rug of various colors.
She had given it to him on his birthday. It was snow-soft,
deep and luxurious, and he had given her a sensuous massage, a goodbye loving before she left on assignment.*

The fireplace was lit and the warm glow from the fire cast

*a reddish gold hue to their bodies as he made love to her,
their bodies slick with the oil. He was wild, unwilling to let
her come down as the hours ticked to dawn, and she let him
"punish" her, again and again.*

"This is for not wearing underwear," he told her as he slid
deep inside her, her legs over his shoulders. She came.

"This is for crossing and uncrossing your legs," he said as
he nudged her apart from behind and possessively thrust into
her heat. She came.

Much later, still buried in her, he parted her legs draped
over his thighs. He drew his legs up until she was wide and
exposed, facing the fire. A muscular arm wrapped around her
forearms and chest, keeping her captive. She knew she was in
trouble then.

"And this," he drawled into her hair, tangled all around
their bodies, "is for heating me up like that fire. This is for almost making me come apart when you shifted your skirt."

Warm oil. Slippery fingers. She was already swollen and
sensitive from all his loving. His slick fingers moved slowly.
She cried out, trying to catch her breath, as he tortured her.

Trapped in that position, she couldn't shake his hand off.
She couldn't close her legs. And every time she tried to throw
her hips up, she was made very aware what was heavily nestled between her legs, still inside her, still demanding her attention. His fingers worked their magic where she burned,
and she stared into the fire in helpless pleasure, riding him as
he grew thicker. Her whole body seemed to spasm from the
inside out.

"Were you wet like this when you were watching me,
hmm? Answer me, baby."

"Yes," she gasped out.

More oil. Mixed with her essence. He had slowed down to
an agonizing pace, just barely putting pressure on that
screaming spot. He was making a point. What? What? She
didn't even know she screamed out the question. He soothed
her down, then brought her back to near peak. Her thighs
throbbed from being parted that wide. She sobbed as he
slowed down again.

"Should I leave you like this, wanting to finish off, so I know you'll come back for me?" She shook her head. *"No? You won't come back?"*

"Yes, yes, I'll come back!" she screamed, struggling earnestly now.

"Good," he whispered. *"Now you can come, then come back to me."*

She came. She convulsed. She pulled at him inside till he started to tremble under her. Till both their cries mingled into one voice.

Nikki screamed her release, thrashing water left and right. The bottle of bath oil floated away as his glistening fingers kept its lazy pace. She kept coming.

The fire flickered fiercely as she came.

"Promise to return safely," he ordered.

"I promise."

Rick loved watching her like this. Giving her pleasure. Taking what she so generously gave. Her sexy throaty cries just for him, calling his name. She sank weakly against him, letting him take her wherever he wanted.

"Do you remember?" he whispered against her wet forehead.

She sighed, already out of it. "Yes. I came home," she said.

Rick frowned, but was careful not to push too far. He washed her hair, taking time to savor its texture. She let him take care of her, giving soft sighs of pleasure now and then. When he was done, he pulled the release valve. He sat with her as the water gurgled down the drain. She was already half asleep.

Placing a tender kiss to her cheek, he curbed the disappointment bubbling up inside. She didn't remember.

Later, he watched her sleeping in his bed. So peaceful. So beautiful. This time she hadn't left him asleep. He couldn't ask her if she couldn't remember. He couldn't ask her whether she really accessed files in his computer. And later betrayed him. And their country.

* * *

Nikki became aware of the regular rhythm of somebody's breathing. Every part of her shrank away from the body on top of her in fear. Then she caught his scent, a clean, masculine tang mixed with that indefinable ingredient that was meant to heat up her awakening senses. Her initial panic receded. Only one person in this world could do this to her.

"Rick?" she said, very softly, not wanting to wake him up if he was asleep.

He was lying on her, covering her body with half of his, as if he was afraid she would disappear when he drifted off. She wondered how she could have slept like that—she had never been able to let anyone be on top too long. It was the loss of trust, a suffocating fear.

Yet, this morning, there was a man in the same bed with her, his big body blanketing hers. The sound of his muffled heartbeat, the rise and fall of his chest against her cheek, the air that fanned her hair every time he exhaled—she wished they could lie here like this, undisturbed.

Here was the center of her universe. This bed, with this man, with this velvety silence. Out there was pain. Out there was something she didn't feel like dealing with. She didn't want to talk about things that hurt. Yet she knew it would be impossible.

When she had accepted this final contract, she had set the wheels in motion. She had wanted some closure to her past, both the missing chapters and the parts that haunted her. She had thought herself ready after all this time. A decade of healing. Surely she would be strong enough to face the truth.

"I dream about you sometimes but never dreamed of waking up to find you in my arms." Rick's voice was sleep-husky as he shifted. The warm imprint of his body heat was more pronounced now that she felt the cool air in the room against her warm skin. "I'm still telling myself that this is real, that I won't wake up and find you gone."

He turned her on her side, so that their bodies faced each other. She suspected that this was how they used to sleep—

her petite body tucked against him, her face buried in his chest as he tucked her under his chin. It felt right.

She lifted her head to look at him. Warmth stole into her cheeks at the look in his green eyes. They saw too much. They knew things about her that she couldn't recall. A thousand questions. Would he tell her everything?

"I'm real," she told him softly, "but am I real to you?"

He laced one hand in her hair, parting the long strands, and she vaguely remembered him combing it last night. She had been half asleep from sheer exhaustion after they had made love. His babying her had been narcotic, a form of mind seduction because she knew he had looked and touched her everywhere. Rick wasn't a person who would do things in half measure.

This much she remembered and knew about her husband—he would be thorough in his search for the truth. She knew he would have checked for all the little things on her body that only he was familiar with. There were fleeting images of his lips on her back, on the mole near her ear, of a slow exploring hand with a towel, and yes, the sensual comfort of his combing the tangles out of her hair. Even now, his touch rekindled an answering flame in her.

"You're real. It's hard to believe it but you're real." His hand combed her hair, letting the heavy strands fall on top of his body. "Why has it taken you so long to come back?"

Rick kept his voice mild, soothing. There was so much between them. Years and years of questions. He must act with care here or put their relationship at risk. He was eager to find out what had happened but he forced himself to slow down. She had no full recollection and he had to broach cautiously. Be patient. Resume the game they had started the last few weeks.

"Ten years, Nikki." He kept touching her, tilting her chin so he could see her expression. "Where have you been?"

Her eyes were troubled and he frowned. One of her eyes was dark brown, the other . . . He had forgotten about the first thing that had thrown him off. "Contact lenses."

She hesitated and reached up, touching the one eye. "Yes.

I can't see very well out of one eye, and afterwards they recommended a change of eye color, just to try out."

He ignored the second statement. "Can't see out of one
eye," he prompted. When she hesitated again, he added,
"You have to tell me, Nikki. I need to know what happened."

He had never known eyes could fill with pain the ways
hers did. He almost said it was all right if she didn't tell him,
after all. He bit back the words. No. He had to know. There
was no way around this.

"Rick," she said and gently caressed his face, as if to
ready him. It seemed so incongruous that she was comforting
him. "They hit me and connected with my eye. It sustained
some kind of bruise, I'm not sure. Then I was kept in the dark
for so long my eyesight adjusted with it. The good eye sort of
took over. The ophthalmologist told me it was natural for the
body to do that, and now I need correction lenses. It hurts
sometimes when it's too bright. Or when I'm tired."

She said the words in a matter-of-fact voice, using it as a
way to cover the emotional aspects behind them, but they
tore at him like sharp claws. Someone hit her. Someone hurt
and humiliated her. Someone ordered her to be locked in
darkness.

He was a trained operative. He understood the minutiae of
emotional and physical torture. The enemy might speak a
different language but they all used the same book. But
studying it, going through the motions of it, even observing
videotapes of it, was not the same as having your loved one
put in that position. The former had only evoked a rage for
justice on the behalf of the victim. But this was his Nikki.
And the venomous blind fury snaking through him wasn't after justice. He just wanted to find out the names—all the
names—and strike. Maim. Kill. No one hurt what was his.

"Rick, you're hurting me. You're going to start bleeding
again, if you aren't careful."

Her words brought him back and he saw that his clenched
fists were tugging on her hair. He let go immediately, turning
his hand over to stare at the cut.

"I couldn't do a damn thing." He swallowed the bitter

taste of memory in his mouth. The shock of listening to the shouts of warning over the wire. The fear when he had realized the covert operation had been discovered. The grim moment when he heard the wire snatched off one of the operatives and the accented voice coming on, informing them that everyone had been captured. "The whole thing went down so quickly and so badly, they weren't able to send in a warning. They just decided to close the whole thing down, shut the operation right after your team disappeared at the rendezvous point."

Rick paused, trying to control his anger before continuing. "It was very obvious the location had been leaked but no one up there wanted to listen to me. There was a quiet internal investigation and that was it. Every operative from that team was declared dead. Gone, just like that. Then we received the ultimatum that all of you would be killed off but no one here wanted to deal with the hostages. Not a fucking one of those bureaucrats would allow any action. They feared UN censure. I wasn't allowed access to the files. I couldn't read the message they sent so I could find out where they had you. I had never felt so helpless in my life."

"Rick—"

The sympathy in her eyes overwhelmed him. She was so soft and giving, so willing to accept all that had happened. He couldn't do that. Cupping her face, he gazed fiercely into her eyes. "The day they told me every one of you had been executed, I made a vow. I would find out what happened, and where they had buried you. I would keep requesting the government to get your body home, even though I knew that wasn't going to happen. I would dig for the truth and bury Gorman and the rest of them."

"Gorman," Nikki breathed, and she was suddenly alert. "Rick, I need you to tell me about Gorman and you. What does he have on you?"

Was he that transparent? All these years, he had played his part so well, and this woman had seen through his charade in no time at all. "He has nothing on me," he lied.

"But you brought his name up."

"I just know he was involved in it," Rick hedged. He couldn't reveal the truth to her when he didn't even know what it was.

To divert her attention, he rolled onto his back and took Nikki with him. Her hair spilled out around them as her sleep-warmed body spread out over him, and her sweet clean scent tantalized his nostrils. Waking up in the morning with Leah's long, long hair, being a prisoner of her hair and scent, arms and legs. He had never been able to resist her when she weaved that spell around him. His body apparently had forgotten it was no longer that of a younger man's, responding like a teenager being rubbed for the first time, the rush of desire so swift that it hurt.

Surprised, she lost her trend of thought, pausing for a few moments before she became aware of his physical reaction. She caught her lower lip with small even teeth when he pushed her thighs apart. He just wanted to nestle against her heat. Like that. His hands spanned her waist.

"You aren't telling me something," she whispered, her eyelashes fluttering rapidly as he started positioning her. "Rick, you're keeping things from me."

He was. But he couldn't explain what he couldn't understand. And she couldn't give him answers about events she couldn't remember. It was a catch-22. All he could do was make her mind open up to the past. What if it was true? What if she had really stolen those files so long ago? The old doubts that had eaten at him for eons were difficult to banish.

He arched up into her softness, and held her down onto him. Ever so slowly. He would never let those suspicions win. He would find proof, even if it took another ten years. Her eyes closed as she absorbed his thick length. It was slow sweet torture for him and she drove him half-crazy each time she adjusted position. Was she remembering? It was the only way he knew to connect her to him—her past with his.

"Rick . . ." Although she protested, Nikki didn't try to stop him. She opened willingly, greedily, needing all of him. Her body was so hungry and similar to the way her appetite had gotten—it was unstoppable now that it had found what it was starving for. Not food. This. This man. *Her* man.

She was a GEM operative, trained by the best in NOPAIN, nonphysical persuasion and innovative negotiation. She knew an evasive ploy when she saw one. Before she had married him, Rick Harden had been one of the best in the business when it came to the games of seduction. That was why she had known that I.I. couldn't have succeeded by trying to tempt him with sex. Part of her had remembered how good he was, and of course, she was a different woman now. Her agency's NOPAIN training gave her insight into how her husband's mind worked.

Right now, her body was primed for loving. She couldn't help that because she loved this man. Her mind, however, continued to analyze him. He had grown so tough without her, so used to finding things out without any cooperation that he was just going to take care of this whole thing his way. He would seduce her while he searched for the answers himself.

She understood him only too well. It was his way of protecting her now because he couldn't back then. Her self-made bureaucrat was still trying to dig through all the paperwork after all these years to find something that was missing. He hadn't accepted her death for what it was and had made up his mind to look for the details surrounding her demise. Not just her. But for something she couldn't remember. That bothered her, just as not being able to remember him while she was in that cell bothered her. Were these two things linked?

All analysis scattered as Rick began an escalating tempo where they were now physically connected. Closing her eyes, Nikki gave in to his demands. For now. Her body was too ravenous, and he was the feast. The rhythm grew faster. She panted. He twined her hair round and round his hands, bringing her face down to him. She braced her hands on his broad chest that rose up and down as he went faster and faster. She shook like a rag doll as he urged her to the edge. She felt his fingers reach between them. She keened. No more.

"Oh yes, more. Tell me you want more."

Of course she did. She rode his erection with a desperate need, riding on crest after crest as erotic flashes of memory of them coupling tumbled like picture cards in her head. How could she not want more? He owned her body and soul.

He muttered her name. She collapsed onto him. As their breathing slowed, she kept asking how she could block this man from her mind for so long. What was she hiding from herself?

The phone rang, and Rick curled a lazy hand on her back, keeping her with him. She heard the deep rumble of his voice in between his heartbeats. The tempo quickened slightly, and she frowned. He hung up.

"What is it?" She raised her head.

The sexual afterglow had disappeared. "They are sending a car for me. They went to Denise Lorens's apartment when she didn't show up for the review board yesterday and didn't call in today. She was found dead in her apartment, and my fingerprints are all over her."

Chapter Seventeen

Rick stared out of the window, taking in the scenery down below. It faced the courtyard where many of the employees enjoyed taking their breaks—a peaceful place amid war strategizing. And up here, in his office, a thorough mess. Just like his life.

But then nothing was normal anymore. He used to think that his life was one big metaphorical knotted ball. No matter how hard he tried to unwind it, the tighter the knot became, until the tension of being what he had chosen to be was squeezing the life out of him. Everything had become functional—yes, no, and sometimes, a shrug. He didn't care much, except when he thought he had found another clue to explain his past. It was a painstaking process—the slow gathering of files and evidence.

His bitterness grew to self-disgust when some young SEAL sent by Admiral Madison so easily caught the very person he had been after all these years. In a space of a few months, that brash military-turned-TIARA operative had cornered the traitor and along the way, found the love of his life.

Rick's lips curled with ironic mockery. Steve McMillan and Marlena Maxwell. He would not forget that pair soon. They had made him see what he had become. They had reminded him of what he was. And his envy and years of bureaucratic tunnel vision had blinded him so much that he had lost the chance to be the one to hold the evidence over Gorman. If he hadn't been so stupid, he would have had something over the ex-deputy director.

Instead, the traitor was locked up, with a whole cache of secrets that no one knew how to pry out of him. All Internal Investigations wanted was negotiating one thing—the names of the network of rats. Rick wanted something more personal. He wanted to force Gorman to tell the truth about the past. After Gorman was incarcerated, the knot had become the rope around his neck. He was going to be hanged for all these years of playing the yes-man to ex-Deputy Director Gorman. Everything looked pretty hopeless.

He turned from the view and observed Nikki sitting serenely at the desk. There was concern in her eyes. He realized now that she never said anything until she needed to. It made him wonder what else she was keeping from him.

Had she known what his life had become without her? A fucked-up ball of knots. She had reappeared out of nowhere, took the whole yarn of deceit he had woven, and had gently, patiently unraveled his life out of it.

"You recorded the whole thing," Rick stated rhetorically, and even now, in his office a couple of hours later, he couldn't quite believe it.

"Yes."

"Did you plan to record the night we were going to share or was it a spur of the moment thing?" he asked.

Curiously enough, he didn't feel deceived. Or angry, even. The other night he had thought he had Nikki Taylor where he wanted her, and he found she'd planted bugs on him. She had sat in her car listening in on his conversation with Denise Lorens and hadn't said one word of it before now. A GEM operative, he reminded himself. She was now one of those witches who couldn't be seduced.

Her blush did something to his insides. She looked down at her lap. He was torn between tenderness and suspicion, need and questions. How much of her was trained? Did they reshape her into this, using her partial amnesia? He couldn't help it. She was here, yet she was still stolen from him.

"I'm always prepared for the unexpected," she answered.

"I can see that." He left the window and moved around the boxes strewn about the chaos that used to be his office. "Are there any more surprises you have in store for me?"

"You mean, I'm not a constant surprise enough?" she returned lightly.

He pulled a nearby chair and sat down in front of her. Taking one of her hands, he placed a kiss on her wrist. Her pulse jumped to life. He couldn't help it. He had to be near her. Touch her. Feel her.

"Look around you, Nikki. This is my world—or was—until it fell apart. This is the second time everything around me had turned into chaos. The first time was when you disappeared."

"Is this time my fault too?" she asked.

Her pale slender hand was small compared to his. Did she know what power she held? "I'm not assigning blame. What I'm trying to do is make sense of things."

"Don't you want me back?" There was a slight catch in her voice, as if she couldn't bear to ask the question.

He squeezed her hand. He had to keep reminding himself that she couldn't remember everything between them. "Didn't last night tell you anything?" He smiled at the self-conscious heat in her cheeks. A thought occurred. "Or maybe you were just recording that too?"

"No!"

Her denial brought a moment's shame of his thoughtlessness. He kissed her hand again and leaned closer. She looked at his lips, and the need and hurt in her eyes made him groan. "Ten years, Nikki. I'm now hard and selfish and distrustful. I question everyone's motives and I operate solely to gather data for some stupid obscure future date. I—"

She silenced him with her free hand, covering his mouth lightly. "Rick, don't." Her plea came out in a hush, even though they were the only two people in the room. "We can't change what happened to us. I don't want you denigrating yourself because you think you could have done something to change the past, or because you are what you are now."

Rick removed her hand, held them both tightly. "What I

am now," he told her, bitterly, "is a used-up bureaucrat that they will try to demote again. What I am now is someone who hadn't lived up to expectations, who couldn't do his job right, who didn't really care about anything in this whole universe except to find—"

He stopped. He was going to say to find "her," meaning Leah. His whole existence was to find out about his dead wife and to bring her body home, and to search for information to prove that she wasn't the traitor. That was what gave him the incentive to carry on.

But his wife was here. Home. And maybe if he just let them shoot his career down, he wouldn't need to dig up what happened that night when she left. He wouldn't need to care about justice. Let them put all the black marks in his file. Let EYES blame him. It would be his cross to bear. And Gorman would still be in prison.

"Except to find what, Rick?" Nikki prompted.

He gathered her close, half dragging and half lifting her out of the chair into his arms. "It doesn't matter now," he said, taking a deep cleansing breath, filling his lungs with the scent that clung to her hair and skin. "I have you back. You're my whole universe. Always."

Nikki blinked away the tears that gathered. His universe. And he made her feel like she was his center. She had never felt this protected and needed. Yet she couldn't help but ache for the underlying meaning in his declaration. All around her was what remained of Rick's world, what had been important to him for so long—in boxes and upturned drawers.

His entire office was in shambles. All the files were gone. His desk had been rifled through. They didn't even leave his paintings untouched—they were on the floor, after it had been ascertained that nothing was hidden behind the frames. Internal Investigations had been very thorough.

Yet they didn't know her man. He was just as thorough. Just as determined as they were. He was also innocent. Nikki knew this in her soul. He wasn't an accomplice to Gorman or any traitor. He had chosen to be seen as a yes-man for a reason, and she knew it had something to do with her. But he wouldn't tell her. What did she do that was so bad that he decided to keep it a secret all these years?

She had the advantage of most of the review board. They had been given the redacted version of Rick's files, but Admiral Madison had gotten his hands on the real thing, with all the details. When she'd received it, her heart had leaped into her throat. This was it. Since her own file was nowhere to be found, Rick's was her only link to her past. This was like her own personal *Tung Seng*, the Book of Knowledge, filled with lessons and information.

However, like the *Tung Seng*, it was also cryptic, open to interpretation. She had read it through quickly, then slowly, and then once more. So much left unsaid. So much deception between the lines. She might not be able to remember everything but she could still tell a lie and detect a cover-up.

"You're what matters most," he told her, stroking her back.

She closed her eyes, welcoming the comfort of Rick's strong arms enfolding her. She wondered whether she could ever mend this broken man, who thought he had failed her somehow. He dismissed his own strength of will so easily. Set on his mission, he had obliterated so much of himself to fit into this mold he now wore with deceptive ease. She had enough memories of him now to know that the old Rick was no bureaucrat, had despised paperwork, and had no conscious agenda other than to serve his country.

"But you still want me to tell you where the bug is planted," she guessed.

"And when you did it."

She hid her smile, burrowing in his warmth. Thorough. Constantly assessing. He would not rest till he found her little bug. "It's one of my hair clips," she told him. "I put it on your collar, behind your neck."

"When I was carrying you, talking to Denise."

"Yes. I didn't want to leave you alone with her."

"Were you listening?"

"Yes. Does that bother you?" It had disturbed her when she was outside his apartment building, listening to Denise's attempt at seduction. Jealousy, she had discovered, wasn't green. It was a blinding vermillion. She didn't think she took a breath until she heard Rick pushing Denise away.

His massage paused a moment, then resumed. "Would it have bothered you if I had gone along with it?" he gently asked.

"Yes." She knew it would have hurt.

"I don't like blackmail, little bird." His voice hardened. "I'm sorry she's dead. No one deserves to be murdered for information, but she was burning her bridges, playing both sides."

Nikki caressed his jaw, feeling the tension pulsing there. "In her way, she liked you, Rick. Wanted you. She thought she could have you and power, too."

He turned his face and nibbled her palm. "She didn't know you have both, little bird."

His words evoked a glow inside. She felt him nudge her and willingly turned up her face to meet his lips. The glow burst like sunshine, and she returned his kiss with fervor. They sat together like that, and she could feel the silence vibrating with a harmony that she associated with when she heard her *chuung*. It was the most beautiful quiet she had ever heard.

A knock disturbed their momentary peace. Usually Greta would buzz the intercom, but everything had been disconnected or was under some pile of papers.

The heavy office door cracked open and Greta peeked in. She studied them for a moment and spoke hesitantly, "Mr. Harden, they are here. Admiral Madison said it would be better to use the conference room down the hall than your office."

"I wonder why." Nestled comfortably against his chest, Nikki couldn't see his face, but his voice was laced with sarcasm. "We're missing a few chairs. There is plenty of room on the floor, though. We can all have a pow-wow in the middle of the room."

Nikki couldn't help it. She chuckled at the ridiculous image of the uniformed admiral, the congressmen, and the heads of the various departments sitting cross-legged among the jumble. She felt the answering rumble of Rick's silent laughter under her ear.

"Sir . . ." Clearly the secretary was nervous that she had to convey that message back to the VIPs.

"We'll be right there," Rick told her.

"Yes, sir."

"I wonder what their decision is," he said, as he helped her on her feet. "Your tape doesn't exactly show EYES in a good light."

Nikki looked up at Rick. His eyes were the same intense green that had haunted her when she sat in darkness so long ago. It was the color of life, calling to her. She just didn't know then that it was also Rick in her mind. The truth had always been in her. Her grandmother's prophecies were becoming more and more important. Why had she ignored them for so long? She had wanted knowledge and yet didn't even try to understand her own spiritual anchor. She wouldn't make the mistake again.

Feeding the hungry ghosts. Setting the truth free. Nikki hoped they wouldn't continue burying it. If they did, they buried her past, too.

A dead CIA agent. No police questioning. Instead, a private conference with two congressmen on the intelligence committee, EYES headhunters, Admiral Madison, and the deputy directors of TIARA could only mean one thing. There was going to be a major cover-up. Rick had gone through something similar before.

It was bureaucrat time. He didn't need to analyze the situation. He could list all the political reasons from memory. It was an election year. Funding was at stake. TIARA could be eliminated. The agency would handle its own, take care of this situation before it blew up in its face. A major shake-up would not be good for its global reputation. It would also put all overseas connections at risk.

The air-conditioned conference room, along with the mood of its occupants, added to the morguelike atmosphere.

Rick put a protective hand on Nikki's lower back as they entered. He would break them if they made one move against her. He hadn't been collecting data all these years for nothing. She didn't owe them a damn thing.

There weren't many initial pleasantries except for an exchange of smiles between Nikki and Admiral Jack Madison. Rick noted that they liked each other, catching the concerned gleam in the other man's eyes. He remembered that the admiral had recently gotten married. Good. He didn't need to get on the bad side of the man yet another time by warning him off his wife.

"Here are the facts, Agent Harden."

Here we go, Rick thought.

"There is a list floating around, or at least that is what Gorman said. Denise Lorens told you she had the list, and according to this tape we just heard, she'd manipulated it to entrap you. Those were her words, but we cannot confirm her motives because she is dead."

"In other words, you don't believe that she actually contaminated the list," Rick said.

"We found the files in your system. That's why you need an attorney, Agent Harden."

"Let's cut to the chase," Rick said. "What's the deal you have to offer?"

They always had a deal. They did the last time. *Take the offer we give you and the agency will take care of everything else. We will do our best to extract your wife but we need your cooperation or the news media would dig things up that might jeopardize operations.*

Across the big conference table, the EYES representative leaned forward. He was a big man, easily six-foot-four, with snow-white hair. Rick had never seen him before, but he was obviously the one given the power to negotiate. He looked at the man's badge.

"I have looked through your file, Agent Harden. You have been through a similar leakage investigation before. It's going to look bad, what with that bad rap from the last time. How is it going to look now, with the leaks that have been found to be coming out of Task Force Two all these years, with you at the helm? Now that Denise Lorens is dead, and listening to this tape you gave, it can be seen as your motive to shut her up after she threatened you."

"Wait," Nikki cut in. Something in her voice made Rick look at her closely. "How did you get to that conclusion with my tape? It was very clear that Miss Lorens was attempting to blackmail and entrap Agent Harden."

"She isn't here to give her side of the story."

"I'm sorry she's dead but that doesn't change the fact that she clearly overstepped her role as an EYES operative and that she had been a double agent for years," Nikki said levelly.

Lips pursed tightly, the man straightened in his seat. "Nothing has exonerated Agent Harden. There is a list found in one of his computers and we have no other list. He has a history of information leakage. One of my best operatives is dead and he has the motive. And, we have matching fingerprints. I'm sure we'll also find matching carpet fibers."

"You heard Agent Harden saying no to her offer at the end of the tape. You heard her fighting him after that. That's the reason for those fingerprints and fibers." It was the admiral this time, his voice filled with disgust. "You're telling me you still won't go beyond covering your own asses."

"Jack," one of the congressmen chipped in. "We have to see how to save the situation here. We can't have the whole agency come tumbling down on account of one man. Agent Harden isn't indispensable."

"I was hoping you wouldn't do this," Admiral Madison responded, his blue eyes blazing. "Gentlemen, it's not Agent Harden who is stinking up the whole United States covert organization—it's Gorman and the rest of the traitors in his network. I'm telling you, I won't tolerate a cover-up."

Rick had to admit that the admiral was intimidating when he chose to be. He cut an authoritative figure in his stark uniform with those shiny medals. Very few men could meet those piercing eyes and not be the first to look away. Rick was glad he was on his side here.

"Jack, let's hear Mr. Stadler out. Internal Investigations should have the final say."

"Not if they aren't doing their job. Not if there are lives at stake, and I assure you, the more you allow these infiltrators in the system, the more you put my men out there at risk. You're not using the Intel gathered by Task Force Two to make friends here."

"Look, Gorman is in our hands. He won't be making problems."

Admiral Madison's chair creaked in protest as he swung sharply around. "Problems? Mr. Stadler, my dead men aren't problems."

"They are collateral damage." Stadler wasn't backing down, staring back at the admiral. "You're a man of action, and I understand that, but the big picture is what matters here. If we don't have a quick scapegoat, the media will eat this one alive. A whole list? They would devour the president, and you're a friend of his, aren't you, Admiral Madison? He doesn't need this as a reelection issue."

"Don't threaten me, Mr. Stadler."

"Your opening an independent committee on national security is a threat to Internal Investigations as well as every agency, Admiral Madison. If you would back off, I. I. will clean house without the publicity and the president won't be embarrassed by it. Right now, we have a whole can of worms with the reappearance of Leah Harden. Do you think publicizing the list won't bring up that particular operation and why it failed?"

"Exactly. I, for one, am very interested in that particular operation and why it failed. All these redacted copies tell me nothing." The admiral sank back into his seat, his eyes narrowing into slits. "You know, Stadler, besides this fear of my independent committee, you're making me more and more curious about this operation with Nikki Taylor—Leah Harden—ten years ago. There wasn't a . . . cover-up of this case, too, was there?"

As he sat there listening to the heated exchange, Rick noted that Stadler's face turned interestingly bland. "There is a procedure to open these files, Admiral Madison," Stadler said coldly. "It takes time to check out everything that Miss Taylor had claimed. We're an investigative branch and cannot simply let any individual come in with a story without any proof. The fact that she hadn't done a thing for ten years makes things . . . difficult. I suggest you go to the attorney general, state your case, and get the file reopened. Miss Taylor will have to undergo a routine interrogation and debriefing, as well as psychiatric examination. As an EYES officer, I would also recommend hypnosis and other tests, perhaps a truth serum. We can then find out more about what exactly happened to her after her capture and her subsequent extraction by COS commandos. I understand access to the Covert Subversive Center is almost impossible, and that their commandos are a law to themselves. As you can see, a thorough investigation will take some time.

Rick had heard enough. What Stadler said was the bureaucratic red tape with which he was familiar, the best delay tactic in the world. It would give I.I. enough time to get its story straight, and mount a cover-up campaign.

"No one is taking my wife into interrogation. No one is giving her hypnosis or any truth serum," he interrupted softly, his gaze on Stadler. "I'll listen to your offer and consider it."

Stadler's smile was knowing, as if he had expected this. He opened his folder and took out some papers, followed by several pens. He turned them so the writing faced Rick.

"EYES will take care of everything. All you need to do is sign here. We will work out a deal with Gorman. You'll retain legal counsel, who will then advise you not to say anything during this whole investigation. In the end, you'll be reprimanded and be given another position. Or you can retire, which is highly recommended. In return, you won't be tied with Denise Lorens's death. There will some kind of released statement to exonerate you."

"What about her murderer?" Rick asked.

Stadler looked across the table. "That won't be your business any longer."

"And the people who worked with Gorman?"

"We will get them, but the press needn't know when we do. Once the Gorman situation dies down, of course. Meanwhile, you again helped the department to stave off scandal, saving the president from embarrassment. TIARA won't be subjected to any funding cuts for another year and—"

"And our overseas covert operations won't be jeopardized. I'll have saved countless lives," Rick ended woodenly. They must all memorize the same spiel in EYES school.

He had spent all this time trying to retrieve his wife's remains. Trying to find proof that she was innocent. But she was alive now and Gorman was in jail. Ending this now would mean another black mark against him. His career would basically be finished. So what?

Rick picked up the pen. Sign it and he could sign away the past.

"No." Nikki placed a hand on his elbow. "Rick, I want to know what happened."

His lips straightened into a grim line. "What is there to know? I can tell you right now what's classified. It says in there that I disclosed information due to negligence. Ten years ago, I.I. believed that could be the main factor that caused your operation to fail. I accepted the blame, took my punishment. The demotion was appropriate."

Take the deal, Harden. Investigating this will take months and months, and who knows what will happen to your wife while they are assigning blame? With you reprimanded, we can concentrate on the operatives' lives, which is the most important thing, right?

Nikki's hand tightened on his arm. She glanced around the table and made eye contact with Admiral Madison. "I've read the unredacted version."

There was a muffled curse. A snort of disbelief. Sounds of consternation from a few of those present.

"How—"

"Do you mean to say you read what would normally take months—"

"Our copies were redacted, so who—"

"That's why you need an independent contractor like me, gentleman. I don't let your red tape stand in my way."

Rick didn't know whether to be amused or shocked. A roomful of bureaucrats against a GEM operative was quite an experience. That the operative happened to be his wife made him cautious and proud all at once. One thing stood out. She said she had read his file without the blacked-out details. Then she saw that everything he had just said was true, that he was solely to blame, so why bring it up now?

"Now about this deal," Nikki said, after she had gotten their attention.

The change from wife to operative intrigued him, too. There was a subtle narrowing in her dark eyes, a challenging edge to her voice. The slow smile she directed at them all raised his blood pressure. He must be nuts. His career was going down the tubes and he was getting aroused because his woman was working. How many sides of her were there?

"No one seems interested in what I want, and I'm the dead woman in that file causing all these problems. A talking dead woman would interest the press, too, don't you think?"

"Good job, Nikki. I'll talk to you later," Admiral Madison said. Save for Rick, he was the last one to leave. Hand on the doorknob, he turned to her very quiet husband before walking out of the conference room, "You're damn lucky to have her back, Harden."

Rick didn't reply, merely watched everyone leave. Nikki turned. And started backing away. He stalked her in measured steps across the room and as she reached the entrance, he leaned a hand over her head, effectively halting her escape. He moved in. She flattened against the big oak door, forcing herself to look up defiantly.

She was a little mad at herself. He had this effect on her that no one had. Powerful. Dominating. It drove her weak when she should be strong. She lifted her chin higher.

Rick's green eyes glittered like gems, and she had the absurd feeling that he wasn't angry with her for foiling his plans. There was so much unresolved between them and she didn't know where to start to break down the wall he had erected. She felt the hand above her head slide down the wooden door till it stopped next to her ear, and he leaned even closer. His fresh masculine scent teased her senses.

"You didn't tell me you read the unredacted version of my file."

She stared at his sensuous lips that could cause such havoc to her entire being. "You didn't ask."

"Remind me to make a list."

"Things happened so fast, Rick." Her heartbeat jumped when the hand moved and wrapped around her neck. He stroked her pulse with his thumb as he leaned even closer.

"Were you ever going to tell me?" His lips were a mere breath away from hers. "Maybe after the review board? As that EYES rep put it just now, you're jeopardizing your assignment by revealing yourself to the world. Now you can't be fair and unbiased, can you?"

Tell him. Tell the world. She knew he wanted all the answers. "I can't have them sacrifice you," she whispered.

"Why not?" he countered softly, his breath brushing her lips like a kiss.

"Because you're my husband."

"How much do you know, Nikki? How much are you still hiding from me?" He searched her face for answers. "Why did you finally come back?"

There was anguish in his voice, and Nikki could only stare back helplessly at him.

"Damn it, answer me!"

"It was time to face my past," she told him, trying to put into words all her fears and longing. "I couldn't before. Every time I tried, my mind drew a blank, and it hurt, and even though I knew the facts, nothing added up."

Rick pushed off the door, turning his back to her as he walked back to the conference table. "Ten years, Nikki. You left me here thinking you were dead." He picked up the papers left by the EYES representatives, shuffling them slowly. He seemed weary as he gathered them under his arm.

"I couldn't help it," Nikki said, wrapping her arms around her. "For a long time, after my extraction, I wasn't sure who I was. I stayed where I was, with my rescuers, because they made me feel safe. The new agency fit me perfectly—people working undercover, with new identities, but it took a long time before I even thought about having one. I was a mess— everything was jumbled and the only focus I had was what was inside me." She pointed to her chest, and added, "Do you understand? I could only trust what I had in my mind because I wasn't sure whether what was out there was real. What if you haven't seen green grass for an eternity and you find yourself staring at a tree or a blade of grass until someone stops you? You realize you're totally unable to function, that you will have to start somewhere or be nothing. I couldn't remember you, Rick. Is that what this is all about? You can't forgive me because I'm not her, not the wife who left you."

He turned to face her, the deep green of his eyes reminding her of those days when she couldn't understand why she was so drawn to that color, why she needed to keep looking at it to find an answer. She understood now. She had been trying to find him in her head.

"Come here." There was a brooding dark edge to his voice.

Nikki shook her head. "No."

"Why?" he asked, as he retraced his steps back toward her. "Are you afraid how every time I touch you, I keep proving you're still her? Are you afraid to remember how you were?"

He stopped a few feet away, giving her room to move aside if she wished, but he had her cornered, and he knew it. She was here because she wanted to remember. Yet a part of her was fighting it, reluctant to let go of what she was now.

"I feel as if I'm in competition with her," she finally admitted. "Everything you have done all these years is for her."

"For you," he corrected. "But you won't see her as you."

"So what are we going to do now?"

He gently drew her away from the door. She wished he

would hug her, but he didn't. Instead he gave her some of the files and papers he was holding.

"Go find out what you want, Nikki." He lifted her chin with a finger. His eyes held hers. "Just don't forget you will always be mine, whoever you decide you want to be."

Chapter Eighteen

The trouble with women, Rick reflected with grim humor, was that, dead or alive, they still managed to grab you by the little hairs. There was his wife, who was dead, but who was alive, and yet was still technically dead. And there was Denise, who was dead, and once he received personal confirmation from his sources, he would then believe to be really dead. If he had to explain the situation to anyone but himself, he was sure he would be the butt of all departmental jokes. Not that there weren't some of those already out there.

Rick strode up to his floor, ignoring some of the looks cast his way. The little anonymous emails they sent each other would be full of gossipy headlines. *Hard-On Had It Coming.* In the elevator, he stared at a colleague till he looked away. *Hard-On Kicked in the Balls. Hard-On All Hung Out to Dry.* He couldn't begin to guess what they were saying about Nikki. Everything that went on in a review board was strictly classified, but rumors were bound to fly after what had happened.

Lastly, throw in Denise's death, and he could imagine all the antacid being popped by the bureaucrats in the building. One thing to avoid at all cost in the bureaucrat rulebook was scandal. Scandal bred questions, which bred more questions. No one wanted to be held accountable.

Well, now he was a failed bureaucrat, too. Lately his very safely uncontroversial life had turned into a scandal-filled one. How could one woman move his world the way Nikki

Taylor had? She just showed up, and everything blew up. Everything.

He nodded at his secretary, opened the door to his office, and surveyed the mess for a moment. Greta was probably the only one who could still find anything around here.

"Greta, I'll be unavailable for the rest of the day, except to Agent Candeloro."

"Yes, sir."

He pulled out his cell phone as he headed for his cluttered desk. "Agent Candeloro? Meet me at my office at once with Miss Ostler as well as your laptop." Rick tossed the files down and swept the rest off onto the floor. "And Cam? Bring your damn snacks. I'm planning to stay late."

Rick opened and closed drawers till he found some screw-drivers. He kicked some of the wires and extension cords out of the way. Where did they plug the phone lines in this place, anyway? He found one and followed it to the jack on the floor. Sitting down on the carpet, he loosened his tie.

He reached into his breast pocket, pulling out a slim leather slipcase. He took out the small reading glasses, stretched out the malleable frame, and with a practiced twist, unconnected one of the earpieces. He laid the small curved part to one side. Picking up the screwdriver, he unscrewed the panels off the phone jack and began loosening wires. There was a knock at the door, and his secretary informed him that Agent Cande-loro and Patty Ostler from records were there to see him.

"Send them in," Rick said, and didn't look up when the door opened again. There was silence for a few seconds, then a cough. Rick kept his eyes on his chore as he asked, "I didn't ask you to come here to stand guard at my door, Agent Candeloro."

He heard their approaching footsteps, then Cam's shoes came within his peripheral vision. "Sorry, sir, it's not every day I see an office worse than mine."

"I'm sure Miss Ostler is in shock too," Rick observed dryly, finally giving them his attention.

Dressed in pristine white, the woman looked her usual im-maculate self, standing in the middle of the shambles and staring wide-eyed at the surroundings. Rick suspected she would look just as spotlessly neat in a tornado.

"They really took the place apart," she said, clearly uncomfortable with the state of the room as she gingerly walked around different piles.

"Ummm, sir, are you all right?" Cam seemed more concerned with his O.C..

Rick cocked a brow. "Do I look ill?"

Cam shrugged. "Well, you're not acting yourself, sir." When Rick continued staring at him, he shrugged again. "You're sitting on the floor with your tie looking like mine. You asked for snacks. I've never known you to eat anything but real food. Besides, what happened yesterday was pretty damn shocking to the system. I mean, it's not every day someone you care for comes back from the dead. The whole team's concerned, that's all."

Put that way, Rick supposed his men had reason to wonder about their operations chief's mental health. He hadn't been aware of how predictably straight-laced his men thought he was. "I'm fine," he informed Cam quietly. "I don't know whether I'll be coming out of this fine, but I intend to at least have the truth on my side."

"How's Mrs. Harden?" Patty asked, setting down her laptop on the chair nearby.

"News travels fast," Rick observed wryly, wondering how Nikki was doing out there, with all this talk swirling around her and him.

"I didn't tell her, sir," Cam said.

"I know. It's difficult not to be the topic of discussion when you're bleeding and carrying a woman out of the building escorted by your men," he agreed.

"I'm from records, sir," Patty countered. "I make it my business to know things that happen around here."

"A good person to have around me," Rick said. He shrugged out of his suit and gave them another dry smile when they exchanged glances. "Look, get comfortable. We're going to be here awhile, and looking up at the two of you is giving me a crick in the neck."

"Okay." Cam started moving things out of the way.

"Did they find what they were looking for?" Patty asked, gesturing at the space where the missing computers and fax machines used to be.

"Not in here, but they found the same list we dug out of the other computer. Of course, they broke the encryption faster than we did, since they had Denise's h . . ." Rick's voice trailed off. He frowned. When did they get Denise to help them?

"Agent Lorens's . . . ?" Cam prompted, squatting down after clearing some space for himself. He peered at what Rick was doing with the phone jack.

Rick absently nodded, not really seeing, as his mind worked out what had suddenly occurred to him. "Agent Lorens's dead," he informed them.

"Dead?"

"Dead? How?"

Rick leaned back against the desk, pulling his leg up so he could rest an elbow on his knee. "She was murdered. And I was, until an hour ago, the number one suspect. But the point I had been about to make was that EYES had broken the encryption with her help, but that's impossible." He cocked his head, talking more to himself than to Patty and Cam. "She was dead when they found the list."

"Which means someone else did it," Cam said.

"Not only that. It means someone in EYES knew whom to go to to get it done. Denise was their main line, working undercover in the Department of Intel, but without her, who made it possible to get the encryption broken so quickly?"

"Wait, wait a minute, sir. Agent Lorens worked for EYES?" Cam asked. "I'm getting confused. She was both EYES and Intel?"

Rick nodded. "I guess I'd better give you more data on the case."

"It's a case now, huh?"

"For me it is."

Cam grinned. "I'm damn glad we're back at work, sir. It's

been dull being in limbo. Paperwork is no fun." He slanted a glance at Patty. "Well, some paperwork. Right, Patty?"

Patty Ostler reddened and turned away from them, opening the laptop. "Don't push your luck, Agent Candeloro," she muttered. "Your report is still in my care."

Cam dramatically clutched at his heart area. His eyes were twinkling. "If you only knew what else you have in your care." His voice was teasing, filled with laughter.

Patty pursed her lips. Rick could see she was trying not to lose her temper while he was sitting there watching them. It was strangely comforting to see these two. In contrast to Rick's careful handling of Nikki, Cam just went for it, so sure that Patty was going to succumb to his charms in the end. He wished he could be so certain about his own love life. He grimaced inwardly. Love life. A month ago he would have never thought that would be his major problem.

"Besides, I care, too," Cam continued, patting the space beside him. "See, I cleared a nice area for you."

Rick chewed on the inside of his mouth as he watched Patty Ostler debate silently whether she wanted to sit on the carpet and wrinkle her white skirt. Finally she sighed and after stepping out of her heels, she did so gracefully, tucking her legs under her primly. Cam leaned close and whispered something in her ear.

"I'm going to punch holes all over your black heart, just like your report, if you don't stop," Patty warned. She was blushing so hard, the tips of her ears were red. She cleared her throat and with a determined lift of her chin, changed the subject. "I bet Agent Lorens's death complicated things. There's no one to catch or confront, nothing."

Rick took pity on her and came to her rescue. She obviously had never worked with Cam before. The younger man didn't have a serious bone in his body, but through the years, he had shown a remarkable eye at catching details. There was a lot more to Cam than what he showed the world. But that was for Patty Ostler to find out. His own plate was already full.

"If possible, I'd like the report airtight, please," he interrupted. "Cam, I didn't want to, but now I think it'd be better if you come and testify by my side." Rick paused. He hated sounding like he needed their help. Things were falling apart, and bringing others into his mess could make it worse.

"Don't worry, sir," Cam said, settling back against the wall. "We'll get this thing done. We want our team back working, and I don't care what EYES or that review board wants, we're going to get you back as our O.C. Now, what're we doing with that phone jack? Patty, uh, can work on the report."

"Excuse me, this is *your* report. I'm only helping you," Patty said, wrapping her arms in front of her.

Cam gave his "gotcha" grin. "Okay, how good are you at screwing the phone jack?"

"Children," Rick interjected, shaking his head. He was just going to have to work alone later. These two obviously didn't have work on their minds.

"Sorry, sir. What're we doing again?"

Rick flipped the screwdriver in the air and caught it. He felt strangely lighthearted and he gave them a wicked grin. His smile widened at the shock on Cam's and Patty's faces. "We're going to screw with the EYES computer files for a while."

"Cool." Cam pumped a fist.

"Won't they know?" Patty asked, pushing her glasses up her nose. "Can't they trace it back to here?"

"Not if we do it right, princess. If they start tracing, they will get to lots of different numbers first. Right, sir?"

"What are we looking for?" Patty leaned forward, holding on to Cam's arm for balance.

Rick poured out tiny flakelike chips from one of the ears of the fake glasses. "I want to find out who Denise's handler is. Files, memos, logs of any cases connected with what we've done the last few years. If we can find Denise's password, even better. We can access her personal files and see whether there are any clues to the whereabouts of the real list."

"Oh yes, that should take about . . . forever . . ." Patty sighed, smoothing her skirt as she sat back. She turned on the laptop on the chair.

"We've got to start somewhere, princess," Cam pointed out gently. He glanced at Rick. "Didn't know you knew how to do the fancy electronic stuff, sir. You always had Arms and Jones."

Rick quirked his lips and didn't answer. He had been Hard-On for so long, everyone had forgotten he was an EYES operative first. There was some other file he intended to access tonight. The thought had occurred to him as he had sat there listening to Nikki this morning.

She had mentioned that she didn't mind being a 'damaged wing,' but she had hinted that her group hadn't been abandoned because they were caught. If that was so, the implication was that they were given up intentionally.

"Damaged wing" was an asset abandoned because there was no way to save it without loss of manpower or cover. It was an accepted practice in covert life; all operatives knew the risk of being abandoned. Because of what had happened, the whole crew, including Leah Harden, was considered "damaged wings"—unsalvageable.

But Nikki had worded her warning very carefully. Enough so that EYES had stopped pushing him to sign the agreement. What had she found out about that operation? He was going to pull out the old original file that Nikki had and read it himself. Something in her story didn't coordinate with his version at all. He thought he knew what his truth was, but now he was no longer certain.

"Grandmother, I'm scared. I don't like these prophecies."
She was brushing her grandmother's fine silvery hair. She stood on a little stool so she could reach the top of her head, pulling the round hairbrush from the hairline gently all the way down. Her grandmother's eyes were closed, enjoying the soothing comfort of each stroke.
"What happened when the Manchurians stormed the last real empress and her consort?"

She had all the old historic fables memorized. She loved the ancient Chinese romances, passed down from old to young. Her grandmother had a gift of telling stories of Chinese warriors and dynastic struggles. The story of the last empress and her consort was famous. Her grandmother, like all the older generation, considered the Ming Dynasty the last real dynasty. The conquering Manchurians, like the Mongols, were barbarians.

Dutifully, she replied without hesitation, "The Manchurians gave them one night to think of signing their kingdom away, and they would then be allowed to live under their protection as long as they did as they were told. Rather than betray their honor, the last empress and her consort drank poison."

In the oval mirror, she saw that her grandmother had opened her eyes. They looked at each other for a few seconds. Then her grandmother lifted her hand and stopped her brushing. "Do you think they were scared?"

"Yes." *Who wouldn't be?*

"Why didn't they take the easy way out? Signing an agreement isn't that bad. They get to live, and still have money."

She wrapped her arms around her grandmother's shoulders, hugging her from behind. One knew these things from reading Chinese historic romances. "Because they wouldn't be happy without honor, Grandmother." *The good guys might fail, but they always had honor.*

"Do you remember how the Manchurians finally managed to take China?"

"Yes. They had a spy working inside. He snuck out and opened the gate in the Great Wall. That's how the Manchurians finally overcame the Great Wall's impenetrable defense."

"And what happened to this Benedict Arnold?"

"To this day, his name is never used by the Chinese people to name their sons ever again," *she recited. She cocked her head.* "Okay, I see. He brought dishonor to himself forever. Right, Grandmother?"

Her grandmother smiled and patted her arm affection-

ately. "*All about being* chuung-sum, *my girl. The last empress knew that even if she had chosen life, she would always
be dead to her people. Nobody is more hated than the traitor.
Traditionally, we should spit when we say his name.*"

She rested her head against her grandmother's and
viewed their reflection in the mirror, her dark hair against
the wispy gray. "*He must be a sad ghost, Grandmother. Nobody to feed him anything but spit.*"

Her grandmother laughed, as if that hadn't occurred to
her. When she stopped, she gave a nod of approval. "*You see,
there are worse things than being scared.*"

Nikki stirred her third cup of hot tea. She should be tired.
It had been hours since she left the morning conference. She
wondered what Rick was doing. He hadn't called her on the
cell phone. She couldn't have joined him for lunch anyway,
since she was nowhere nearby. She checked to see what Erik
was doing. He was still busy playing with the laptop since
she had gotten permission from Admiral Madison to do what
Erik wanted—which was . . . not exactly legal. That was
why they were doing it from his apartment. If they were
caught—and Erik had arrogantly assured her that they
wouldn't be—she could say that it was part of her report on
security.

While waiting for Erik, she had been busy writing, but it
had nothing to do with her job. She reread what she had written, wondering why, of all things, this scene stirred in her
mind. Memory was a strange thing. In her darkest hours, she
couldn't remember her own husband, someone with whom
she was most intimate, but the sound of a wind chime
brought her grandmother back. Her childhood remained
clear as the melodic tune that echoed in her cell and gave her
the courage to live, despite the fear and the filth. She was a
forgotten soul.

Then one day she was rescued and was taken to a place to
heal. She was free, but her mind had remained a prisoner. She
still couldn't remember key things—her name, her home.
The strange thing was, she had remembered her interrogation, remembered what they did to her. The doctors had

called it selective amnesia, more common than total blanking of the mind. She had accepted it. It was easy to accept things when one had gone through a lot of pain.

They had asked her to try to remember her name. She tried. The only name that stuck was Nick, and they had called her Nikki.

Her rescuers were specialists in covert warfare. They hadn't come for her. While on their mission, their leader, Jed McNeil, had heard about American prisoners from an insider. It was Jed who had decided to check out the cells his source had talked about. It could have been a trap, so he had gone in alone. He came out with Nikki in his arms. When she'd asked, he had told her there was no one else. Nikki had accepted that, too. She told her rescuers what she knew and, from habit, kept parts of her assignment secret.

She learned that they were a special branch in the government, with a lot of autonomy. She had never heard of them before that day but the fact that they gave her a choice whether to keep her rescue a secret told her how much power they had. They had extracted her because they wanted to, not because of some direct orders from the top.

It was a long time later, after her facial surgery, after undergoing therapy, that they finally discovered who she was. She had been signed off as a damaged wing by the government after her captors had threatened to kill off the prisoners when their ultimatum had been ignored. She had been pronounced dead in the line of duty.

Through the haze of trying to adjust to living among "friends" again, she had only one anchor—Jed McNeil, a man who seemed to hold more power than a mere government operative. He had told her about her old life. She even had a husband. They gave her pictures, files, information. Rick Harden. They told her she could have meant Rick when they had asked for her name. She was Leah, not Nikki. She had looked at her own photo and then at her reflection in the mirror.

"No," she had told them. "I'm Nikki now, tailor-made."

It had hurt every time she opened that file. She couldn't

remember anything, and it hurt. The man in that file had gone on with his life; to him, she was dead, a damaged wing. What would going back to her old life give her? Nothing. She couldn't remember what it was like, anyhow. She was dead. No one out there was thinking about her.

She had been scared of going back, so she had chosen death, an option her new agency had given her. They had seen her old files and knew her capabilities. She had a new face, new identity, and she could be an asset. They would rebuild her. Nikki had accepted that, too.

There are other things worse than being scared. Her grandmother's advice whispered in her mind like a soft breeze.

Nikki sipped her tea, savoring the soothing taste of chamomile and honey. How did one explain the pain and the fear of the unknown to someone who had become that unknown thing? She had been afraid of everything—the dark, the touch of a man, the proximity of strangers. It took months and months of careful training and mental help before she came out of her shell.

She was strong now, capable of many things that grew out of her weaknesses. Jed had helped her because of his experiences, and through him, she had learned to trust a man's strength again, to function within a man's world without going insane. Her sense of self had grown. She now liked being alone, liked the knowledge that her thoughts were hers and no one's recollection. Most of all, she enjoyed things that meant a lot privately—bathing, eating, touching green things, listening to sounds. These little freedoms were like gold to her because they were the things that made her cling to her humanity in those dark days. But it was a slow journey back from hell. Years and years . . .

"Damn!"

She looked to her left. Across the room, Erik Jones sat in front of his laptop, rubbing his jaw, a look of disgust on his face.

"Can I help?" Nikki asked.

"No." He waved her off absentmindedly. "Continue what you're doing. I thought I broke through but . . ."

His sentence remained unfinished as his train of thought swerved back to more important things. He snapped his fingers and started to pound the keys in rapid succession.

"No, I'll not accept your stupid negative commands, you idiot program. I know a trap when I see one. Ha! Beat you there!" he talked to the laptop after hitting one last keystroke.

Nikki smiled and turned away. For once Erik wasn't playing at being an agent; he was one now. He was in his element—encryption and decoding—something at which he was obviously very good. No wonder he felt wasted in administration.

She looked down at her writing. While the young man battled with some cyberspace phantom, she had taken a time out to think about where she was now. Rick deserved an answer. Why so long? And why now?

She had accepted so much, but it was a passive acceptance. Until she finally made the effort to look into the matter itself, she had moved on in her new life as Nikki Taylor. Maybe it was just time or karma. One day she had opened that file and reread its contents and her grandmother's prophecies kept repeating in her head.

With her agency's Intel systems at her disposal, it didn't take long before she pulled out things that weren't meant for public eyes. Her file, she had discovered, had been designated damaged wing *before* that fated operation. For years afterward her husband had continued looking for her remains, sending request after request for her lost files. Following personnel files, it was clear that he had been partly blamed for the death of her crew. Something about that last bit of information didn't sound right. Why had he refused to answer questions? What had he done to betray her?

She had looked at the picture of Rick Harden again, and as always, felt that strange need to trace his face. After ten years, he was even more a stranger, but she was drawn to him nonetheless. His strong, sensual mouth had frightened her. His search for her had frightened her. But his questions made her realize something else. *You're wrong. Someone never forgot about you. Him.*

Again, fate or karma had interceded when they offered her this contract. She had taken it, knowing full well all the possibilities ahead, but she couldn't afford to be afraid anymore. Her grandmother's prophecies had prompted her into action. She must stop fearing the past. Fear had robbed her of so much, especially the truth.

Nikki finished her tea, setting down the cup on the table. She had to find out. Was she like the traitor who opened the gates for the enemies? Was that why she couldn't remember? If so, why had Rick gotten a censure for information disclosure? Was he the traitor? Her mind rejected it, but why didn't he fight it? She thought of the flashback she had when they made love—by the fireside when they had been together one final time.

Rick had an intent look in his eyes when she told him she remembered that last night together. It was as if he had expected to hear more, and she could have sworn she saw disappointment before he masked it. What? *What?* She thought of his hands touching her intimately, moving over her naked body in the firelight. She remembered his soft moans in her ear as he had fought for control while he gave her pleasure over and over.

Nikki's body tingled as if he were doing it to her now. She closed her eyes, imagining the whole scene. Heat from the fire. His slow burning touch from the knee to the thigh, then between her legs, and staying there. Heat from his fingers. She was writhing and moaning, straining against his captive hand. She felt flushed, weak. Then . . . she had said . . .

Nikki held her head between her hands. She groaned from the weight of the pain exploding suddenly.

Chapter Nineteen

"**N**ikki? Are you all right?"

Erik's voice sounded far away. The pain blurred her vision. Red lines and white spots. Erik's face suddenly floated before her.

"Nikki!"

"I'm okay," she replied, her voice a mere thread as the pain slowly receded. She blinked rapidly.

"What happened?"

Nikki moved away from Erik. He was standing too close. "It's okay. I'm all right," she assured him, trying to stand up and stumbling.

Erik grabbed her upper arms to steady her. Although part of her knew he meant no harm, she jerked away in panic. He misunderstood, coming closer to hold her more firmly.

"No!" Her strangled cry was followed with a practiced move driven by instinct. She had the young man on his back before she knew what she had done, her elbow cutting into his throat. His eyes went wide with shock and surprise. He gurgled. Realizing the pressure from her elbow was hurting him, she let up, confused and apologetic.

"I'm . . . sorry," Nikki said. She released him and stood up swiftly. She took a deep breath. "Are you all right?"

Erik stared up at her, his hand rubbing his throat. He tried to speak, then coughed several times. "I asked you first," he finally managed to say. "What happened? You seemed to be in pain, and now I am."

Nikki didn't try to explain. "I'm sorry," she repeated. "I really didn't mean to hurt you."

"Yeah. Sure." He slowly got on his knees. He coughed again. "You're stronger than you look."

She could have killed him. She bit her lip, regretting her loss of control. Usually she was able to tolerate the occasional contact and close proximity of others. She suspected that she had let her guard down since finding out that Rick's touch didn't affect her.

"It's all right." Erik attempted a grin, still rubbing his throat. "I'll survive. What did I do, though, to set you off like that?"

"It wasn't you. I . . ." Nikki shook her head, unable to explain the confused swarm of emotions that had attacked like stinging insects in her brain. She was bewildered by how quickly her flashbacks were returning, like some television channel she could now switch on. But every time, the joy of discovery seemed to be followed by pain. "It's complicated."

"Does it have to do with yesterday?"

She frowned, "Yesterday?"

"I heard you fainted yesterday, and I saw Agent Harden carrying you out."

She nodded slowly. Erik was right. She had captured a moment of a younger, smiling Rick before that awful blinding pain smashed into her, blanking her mind. The same thing had just happened again. What was happening to her?

"You're hard to talk to," Erik grumbled. His voice was almost back to normal. "You never say anything, even when I'm trying my damnedest to get something out of you."

Nikki smiled. "That's because I have nothing to tell you."

"Or maybe I'm asking the wrong question." It was a rhetorical statement, as if he knew by now that he wouldn't get a reply. "You sure you're all right now? I'll get back to work."

"Yes, I'm sure. I'll sit by and watch you again, if you don't mind. Maybe I'll learn something." She needed some kind of distraction. The frequency of her flashbacks gnawed at her whenever she was alone and thinking.

"Sure."

He got a chair for her and after settling down beside him, she watched him quietly for a while. "You're good at this," she finally remarked after witnessing him dismantling one of the string of codes.

"Well, it has to do with your laptop, too," he said. "This baby is some toy, Nikki. Do you know how powerful it is?"

She had an idea. Jed had given it to her, and anything connected with Jed McNeil was powerful and secretive. Shrugging, she asked, "If they catch you breaking into the system, what would they do?"

"They will first try to slam shut any open ports at that time. Rather, we would," Erik corrected himself, grinning. "If I were in charge, I would be tracing us back to here. But a good hacker will use several different ways to elude a trace."

"Piggybacking," Nikki said.

"Yes, that's a popular one. The amateurs steal someone's password and hack that way. Or the smarter ones piggyback a server. The bigger the server, the harder to find them. Sometimes they send out false leads, and anyone chasing them end up at different locations."

"Like some weird addresses overseas," she said. She knew enough about the perverse art of hacking, having seen some of her friends at work. "So, are you doing that?"

"Of course not," Erik scoffed. "I'm inside, remember? I have the advantage of knowing some of the firewalls and passwords already. Speed is the name of the game here, so I'm going in to grab what we want and leave immediately. Most hackers can't resist staying around to leave a calling card, or to explore more. That's how we catch them."

"You mean you set traps for them."

"Bait, traps, whatever . . ." He shrugged as he typed away. "Most of them are nuisance hackers but we also get the sophisticated criminal who steals information to sell. Those are the ones we try to get."

Nikki watched his avid attention to the numbers on the screen. "You really enjoy this," she observed.

"This is great fun for me," he acknowledged, slanting her a glance.

Yet he wanted to be James Bond. Nikki hid a smile. She didn't think he would be pleased if she told him that the infamous legendary spy rarely sat at a desk dueling with invisible foes using strings of computer codes. She preferred her job over this one. Hers wasn't some covert game of transferring electronic files from one place to another. No wonder she couldn't solve the mystery of her files alone. She needed someone who understood this kind of warfare. She studied Erik's profile. She wondered whether he was as good as—

"Holy shit!" He stared at the screen for a few seconds. More curses followed.

"What, Erik?"

"Shadow Firewire." He tapped some commands. "I can't believe it. It's on top of us! Man, it's fast."

Nikki touched Erik on the arm. "What's firewire? What's it doing?"

"I think we've been caught," he breathed. "No way. No fucking way."

"Why are the string codes echoing each other, sir?"

"It seems we're not alone. Let me try something." Rick typed in a command. "Now we sit and watch."

"What's happening? Have we found what we're looking for?" Patty moved around the furniture to get a better view.

"No, princess. We're tracing someone's dataline. Someone's typing in the same sequence of commands and we're catching the echoes. That means there's someone else in the room."

"So we've been caught?"

"No, no, the other way around. We caught them. Sir, why are we monitoring them, anyway? Maybe it's just someone from EYES."

"Hacking into their own system and accessing the files we want with trolls and fake command strings? I don't think so." Rick sat back, frowning. "But this person knows what he's doing, though. He's very specific. Look at that—he just downloaded without even any use of hacking sequences."

"That means the person isn't using any electronic means to try to randomly find a password, princess."

"I know what it means. I have read about ATM machine robberies, stuff like that. Shouldn't we call somebody to catch this person, then? He might be one of the people on Gorman's network."

"No," Rick said. "Let's see what he's downloading first. We'll follow what he's after and take those files. It's too strange that he's here at the same time as us, don't you think?"

"Yeah, but downloading what he's after would be tricky, sir. To do it once without being caught is pretty nifty but if we repeat the same codes, it'll trigger a warning in the EYES system."

"We'll just have to be niftier, won't we? Ever use a firewire?"

"Not while hacking into the government, no, sir."

"Okay, that's not a term used in ATM robberies," Patty chimed in.

"Princess, we aren't exactly hacking into an ATM machine. It takes a lot of time to download files from someone's system, especially when that someone is our very own Uncle Sam. They have firewalls and protection circuits and . . ."

"Firewire, Patty, is a lightning fast program to download from one site to another. It's used mostly in recording CDs—music files zapped quickly from one music medium onto CD. We'll use a new tech called Shadow Firewire."

"Thank you, sir, for not giving me a lecture on computer firewalls like Agent Candeloro. So, we're firewiring, if that's a word."

"Sir, how would that keep the EYES alarms from noticing two repeated sequence?"

"Simple. We go after Mr. Know-It-All here and download all his files from *his* system."

"Wow."

"Oh wow."

"See, princess? We can agree sometimes. Ouch."

* * *

"This just isn't possible."

Erik's horrified voice told her how serious the situation was. She didn't pepper him with any more questions. Whatever was happening, it was apparently too late to do much.

He turned to face her, his face a little pale. "Nikki, whoever that was zinged us with something high speed and downloaded everything that I've just loaded into your laptop."

Nikki frowned. "I don't understand. Why would they take what they already have?"

Erik shook his head. "You don't understand. This guy is good. He trolled into my territory and stole all my files . . . and . . . whatever else you have in the hard drive, Nikki. I'm sorry. I didn't think . . . We're really up shit creek now."

"Why are the sequences repeating, sir?" Cam rubbed his eyes. "God, I feel like I'm being bombarded by evil cyber energy."

Rick squinted, trying to read the codes quickly. They were scrolling too fast, but what he caught didn't read right. "It's a deliberate signal," he finally said. "We've been caught."

Her hard drive? Nikki's frown deepened. "They downloaded everything in my laptop?"

"Yes." Erik's face had turned a bright red. "Is there anything in there that's classified?"

Her personal writing was in there. Some files. "A few," she replied slowly, "but nothing that would jeopardize national security. What's it doing now?"

"I don't understand what's happening now." He pointed at the codes in the screen. "This and this are just repetition and shouldn't be happening. I've been very careful with the download, Nikki. No one could possibly have known what I was doing, but I know for sure we've been caught."

"Well, turn the laptop off. Pull out the phone line."

"And then what?"

"We wait, and see who's caught us."

* * *

"Ummm, Cam, did I hear that we've just been caught?"

"Princess, don't worry. I'll take care of this. Why don't you go off now? Just in case EYES are sending some personnel over here."

Rick waved a hand, interrupting the two of them. "Go. Both of you. I don't need you here." He didn't feel any panic at all. He had never been caught before, but this still didn't look like any tracer program he'd ever read or played with. It looked as if it was . . . He started typing quickly. Waited. Then he repeated the same command again.

"Sir, shouldn't you just turn it off and let's get out of here?"

He shrugged. "This looks interesting."

"Interesting?" There was a scrunching sound as Cam tore open a bag of chips.

"Yes. Look. It's repeating my nonsense."

"Like it's mocking you or something! Hell, what fucking game is he playing? Shouldn't he be tracing us for downloading from his laptop?" More noisy crunching.

"No. I think this isn't our first perp." In fact, Rick was sure it wasn't. This one was of a higher caliber; he had somehow been hiding in the wings and then inserted a virus program during his download.

"I don't understand. Cam, what's happening?"

"Not sure, Patty."

Rick finally looked at them. He was surprised they hadn't run off. Being caught with him would end their careers. "Some form of troll with a virus came in with the download we were stealing, and it connected to some source online immediately. There was an immediate trace but I don't think it's from EYES. It's from whoever put the virus into that download, with a command to signal him if someone triggered something in those files. When I went in and took everything from the hacker's hard drive, there must have been a hidden virus in there." He patted the laptop. "Whatever it is, we still have the files because I loaded it into an alternate zip site that will copy them several times. Even if this virus destroys what we downloaded, it won't know about the backups."

"That's cool," Cam said. There was a sudden whirring sound. "Oh-oh. Is that destructo-virus?"

"Ye—" Rick stopped, cocked his head. Now he was truly intrigued. "No, it's transmitting a . . . fax?"

Twenty seconds. That was how fast the virus was. Suddenly there was an open window on the screen, with a YES option for saving to file.

"Holy shhh . . . sorry, princess. This is freaking amazing! Sir, are you going to accept it?"

"Yes."

It came in encrypted. It had a subject title—FYEO: time to ask some hard questions.

Patty read it aloud. "For Your Eyes Only. Sir, does that mean he knows it's you?"

"Yes." Whoever it was liked mind games. Rick decided to open it later when he was alone. "We've done what I wanted for the night. Let's look at the download quickly."

They made backups, working through late afternoon. Greta brought in some beverage and snacks before she left.

"Hell of a show, sir, being caught stealing from someone stealing from EYES! I'll get the report rewritten ASAP. Good night." Cam finished his drink.

"Bye, sir. Tomorrow I'll use that code sequence you gave me and find out whose password that is. It's safer from my office. It'll look like part of a departmental request."

"Thank you. Good night, Cam, Patty."

Rick adjusted his seating position. His rear end had died on him some time in the last hour, but he had paid scant attention to it in the midst of all the excitement. Now that it was over, with the rush of adrenaline receding, every cramped joint was protesting.

His bureaucratic butt missed the nice soft leather chair. His bureaucratic back didn't like the hard metal cabinet with its sharp corner that kept pressing into his right shoulder. His bureaucratic neck couldn't take the patience of leaning down and playing with wires and chips. They would rather do all that in his study at home, with all its high-tech toys. All this was back-to-basics, like lifting barbells after using weight machines for years.

He had chosen to do it here instead of back home for several reasons. First, he was in the mood. It was a hell of a time to choose to take his good bureaucrat jacket off, but Nikki had unknowingly provided the incentive. She wanted her past. Fine. He couldn't make her remember it herself, so he would try to get those damn files back for her.

Second, he did it out of a sense of perverse irony, like playing too close to a roaring fire. He had enjoyed himself immensely, even though someone out there had caught him at it. He knew it couldn't be EYES. They would never suspect that he was hacking into their system from the inside. Besides, he had activated his password on his own computer, starting an autosearch program that activated movement through various departments before setting up the real laptop for what he had in mind.

So who was the troll who sent him the encrypted file? Another challenge, to test whether he could break into it. Rick glanced at the time at the bottom of the screen. Nikki hadn't called him all day. He would give her another half hour and then go look for her. Meanwhile, he would play with this encryption.

It didn't take him long before he got the file to release its zipped contents. Rick stared at the screen. The surrounding boxes, scattered piles, and furniture receded from his awareness, and there was a kind of muffled silence as his brain acknowledged what he was seeing. The loud thumping must be coming from inside his head. It couldn't be his heart because it had just stopped and died.

It was a picture of a smiling Nikki on a couch. A man sat beside her, with silver eyes that stood out because of his tanned face. At their feet, a young half-Asian little girl was on the floor between them, smiling toothily.

The caption underneath read HARD QUESTIONS GIVE HARD LESSONS.

Chapter Twenty

"Where are you?" The low masculine voice coming from the speakerphone, as always, sent a warm, tingly sensation through her.

"I'm on my way to you," Nikki said as she maneuvered a left-hand turn. It was much later than she had thought, and she was surprised he had not called her all day.

"Where are you coming from?"

"I had to stop back at my apartment to pick up some things." It was an evasion, but she didn't want to talk about the day's events over the cell phone. She hesitated, then added, "That is, if you want me to go back with you?"

She had wrangled over the decision, whether to stay where she was and wait for him to tell her, or to go to him on her own. She had been alone for so long, she was afraid of letting go of what made her feel secure. Going to him meant more than just taking on a lover or a man in her life. This was Rick Harden, whom she had avoided thinking about all this time. Going to him meant giving up part of herself to be somebody else. She shook her head. To be *her*. Leah. He saw her as Leah, and she wasn't that person any longer.

There was such a prolonged pause that she thought the call had disconnected. "Rick?"

"Yes, I want you," he replied. "It's raining here, so drive carefully. Just wait for me in the car and page me when you get here. No need to get wet and go through security."

He rang off. Enigmatic as always. What did she expect? "Hi, honey, how was your day?" She smiled, then bit on her lip. There was a time he had asked that question, she was sure of it. Was their relationship back then as normal as it was tense now?

It started drizzling, then turned into a steady rain as she drove on. She went through the checkpoint that led her into employee parking and after finding an open space as close as she could, she called his beeper and waited. She left the headlights on so he would know her location. The windshield wipers went back and forth as she stared at the brightly lit entrance. It made the rest of what she could see appear darker and less recognizable.

That uneasy feeling that encompassed her every time she focused on this building gnawed at her again. It looked like any ordinary federal structure, with its lit windows where people worked late. Yet the dark shadows cast by light and reflection appeared menacing to her overactive imagination.

Again an earlier odd notion rang in her brain. *The building was sick.* How was she going to transfer that sort of reaction into proper bureaucratic wording in her report? EYES would sneer her out of the committee meeting. She wondered whether they would use her past to question her conclusions, say that she was not quite right in the head. Or maybe they would use her relationship with the O.C. of Task Force Two to undermine her objectivity.

Speaking of which, the operations chief was walking in the rain toward her. She would recognize that proud stride anywhere. The headlights put him in harsh relief against the black and gray background. As he came nearer, she could see the lines of rain falling hard on him.

He opened the passenger door and climbed in. The interior lights caught the harsh planes of his face. The flash of green eyes with wet eyelashes. Then the door slammed shut and the streetlight nearby muted all the colors. It didn't lessen the tempo of her heartbeat at the sight and smell of him.

"You should have told me you didn't have a raincoat or umbrella," she said.

In answer, he turned and reached for her. His kiss was hard, bruising her lips. His hand held the back of her head firmly as his tongue swept into her mouth. He tasted of the storm. He kissed with the same ferocity of one, leaving her breathless.

Lifting his head, he raked fingers through his rain-darkened hair, shaking drops of water onto the seats. "I didn't want you to turn around to get me one."

He drew her closer still, uncaring that his wet clothes were damping her dry ones. The dark interior of the car reminded her of how good he was in small spaces, and her body quivered at his possessive marking. Her lips. Her breasts. Every part of her responded at his touch.

"You didn't call me and I wasn't sure whether I . . ." She wished she could see his expression, tell what kind of mood he was in. She whispered, "This isn't easy for me."

"We haven't had time to talk," he agreed, "but you're still coming home with me."

There was an edge to his voice that suggested he wasn't willing to compromise on this one point. "You can't expect me to just move in and continue like nothing is happening. We're already arguing over what we want to do—this morning, and now."

His thumbnail caressed her pulse, an oddly possessive gesture, as if he wanted to unnerve her. His voice dropped an octave. "I know how to stop your arguing."

His lips hovered inches above, his heated breath mingling with hers. She inhaled the musky scent of man and ozone, suddenly aware that there was a storm brewing that had nothing to do with the weather outside.

Pulling slightly away, she said, "You can't use sex for everything, Rick." Her voice came out breathless. It was too easy to think of Rick and sex.

His hold on her neck tightened. Then, as if he changed his mind, he released her. He leaned over and fastened her seat belt. Her breath caught where his hand touched her hip, as it provocatively slid down her inner thigh, evoking memories from a certain night. She eyed him warily as he paused. He moved, fastened his seat belt, and placed his hand back where it had been. That whole leg seemed hotter than the rest of her body.

"Let's go home, darling. It's late," he said, in that dark, edgy tone.

As she started the car, shifting gears, she was very aware of that hand resting firmly on her leg. Another possessive gesture.

Rick studied her for a few seconds. *Ask her*. "So, tell me about your day," he continued.

"I found some things that might help me," she told him guardedly.

"Good," he said. She was nervous, probably gauging how much to tell him of what had happened today.

Ask her. Or maybe he should tell her. Tell her that it was he who had snatched the files from her laptop today. He knew now that it belonged to her.

He was supposed to start working on the encrypted files downloaded from EYES. Instead, that faxed photo had sidetracked him. He had started reading the contents of the other files, and there could be no mistaking the owner. A romance manuscript. A file documenting departmental duties and security stopgaps. And lastly, the second most painful discovery of all—his own file, dated almost nine years ago. Nine years. She had known about him for nine years. And instead of contacting him, she had—

That photo in his laptop burned a hole in his brain. *Ask her*.

"I have several encrypted files for you to look at."

"How did you get them?" he asked casually. He felt her thigh tense under his hand.

"It's better that you don't know," she replied carefully. "Your job is still at stake, and if they questioned you—"

Was she trying to protect him? The old doubts resurfaced. After all, she read his files without permission before she went on that ill-fated operation. For whom? He had spent all this time trying to find out the truth, to prove that his doubts were wrong, but now he feared that maybe, just maybe—no. Leah loved him. She would never have tried to hurt him in any way. But who was the man with her, and what had she been doing with him all these years *when she knew where he was?*

Ask her.

"Yes, of course, you're right. What I don't know can't hurt me." Her leg tensed like a coiled spring and she inadvertently stepped hard on the gas pedal, speeding up the car jerkily. He gave her a light squeeze, bringing her attention back. "What's wrong?"

Nikki swallowed hard. "Nothing. Your hand distracted me."

She kept her eyes on the road, refusing to glance in his direction. She wasn't lying, not really. She couldn't think properly when she knew how intimately close his hand was. His fingers curled possessively every time she changed gears, subtly caressing the inside of her thighs. The thin layer of clothing she had on didn't check the warm curling heat gathering and tightening in her.

Those words. That was what she heard this afternoon. *What he doesn't know can't hurt him.* Had she said that? When and why?

"What else distracted you?"

He was sure she was lying. That nervous flick of her tongue betrayed her. The slight trembling of her leg betrayed her. She didn't want him to know something. But then she didn't want him to know lots of things about her. He frowned, recalling what he'd said—*What I don't know can't hurt me.* Was she thinking of that man in the picture? And the child? He smiled grimly in the dark. *Ask her.*

He turned to study her profile. He wasn't sure whether he wanted to hear that she had made another life with another man. His chest tightened up and the questions burned with agonizing echoes.

At the next stoplight, slowly, deliberately, he slipped his hand between her legs. She gave a soft gasp and lurched forward. She finally darted him a glance, her eyes wide—yes, there was desire there. He pulled on her zipper. Hands on the steering wheel, she stared back helplessly, a small sound escaping her lips when he slipped his hand inside.

She was already wet. He stroked her with his finger. She gasped again, and that coiled anger in him formed into a solid determined ball. It didn't matter about that photo. Tonight he would make her tell him she was his. He would make her answer his questions.

"The light's green," he told her softly. "Drive slowly."

He opened a sensual world that went beyond what Nikki had ever experienced. At least in her limited new life. Where once, just the thought of growing comfortable with touching and being touched was an ambitious goal, she found herself yearning for Rick, and Rick alone. His touch melted the cold corners of her awareness where she had always feared to tread.

She quivered with both need and vulnerability. Part of her couldn't believe this was happening. He could have her anywhere and she couldn't deny him.

Here in the car, as he teased her at every traffic light. Red, and her heart beat in anticipation at what that hand was going to do when she braked. Green, and her whole being protested as he ordered her to start driving again.

This couldn't be her, Nikki Taylor, who had sworn to be the mistress of her own fate. No, this was Leah Harden, greedily forcing her identity back into her psyche. And she couldn't fight herself and the sensual journey Rick was initiating. There was another red light ahead. Her lips parted, her lower body tensing up. It was sheer torture as the car slowed down . . . and her body started up. He controlled her desire all the way to his place, and she let him.

No, she couldn't deny him. He turned her on like no other man.

Here in his bed as her wet clothes melted off her body like magic. Dark magic. He kissed her from head to foot as she lay there on his big bed, waiting, waiting for him to finish what he'd started.

"Are you still afraid?" she heard him ask.

She stared into his green eyes and saw her hunger reflected in them. "A little."

"Tell me what they did to you."

Caught by surprise at his question, she jolted up, but he easily stopped her with a kiss, pushing her back against the soft pillows. He tasted of the storm outside—wild and demanding. She almost forgot his query when he reached down and resumed her sensual climb to oblivion. He bit her earlobe and her head lolled to one side submissively as his teeth found the most sensitive spot in the hollow of her neck. She moaned softly.

"Tell me," he insisted in that dark, edgy voice. "Tell me what haunts you, Nikki."

She shook her head but realized now that there was no escape from his lips, his hands, his steely determination to get what he wanted. He sucked on her breast as those fingers between her legs urged her higher. Release was so close. He paused.

"I . . . was tied down at first but they didn't need to after a while," she whispered, desperate for his touch. He nibbled his way back to her lips. "They called me names. Hurt me. They laughed. Rick, don't make me go on."

She didn't want to say out loud what her body had suffered. Seeing it in her head was enough. Still having nightmares was enough.

"Like this?"

He tugged one of her arms above her and tied it to the bedpost with one quick twist. Just one hand. His eyes never left hers as he slowly moved down and put his mouth between her legs. "Like this?" he repeated softly.

Dear Lord. No, not like that. She gave him a strangled reply and arched up against his teasing tongue. He stopped the torture, nibbling the soft flesh of her inner thigh as she waited . . . waited . . .

He climbed back over her, took her free hand and put it over his hard erection. "Put me inside you, Nikki," he rasped out.

He was doing something to her fears, changing that hated emotion to raw desire. How could she like this situation? She should be afraid—she shouldn't like being tied up, held down. But he gave her his most vulnerable part to control. It was hot and heavy in her hand and she owned it. She squeezed him tightly. He hummed with approval, waiting for her to do as he wanted.

It was a matter of taking control. She guided him to her heat and he nudged her open and slowly took over her willing body. He removed her free hand, lacing his fingers through hers as he pushed deeper. She welcomed him eagerly, her whole being centered where they were joined. He felt so good.

"Like this?"

"No." He was dissolving all her ghosts. Those faces filled with ugly lust and those cruel hands. The pain of being forcibly taken. The humiliation of being nothing more than flesh. There was only Rick right now. The scent of Rick. The taste of Rick. And this sense of belonging. The force of his hips pushed her whole body up, sliding over the dampened bedsheets . . . and suddenly the room plunged into darkness.

He'd turned off the lights. Still embedded in her, he stretched out her remaining free arm over her head and secured it like the other. Her breathing quickened.

"Turn on the light." In the dark and being tied. This was too close to her nightmares.

He didn't comply. Instead he started to glide in and out of her in a slow rhythm. "How long did they leave you tied up?"

He tilted her hips, placing a pillow under her, and he was thicker and longer in this position. His rhythm was steady, a slow tortuous dance of entering and withdrawing. It also left his hands free, to do as he pleased. He reached down and parted her, exposing the little bud. She waited for his touch.

"How long?"

"Please . . ." She wanted him to go faster as she wrapped her legs around him tightly. But his hand wasn't moving. He was waiting for her answer. "Hours."

Too late, she realized what he meant to do, where his

questions were leading, and she started to tell him that she was afraid, but could only cry out his name. His finger. It was stroking her, using her wetness ruthlessly to turn her protest into cries of pleasure as she peaked. Up, up. And his long finger skimmed back down. He kept that slow tempo, drawing her climax out, and the ecstasy was so long and so hard, she forgot what she wanted to say.

He slid out of her and parted her legs wide for another invasion. His mouth. His skillful tongue tasting her, pressing hard against her already sensitized nub. The sensual assault was too much. She started to scream his name in the dark.

No, no, she didn't scream his name. She mustn't. Not ever. They would torture her some more just to know more about him. No, never scream his name.

She sucked in long breaths, hearing her racing heart, trying to understand her flashback. Felt him moving lower. He tied her parted legs. She was now spread-eagle.

"Like this?"

She understood what was coming next. "Don't leave me," she implored, too exhausted to move.

"I'll never leave you, Nikki. I've never left you." She felt his damp muscular chest against her breasts as he pressed soft kisses on her lips. Caught the musky scent of desire as he entered her again. "You're mine. Tell me you're mine."

She couldn't deny him anything. Not when he possessed her soul as he took her. Not when she knew he was trying to help her forget. "I'm yours."

"Say it again," he ground out.

"I'm yours."

He came violently, calling her name between clenched teeth, rubbing his scent on her body, pouring into her.

"Mine, mine, mine." He continued climaxing and then dropped down, breathing harshly.

Nikki closed her eyes, savoring his weight, loving the feel of him still inside her. After a few minutes—an eternity—he slowly shifted, still pushing deeply inside, as he propped up on one elbow. She responded eagerly, gripping his length possessively, not willing to let him go. How could she still want him so? She heard a drawer open and whimpered an objection as his hardness glided out of her.

"Shhhh." His fingers found her nub again.

It wasn't over. There was more. Very, very gently, she felt a slow invasion as his fingers entered and explored. Very, very gently, he stroked, and she shivered in delight as he found a particular spot. A vibration started.

"Oh!" Nikki arched up, but she was tied. "Oh!"

"I'll make dinner, then I'll be back," he whispered in her ear, and his weight left the bed.

Alone. Tied up. In the dark. *She can't call out his name.*

"I'm not leaving you. Think of me coming back for you, darling."

He tugged something down there. Molten heat exploded into bright flaming stars. A moan escaped her lips as waves of incredible sensation took over her mind. She felt that tugging again. Then he placed a long hard kiss on her clitoris.

"Rick! Rick!" She forgot her fears, called his name. There was only his scent. His memory. And intense pleasure.

Chapter Twenty-one

Truth. That was all Rick ever wanted out of life. It was the kind of sarcastic credo he liked to use in moments of despair. He lived in a gray world and expected truth. How utterly ironic.

He expelled a harsh breath as he slowly closed the bedroom door. He couldn't afford to be gentle with her any longer. That photo in his laptop was the last straw. He was aware of how unfair it was to expect Nikki to be alone all this time, but damn it, he had the right to the truth. She wouldn't—or couldn't—tell him. He *would* make her. Right now, he couldn't bear to have her gone again. Right now, he couldn't bear to live another lie.

What right did she have to return into his life just to use him as a tool to find her missing files? It was obvious now that he was a means, and not an end. Someone had sent her back to him and she was a willing accomplice, not because she wanted her husband back, but because she was promised those damn files.

That hurt. It hurt so damn much he couldn't even focus on those downloaded files he had stolen for her. That photo, with the man and child, embodied everything he had lost, *and she had been living it*. She had a life with that man—it was there clear as day. And the little girl—Rick closed his eyes—she was the biggest betrayal of all.

A soft moan broke through his bitter reverie and he resisted the urge to rush in there, though he couldn't seem to leave her alone. He stood out here, listening, making sure she was all right. His lips twisted. Oh, she was definitely all right, because he was an expert in this and he knew her body better than she did. Theirs had been an intensely sexual relationship. *So why couldn't she remember him?*

The man with the light eyes—how well did he *know* her? Rick angrily turned from the room and stood on top of the small landing. His hand clenched, unclenched. He just couldn't seem to walk away and leave her in there. He was a fool.

She had been all he had.

He stared broodingly down the stairway, torturing himself with what she had been doing for ten years without him. All he could think about was the fact that she had knowledge of him all along. He curled one hand on the banister at the unexpected pain that slashed at him. All that time, when he had no knowledge of her, he had been *looking* for her. A missing loved one was a devastating experience he wouldn't wish on anyone. Even getting her remains back would have meant something.

He had been ready to give up before Nikki had suddenly appeared; she became a lightning rod to a new life. How wrong he had been. A soft brittle laugh welled up. What did he expect? That suddenly, after a decade, he could simply don a white hat, and everything would morph back to the way it was? She came home for a reason, and it wasn't for her lost love. He wanted to spit at the word.

What an utter fool, to even harbor any hope that he could turn his life around. He was now another man, doing things he had once abhorred. He grimaced. No matter what, he was still good at one thing—the continual need to expose every layer of those around him until there was nothing but the truth. This one skill had stayed with him.

Hard-On. There was no turning back. He didn't get that name because he was an easygoing guy. A compliment from the women and an insult from colleagues, it was still his core, what he was under all these layers. A prick had no other agenda other than to satisfy his own needs.

His agenda had always been the truth, and truth had no emotion. He forced all feelings out. Time to go back in there and do what she had set him up to do. Peel her layers. Expose her for what she was. He never had any intention of leaving her in there for hours. The power of suggestion was meant to prolong an emotion, and fear was the key here. This was the trigger-point in psycho-imprintment, a deliberate push at the psyche.

Through the crack, he heard her call out his name and stood frozen, his hand against the door panel, for what seemed like an eternity. Every muscle bunched into knots as a cold tingle went down his spine. He hadn't heard those purrs in a long, long time. Every nerve in his body lit up, as if someone had thrown on a switch.

Dear God. It was Leah calling him. It was Leah's deep-throated moans he was hearing. So dearly familiar, and yet—

Enhanced pleasure was like entering a different level of consciousness. There was a point in the throes of passion when a person couldn't control body and mind, when she became totally focused inside, and it was what was hidden inside Nikki that Rick hoped to release.

And yet—his search for the truth might come up with something he wasn't prepared to face. He didn't want Nikki to just remember facts and figures of her past. He wanted her to remember their lives together with the same emotional depth as before. Without it, he couldn't reach her, couldn't get her to tell him the truth.

It just wasn't enough.

The chemistry was still there, so palpable that it left him craving for more. Her body recognized his, and she had even admitted as much, that being with him had awakened powerful, emotional revelations that had shaken her.

Well, he was shaken, too. Having her back in his arms was heaven and hell. She was here, and she wasn't. She had no memory of how it had been between them. It was strange how one could have one's wish granted, but it wasn't quite the same anyhow.

A prolonged session of pleasure. And a miracle. He could

easily provide the former, but he had ceased to believe in the latter happening. He stood there in the dark, in *his darkness*, wondering if truth was really worth the pain sawing through his gut.

"Rick!"

He switched on the light, adjusting it to a soft glow. His nostrils flared at her scent. His pulse raced at the sight of her lying there, the pillow beneath her pushing her hips up provocatively. Part of her face and body were covered by her beautiful hair.

Rick swallowed hard. *My God. She looked like that in his nightmares.* Lowering down onto the bed, he slowly combed the long, thick strands away. His heart thundered. Everything seemed to be in slow motion.

Nikki's face was radiant, her lips parted, her eyes dreamy and half-closed. She purred at his touch, tossing her head back. He turned off her source of pleasure, loosening the ties, and she stretched like a cat.

"Love me," she whispered.

Leaning closer, Rick stared down at her. Fascination and dread tugged at him. Every sigh, every low moan, was an echo of his dream. His ghost was alive.

"Love me," she repeated, moving sinuously against his hand. "You promised to come back and love me."

"Leah?" he queried in the softest of whispers.

Her eyes opened wide. Tears of frustration shimmered in them. "It's Nikki." Reaching up, she dragged his face down and kissed his lips with an ardency that was Leah's. Even though he didn't want to, Rick pulled back. He studied her face, searching for clues. She tugged at him. "What's the matter? Don't you want me?"

"I do," he told her softly.

"But you want her more."

He wanted his wife back, but it wasn't the time to explain. She was disoriented by what she was remembering, and he needed to push her. Those dark eyes stared up accusingly. Like the beautiful ghost of his past, they held secrets from him.

"She is you, Leah," he said deliberately.

She shook her head violently, her tangled hair falling heavily over his arm. He looked down, spellbound at the way it imitated those dreams.

Unable to stop himself, he repeated the same words burned into his brain. "Liar."

But unlike his dream, she didn't laugh. Her tears flowed freely and she emitted a tiny sob before biting her lip. He clamped down on his traitorous emotions, refusing to give in. "Liar," he told her softly. He had to push her hot buttons. "And yes, I want Leah more."

"What about me? Nikki, not her. You lied to me," she said, still crying. "You told me it didn't matter."

It was like reading off a script. He had repeated the same lines over and over whenever he had that nightmare, except that he was now saying it with an entirely different meaning. "You're the one who lied to me. You betrayed me. Don't hide anymore."

Her whole body stiffened and her face mirrored her shock. She closed her eyes for an instant. When they re-opened, the sultry expression in them made him shiver.

"Then love me. Now." She was insistent, hands and feet staking their claim on his body.

This was totally unexpected. She looked like Nikki and demanded like Leah. It was hard to resist a dream that had somehow invaded his reality. He ran an exploring hand down her silky body, half expecting to wake up from this tangled mess. Instead her hand covered his and pushed it between her legs.

She was wet. She arched up wildly, greedily. Just like in the dreams, she wanted sex. Wanted him to take her. His own desire clamored against his will, seeking fulfillment. He never took her in those dreams. He would push her away and she always ended up dead.

She whimpered as he slid his fingers inside her. She was hot, so hot. And she was very, very alive. He could barely think above the roaring in his head as she climaxed, her sensitive channel needing no further coaxing.

"Who are you?" he demanded hoarsely, desperate to end this. This wasn't part of the dream. He would have woken up by now, with that dead emptiness nestling inside. More than anything, he wanted to thrust into her moist heat, to feel again that rush of happiness, but he ruthlessly forced himself to be still.

But this wasn't Nikki. This was his Leah, the aggressive minx who knew his body too well. She reached down and grabbed him in urgent demand, her focus only on what she needed at that moment. Then she squeezed tightly, sending him into overdrive.

He jerked away, trying to put on the brakes before he gave in to the rapacious hunger growing like wildfire, but she held on possessively. Her hand was slick from her own heat, and she traveled up and down his length with a knowing rhythm. The rush of pure male desire was almost too painful to bear, and he shuddered in her grasp.

"Please," she pleaded, as if he wasn't the one at her mercy at the moment.

He couldn't resist her, but he hadn't done this to her to satisfy his own unruly hunger. He was this close to pushing her over, to getting her to tell him the truth. He wanted to laugh out loud. It was that stupid irony thing again. Sure he had her under control, but he damn sure seemed to be lacking it.

"Rick!" she breathed out, her frustration vented out in his name. "Can't we talk later?"

She sighed in welcome relief when he acquiesced and climbed over her yielding softness. Any thought of control disappeared as she guided him impatiently. Heaven surrounded him in a hot and dark sensual haze, filling that gaping hole in his soul. He groaned at the exquisite feel of her. He didn't need her to tell him who she was. He knew. *Because he belonged to her.*

Her hands smoothed down his back, urging him to lower his weight onto her. He did so. She wrapped her legs around him, cloaked him with the silky softness of her long hair, murmuring his name over and over.

"Love me, love me."

With a groan, he did so. Unlike his nightmares, she didn't laugh at him, and he didn't call her traitor. She rose up to meet his every plunge, and it was Leah's voice that urged him on. Just then, she tilted her hips a certain way that took both their breaths away. He stopped, buried deeply, their bodies molded together. Her eyes were closed but she had the expression of a woman discovering nirvana. She dug her heels into his back and swiveled her hips again. He heard his grunt along with her gasp of delight.

Her eyes flung open and fear flickered amid the smoldering heat. "Oh my God, Rick."

He understood. He had taught her that little trick eons ago, and she had done this out of instinct and *memory*. That was the trigger point setting free both mind and body. Nikki was in the throes of a flashback. Her nails dug into his flesh and she gasped out incoherent words, but it was too late to talk. Dragging her hips higher than the pillow propping her up, he proceeded with the rest of the lesson from long ago. Her climax was long and violent, and Rick closed his eyes as he, too, let go. This was no dream. His ghost had disappeared; his wife was really, really here, and he poured everything—dreams, hopes, doubts, anger—into her.

Later. Later they would talk. And he would check his hands to see whether they were bloody, just to make sure he hadn't been dreaming.

Who was this woman whispering earthy suggestions to her lover? It had to be a stranger doing this—no, it was *she*—but that wasn't possible. She didn't know a man's pleasure would be enhanced if she did this to him. She didn't know a thing about ancient *tantric* breathing techniques. This woman wasn't she, this stranger who was attacking sexual pleasure like it was a magnificent feast.

She was Nikki Taylor, a self-made person who strove for balance and control in her life as a way to banish those dark memories. Not this wild creature that couldn't get enough of this one man who had the ability to take her where she dared not tread.

Beware the center.

Therein lay the painful truth. Her center, her *chuung*, was lost amid the clanging lies, and her fear was just an excuse not to go further. Every time she came close, a part of her ran away. It was easier to drift along in her new persona.

She came home to seek her *chuung* and found that centered on one man. He was now relentlessly pushing her toward that dreaded point where she always turned back. Familiar fear swamped her, trying to halt what was happening, but she couldn't stop his persuasive hands and lips. He was taking over her mind and body, demanding a price for the pleasure he promised. The few minutes she'd managed to break free and not give in didn't last long.

"Traitor, you lied."

His accusation was unacceptable, and she sought to regain some sort of control but her body was busy betraying her. The stranger in her was some sexual beast, wanting more. No, no, this wasn't she.

"Oh my God, Rick."

A host of images fanned out like playing cards in her mind and it was easier to escape by giving in to the pleasure. She was totally out of control. Out of balance. All her senses reeled as she embraced the loving and recoiled from the horror all at once.

With a muffled cry, Nikki gave in. Leah Harden rose like a phoenix from the ashes in her center and took charge. Her husband. Her lover. And how long that had been.

Beware the frozen heart.

There was no stopping the greed of this woman's boiling hunger for her husband, and too late, Nikki understood what price she had to pay. She was always hungry for food, ignoring her heart. Now the woman she had been, after being buried in some dark recess for so long, had been set free. This was Leah, and like some possessing entity, she was making herself known. She was no Nikki Taylor, timid and frigid, forever frozen in fear. Leah was hot and lusty, and very intent on reclaiming her husband. No made-up persona was going to stop her. She also brought with her all her memory intact—

of things done to her, of all the hours of torture and pain, and of what she had done.

Nikki could only hold on to Rick. Her head was spinning, as if some pressure valve had been released. Her body radiated with pure pleasure even as her mind screamed at the sensory overload. And her heart was bursting from the weight of both pleasure and pain.

Feed the hungry ghosts.

She was doing things that she hadn't even known she liked, climbing over her husband like a rampaging Valkyrie, using her hair to seduce him, knowing instinctively that he loved it. That she could tie this man in knots. That she knew how and where he wanted to be touched.

He lay on his back, watching her with eyes that glittered with suppressed emotion. They had darkened into a deep jade green, the color that she had yearned to see while she lived in total darkness, that rich green that couldn't escape her memory, even though she didn't know it was her husband she was missing. In her despair, she just knew that color was important to her life and she had prayed to look at something green again. Her first source of pleasure had been the blade of grass she managed to get her hands on, and when she was finally freed, it was the dark, rich tones of the trees that had called to her.

She had been looking for her husband's eyes. He was the ghost in her past, hungry for the truth. All her grandmother's prophecies had finally come about. Now she understood.

"I don't follow, grandmother."

"Of course not. All of you are still alive. Wait till you've lost your center. Wait till the fire melts the frozen heart. Then you will find many ghosts to appease."

Her tears plopped onto his chest as she kissed her way up his neck, and she rained urgent and desperate kisses up the side of his face, on his cheeks and eyes, trying to communicate all she was feeling without the pain of words. He suddenly tasted so familiar that she started crying harder. How could she not remember this? How had she been able to live without him?

She'd betrayed Rick. The growing horror inside threatened to spill out, as Nikki cried for all they had lost. They had both suffered so much, kept apart by circumstance beyond their control. Running her hands down his broad slick back, she reveled in the play of muscles as he shuddered and climaxed. He hugged her to him, their limbs tangling with the sheets. She still couldn't believe that she didn't miss pleasure like this. She had walked around half alive, unable to grasp what was missing. Everything was so clear now.

"There was no other choice when I was taken prisoner. I had to shut you off—you must understand that," she began, as she kept caressing his back. She kneaded at the sudden tension under her fingers. "They were questioning and questioning. When no rescue was coming, they didn't need to be nice about it any longer. Someone had betrayed the operation. They knew our logistics and how many of us there were. They singled out the few who had the most senior ranks—I knew they would show no mercy to get what they wanted—names, dates, places."

"Continue." She couldn't see his expression. She tried to look up but her hair was in the way. He didn't move; instead, he tucked her under his chin, shifting enough weight off her so she could turn into his warmth.

Pleasure could be a double-edged sword. There were other things tumbling through her mind that had nothing to do with the gentle lapping waves of satiated comfort coursing through her. Normally, she would curl into a ball and try to block out the images. Yet, in Rick's arms, with him still in her, her body still quivering with tiny sparks of pleasure—she found herself able to deal with those dark memories. She could hear his strong beating heart as its rhythm steadied back to normal, and she placed a kiss there on his chest. She was going to need all his strength. Closing her eyes, she began.

Her whispered tale tore Rick to pieces, but he didn't stop her. This was Leah telling him how she had mentally resigned herself to be used by other men. This was his wife revealing how she had silently bid goodbye when she saw the drugs they were administering. They had been trained to resist drugs used to induce information. Alternate reality became her truth as a means to survive—she was safe as long as she didn't tell them everything. Now he had forced her to remember it all.

"Rick," she called him back to the present. "They aren't hurting me anymore."

She shook her head and he realized that he had taken fistfuls of her hair while she was relaying her tale. He immediately released them. When she looked up at him, her eyes were darkened pools, and he wished he could forever chase away her pain.

"They cut your beautiful hair."

"The first thing is to take away your identity, you know that."

It didn't matter that he knew the aspects of breaking a person and making him talk. Somebody broke his wife. Somebody took away *his* life. Somebody was going to pay.

"They took more than that."

The lethal quietness in his voice sent chills through her. Something wild lurked in his green eyes that reminded her of a caged wild animal she once saw. It had been biding its time, waiting for someone to open the door. She had asked about it because she hated the idea of something so proud in captivity. They shot animals like that, she was told, because it was only a matter of time before they turned on their masters.

"I only want my files back, Rick. I wanted them to acknowledge they did this to me." Suddenly she feared for his safety. "Somebody already killed Denise. Don't make them come after you, too."

He lifted his hand and stared at it for a long time. "You know, if I had strung her along a little longer, she might be alive today."

"She was going to double-cross Gorman," she reminded him. "There was nothing you could have done, Rick."

He shook his head. "Not Gorman. The list has some bigger names. The only thing saving those people from discovery is for EYES to find it before we do, and—" He stopped.

"And?" She watched as he worked his jaw. The green in

his eyes deepened into a glittering dark jade. She could feel the muscles in his body tightening; her wild animal was braced for an attack.

"And the fact that you haven't told me the truth." His breath came out in a harsh rush.

She had to tell him herself. Rick couldn't bring up the incident because it was crucial to see things from her point of view. If she omitted any part, then either she was lying or something was not the way it seemed. It was going to be her truth and he would hear it first.

"If I tell you that what I did back then, I did out of the foolish notion that it would save you from EYES, would you believe me?"

Her voice held uncertainty and a hint of self-loathing, and he tightened his hold on her for a second. He understood both emotions too well. "Yes." She hiccupped a couple of times. Rick wished to let her sleep, but he couldn't. The barrier was down. He sought to encourage her to talk. "I love you, Nikki."

The words were equal to a magic spell releasing him from some enchanted imprisonment. Peace as he hadn't known in ages spread like a cool mist inside. He inhaled, welcoming the lightness of being. It was easier to say it now that she remembered. He didn't feel comfortable before because she had thought herself two different women, and he loved the same one. In response, she began crying against his chest again, harder than before.

"Oh Rick, I never meant to hurt you in any way. I don't understand why it made sense then, but I thought . . ." She paused to catch her breath as her hiccups continued. "I just thought I could explain when I got back . . ."

Of course, she never did come back. Nikki couldn't stop the flow of tears, grieving for so much lost for so long. In spite of all this, he said he loved her. It was humbling. He had steadfastly continued to search while she hadn't lifted a finger to help herself. She had done him so much wrong. Would he forgive her if he knew the whole truth? That she hadn't even wanted to return for fear of being rejected? That she had preferred to live life without the pain?

"Don't cry, baby. It's over."

"No, it's not," she sobbed. She was a coward, running away from everything. "It's not over. Look at me. I'm not the same person you loved and I don't think I can ever be. I'm not as strong as you think I am."

"No, you look at me." He forced her to meet his eyes. He gently wiped away her tears. "You're a survivor. You're still the same person inside, Nikki. Many would have been broken by your experience, but instead you rebuilt your life."

Without me, he wanted to say. That was still too painful to accept but he must try to see things from her perspective.

"I lost you. What good is surviving when I chose to sacrifice the best part of my life?"

Her continued crying broke his heart. There was nothing to say because he had been dying without her, too. "I know, baby. Losing you was like having a limb torn off but it was worse because you were just missing. Everything was relayed to me from another party and as time went by, I couldn't trust their version anymore, especially Gorman's."

She stiffened at his name. "How can one man be responsible for so much pain for so long and not get caught?" she wondered.

"What do you mean?"

She sniffed and wiped her eyes with a hand. "God, it's been so long and now I see it like it happened yesterday. Do you remember how it was back then, Rick?"

"The two of us were very happy. We made love every day. I was going to make more money so we could start a family."

"Stop right there. The last part. How were you going to make more money?"

Rick drew himself up, propping a pillow against the backboard before settling her against him comfortably. "I was different back then, Nikki," he answered, trying to see where she was leading him. "We had these big plans." All dust. All ruin.

"One of them was to get promoted."

"Yes."

"Your chief rival was Gorman."

"He was on my team and yes, I knew he was one of the top candidates." He didn't like him then, either. There was something about Gorman that was too smooth, but he had been a good asset to the agency and they had worked together a couple of times.

"Rick, two weeks before my assignment, I accidentally heard Gorman on the phone with someone. I was checking up some data in the library and there was someone talking softly back there where I knew few went. I got closer and overheard most of the conversation. He was talking about you, reporting on your activities."

"Jesus." Why didn't she tell him then?

"He said the sting operation wouldn't have worked because you were a"—Nikki closed her eyes, remembering the scene vividly now—"because you were a 'careful bastard in spite of acting rashly when it came to regulations."

Rick recalled that as his reputation back then. "I was under fire a lot because I didn't follow some of their damn red tape." He ran weary fingers through his hair. "I was a far cry from what I am today, Nikki. I ignored so many warnings, I thought there was no way I could even compete with Gorman for the promotion."

"Yet someone nominated you as one of the top two. Gorman was the other."

"Yes, he got the promotion too, not long after." History sometimes tasted strangely bitter. He left unsaid that the black mark against him was the death knell to any sort of career with EYES. He was demoted to a desk job until Gorman was promoted again a few years later, as deputy chief director of Task Force Two. Gorman had picked him, of all people, to be his operations chief, and Rick had seen it as a way out of EYES and a way to work up the bureaucrat ladder to find out what had happened to the disastrous operation.

There was a pause, and even though more questions arose, Rick let her sift through her mind as she connected the past with the present. He had waited ten long years. A few more minutes didn't matter.

"I heard enough to know that he was planning with someone higher up with access to your personal files, and that they were coordinating some kind of sting operation against you. The setup wasn't clear but it had to do with your last case." She sat up, her eyes darting restlessly as she stared into space. Frowning, she bit her lower lip as she gathered her long hair in a bunch and began braiding it.

The gesture was so familiar that Rick had to stop himself from pulling her back into his arms. Leah used to braid her hair when she had something on her mind. He lay there watching Nikki, absorbing the picture of her naked in his bed, her fingers busy, her brow puckered as she brooded. He reached out to stroke the top of the braid, and she smiled at him tremulously.

"I can't remember what your last operation was," she told him.

It was now his turn to sift through his memory. "The one they were referring to probably had to do with the big stink I raised over losing the foreign asset assignment. I was so angry they didn't pick him up immediately. I broke a few rules, didn't get the right paperwork done, and when they threatened to censure me, I countered with information against those who falsified red tape. I told EYES I would expose their little network of lies." Rick shrugged. He was younger then, very sure of himself and his ability to escape any situation. "I had no intention of doing that, of course, since that involved months of paperwork, but it was a good way to get them off my back. That's why I didn't understand how I was even considered for that promotion, seeing that I just raised their hackles up with my wonderful tact."

Seeing her almost finishing her task, Rick opened the bedside drawer and pulled out the silk purse she had brought on her first visit. He had opened it that night after he'd let her go. It contained her hair ties. "Let me," he said softly. She scooted closer as he drew out the ties. "Do you remember me playing with your hair?"

"Yes," she replied just as softly, and blushed. "But you always took too long."

"I missed the little things the most." Rick played with the braid with sure hands. "Like watching you comb your hair at night. Tying it for you. Waking up with you in my arms."

He wanted her to admit that back to him, too, but of course she hadn't missed any of that the way he had. But she was here now, and he ought to be satisfied.

"Tell me the rest," he urged, abruptly interrupting the direction of his thoughts.

Nikki closed her eyes. It was like watching a mini movie in her head, with herself as the main actress. Not any different from the way she plotted her novels, she mused. Except that her heroines never faltered as she did. Or allowed themselves to be used as pawns.

"I did the worst thing possible in that situation. I went to EYES to report this obvious corruption of the promotion process." She opened her eyes and laughed hollowly. "I thought, 'Internal Investigations will take care of this person who is trying to influence the board.' They told me to keep it quiet while they checked it out. A few days went by. You didn't say anything. No one said anything. I was so frustrated."

"Why didn't you tell me then what happened?"

"I knew you would go and confront Gorman," she replied, misery swelling in her chest. "If there was an active investigation, and with another altercation on your record you would be censured. I wanted a fair review of both your records, and I thought I could do it the right way, the way they wanted you to do things—through red tape."

Rick pulled the tie into a bow. He wounded the thick braid around his hand several times, slowly pulling her close. "There is no record of the complaint," he told her quietly.

She had to lean over him to keep her balance. "I know that, too. After a week of silence, I couldn't bear it any longer, so I checked with several sources. They never saw anything passed through their departments."

"And?" he prompted. He needed her to explain the most important thing of all.

She sighed and planted a kiss on his lips. "I committed the second stupid act after that."

He pulled at her braid, and she gave in and landed on top of him, her body fitting against his male contour. "And?"

"I . . . drugged . . . you." Her eyes were haunted, miserable. "While we made love the night before the assignment. I downloaded some files from Gorman's computer into a disk and then transferred it to your link. I didn't have time to look through them to see what they were investigating, and I didn't want to make waves for you. I thought once I found out what they were up to, then I'd also find out why they were ignoring my complaint. But with the assignment coming up, I barely had time. So I . . . drugged you."

Chapter Twenty-two

*S*he didn't betray him.

Rick had bet his life and career on the fact. He had lied to cover up for her because he believed that ultimately, the truth would prove her innocence. Yet sometimes, deep at night, doubt had crept in and nibbled at his determination. He had even dreamed of killing her often, because he felt betrayed by everything.

Not anymore.

The morning air had the crisp freshness of days when nature encouraged one to take the day off. So he did. He had no current duties at the task force anyhow. What he had were encrypted files that were best deciphered in the privacy of his study.

"Come on, slow poke."

Rick looked ahead as he jogged on the trail. A smile tugged at the corners of his mouth. First things first. He felt strong as a horse, light as mountain air, and giddy as a drunken teenager. And all because the woman he loved was beckoning to him with a grin that radiated mischief and seduction.

"You're on a bicycle," he pointed out as he advanced toward her at the side of the path. "It's a little sadistic, don't you think, to ride fast ahead for a quarter of a mile and then yell obscenities at your husband for not keeping up on foot?"

"You're the one who wanted to do this ungodly exercise," Nikki called back as she tapped one foot impatiently. "I didn't want to get out of bed."

True. He was the one who wanted to jog. He also didn't want her out of his sight. Danger and uncertainty lay ahead, but he didn't voice his fears. There were still unfinished things between them, but a human body can take only so much. The toll of the last few days reflected in the bruised shadows under her eyes, and he was determined to chase them away for a while. So he had called in for them both. Fuck Internal Investigations.

All his years alone, the best way he had found to refresh a tired mind was to go out and punish his body in relentless running. He ran from his troubles as well as the pain inside. Today he was going to start anew and run for joy.

Nikki turned as soon as he reached her in a mock bid to fly off on her bike again, as she had done several times already, and every time he had caught hold of the handlebars and tipped her into his arms. He barely paid attention to the familiar joggers going by who stared at them in amusement as they kept passing the same scenario of the two of them kissing passionately every quarter of a mile.

"Drop your bike by the side of the path and jog with me," he ordered, his nose buried against her hair, taking in the sweet scent of shampoo and woman.

"Uh-uh. Jogging dislodges your brain. I don't have much up there left to waste." She smiled again, with that same glint of mischief that he hadn't seen for a lifetime, and added in a soft shy voice, "Unless . . . you want to jog in bed?"

Rick gave a short laugh. There was something devastatingly seductive in this woman who seemed to be both his wife and not. The self-conscious touch in her sexiness only added to his hunger for her. She would always remain a little reserved and secretive.

He tilted her head back and gazed down. How was he changed for her? Unlike her, he had become someone even he didn't like. He wasn't the Rick she had loved. Maybe that's why she hadn't told him . . .

"What's wrong?" she asked, her smile disappearing. "Jogging in bed makes you frown?"

Rick shrugged away his thoughts and gave her a reassuring

smile. "No, but if you keep interrupting my run every quarter mile, we'll never make it back to bed. Come run with me."

"Someone will steal my bike," she said, as an excuse.

"I'll buy you another one."

"I'll be too tired to walk all the way back once we reached the end of the trail."

"I'll carry you back"

"You really want me to jog?"

Rick touched her cheek with his knuckles. "I want you by my side, not like some illusion up ahead all the time. I want to hear you breathe hard, so I know this is real."

Her dark eyes shone with an inner light that warmed him more than the morning exertion. "Do you know at moments like these, if you close your eyes and listen, you can hear your *chuung*?"

She hadn't said a word when he told her he was the one who had interrupted Erik's little game yesterday. He admitted to reading her notes and story on the laptop, but omitted the fax that came right afterward. She wasn't angry at all, as he thought she would be. She knew him for what he was, after all—a man who had no conscience.

Her reference to these private things, like her grandmother's tales and references to some prophecies with something called *chuung*, of her hero on the run and the heroine who saved him, humbled him. She was forgiving and generous and he was a bastard. No wonder she still hadn't decided whether she still loved him enough to tell him everything.

"Can you hear it?" Her eyes were closed.

"Yes," he lied, watching her, loving her, and filled with the need to make love to her. "How come you aren't angry that I went through your files?"

She opened her eyes and regarded him with her dark expressive eyes. There was a gentle sparkle in them, as if she had been waiting for his question. "Because I've been writing about you. It's always been about you," she told him. She pushed off him and guided the bicycle next to a birch tree. "I'm really going to regret this."

Jogging in unison. This used to be his lone activity, where he could reflect on and not lose sight of his goal. It reminded him that like jogging, it would hurt while he was doing it. He darted a look at Nikki, her face flushed, lips parted as she moved beside him. There was his goal, right beside him. His heart swelled at the sight of her. Maybe this was what she meant by hearing his *chuung*, that perfect pitch of sound and sight.

Nikki suddenly faltered and stumbled. Rick grasped her elbow to steady her. Her stunned expression made him realize that she hadn't tripped. He followed the direction of her gaze.

A lone male stood nonchalantly at the end of the trail, studying them. Even from here, Rick could see those strange light eyes gleaming out of the tanned face. He was silent, waiting for Nikki to make the first move.

"Jed . . ." She said his name like a woman greeting a lover, the initial surprise on her face changing into an expression Rick didn't care for. He watched her walk slowly toward the figure.

His soaring heart descended like a heavy rock in churning waters. Oh no. His hands fisted at his sides. He hated this helpless feeling of inevitability. The photo of Nikki and this same man with the young girl swam in his eyes, mocking him. A silent denial rose out of desperation. No, she wasn't going back to the stranger. He couldn't accept that. But she was already halfway to the waiting man she called Jed.

He didn't like him already. The stranger didn't change his stance, continuing to lean against a big wooden sign that posted the words STOP. END OF TRAIL. Arrogant bastard.

Jed. The very last person Nikki wanted Rick to meet.

The very person who had brought her back from the dead was as shadowy and unexpected as Death himself. Jed McNeil was the leader to a special covert group of nine commandos who infiltrated enemy networks like a virus, destroying from within. During one of these operations, he had heard about the few prisoners and had sought them out. She had been the only one left. Her heart filled with warmth as she took in the familiar angular features, with those striking eyes and the deep dimple in the chin. His lazy slouch against the post didn't de-

ceive her at all. It hid lightning speed and agile strength that
could carry a body for miles down mountain terrain. There
was only a very thin veneer of civilization masking the former Airborne Ranger.

She looked over her shoulder. She had assumed Rick
would be right behind her, but he wasn't. He had a grim air
about him, his light mood all but gone. She glanced back at
Jed. He hadn't greeted her yet, but that was just like him. Jed
McNeil never did anything one expected him to. She didn't
even question how he knew she would be jogging here on
this trail. Jed always seemed to know things. She was close
enough to catch the glint of humor in his eyes. She frowned.
What was he up to now?

She turned back. "Rick?" She held out her hand, and after
a moment's hesitation, he came forward to join her. His eyes
were very green, and they weren't smiling like before.
Maybe it was the morning sun, but the play of light and
shadow flickering across his face gave him a menacing appearance. Her frown deepened. "What's the matter?"

"Who is he?" His gaze didn't leave her face.

"Come meet him," she said quietly. One couldn't just explain Jed in a sentence. It was simpler to introduce him. "It's
okay. I know him."

"Did you tell him you would be here?"

"No."

"How did he find out where we are?"

"Because he's Jed." She squeezed his hand lightly.

She could feel the tension in Rick, and Jed wasn't helping
with his usual quiet amusement. She didn't know why he
was here but Jed always appeared at a time of his choosing.
He was the most unpredictable person she'd ever met. Despite the feeling that an explosion was pending, she couldn't
help smiling at the sight of him leaning against the sign. He
hadn't changed, still playing mind games.

He was in his favorite getup—a jean jacket and faded
jeans—and judging from his tan, he must have just come
back from somewhere tropical. Rugged and powerful, he
was the only man who evoked a responsive chord in her in

the aftermath of her imprisonment. She didn't know how she was going to explain him to Rick.

"Jed." For an awkward moment she found herself unable to take the few steps for a friendly embrace because Rick was purposely slowing their approach by pulling on her hand.

"Nikki." His familiar husky drawl said her name in a soft greeting. Nothing else. He didn't move any closer, either.

She realized that Jed was putting the burden of introduction on her and her eyes narrowed a fraction as she tried to gauge his motives. He was his usual unreadable self, his silver eyes gleaming in the morning sun. They roved over her in a lazy, thorough, head-to-toe inspection, and she felt Rick's grasp tighten even more.

Nikki licked her suddenly dry lips. Jed McNeil never showed up for a friendly hi. This wasn't going to be the first time, either. "This is a surprise."

"It's time to check up on you." He cocked a dark brow, still waiting.

"Rick . . . this is Jed McNeil."

There was an interminable pause as both men didn't make a move.

"You can't leave the introduction hanging, Nikki," Jed finally chided. " 'This is Jed' isn't enough for a man holding your hand like that. And especially"—he looked at the man behind her, a corner of his mouth lifting—"for a man who's more than a friend."

Damn. Nikki didn't curse often, but this was one of those times. *Damn.* She had forgotten Jed had an innate love of double entendres. She didn't want to do this now. Not yet.

But she was standing between two of the most uncompromising men in the world—one who had forced her back into living, and the other who was her life, who made her feel alive. She was unwilling for them to meet. It was like . . . acknowledging she had failed both of them somehow. She couldn't be what either of them wanted. Not a woman for Jed. Not a wife for Rick. Neither Nikki nor Leah, she realized.

"Be brave, Nikki," Jed scolded softly. It was a phrase he

used often between them, a private communication that meant a lot.

"Leave her alone," Rick cut in brusquely.

"Too long, it seems." Jed straightened up and for the first time acknowledged Rick. "Being a bureaucrat has made you soft, Harden. All this time I'd given you, and you haven't figured out a damn thing."

"What the hell do you mean, given me time? I don't even know you." Nikki had never seen Rick so angry before. He hadn't raised his voice, but the glacial edge to it would intimidate a lesser man. His hold on her hand was firm to the point of forceful, and it made her wonder whether it was just because he didn't want her to give Jed a hug.

"But I know you. I kept waiting for a sign that you really cared for her but all I saw was a bureaucrat staying within the safety confines of rules. You were paper-trailing yourself to death, man, and there was no end in sight. How long were you going to wait before you made your move? Another ten years, perhaps?"

"How long have you been watching me?"

"Years. We were both on the same quest, it seemed, except"—the well-cut mouth quirked up slightly—"I had your wife with me, and you didn't."

The words had the desired effect. Nikki's hand was freed as she watched her husband lunge out at Jed. It happened so quickly she was momentarily stunned with dismay. Jed had deliberately taunted Rick, and Rick fell for it.

"No!" She ran forward to come between the two men. This wasn't the balance in her life that she was seeking.

Rick grabbed Jed by the shoulders. The son of a bitch didn't flinch or back off. In fact, he didn't even move an inch. Only the gleam in his odd eyes warned him that this wasn't a man to be trifled with.

Not that Rick cared. Jed McNeil could show up armed to the teeth and Rick still wasn't going to give up Nikki, not without a fight. The way Nikki had looked at him was telling. This was a rival who could do the ultimate damage. He could take Nikki away.

"Rick, no!" Nikki tugged on his sweatshirt. Rick glared at Jed. The urge to draw blood stretched like a wire inside him. She gripped his tensed arm and added, "No, it'll only make things worse."

But it'll feel so good.

"Go on," Jed said, a hint of challenge in his voice now. "A little bit of action might loosen those atrophied muscles."

Rick didn't like the way the other man stood totally relaxed, looking at him as if there was nothing important going on. He hated feeling disadvantaged that his opponent knew more than he did. About Nikki. About his own past.

"Fight. Or let go," Jed said, then cocked an eyebrow. "Kissing is out of the question."

Rick sensed that Jed wanted him to lose his temper and start a fight. He pushed off and stepped away from the shorter man, who still somehow managed to stand there with his hands in the pockets of his jeans jacket. He wouldn't play this game.

"Jed McNeil?" he repeated the man's name. "Where have I heard that name before?"

"Ah . . . finally, memory and common sense kicking in."

"Jed, don't." The soft appeal in Nikki's voice grated Rick. "I promise I won't hurt him, darling."

Darling. That was the last straw.

Rick dragged his gaze away and turned to Nikki. "Who is he to you?" he demanded.

Behind them, approaching sounds warned them of other morning joggers. Nikki continued talking hurriedly. "If you get into a brawl, those people will call the cops, and we don't want any more attention drawn on us right now. Please, not now, Rick. Jed isn't here to fight you."

"I don't need to," Jed said. "At the rate he's going, he'll be fighting with everybody else. Let EYES destroy him. Let Gorman make mincemeat of him and Task Force Two. He thinks he can handle everything and everyone on his own. Ricardo Harden against the big bad world, isn't that right, Agent Harden?"

Rick blinked. He had heard those words before but from a woman's mouth. "How are you connected to GEM?" he demanded. "And don't tell me you aren't because you've just repeated a conversation I had with T."

"Rick, Jed is sort of T.'s commander," Nikki explained. "His group works with ours."

"Does that mean you work for him too?"

She hesitated, looking at Jed for tacit approval. "Yes." Her smile was tentative, unsure. "I can't explain things till it's time. Don't fight, okay? Jed is testing you."

Rick didn't like the way they communicated with their eyes. Why was she so damn worried about Jed? "Who is he to you?" he repeated.

"Maybe she doesn't want you to know," Jed drawled. "Maybe it's none of your business."

"That's not true! Jed, stop this, you're making it worse."

"You wanted answers about your past. Coming back here meant answering some hard questions yourself—you know this, Nikki."

Hard questions. Hard lessons. "It was you!" Rick accused. But why did he send Rick the photo? Why was he monitoring both him and Nikki separately?

Jed returned his regard coolly, not answering. Frowning, Nikki asked, "What—have you two met before?"

"Not personally," Jed replied, "but I grow tired of the two of you wasting time."

Rick hadn't said anything about the faxed image because he wanted her to come to him freely, but this man's presence was forcing the issue out into the open. He should be happy, but he wasn't. He never liked being manipulated.

"Care to explain that last comment?" he asked quietly.

"Even my patience has limits, Agent Harden, and after the Gorman incident, it seems I have to force something to happen before I get my job done. You were too eager to hang yourself." He looked at Nikki briefly before continuing, "I didn't return her to you so you can spend time jogging."

Rick rounded on Nikki. "What does he mean, return you to me?"

Her expressive eyes were startled-wide, like a doe caught in headlights. "Rick . . ."

"Those files I pulled from your laptop—there was one about me. It was dated about nine years ago, Nikki. You found out you had a husband but you didn't come back. Why?"

"I . . ." She hesitated, then sent Jed a desperate glance. Rick pulled her around to face him. "Why do you need his permission? Even though you couldn't remember, like you said, didn't you think I should be informed that my wife is alive? Why didn't you come back?"

She stared up at him, biting her lower lip hard.

Rick shook her. "Why? Who is he?" he thundered. The image of Nikki and Jed with the little girl taunted him. The possible answer tore a hole in his gut.

Movement caught the corner of his eye. To his surprise, Jed McNeil was almost ten feet away, heading toward the park area off the jogging trail. *He hadn't even heard the man move.*

As if he knew he had Rick's attention, Jed turned and called back, in a mocking drawl, "Don't stop now. You're heading in the right direction with those questions, Harden. I'll be picnicking over there when you're ready for more." He cast a strange look in Nikki's direction, and added in that soft tone, "It's time, Nikki. Be brave."

Nikki stared after Jed, exasperated at how matters were taken out of her hands. She knew that was the closest Jed McNeil would ever come to apologize for the havoc he just had wreaked.

She had known coming back was a big risk. For so long, she had convinced herself that life was ahead, and looking back at the past wasn't healthy. She died in that hellhole. She didn't have any memory, save that of her grandmother. Besides, there was nothing worth going back to, since her agency had betrayed her. She hadn't felt like reliving her nightmare by confronting those who had abandoned her. Rick's tortured eyes denounced her cowardice. She knew there was no way to escape telling him everything now, not with Jed stirring the pot.

"Jed saved me from that prison," she said, "but that's not what you want to know, is it?"

He shook his head. "No. He is more than your leader, isn't he?"

"He's just my commander now," she offered, and touched his chest gently. "I was little more than an animal for a long time, Rick. I had no memory. I was afraid of everything, especially of men. I could barely speak in complete sentences. Jed took me under his wing, nursed me back from my hell because he had been a prisoner of war before. He understood me."

"How long?" Rick asked woodenly. "How long were you with him?"

Nikki clasped her hands in front of her. "Eighteen, nineteen months."

Dropping his arms from her, he strode to the post where Jed had been leaning and glared at it as if he was going to punch it. "That means by that time you already knew you had a husband looking for you. My file you had was dated before that." He swung back around, green eyes flashing. "You knew and still continued a relationship with him."

"Knowing and having memory are two very different things," Nikki said, swallowing the lump in her throat. Her voice sounded strange and hoarse. "I knew, but I didn't feel anything. How could I have a husband if I couldn't even recall what he looked like? And . . ." She hesitated, then rushed out, "And I didn't want anyone else to touch me."

Rick closed his eyes for a few seconds. "You let him touch you, even after you knew your identity, knew about your past life, knew that I—" He opened his eyes and looked at her as if she was a stranger. "—that I was here looking for you. You left me thinking you were dead, Nikki. Why?"

Her eyes had a hollow misery that pleaded for his understanding, but he couldn't let it go. This was about what could have been. If he had had any tiny hope that she had been still alive, he wouldn't have gone down the road to end up like this—a man she scarcely recognized as her husband. *Either way, she wouldn't have recognized you.* He ignored the voice sneakily reminding him of her amnesia. "Why?" he demanded again, fiercely, ignoring the couple of joggers who came and went.

"Why would anyone want me the way I was?" Nikki countered in a low voice. "You don't understand what it was like to look in the mirror every day and see nothing but a broken thing. I had a choice, either to let go of everything or go insane with the memories. They repaired my looks. The physical scars eventually healed. But I have to be the one to take care of my mind. I'm the one who has to deal with the demons."

"I'm not asking about the pain of what you went through, Nikki," Rick said. "God forbid I would be such a bastard as to demand that everything be all right the moment you found out about me. I'm trying to understand. When you received the information, it was a year after you were freed. I assumed you would be curious about your past life, about anything or anyone connected with it, but you didn't do anything, Nikki. You didn't even give me a chance."

"I'm sorry, Rick," Nikki said. "I thought it was for the best then."

His heart hurt. "I know what you're leaving out," he said starkly. "You had a new life. A new man. You didn't want to drop everything to start anew yet one more time."

Her eyes filled with tears. "I couldn't. I couldn't bear the thought of—" She bit her lip.

Rick finished for her, the words torn out of him. "Of having another man touch you. Yes, of course. I see that now. It makes sense." He turned away.

"You make it sound so . . . wrong. It didn't happen overnight, Rick. I couldn't take care of myself, didn't even know what the next day would bring. Jed brought me back without the usual medical solutions for someone in deep depression. He was adamant that I wasn't administered any more drugs. He was the only thing solid at that point—"

"Spare me the details," Rick cut in, then instantly regretted it. He *wanted* the details, wanted the torture of hearing all about wonderful Jed McNeil. He stared into the distance. He could feel her coming nearer behind him, but he couldn't let her see him right now. All this pretty sunshine, and he felt wintry-cold. "I suppose I should thank *him.*"

His bitter laugh ripped through Nikki. The last thing she had wanted to do was hurt him, ever. She loved him. Always had. Always would. It was so simple now, standing here in the open fresh air. When there was nowhere else to hide, the truth always shone. Didn't her grandmother say so?

"Rick, don't fight with Jed, please."

He swung around, and she inhaled sharply at the stark pain in his eyes. "Why? You think I can't win you back? You think I'm exactly what he said I am, don't you? A bureaucrat who can't do a damn thing anymore."

She stared at him, shocked that his perspective was so *male*, so utterly out of her hands. Fighting for her. She hadn't even considered that fact. All she had wanted was to regain knowledge of her past, but of course, she had been short-sighted. One couldn't regain knowledge without dealing with everything else in her past.

"The hungry ghosts," she muttered.

"What are you talking about?"

She hadn't realized that she'd spoken aloud. She shook her head, at him as well as at herself. She was getting dizzy going back and forth like this. "I'm asking you not to fight because you're both good men, and it's I who have caused this wrong." To you, she added silently, but like a coward, dared not say it out loud.

Her words took the anger out of Rick. What right did he have to be feeling like this when she had gone through so much? But the hurt remained. To be forgotten was one thing, but to be put aside, like something unimportant . . . He swallowed. "You've done nothing wrong." He sighed. What was there to say? "Maybe the fact that you hid the truth from me, that you never wanted to come back to me."

"Rick, I didn't know!" Nikki cried. He was standing close enough that she could step into his arms and hug him, but it was as if he had erected a wall between them. She couldn't seem to reach him. "I didn't know how I would feel."

"And your agency sent you back here. It wanted you to use my feelings for you to get something. What is it?"

He had swooped down on the truth so suddenly, she stared back at him wordlessly for a few seconds. Laughter from strangers jogging by. A chainsaw buzzing in the distance. The rustle of leaves against branches. Yet it was the silence inside her that grew loud as a boom box, a crescendo that had built into a bursting sound wave. The moment of truth was the perfect *chuung*. If only it wasn't killing her to have to tell it.

"Your relationship with Gorman," she replied, gazing directly into those green, green eyes. "What he has over you."

He nodded crisply, as if he already knew. "And once you found this information out, and your assignment was done, what would you get out of it?" There was a businesslike tone to his voice, much like when he talked to his subordinates.

Very slowly, she replied, "I retrieve the files they had of me. I get to know what really happened that day. I read about all their reasons for the decision to make me a broken wing."

"I see. Then you—what—go back to Jed McNeil and live happily ever after? Isn't that the romantic ending you seek, Nikki?"

He was still speaking in a monotone, and she couldn't stand it. "Jed and I haven't been together for a long time, Rick," she told him. "This was years ago. Can't you forgive me for that? He's just a friend now."

"I told you, you've done nothing wrong," Rick said woodenly. "It was to be expected. He was there for you and I wasn't. Now, let's go see your Jed and see what he wants."

Nikki felt a swelling of fear. "What do you mean?" she asked, touching his arm for the first time. He jerked and turned toward the path heading to the park.

"So I can be clear on how to help you get your past back," he answered, still in that very polite voice. "Everyone wants something from me, it seems. I'll gladly do my best to give it to all of you."

Nikki stared after his retreating back. She didn't want her past. She wanted her future, and he was walking away from her.

Chapter Twenty-three

Everything was crystal-clear now. What a reminiscing fool he had been. Rick strode down the path, looking neither left nor right, as he headed for the open area beyond the clump of bushes that screened the path from picnickers.

It was a weekday and early in the morning, and there was unlikely to be many people about. He spotted Jed immediately. Who wouldn't? The man was everything he wasn't, obviously. He didn't look like he spent a day in an office or much time in a suit and tie, or drank martinis for lunch. He didn't look like the type who would be hindered by red tape. In fact, he didn't look like he needed to jog for the sake of getting out of the stupor of dealing with bureaucratic games.

The Hard-Ons of this world couldn't compete with the gangly man sitting casually at the picnic table, legs thrust out, sunglasses pushed up on his dark head, tanned face turned toward the morning sun, as if he had every right to enjoy life, as if he had no worries for his future. Rick unclenched the hand he had unconsciously fisted.

Life reflected the truth all the time. All Rick had to do was look for it. He was looking at it now. He had wanted to go back, grasping at a past that shone like a mirage in a desert, but reality had finally shown itself. He was Hard-On. Accept it.

He squinted in the sunlight as he studied Jed. He looked thoroughly relaxed but Rick doubted that the other man wasn't aware of his presence. From what he had seen of them, these GEM operatives were good. Marlena Maxwell's undercover persona had fooled him. Diamond's cool handling of the first Gorman interview had impressed him. Rick's lips curled derisively. And Nikki had certainly done her job well; she had found the crack in his armor. And this man, in plain jeans, was their almighty leader. He didn't look it but the aura of danger clung to him like a second skin.

Jed opened his eyes. "Have a seat," he invited. "Nice day for a picnic."

"I'm not hungry," Rick said. He didn't sit.

"Food for thought, Agent Harden, can be just as calorie-filled."

"You can stop the NOPAIN shit, McNeil, if that's your real name. I'm immune to your manipulations."

Jed's silver eyes glinted in the sunlight, a startling contrast in his tanned face. There was an aloofness in them that Rick had seen before. He had interviewed men with that same look. Killer eyes. Merciless. So here was the operative gazing back at him. The eyes blinked and there was nothing again, just a cool, easy expression.

"Why would I use Non-physical Persuasion on you, Agent Harden?"

"Marlena tried. T. Nikki. I see a pattern here," Rick replied. "The Agency has similar programs, not as advanced as your group's training, but then we don't specialize in trickery."

"We're all on the same side, Harden."

Rick cocked his head. "The same page, McNeil. Rarely do different agencies have the same agenda."

"Spoken like a real bureaucrat." Jed crossed his arms and stared out at the distance. "So where's Nikki? On the same page with her yet?"

She hadn't come with him. "Is that what this is all about?" Rick countered quietly. "For all of us to be on the same page? What do you gain from this?"

"We all want to know about the past, don't we?" Jed replied enigmatically.

"Quit fucking around. I know why you faxed that photo." Rick paused, waiting for Jed to question him, but when he remained silent, he shrugged, and added, "What I want to know is, why were you lying in wait for Nikki's computer to download the files? Why were you shadowing her trail? After all, if you're in charge, shouldn't you be the one authorizing that risky move she made?"

Jed's lips curved, giving a hint of a smile—or maybe it was a sneer, Rick couldn't tell—as he looked into the distance again. "We don't do things like Task Force Two, Harden," he said softly. "We don't get any glory for being successful or any blame for a snafu. In other words, we get things done."

"No, in other words, you guys don't have any accountability."

"Accountability?" Jed shifted his gaze back to him sharply. "Who's accountable for Nikki's being what she is now?"

Rick snapped back, "You don't know yourself."

"But we're talking about accountability, not which agency is better at finding the truth, aren't we?" Jed asked.

"You're fucking playing with words again. Fine. I work in a situation that hindered my personal investigations, but I *will* get to the truth."

"Not if EYES has reasons to stop you."

Rick heaved a sigh and sat down at the end of the picnic bench. He looked out at where Jed was gazing, and saw in the distance a few people playing a game of horse on a basketball court. "It's beginning to look like they are part of the network," he admitted.

"Some elements in them are," Jed agreed.

There was a pause as they both watched one of the players put the ball through the hoop consecutively. When he finally missed, Rick asked, "And was Nikki hired as the independent contractor to smoke them out?"

"No. Admiral Madison wanted an independent report for his committee for national security because of the number of leaks putting his SEAL teams in danger. Nikki's specialty is finding how a system fails—where the possible weak links are and how to balance those with changes. She was, after all, part of a failed system, and knew firsthand how things get buried away. Besides, her past knowledge of having worked in the directorates gave her superior advantage at getting information. The risks she took, you see, weren't risky at all. Nikki knew how far in the system she could go without being caught."

"And of course, you know her so well," Rick added bitterly. A failed system. Did she see him that way?

"Yes."

"You don't give an inch, do you?"

"Neither do you, Agent Harden. Or I wouldn't have risked Nikki's happiness just to save your ass."

Rick clamped down on his anger. Responding to the baiting would just please the other man. He glanced coolly at Jed's profile. He looked so engrossed in the scene over there, one would think they were here casually discussing sports.

"Let's spell out 'horse manure,' shall we? Let's see how many points I get for the reasons you're so interested in my ass. What does GEM want from Ricardo Harden, the most likely suspect in treason at the moment?" Rick asked, injecting careless mockery in his voice. "Point, your agency's prints are all over the place on this one, starting with Marlena Maxwell going after Gorman not so long ago. Your side had obviously been targeting him for a long time, what with Miss Maxwell's two-year undercover work.

"Point, I should've known there was something bigger than Gorman brewing, when right after he was caught, another agent from your outfit whisked him away without a single squeak of protest from EYES. No red tape, nothing. That means you have more power than EYES. I'm thinking the General Accounting Office.

"Point, with Gorman gone, I'm suddenly your target, so you sent another operative after me." He paused to take a deep breath, betrayal tasting like a dry bitter pill. "Nikki Taylor showed up conveniently as an independent contractor brought in by Admiral Madison, who had also recently infiltrated my task force team with his SEAL, Steve McMillan. Coincidence? Or maybe he'd been working hand-in-hand with GEM. He had netted Gorman and now has a case for his national security committee. So the magic question is, what do you want with me, McNeil, that you sent Nikki after me? How am I doing with the game?"

"You're scoring well," Jed replied, finally taking his eyes from the far-off game, "except for one thing. If you were a traitor, I'd never even consider sending Nikki into this assignment, Harden. I'd have come after you myself."

Rick unflinchingly met those cold eyes for long seconds. In another time and another place, they could have been friends. They were both, after all, protective of those they loved. In this time and in this place, however, it happened to be the same woman. He knew if Jed had found any reason to destroy him, he would. The veiled violence he had sensed was very real now, as if the other man wished to reveal just enough to let him know who he was dealing with. Yet Jed had triggered a series of events from his actions, and it wasn't just his choice of Nikki for this assignment.

"Why did you fax me that picture?" Rick asked suddenly. "Why now, when you could have done it sooner? Years ago? Months ago?"

Jed nodded. "I wonder when you're going to ask some good hard questions," he mocked. "You seem a man in search of the truth, but are you ready for it?"

"You think I can't handle the truth?" Rick countered harshly. He told himself he could. When Jed laughed softly, he warned, "Don't fuck with me, McNeil."

Jed pinched his bottom lip as if to erase a smile. "Point," he said, in the same soft tone, "the faxed photo pushed you into action, as I meant it to. Sending it earlier didn't serve any purpose. Nikki wasn't prepared to tell you who she was and I wasn't going to betray her. However, after she revealed herself to the review board, I wasn't bound by her secret any longer.

"Point, her secret lies in her past and her constant need to find herself through her writing. I could make her remember without your help, Harden, but that, too, wouldn't have served any purpose. Nikki chose not to remember, and I honored her wishes. However, when she chose to tell you who she was, I couldn't justify not pushing her any longer. So I dumped her files on your lap. Her secrets. Her personal musings in her plots. You don't think I was romancing you, do you? Those files *are* her past. I don't have time to sit and fill you in on ten missing years. You're supposed to read them."

"I did," Harden interrupted. He had been intrigued by Nikki's writing. It was wrong to do it but he hadn't been able to stop himself. He had to know this new woman who was also his wife from long ago. He had searched for a hint, any references to himself, but found nothing direct. Just that damn file with his name, with the date that told it all.

As if he could read his mind, Jed said, "Of course you did. You're an information addict. You need to know. That's your strongest and your weakest point. Nikki writes about you all the time, or are you simply that blind?"

Rick wasn't going to agree with him. "You break into her files and read her personal stuff and think I'm condoning it because of your explanation?"

"You break into everyone's files and read their personal stuff," countered Jed. "Don't be naive. Nikki knows what I'm like. She has no problem with it."

"You bastard. Quit bringing that up to get me."

"Quit being so easily distracted."

"We're not going to settle this by talking." Rick wanted to bash the man's head in, see some bruises on that nice tanned face.

Jed shrugged. "I'm not here to settle anything with you. You're a means to an end, and I'm just doing my job. You want to fight, we can do that later, but the business at hand is to get hold of that list."

"You don't need me for that," Rick pointed out. "Plenty of hackers and code breakers out there besides this burned-out bureaucrat. Cut to the chase."

Jed bent down and pulled a weed out of the ground, studied it, then proceeded to break the plant apart. "Three and a half years ago, during an operation involving arms dealing, some members of my group were betrayed in a way similar to Nikki's assignment." He twisted the flowerlike heads off.

"A couple of them are still missing. Everything pointed to an internal mole."

He snapped the thin stems off the weed methodically. "It took two more years before we could trap this arms dealer again, with T. working inside and M. working outside. When M. arrived at D.C., we had two objectives. One, get the inside mole. Two, sell our arms dealer something we could track. Gorman's theft of the laptop gave us an opening. He needed a middleman, so we sent in Marlena. Once she retrieved it, Tess gave her a tracer laptop we'd set up." He pulled the two remaining leaves off.

"Point, we finally have Gorman but he isn't talking. Someone else is still running the show, and we need that list that Gorman is dangling in front of EYES. Internal Investigations has been acting suspiciously at every turn and we have reasons to believe they don't want the real list out. You already know you're going to be the sacrificial lamb."

When Jed arched a brow inquiringly, Rick nodded and dryly noted, "My hindering McMillan and Miss Maxwell didn't endear me to you, I presume."

"T. was in charge. She knew enough about your past to negotiate with you to let McMillan out of custody."

"She told me in the end Gorman would be mine. She said the past was catching up," Rick murmured, remembering that conversation with the operative who had hinted about his past. "Is there no one in your agency that doesn't play word games?"

Jed acknowledged the sarcasm with a small quirk of his lips. "Nikki doesn't."

Rick looked at what remained of the weed in Jed's hand. "So where do I fit in this grand scheme of things?"

"Simple. I know you aren't the mole. Your actions looked more like you're protecting someone important to you. That tells me more than all your bureaucratic hide-and-seek how much you really loved your wife, dead as she was to you. Tell me what Gorman still has over you, Harden. We'll get the list decoded and I'll make whatever you're afraid of go away."

"So sure? What if it involved Nikki?" Rick countered, reassessing the power of this man. "She's so adamant about getting her files back. What if her files show something that would destroy her?"

"It's your job to make sure the truth doesn't."

Rick stared into those silver eyes for a long time. "You aren't going to take her from me," he finally stated carefully.

"I rarely give any opponent the chance to take anything that's mine."

"So the kid in that picture . . ."

"Is mine. She's right now doing her sophomore year in college."

Relief washed through Rick. Nineteen . . . too old to be Nikki's child too. "You son of a bitch. You purposely wanted me to think you and Nikki had a child."

Jed shrugged. "Nikki isn't the only one needing prodding."

He had been thoroughly played. That photo had pushed him into drastic measures. Was he so predictable that another man could second-guess what he would do to Nikki? "You're making this awfully easy for me," Rick said testily. "Save my career. Give Nikki back her past. And you out of the picture. Give me a reason to trust you, McNeil. How do I know it isn't just another of your NOPAIN games?"

"I seldom repeat myself, Harden. I told you, I don't give anyone the chance to take back anything that's mine."

The man had this thing with cryptic lines. It grated at Rick's nerves. It had to be done on purpose, to keep everyone off-balance, while he remained in control. Not going to happen to him, Rick decided. "You gave her my file all those years ago," he said coolly. He could analyze a situation just as well as the other man. Time to attack instead of giving ground.

"Yes."

"Why? I wasn't around. You didn't have to tell her anything about me. You could keep her, or were you already tired of her, wanting to get rid of her?"

Rick studied Jed for signs of anger but the man's control was superb. Nothing. Not a shred of emotion in those eyes. His reply, when it came, was shockingly simple.

"I gave her your file because she was a married woman, Harden." Jed stood up and looked down at Rick. "She belonged to someone else, and as long as she refused to deal with it, I had no choice but to give her room to grow, to be whomever she wanted to be."

"So you waited ten years to send her back to me?" Rick asked skeptically.

Jed twirled what was left of that weed in his hand then dropped it on the ground. "It took two years for her physical scars to heal. Two more to train her to be a good GEM operative. Four years of being on her own, besides surviving. She went into retirement and on her own, after a year, she decided that it was time. Read her stuff, Harden. What's the color of her hero's eyes?"

"Green."

"What does he do?"

Rick didn't like the tables turned but replied anyway. "He works for an agency and is being set up."

Jed nodded. "She's been following you for a year without anyone's prompting. Surely that tells you something. My facilitating her new assignment is just a matter of course. I'll help Nikki as much as I can. It's now up to you, unless—" The dark eyebrow rose a fraction. "You would rather return her to me? She remembers everything now, so I won't be taking advantage of her, and I must admit, I miss my Nikki a lot."

"Fuck you," Rick offered rudely.

For the first time Jed laughed, a surprisingly rich, genuine sound. He crushed the plant under his boot. "I have other plans," he said, and the amusement disappeared like a magic trick. "I want those who killed my men, Harden. Five years, ten years—I'll get them."

Rick stood up. Sitting down while this man was around wasn't a good idea. "I win on that account," he told him. "I have waited ten years to get Gorman."

"Point, I have had ten years watching Nikki. By the way, Non-physical Persuasion is just the first part of NOPAIN. My talents lie in Innovative Negotiation, Harden, remember that."

They stared at each other. Rick understood the hidden message very well. Jed McNeil never lost a fight; he wouldn't have let go of Nikki if he'd found anything about Rick that proved him guilty. He was warning that he would be watching. Rick nodded back. He would make damn sure the man stayed far, far away from his woman.

To give the men some time, Nikki went back to get her bicycle. She knew Jed wanted to speak to Rick alone or he wouldn't have taunted him that way. Besides, she needed to sort out what to do next. What Jed chose to reveal worried her. She suspected Rick somehow already knew about him— the antagonism he'd shown was raw and abrasive, as if he hadn't been able to control himself. Jed would undoubtedly use that emotion to get what he wanted; he manipulated everyone like that.

She sighed. Men. She was afraid of them. Their size. The way they casually used force to solve a problem, be it pounding a hammer at a stubborn nail or showing their fists at each other. The careless power they could wield over women, with intimidation, physical or emotional, or sex. Her grip on the bicycle handles tightened. She knew how a man could break a woman.

It had been ten years and she still couldn't run away from her fears. Jed had called it her emotional garbage that she needed to throw out, not sneak it around inside her, like guilty dirt thrust under the carpet. She held on to the bike like an anchor as she looked indecisively at the jogging path.

The two men back there were honorable men. One saved her, saw her through the worst of horrors. The other wouldn't hurt a hair on her. Yet she didn't trust them enough to face them with any of her emotions. Partly it was because they both had a knack of seeing through her calm façade. She had erected this wall to stop the pain of humiliation, to evade men who had violated her out of greed and power. For a long time, before she did so, a man's hungry look would drive her to nausea and near hysteria. Allow anyone too close, and her whole being would scream in warning.

Nikki took a deep breath. She felt safe behind this emotional barrier, but it also isolated her from the world. She had kept out people who offered friendship and love because she had been afraid. Unless she took down this wall herself, she would never learn to trust, and wasn't that the most important thing in finding balance? To trust again?

She got on the bicycle and retraced her path, passing the joggers and taking in the scenery. She smelled grass and sunshine in the air. It all brought home a point. She wasn't alone trying to survive the next session of question and torture any longer. She didn't need to lie awake at night and think of deep darkness without color. If she would just reach out her hand, there were colors everywhere, and she could, if she dared to hope, touch a warm body next to hers. And she wouldn't have nightmares of sweat and tears because the strong arms that would envelop her belonged to the man she loved. It was a nice daydream.

Nikki braked slowly. The bicycle came to a standstill in front of the two men at the end of the path. They had been talking but turned in unison toward her, both aware of their surroundings. She teetered on her seat, keeping the bicycle balanced for a moment, as she looked from one face to the other.

Tension still emanated in waves from the two of them, but they hadn't been arguing when she saw them. She knew Jed had gotten what he wanted; he always did. As her gaze settled on Rick, she tried to hide the anxiety in her eyes. He looked formidable, and a strange coldness invaded her belly. She wondered whether she had lost him.

"I won't let the two of you run my life," she broke the silence quietly. "I'll decide what I want to do and how I want to live."

"Nobody's running your life," Rick said, but his eyes had the look she had begun to recognize too well.

"No, but you want to save me, just like Jed did," she said. "This is my quest, my life."

"I'm part of it." The stiffness in his jaw didn't bode well.

"I know." She attempted a smile. "But you can't slay all

my dragons. This was done to me, my body, my mind. I have to be the one behind the wheel. From what I can gather, you're both working around me, as if I'm Humpty Dumpty on the wall. That was fine before. I can see why you both think my amnesia is some kind of fragile ornament. If anything, it's like a mirror, reflecting my reality. That mirror was shattered a few days ago and I'm still here, and I'm fine."

"Are you saying you don't need me?" Rick asked.

It wasn't easy to look from one pair of intense eyes to another that was equally penetrating. Men liked to be charge. She reminded herself that these two had been in charge of her in one aspect or another in both her personas. Jed had let her go years ago, but she knew him well enough to realize that he had kept an eye on her. She gazed longingly at Rick, wanting to go to him and smooth that frown away, but that was the point. It would be doing what they wanted her to do—let them handle it.

No more. She turned the bicycle around and started pedaling back. "I need you both," she said quietly, "to let me do my assignment."

Rick watched his wife pedaling away from them. He was angry that she didn't make a choice. He wanted her to come to him and show him that it was he she wanted. Instead, the woman cruised off.

"So you want to play another game of horse shit?" Jed asked nonchalantly as he pushed his sunglasses down on his nose.

Rick told him where to shove it.

Nikki heard Jed's laughter behind her and sighed inwardly. Not good. It was risky leaving two explosive chemicals side by side like that. It occurred to her that she was the only thing keeping those two in balance.

Chapter Twenty-four

"I don't share."

The declaration was made quietly, without heat or inflection.

Nikki had waited for some sort of explosion since their return, but Rick had drawn out the tension by going into his study immediately. The door was still closed forty-five minutes later when she emerged from the bath and she'd imagined her tiger in there pacing, teeth bared, claws extended. Shaking her head, she'd decided to work on her report in front of the fireplace.

After a while, engrossed in her notes, she didn't hear his soft footsteps. Something made her look up. He stood at the bar, still in his sweatshirt and pants. Seeing him like this sent her heart racing. She was used to him in a business suit and tie. There was something fiercely untamed about him in those old clothes, and she wanted . . .

"You keep eating me with those eyes, and we'll never get a chance to talk," Rick interrupted her wayward thoughts, the ragged edge in his voice the only hint of his current state of mind. He walked behind the bar, as if he wanted to put something between them. "We need to talk."

"I know." Nikki told herself to be brave. "You want to know about Jed. About everything. I haven't been upfront."

"I'm the last person to condemn you for anything, Nikki." Rick pulled out a jug of juice from the refrigerator and poured himself a glass, giving the act a whole lot more concentration than necessary. "God knows I haven't been a saint. But we need to talk about what you want from me. I know what I want, but maybe that's not enough anymore. Maybe I've changed too much for you."

Nikki stared at him but he wouldn't look at her, turning around to put away the jug. "What are you saying?" she asked.

"When you and the team went missing, our side wouldn't send out an extraction team because they knew the international consequences would hurt us politically. I knew from my monitoring system that they were offering negotiations. Then, all of a sudden, you were all dead." He took in a deep breath. "And they wouldn't tell me anything. I couldn't accept that."

Nikki was quiet for a few moments, dissecting the situation from his perspective. "You went looking for me the only way you knew how," she deduced.

"Yes."

"By being a bureaucrat, so you could dig deeper and look for the missing information."

"Yes."

"And that's how you've changed. You've become a bureaucrat, and you think that affects our relationship." She stated her conclusions rhetorically because it was obvious meeting Jed had rattled him. She sighed. Jed would be pleased to know he'd accomplished his goals.

"Doesn't it?" His sipped on his juice slowly, watching her intently.

Nikki pursed her lips. She had never been good at making speeches. That was why she wrote stories. It was less personal, and easier to choose what to say or not to say when she could delete at will. She didn't have that option now. Her tiger was waiting. "You're angry because of what I did, and I don't blame you." She swallowed, willing her voice to be stronger. "It was selfish of me, and yes, I know it wasn't right to let you suffer. I can never make it right, no matter how many times I say I'm sorry. If anything else, I'm responsible for your becoming a bureaucrat. I wish I could change the past, Rick, because I can't bear to see you hurt."

"Make me understand. Was the thought of having a husband so frightening that you would deny my existence for nine years? Was there never a moment when you were curious at all, just to even want to talk to this stranger who knew you?" Rick carefully finished his glass of juice and placed it in the sink. "Was I just nothing in your mind?"

She wanted to be truthful, yet was reluctant to hurt him even more. She had to be very careful here or everything would blow up in her face. "I don't know what Jed told you," she began, pulling at the pages on her notepad, "but it was over between him and me a long time ago. I just didn't want to commit to anything or anyone, Rick. I had this . . . delusion . . . that I could forget what I couldn't remember, if that makes sense at all. I wanted to be a new person because I felt like damaged goods. Everything was new in the here and now whereas the past was ugly and tainted, and somehow, even if it's not true, you were lumped in there as part of something not to remember."

"I see."

Nikki threw the notepad down. "No, you don't. You're hiding your anger and pain, and I know my words are hurtful and cruel, and nothing I say or do will make it all right." She stood up and began walking toward the bar. "I just let time pass. One day I retired from field work. Another day I decided to write. It was then that I realized my writing was revealing my inner self, and no matter how much I tried, I couldn't run from my past. Jed had been right—there will never be peace for me until I make peace with my past."

She reached Rick, with the bar a barrier between them. She placed her hands on the counter and leaned close. "It's difficult to resist a bait set deliberately for me. Jed dangled it—you, my past, my file, everything. And all in the course of saving my country again. How could I resist? This was my chance to come back and see for myself, whether the sight of you would jolt my memory, whether it was possible to see myself through your eyes." She took a deep breath and exhaled. Be brave, she repeated. "I knew the risks of doing this, that if you found out the truth, all of my investigation could be jeopardized, so I opted for secrecy."

His back against the small refrigerator, Rick regarded her with somber eyes. "But part of the whole thing was to get me to talk," he said in that strange subdued voice. "Your—Jed already admitted that much. So you were sent here to mess with my mind. Get me to make the wrong move. Your agency wanted Gorman, and somehow has concluded that I was keeping something that they wanted."

"That *might* help them to net all the traitors," Nikki corrected. "They want to know what you have over Gorman, and vice versa."

"And what luck that they just happened to have you in their arsenal. They saw an opportunity to get to me and use it, and of course, here you are." There was no sarcasm, just that frustrating monotone.

"It was *my* decision. They couldn't have forced me if I'd refused."

"So tell me, besides the temptation of reading your own file, and maybe seeing your husband without any commitment, besides the luxury of being able to make up your mind what you want for your future—be it Jed McNeil or Ricardo Harden—besides all that, did it ever occur to you that I should have a say in this future?"

She was fast losing control of the situation. He was twisting her words, reading more into her motives than there really was, but who could blame him, when everything he had said was true? "What if you didn't want me?" she whispered.

His green eyes came alive, and all of a sudden, he was leaning over the counter, his face inches from hers. "How could you say that when you knew I had been requesting the return of your remains every year? How could you *think* that when your precious Jed had his eye on me for nine fucking years and knew every detail there is about my life? He knew enough to stay away from you, I'll give him credit for *that*. I asked him why he never contacted me, told me about you, and you know what he said? He said he knew I would never have accepted your being alive and not wanting to contact me, that I would move heaven and hell to find you. If *he* knew how I felt about you, Nikki, how could you not know? The file was there, the information was there at your fingertips. What did you do, check now and then, and see the stupid son of a bitch becoming nothing more than a paper pusher? That it's just not worth reliving life with him? That—"

Nikki pushed her palm against Rick's lips. "Stop," she pleaded, the shocking torrent of words slicing every fiber of her being. "Please, please, stop. It isn't that. It has never been that!"

She trapped his face between her hands, blinking back her tears as she tried to form words that weren't there. "I . . . you . . . No . . ." She released him and slapped the counter in frustration. She didn't want to say it, but she had to. Saying it out loud was horrible, but at least he wouldn't think she sat around calculating what would give her the best happiness. She lifted a weary hand to sweep the hair away from her forehead and took another deep breath. Exhaled. Finally she said, "It's worse. You meant nothing to me for a long time. And I know I didn't try, didn't attempt to reconnect with you or my past, or anything or anyone to do with it. It wasn't decent or honorable or moral. But I never meant to hurt you. Never, Rick, never."

"I repeat, what is it you want from me?"

She looked at him, really looked, and there was nothing but contempt in his eyes. She withdrew, hugged herself because she suddenly felt cold. At one time she would have replied that she didn't want much. Just her file, just something to tell her that she had existed. Now, after seeing and touching—loving Rick—she wanted so much more. But he was right. She was being selfish, taking and not giving back, and expecting him to give even more. She shook her head.

"Nothing? You want nothing from me?"

She rubbed her arms agitatedly. Jutting out her chin, she said, "Nothing you don't want to give me."

"That, at least, is a start," he said. She peered up. His gaze remained shuttered, unreadable. "You said earlier that you wanted space to do your assignment. Fine. But you've got me now, and I'm not some piece of information in your head anymore. You cannot remember. Fine. But what we have now, I won't let you forget. Is that clear?"

How could she forget? "Yes," she replied.

He nodded. "We have to start at a point where you're comfortable remembering. Would you rather be Nikki Taylor, or be seen as my wife?"

She blinked. "Your . . . wife."

"There's no going back," he warned softly. "You know how I am. My future isn't too bright at this moment, either, and could be getting worse, but I also want you to know that I'd do my damnedest to give you everything you want, even a new beginning. That's all I have to offer."

She bit her lower lip to stop its trembling. "Why?"

He didn't pretend to misunderstand. "Because the past you want has a price. What I'm going to tell EYES will put me in jail, but they'll locate your missing file once I take the second deal they hinted at over the phone."

"Grandmother, why does Grandfather need money in the Underworld?"

It was the Festival of the Hungry Ghosts, and Grandmother was burning paper offerings for the dead. Especially the dead relatives, she told Nikki, because they were so annoying when they were alive. Nikki watched as bundles of "money" and material goods made from paper went up in smoke, while her grandmother chanted prayers and lit joss-sticks, filling the air with Oriental incense.

Her grandmother didn't answer her immediately as she arranged small colored paper, called yim bo, into soft, saucerlike shapes and then crowned them with nuggets of glitter paper signifying gold and silver ingots. Her grandfather's yim bo arrangement, she noticed, was bigger than the rest.

"Maybe he isn't a ghost anymore," Nikki speculated.

Her grandmother fed the fire with more paper-money offerings. She gave some to Nikki. "Here, throw some in so the ghosts won't fight over it and get mad at us."

Nikki obediently did so, half amused at the idea of ghosts fighting over paper printed with bold red one million dollar markings. Things must be expensive in the Underworld.

"You have to be generous," her grandmother remarked, *as if she read her thoughts.* "It doesn't hurt to feed the ghosts generously. Some are greedier than others, and you never know what mischief they seek if they aren't satisfied."

"So it's like bribery? Give them more so they don't bother us?"

Grandmother chuckled. "Do you think ghosts don't want material things? They are all hungry for things they can't have here on earth, you know. They're allowed out once a year, so they're very hungry, especially the lonely ones, the ones who have been abandoned. Feed them, child, give them what they want."

"What about Grandpa? Is he hungry and annoying too?" *Nikki persisted in her theory.* "Maybe he's been reborn."

She hrummphed loudly. "Your grandfather kept too many secrets from your grandmother to dare leave me all alone." *She looked around, a little frown puckering her forehead, as if trying to discern his spirit out there.* "He won't be ready to be reborn till he sees your grandmother cross over, and then he'd better have lots of money and things left for me because he's in real trouble."

Nikki laughed. "What did Grandpa do? Tell me! Had he been really bad?"

Her grandmother tossed more yim bo into the fire and chanted another prayer. "Bad?" *She shook her head.* "No, but he did things he thought were best for me, and he passed on without telling me, so he's always going to be hungry, that naughty old man. And serves him right if I don't feed him."

She turned to Nikki and continued, "That's why you always take care of business here and now and not worry about feeding hungry ghosts later. Don't let the past haunt you, child. You get hungry, like the dead."

Grandmother must be haunting her because she hadn't listened closely to her teachings. Nikki fingered the key to her apartment as she made her way to the building. When she was younger, the past was nothing but stories of ancestors and their history. Nothing to fear. No ghosts. Now, she grimly noted, she faced a multitude of ghosts, some of them ravenous.

She had come alone to be debriefed by Jed. When she told him, Rick didn't say anything, but she was all too aware of the undercurrents. He'd let her go without a protest, planting a hard kiss on her lips. He would be in the study working on decoding the encryption, he told her. Then he would be meeting with Internal Investigations.

She opened the door to her apartment. Jed was lounging comfortably in her armchair, eyes closed. Years could go by without her seeing him, yet he always remained remarkably unchanged. The man must have a secret fountain of youth.

"You enjoy these games too much," she chided gently.

"I get no pleasure from them," he said, not opening his eyes.

"And there aren't seven days in a week," she quipped.

His eyes opened. He lazily examined her. "You've lost some weight."

"D.C. diet is bad for me."

"Does that mean you aren't staying?"

Nikki paused in the middle of opening a drawer. It must be fate. Her life was dominated by men who took too much interest in getting her to tell them what they wanted to hear.

"I thought you'd know the answer to that," she said as she pulled out files and papers. "It's your thing, isn't it, Jed, manipulating everyone? We're just puppets in your game plan."

"I just do my job."

She swung around and headed toward him, ignoring the silvery gleam in those eyes watching her. She stood over him, hands at her waist. "You say that every time you want to avoid a confrontation. You just do your job. How many times have I heard that? I think I've even repeated that mantra to others whenever it's convenient."

Jed didn't move, head comfortably resting on his hands, a small quirk forming at the corner of his mouth. "Works, doesn't it?" he asked. "Everyone starts doing things instead of sitting around arguing and wondering about motives and consequences."

Nikki gazed down at him. She would never understand this man, not in a million years. He had always fascinated her with his implacable aura, as if what she was seeing wasn't really there. "That's your job, then?" she asked. "Getting people to do their jobs."

"I'm number nine, my team's commander. There are eight men before me who have to do exactly as they're told before I can come in to finish the assignment. I can't afford having them thinking about the next step or consequences, Nikki."

That was how this complex man saw himself—unnervingly simple in his explanation of what he did. Never mind that number nine was the man in charge of an elite team of men who infiltrated the most dangerous sectors of society. Never mind that the job of number nine was the ultimate soul-destroying part of the carefully constructed mission. Jed McNeil, as he simply explained, did his job. He was the one who did the final act, and an assassin shouldn't think about consequences.

She shook her head. "You're more than that, Jed," she said, and out of habit, leaned down and flicked the lock of dark copper hair that brushed his brow. His eyes narrowed a fraction but she ignored the danger signals. Jed never did like people touching him. She perched on the arm of the chair. "You're always manipulating people and you have a knack for getting them to do what you wanted them to do in the first place. It must be horrible to be right all the time." She smiled. "One day you'll meet someone who will manipulate you right through to marriage, and I'll be the first to cheer her on."

Jed unclasped his hands from behind his head and reached for her hands. She didn't pull away. His thumb traced her palms absently as his light eyes explored her face, looking for signs of her old nervousness. What he saw seemed to satisfy him. "It isn't good to put a curse on your fairy godmother," he told her.

Nikki laughed softly. "You're an evil fairy godmother,"

she said, and sobered up, "but I need all your magical powers to make things right."

"Don't I always?" Jed asked gently, his soft caress traveling up her wrist, then her elbow, then his hand was massaging her shoulder. Testing her courage.

"You always took care of me," she agreed. "But this thing has to do with Rick and what he's going to do. He won't wait, not after you've so cleverly manipulated him."

"If I promise not to tell him, come sit on your fairy godmother's lap and tell me what he's going to do," he invited, his voice low and teasing.

She shook her head. The man didn't know how to behave, always trying to push past boundaries. His touch was gentle as his finger traced her collarbone.

"My assignment with GEM will be completed as soon as you've debriefed me," she said. "After that, I still have Admiral Madison's report for his committee."

"Then you should be happy. You'll have your file, your past and future . . . your man." Jed tapped under her chin with a finger. "Why the long face?"

"He just told me what Gorman has over him." She took a breath as he waited. He pinched her chin gently, prodding her. Finally, she continued, "Perjury. Lying under oath."

Jed cocked his head, dropped his hand from her face as he sat up a little higher. "Something our Justice Department would frown upon. I assume he did this after you and your group went down."

Nikki nodded. "But it's all to protect me. He lied to cover up for me. You've read my report I sent of what I remembered doing. After I drugged him, I went to download the files from his link that I had transferred from Gorman's computer. I didn't have time to look through them, nor could I say anything when I didn't have a clue about what was happening, so I hid those files, and left a note on the computer that I'd explain everything when I came home."

"Only you didn't."

She nodded again. "Gorman somehow traced the link to Rick's, and then to his home computer. He already knew about the complaint I made against him, so he must have panicked." She paused. "Jed, I think he somehow got rid of me, or thought he did, and thought he would use my stupid download as proof of betrayal that I sold out."

She stood up, pacing the floor as she contemplated that long-ago event. She turned to see Jed's gaze following her thoughtfully. Steepling his fingers on his chest, he noted the obvious. "Except Harden lied during the investigation, said he downloaded the link. I've read that case file. His testimony had a lot of refusal to answer, which accounted for the black marks in his report card."

"Gorman threatened to go on the stand to say I downloaded the files and Rick stopped him," Nikki said. She spread her hands out hopelessly. "Rick made a deal with him, said that he would be out of the running for the promotion anyway, and needn't be tangled up by departmental scandal. All along, he still didn't know I made the complaint against Gorman, and he thought he was covering up for me because I could have sold out. He refused to turn me in."

"He refused to believe you were a traitor, Nikki," Jed told her, softly. "There was also your message that you left, promising to tell him everything. He waited a long time, the poor bastard."

Nikki stared at Rick. "It was all my fault," she said, desperately trying to control the tumult of emotions roiling in her since Rick told her the truth. This was a debriefing, and emotions had no place in it. If she broke apart now, she wouldn't be able to function, or get Rick out of this predicament for which she was responsible. "Nothing good came from that one thoughtless act I did ten years ago. If I hadn't tried to do things by myself—"

"You made a complaint through the proper channels, remember?" Jed reminded her quietly. "Didn't work. You were trying to find evidence to substantiate your suspicions. That is the standard procedure before making any direct accusations."

"I stole files!" Nikki exclaimed in self-disgust.

"Correction. You committed a tactical error. You downloaded files using a network with open channels. Gorman, who was exactly what you suspected, caught you. Obviously you were onto something very incriminating, or he wouldn't have taken a whole team down."

She stared at the man looking calmly back at her. Did nothing ever faze him? "Tactical error or not," she said, "I can't have Rick trying to cover for me yet another time. He's going to hear out this new deal with EYES and admit to perjury in exchange for all my files. He thinks without him sacrificing himself, the ones Admiral Madison had gotten will be cleaned up. As a bureaucrat, he knows how that's done all the time."

"Do you think he's given up?" Jed asked.

She worried her lower lip. "I don't know. He was very calm about it, almost resigned. I tried to talk him out of it but he said time was running out, and he wasn't going down by himself. So he's going to get hold of the names, dangled it in front of EYES in exchange for my file and the truth of that operation to come out. But if that were to happen, he has to tell the truth himself, that he perjured. That's going to end his career, Jed."

There was a short silence, and then he asked, "What do you want, Nikki?"

She sat down heavily on the nearby ottoman. Jed's question was an echo to Rick's earlier. Was she such a selfish person that everyone was constantly asking her about what she desired? She had never thought herself demanding before. Mostly she had kept to herself. "I don't think my past is worth so much. I don't *want* it if he has to sacrifice yet again." Her voice became fiercely determined. "I. Won't. Let. Him."

"You forget he's pretty good at this bureaucratic bullshit. He might negotiate a plea that won't be too bad."

"Jed, no more mind games. Are you going to help me or not?" she demanded, and then sat back, shocked. She didn't lose her temper, ever.

Jed's smile was slow and satisfied. He finally moved, swinging his long legs off the sofa. "Stubborn people are like bulls. They don't move till you wave a red flag at them," he remarked.

"Are you calling me a bull now?"

"One bull is determined to throw himself on the matador's sword. Just give up, so to speak. He must love you a lot, Nikki, to do that, since we know how he hadn't given up on finding the truth about you for ten years. Why don't you let him do this for you?"

"Because I love him." She wasn't going to let anything hurt him again.

"Have you told him this?"

"How come you always know what to ask?"

He didn't tease or mock her this time. For an instant, she thought she saw something flare in his silver eyes, but whatever it was, it was extinguished with barely any facial expression. "I just do my job," he replied simply.

"What do I have to do?" she asked, trusting him to help her.

He considered for a few moments. "You'll have to do some serious digging. A complaint sent through regular channels doesn't just disappear. It might be ignored, or buried, or hidden, but the bureau has a habit of keeping files on everything." His lips twisted. "Even though they can't locate it at a later date."

"So it'd still be in records, you think?"

"In those days, email wasn't that popular. They did forms in triplicates. They are hard to delete. The top man might have buried that complaint. He might have called on the second tier to follow orders to ignore. However, the most forgotten department is records. They are overworked and underpaid, and no one pays attention to them unless they need something found. If no one asked about the complaint, and it never was sent anywhere, and if no one brought it up again, it's a safe bet that it's lost forever."

Nikki snapped to her feet. "I won't give him up without a fight. I know one of Rick's men is going out with someone from records."

Jed stood up too, like a lazy panther stretching. "Patty Ostler."

"Can she be trusted?"

"You'll have to take a chance, won't you?" He retrieved

the bunch of papers she had pulled out from the top of the drawers. "I can't enter the building without causing a stir, so it's up to you, Nikki."

"All right. What will you do in the meantime, Jed?"

He buttoned his battered denim jacket and turned up the collar. "Go see the admiral. Update him on the situation. Check on Grace."

"Grace?" She arched an eyebrow. Jed's daughter was a handful. Like the father. "Is Trouble in trouble?"

"Trouble is a sophomore in college. There is ample reason to be slightly concerned."

Nikki laughed. Grace was the most grown-up little girl she'd ever met, a tad too independent and with no fear of anything. Unlike her, she thought. "Tell her I love her," she said. And in a special way, you, too, she added silently.

Jed looked down into her eyes. He was close enough to bend down to kiss her, if he'd wanted. Instead he said, "I'll call from the admiral's. You'd better hurry. You've got your own trouble to deal with."

Chapter Twenty-five

Rick's cell phone was off, and his secretary didn't know where he was, either. After leaving a message, Nikki checked with Internal Investigations. A dead end, of course. They wouldn't confirm whether he was there or not. Finally she decided she would go to Rick's office to leave him a message as well as get hold of Patty Ostler.

She had expected it, but it was still unnerving to have so many pairs of eyes on her as she made her way past security and up to Task Force Two's floor. People working here were trained to break codes, listen to gossip, dissect situations. She was probably Fodder of the Week.

There was nothing to do but to withstand the stares and the knowing smiles. At least no one had said anything yet. She adjusted her cardigan inside the elevator, trying to relax. The constrictive prickly feeling she always had when she was in this building was back. She bumped into Agent Candeloro when she walked out onto the floor. They hadn't talked more than a few minutes but she liked him. With his unruly ponytail and easy demeanor, he had shown his faith in his Task Force operations chief when he showed his support in front of the review board.

"Hello, Mrs. Harden," he greeted her.

Nikki blinked. It was the first time she had been addressed that way. She absorbed the moment wonderingly. There was no fear of loss of identity, of being seen as someone else. She . . . liked the feeling of belonging. "Agent Candeloro," she said, smiling warmly. "Have you seen Agent Harden today?"

Cam nodded and gestured at his laptop case. "He gave me some work to do, which saved me from going to beg for a desk job at another department. Are you looking for him?"

"Yes."

"He has a meeting, you know."

Nikki noticed that Cam was speaking in very broad terms, which told her that he was afraid of being overheard. "I was hoping to catch him before that," she said.

He shook his head, punching the down button on the wall. "I think he went off about half an hour ago, Mrs. Harden. Do you want me to leave a message?"

"I think I'll leave another one with his secretary, but I do need your help, though. I need to speak to Patty Ostler. She's a friend of yours, right?"

"Yeah." He eyed her quizzically but didn't ask for more information.

"Can you take me to her at records?"

"Of course. I'll wait for you here. Hold the door and all that."

"Thanks. I'll hurry."

Rick's secretary was on the phone and Nikki had hoped that was Rick. "No, it's not Mr. Harden. He didn't say when he will be back."

"If he comes back, can you please let him know I'll be with Agent Candeloro and Patty Ostler? I don't know how long I'll be but I'll call again later to let him know where I am."

"Of course. I'll be sure to tell him as soon as he gets in."

Nikki smiled and thanked her, then went with Cam to records. She was surprised when she met Patty Ostler. Dressed chicly in white, with her hair pulled back into a tight weave, she didn't seem the type that would go for someone like Agent Candeloro.

"I wonder whether you can help answer some questions about locating old files and memos," Nikki said to her, after Cam introduced them.

"Sure." Patty moved the inbox tray on her desk back into position after Cam pushed it sideways by accident.

"I'm talking really old memos and files, at least ten years old," warned Nikki, watching Cam lean over to open the candy jar and knock the stapler over as he did so.

"That can be difficult to find but not impossible," Patty said, automatically righting the stapler, then moving the out-box tray before closing the candy jar. There was now a slight tension marring her smooth face. "Some are recorded, some filed away, and a lot of them are sort of lost in a huge mountain in the cavern."

Nikki frowned. "In the cavern?" she repeated.

"That's the vault to us," Cam chimed in, sucking his candy noisily. "When e-data became the thing, much of the updates started 'as of,' with current backups as priority. The goal was to have everything backed up eventually, but that— umm—fell by the wayside in the last few administrations."

"Lack of funding," Patty agreed. Finally, as if she couldn't stand it any longer, she turned to Cam, who was eyeing her with a wicked light in his eyes. "Is there something else that you want to mess with, Agent Candeloro?"

"Only you, princess, but Mrs. Harden really needs your help right now," Cam answered with a grin.

Nikki smothered her amusement. She had thought he was just being clumsy but all those little "accidents" were just to irritate Patty Ostler. She noted the high color on the younger woman's cheeks and thought they made an adorable couple.

Patty chose to ignore Cam's last remark and returned her attention to Nikki. "What are you looking for, Mrs. Harden?"

"I filed a complaint against a certain department. What would be the procedures of keeping the paperwork on file?"

Patty frowned. "Shouldn't that be with the DOJ?"

"Not if the Justice Department never received it," Cam countered.

"Oh."

Nikki nodded. "He's right. The DOJ might not have seen it

since I, and not the department head, filed the paperwork, but there should be copies buried in records. At least, I hope so."

"There should be but with the vault in such a mess . . ." Patty sounded doubtful of a successful find.

"But you found the old Marlena Maxwell files for Steve," Cam pointed out. He turned to Nikki and proudly boasted, "Patty could find anything on anyone, given time. Just tell her as much info as possible, Mrs. Harden. Patty will find the copies, if there are any lying around."

Nikki smiled as Patty flushed with pleasure. The younger woman stole a glance at Cam, who held her gaze with a very obvious message.

"That would be great," Nikki said softly, stepping back to give these two a moment to connect. It was always so nice to see a romance growing.

Rick looked up at the clock hanging over the doorway. He had expected to be kept waiting. This was, after all, Office of the General Counsel, where time was meaningless as the legalities of government intelligence and covert actions were weighed and dissected. The clock in the room ticked loudly, serving as an irritant to those who waited. It was all part of the game. After all, he was the one begging here and not in any position to demand immediate attention.

He had anticipated this and had gone to the bathroom before coming in. Any sign of nervousness or impatience would only play into their hands. They had kept him in here for an hour now, and no one had shown up yet. Finally the door opened, and he studied the man walking in with his assistants behind him.

As he had expected, it was Hal Stadler, the same counselor in charge of the first EYES deal. Internal Investigations loved men like Stadler. He was brilliantly meticulous in his cases, building each one with a chesslike strategy until he had all the angles covered. Of the good-old-boys mentality, he disliked anyone who broke rules and worked outside the box. Rick understood that in the world of EYES, those who did so were frowned upon. Government couldn't run smoothly if people didn't follow policy.

It made sense, Rick reflected with cynicism, until those in the box used their power to cover up their own illegal activities. Then the good old boys would be nothing better than the Mafia policing their own. The Office of the General Counsel trained and hired lawyers who were very good at that. Many internal abuses never made it into the public arena unless there was a huge media outcry. This had happened during the Iran-Contra affairs, and the OGC had been forced to do a lot of things in the sunshine. With Gorman's recent arrest, the media interest in national security was at an all-time high. This time, the OGC must be trying to do damage control before things got out of hand. Rick thought of the list of names in his laptop as well as what he had procured earlier in his study. Denise's password had taken him to several interesting places.

Stadler went straight to the matter. "Shall we begin?" he asked, heading toward a connecting door on the left. Without waiting for Rick's reply, he ordered his assistants, "Check him for listening devices."

The men opened their briefcases. Rick noted with somber amusement that they were using similar gadgetry that had failed on Marlena Maxwell not too long ago. He removed his jacket when one of them pointed to it and watched as the electronic wand was passed along the sleeves and lapels, looking for hidden microdevices.

"Just being careful, you understand," Stadler said, from the other room.

"Yes, I understand," Rick echoed cynically. This coming deal was obviously going to be one made out of the box.

"Do I have clearance to go in with you?" Nikki asked. They had driven to another building. She had checked before leaving with Cam and Patty, but Rick still hadn't returned. Greta must be sick of writing down her messages by now.

"You do. I checked first, of course. Seems Admiral Madison had taken care of all the details," Patty assured her. She turned to Cam. "You, however, can't go into the vaults with us. You can accompany us as long as you don't go into any of the restricted areas."

Cam made a face. "I'm familiar with this building. Spent some time helping the Directorate of Administration clear out space. I'll go with you as far as I'm allowed. It's not like the place down there is going to be overrun with security, you know. Who cares about a roomful of dusty old papers and forms?"

"Hopefully, Mrs. Harden will find what she's looking for there. Dusty old papers are my job, so are you saying nobody cares about what I do?"

Nikki smiled at Patty's deceptively serene tone, her respect for the neat young woman going up a notch. She knew how to handle Agent Candeloro, who was apologizing profusely.

"Princess, your job is the most important in the world because nobody but you can do it," he declared and bowed humbly. "Look at me begging you to let me accompany you down there. It'll be dark and danky, full of dangerous spiders and other assorted insects. You'll need me to hold your hand, guard you against the evil things, be the knight that you always read about in your romance novels—"

"Oh hush," Patty shut him up hurriedly. "Do you have to keep teasing me about the books I read? I'm sorry about this nonsense, Mrs. Harden. Let's go before he drives me nuts."

"It's okay, I read romance novels too. Not nonsense at all," Nikki told her, as she watched Patty slide a security card through a slot in the wall. The door slid open like Aladdin's cave.

"Really?" Patty said, as the door closed behind them. "Who do you like to read?"

"Ladies, don't forget your big bad knight protecting you from behind," Cam reminded them in a forlorn voice as they headed toward another set of doors.

Nikki and Patty laughed.

* * *

"Sometimes, to protect our national security, we have to break certain laws."

"There's a distinction between breaking laws of other countries and the ones in our own," Rick politely pointed out the unspoken rule of all Intel and covert agencies.

Stadler's eyes narrowed a fraction as Rick steadily regarded him. Finally, he admitted stiffly, "There were some mistakes made, but those are aberrations."

"When a miscalculated leak put a whole team of operatives' lives in danger, that is an aberration. When the leak was deliberate, done for personal ambition, I don't think any defender of our Constitution will call that a mistake, Mr. Stadler."

"We're here to discuss an open-ended offer, not the Constitution, Agent Harden," reminded Stadler in a steely voice.

The knot of anger in Rick's stomach tightened even more. Stadler was right. He was here to listen to their offer and counter with his own, not to debate ethics. So far, what he had heard went against every ounce of what he believed in. If he gave in to them, would he be able to put this behind him and start life anew?

"There isn't much to discuss," Rick said with a shrug.

Their "open-ended offer," as they called it, had been thoroughly massaged by lawyers. They would acknowledge the mistake made to Nikki's team ten years ago. They would release the "lost" files, but only under the Classified Information Procedures Act, which meant that only the courts and the Judiciary Committee could read the truth. Due to possible "irreparable damage to national security," the public would get a summary, with no mention of names and certain facts. No admission of guilt.

"This is what we could give you. What is your counteroffer, Agent Harden?"

"It's like a maze," Cam observed. "If it weren't so nicely carpeted, I'd think our bosses keep a dungeon down here. Princess, how many doors do you intend to take us through?"

They had gone down several levels, each time requiring

Patty to insert a special ID card and code. Each computerized elevator then appeared to skip certain levels. Nikki had never been down here but knew that each directorate had use of different sectors. She was also aware of the interrogation areas that everyone agreed didn't exist.

"One more level. We simply have no time to input every file from way back when. The 'dead' files are the least important, so they're way in the back. The scanned ones are with the microfiche. I think they're viewed as backups. It's quite a mess, so it's going to be a pain to locate a complaint triplicate. The only thing going for us is that we have a date," Patty said as she punched in the code. "There's also limited air-conditioning, since no one goes there much. Budget cuts and all that."

"What else has been cut, besides air-conditioning?" Nikki asked. She could use this in her report.

"Lighting is partial and curtailed. Motion detectors have been removed. They used to have people coming down here at least once a day for a routine walkthrough but it was deemed unnecessary since hardly anyone uses the backlog vault except to dump more boxes. So it's now once every two weeks, when a maintenance employee will come down here to look around."

"To nap, probably," chirped in Cam. "No cameras, no records, no real work. Great place to nap."

"Do you ever think of anything else besides ways to goof off?" Patty stopped in front of a steel door. "Here we are. Cam, you can't go in. Sorry. I wish you could. Will you be all right out here?"

She sounded so apologetic, Nikki had to smile. One instant she was cutting the poor man down, then the next she didn't want to leave him out here waiting.

"We'll try to be quick," Nikki said.

"Don't worry, ladies," Cam said. "Take your time. I brought . . . this . . . to keep me company. Have to take pointers."

He whipped out a book from inside his jacket. It was a romance novel. Patty muttered something and walked into the vault. Nikki laughed as she followed. She really found this couple amusing.

"Are you acknowledging that you committed perjury during the review process of Operation Urgent Stealth? You're aware, of course, that this is a serious offense."

Rick gave a negative shake of his head. He was taking no chances here. "I'm *offering* to admit to perjury."

"And what's the asset in having you do that?" Stadler sat back, eyeing Rick cynically.

"Do you really want me to repeat everything from our first meeting? Fine. If my wife's file is reopened, the failed operation will be, too, and of course there'll be a risk of a full-fledged investigation by the Judiciary Committee. As you realize, there is also a national security review board headed by Admiral Madison, given full authorization by the president himself, to analyze and review security issues of operations and agencies. My wife is currently an analyst for Admiral Madison. Her very presence is an asset to the whole review, Mr. Stadler. I don't have to mention all the skeletons that might be brought up, do I?"

Rick watched Stadler's lips thin as he considered the ramifications. A team of lawyers from the Office of General Counsel sat at every major review meeting to aid in covering up anything negative. With Admiral Madison not playing with the big boys and Nikki Taylor an independent contractor, the lawyers had a tough time reining in information that would be fodder for future investigation.

He quirked a brow at Stadler. "EYES knows I'm the only thing that might be able to stave off a big investigation on every directorate. How about that?" he mocked lightly.

Rick decided to keep his ace quiet for now.

The air was a bit stale. Nikki stood for a few moments as she took in the vastness of the room. It was just as Patty had warned her—shelves of documents and file cabinets among boxes of memorabilia from past cases.

Patty's gasp swung her attention to the left. Three figures.

Two were working on something set against the far wall. The third man turned around. It was Agent Erik Jones. He pulled out a gun and pointed it straight at them.

"A letter signifying gross negligence is already in your file, Agent Harden. A case of perjury will turn it into misconduct." Hal Stadler's unblinking stare reminded Rick of a lizard looking at a small insect. "From a personal point of view, I understand the sacrifice of a man in love, but as a lawyer, handing over your head does nothing to stop our current problem. The implication of your ties to Gorman is enough to finish your career. Don't take me wrong, we would prefer your head on a platter anyway, but . . ."

He shrugged, unwilling to admit aloud that the original plan had failed.

Rick allowed a small ironic smile and finished for him, "but the sudden appearance of my wife complicated matters, I'm sure. Not for Gorman, who seems to be having the time of his life behind bars, but for someone else." He cocked his head. "Tell me, Mr. Stadler. Do you have Gorman, or does he have you by the short hairs?"

The lawyer bristled. "Agent Harden, former Deputy Director Gorman is not our business today."

"I'm afraid it's so," Rick told him, clasping his hands in front of him on the table. "You see, if my *offer* of perjury is taken up, then I'll be asked on the stand what the truth is, and my story will sound something like this: The truth will show former Deputy Director Gorman being aware of my supposed lies. He made a deal with me to cover up certain facts about my wife's failed assignment. His appointing me to be his operations chief later wouldn't help his case; he knew this, and that's why since his incarceration, he'd tried to make damn sure that things look bad for me. To save his ass, Gorman started to name names, and warned EYES about a private list. I became dispensable, until a miracle appeared. How am I doing so far?"

"Enough. You're speculating."

"Am I? Remember Agent Denise Lorens?" Rick watched

as Stadler's shoulders stiffened. "She was EYES' setup for me, remember? Gorman in jail wanted me to take the brunt of all the leaks and she was planted to continue leaking information from my links while he's behind bars. Except, of course, the president gave Admiral Madison the authority to have his own independent investigator on board, who turned out to be my wife, and miracles of all miracles, her past is somehow linked to someone on Gorman's list. So now not only does the main man behind all this have to figure out a way to placate Gorman, he has to deal with my wife."

The frown on Stadler's forehead deepened. "Agent Lorens is dead. Nothing she did or said could be of use for your defense. You cannot possibly want to concoct a story that there is another list when there is none found, except one with your name on it."

Rick used his ace. "Except I did get close enough to Agent Lorens, Stadler, to get a copy of that famous list that Gorman has over your head."

Nikki pushed Patty hard. The automatic weapon discharged, and for an awful moment, she thought the younger woman had been hit because she wasn't moving. Instinctively she dove in the opposite direction and heard the weapon discharge once more, its echo strangely loud in the huge vault. The room plunged into darkness.

"Shit! You hit the lights, you idiot."

"Go get them!"

There seemed to be some confusion among her attackers. In the ensuing minutes there was a loud thud and groan. Taking advantage, Nikki crawled toward where Patty lay. She couldn't see how injured she was, but she had the keycard in her hand still. If she could reach the entrance . . . A large hand covered her mouth and she jerked back, reaching for the throat.

"It's Erik." the man whispered. As if she hadn't seen him before he pulled the trigger. She would rip his lying throat out. "Nikki, I just shot at the light, honest!"

She hesitated, and Erik rolled away from her. "I meant to

shoot them, but I couldn't do it." There was misery in his voice. "But I got them in the dark just now. They're out."

"How do you know?" she whispered back.

"I know how to fight," Erik replied. "Now can I turn on the emergency light without you killing me?"

"Yes."

She sat up slowly as she followed Erik's movements around the wall closest to her. He appeared to be groping around for a switch. There was an electronic hum.

"Shit, why do emergency lights always glow reddish?"

Nikki looked around quickly. The other two men were lying on the floor. "Why didn't you just shoot them?" she asked as she went to Patty. "I think I hurt Patty."

"I'm sorry. I just couldn't shoot a man in the back. I wasn't thinking."

"Agent Jones, are you going to tell me why you're down here and why you felt you had to shoot at something?"

"No time to explain. It has to do with orders from my directorate. We've got to get out of here. Those aren't exactly good guys, Nikki."

"The Directorate of Administration?" Nikki lifted Patty's head onto her lap. "Open the entrance and get Cam. We have to call for help."

Erik picked up the keycard and slid it into the slot. After he punched a series of codes, there was a loud click as the lock unbolted. He pushed it open quickly.

"Candeloro, we need you in here. Get the women out. There is a—" Erik started backing away. Nikki looked up. Instead of Cam, a very large man, well over six feet, strode in.

"Finish the sentence, Agent Jones." He had an accent.

Backing away even more, Erik said slowly, "There is an explosive charge in here."

The man nodded. "Yes. You tried, but you're not good at hiding which side you're really on. You make a really lousy spy, Jones."

Nikki screamed in horror as the man calmly shot Erik twice. Erik ducked, then crumpled, gasping and gurgling, blood dripping down his face. She started toward him, but his attacker kicked his shuddering body and stepped over him. Erik gave an odd moan, there was a pause, then—silence. Nikki covered her mouth as she stared up at Erik's killer.

"We'll have to verify this list."

Rick shook his head. "It doesn't take a genius to figure out that Internal Investigations wants to sweep everything under the carpet, Stadler. You want to do your own investigations, make as little noise as possible. That's why you're willing to deal with me. Once you have the list, business is back to usual. Gorman will have nothing. I will be nothing. And this open-ended offer will be dead-ended."

"You distrust your government too much, Agent Harden." Stadler clicked open his suitcase and took out some papers. "I'm a lawyer, not a traitor. It's my job to defend the interest of the United States—"

"Mr. Stadler, spare me the lecture. Hiding the traitors from the American taxpayers isn't in the interest of the United States. Worse, ignoring the problem is going to put our security at risk." Rick waved away a response from the other man. "I know, I know. We're not here to discuss these insignificant matters."

Stadler slammed his briefcase shut. "Think about it, Agent Harden. We've agreed to some of your key points. Your wife's case reopened. Gorman done. That's the deal. Your career"— he shrugged—"that's hardly anything you could do if you're going the perjury route. Put that list in the EYES' hands and everyone is happy, even you. Isn't that what you want?"

Rick had to admit EYES had a point. Everyone would be happy with the results. Gorman would be truly cornered. That was a revenge of sorts, if nothing else. So why was he hesitating?

Nikki kept her eyes on the killer. He kicked Erik's gun away from reach.

"You can always spot the new ones," he remarked casually. "Too many questions, shifty eyes, always trying to please."

Nikki avoided looking down at Erik, blocking out the

memory of blood running down his face where he was hit. The horror of his death hadn't truly registered yet. She clenched her hands that had gone sweaty. She had to keep this stranger talking. "Do you also work for the Directorate of Administration? What did Agent Jones mean about the explosive charge?"

His size intimidated her and she took a step back as he strode closer. "Agent Denise Lorens used to work down at one of the other levels. Guess what a closer examination of her keycard shows?" He looked around. "She spent too much time down here."

Nikki drew in a breath. Denise's record of Gorman's network of traitors. The vault would be perfect to hide a list of names as well as research on past forgotten files of individuals she was going to use to further her and Gorman's ends.

The man flipped open a small cell phone. "Like you said, she's here. Yes, she's alive." Nikki controlled a shiver at his narrow-eyed scrutiny as he continued talking. "The other two won't give me any trouble. Unfortunately, I had to get rid of one of the three you sent down here. He tried to help her. Hmm, let me check."

He continued to aim the weapon at her as he tracked toward the two who were with Erik. He nudged one of them with his foot. The man on the floor elicited a groan. "Yeah, I think they're alive. I'll take care of it. Yes. Not a problem."

He ended the call. He gave the downed man another kick. "Get up, Butchner. Butchner!" The man groaned a reply. "I said, get up!"

He took his eyes off her for a moment to study whatever the men were working on before Erik took them out. Taking a chance, Nikki stepped toward the exit and stopped short at the sound of the weapon being cocked. Her heart in her throat, she met his eyes for a moment. He had the steady gaze of a trained assassin.

"Who are you?" she asked. "You're going to kill me, anyway. Who's behind this?"

To her surprise, he put away the gun as he approached. "Oh no, I won't kill you yet. You're too valuable at the moment."

He reached behind his back. Nikki's eyes widened at the sight of the ugly-looking knife he brandished. Built like a wrestler, he had the advantage of height and strength. With the entrance still locked, there was nowhere to run. He stood over Patty Ostler's unconscious body.

"Come here, and I won't plunge this knife into your friend."

Nikki shook her head, backing a few more steps. "What do you want?"

"Come here or this woman dies." He jerked his knife threateningly. "Slowly. That way, you might listen to instructions."

She had seen him kill Erik in cold blood. She couldn't just stand there and watch him murder again, she just couldn't. She slowly came forward, willing herself to stay calm.

The flat of the blade tipped below her chin and her heart raced as she stared up defiantly. His dark eyes were dead, unemotional. Unless she figured out a way to save herself, sooner or later, this man was going to kill her. She cried out in pain as she was unexpectedly jerked onto her toes. She kicked out as hard as she could.

"Did anyone leave any messages for me?" Rick asked his secretary.

"No, sir, there aren't any messages."

Damn, he'd hoped Nikki had called. He wanted to talk to her about his meeting, tell her that he found Denise's password while she was with Jed. He frowned. She couldn't still be in debriefing, could she?

As he walked to his desk, he called her cell phone. No one answered.

Nikki struggled to loosen her bonds, listening to the soft conversation between her captor and the two men who were back on their feet. She felt her cell phone vibrating against her hip but her hands couldn't reach it. She ignored the pain burning through her wrists as she kept working. Tears of frustration welled up.

"How long do I have?"

"We're about to set it to go off right after working hours, as was ordered."

"Give me another couple of hours."

"Yes, sir."

"We need to clean up, especially the kid's body. We can't have one with bullets found afterward. Too many questions. Dump him."

"Yes, sir."

Nikki strained her neck to see what was happening. She caught the shadows cast by the emergency lighting, and watched them flickering against the walls and carpets. One man was at the far end, still working on the panel. That must be where the explosive device was. Another figure was closer, leaning over Erik's body. She bit her lip as the tears kept coming. She didn't want to cry, but knowing Erik Jones was dead, and maybe Cam, too, was almost too much.

She had put up a fight, but her captor's immense strength easily overpowered her, choking her till she passed out. He had then dragged her to the wide workstation where several computers and printers stood, tying her tightly with electrical cords. With her hands and feet strapped together, her mouth taped, lying several feet above the floor, she couldn't see much. Couldn't move much. Panic threatened and she desperately fought it. She had to stay calm.

The cell phone vibrated again. Rick. She knew it was he and her frustration grew as she tried to reach the only thing that might save her.

"Take the other woman with you after you've administered a shot. There's another man tied up in Room A. I gave him a shot, too, so he should be out still. Be sure to go about your maintenance business, gathering things for the directorates. Put them both in the crate ordered by our directorate and take them with you. You will be instructed what to do next. Meanwhile you'll take care to deliver the packages like you normally do."

"Yes, sir."

"Adjust your clothes, both of you. Be sure you have the

papers with you to show that the directorate ordered the crate for shipment."

"Yes, sir."

"I'll take care of everything else. Leave now."

There was a short silence. The carpet masked the footsteps headed her way but her eyes followed the approaching shadow. Nikki glared at the man looming above her.

"Well, well, tears? Come on, I was looking forward to more fighting."

She heard the vault door open and close. It was just he and she now. He took out his knife again. She started to pull harder at her bonds.

No! She wouldn't let him touch her. Fear blanketed her, and odd things churned at her senses—musty sweat and darkness; rough hands and laughter; pain from bleeding wounds. A scream stuck in her throat. The dreaded darkness that filled her old nightmares fell like a heavy movie curtain.

Rick stared at the computer screen. He had broken the encryption. What the hell was this? Internal Investigations would never allow this to go public. He scrubbed his tired eyes with the heel of his hands.

His brow furrowed as he checked his watch. It was almost quitting time, and still no call from Nikki. Maybe she was avoiding him because of how the morning had ended between them. He had acted like a possessive bastard, responding to McNeil with a juvenile pissing contest, and instead of talking about it afterward, he'd angrily challenged her. He couldn't help it. He wasn't—couldn't be—the old Rick.

He had grown into an uncompromising and suspicious man. It still pissed him off that he'd allowed McNeil to play him like some toy soldier. A soft knock at the door interrupted his thoughts, and he tapped a command on the keyboard before closing the laptop.

"Yes, Greta?"

His secretary peered in. "The package you requested is here, sir."

Rick frowned. "From?"

Greta walked in. He vaguely noted that she must have just gone to the hairdresser's again because her hair was whiter than usual, the kind of brilliant cottony style that reminded him of old ladies in Florida who couldn't remember what color their hair had been. Greta, however, had one of the best memories around here.

"It was a delivery from the Directorate of Administration. The young man said you requested it."

Rick took the small box from her. It was stamped CLASSIFIED and FYEO. The Directorate of Administration was in charge of security and funds, as well as filling out orders for operations. He hadn't had any dealings with them since EYES stripped Task Force Two of its workload. His frown deepened.

"Thank you, Greta. You can leave early tonight. I'm waiting for a call."

When he was alone, he took out a pocketknife and carefully cut the strapping tape through the middle. The top flap of the cardboard popped open.

Rick's breath froze. Every thought came to a screeching halt. Slowly he reached inside the box. Pulled out a long thick coil of hair. A braid the length of a woman's pride.

Chapter Twenty-six

*B*lood had different tastes. Fresh wounds, the kind that were deep enough to bleed a lot, reminded her of sucking on a rusty fork. Her tongue worried her split lip over and over, tasting the fresh blood. She told herself it didn't hurt. She had repeated this enough times, even as her screams mocked her own ears. It didn't hurt at all.

She wouldn't look her tormentors in the eye and let them see how afraid she was. So she stared at them blankly as they stripped her of every dignity. Touching her. Hurting her. Using her for their pleasure.

But then they had handed her over to another man, and he was more sadistic. Her hair. Her beautiful, long hair. What would she tell in exchange for leniency? She had nothing to say.

No, it didn't hurt.

Training and reality merged, and she forced herself to concentrate on her inner self. It was her safeguard against insanity. Some part of her quoted subject headings from training classes in a soft monotone: "Sleep deprivation and mind control." "Verbal threats and physical torture." "The use of humiliation to break a female prisoner." "Drugs and dosages."

She remembered each stage that destroyed Leah Harden little by little, until she was no more, submerged from the daily pain.

Like a panicked animal, her mind crawled to hide in the

depths of her frozen fear, away from what was happening. It would be so easy—and it wouldn't hurt anymore. But something kept calling her back. It was her mini cell phone, buzzing insistently, pulling at her consciousness. Rick. Rick was at the other end, and *he never gave up on her.*

Nikki's eyes flew open. It was almost as if Rick were telling her he was going to find her. She wouldn't be abandoned, like before. A new determination broke through like the first ray of sunshine. Leah might be dead, but she was not about to let Nikki be destroyed, too.

"No, I'm not calling back later. I don't care if he's in a meeting. Put me through to Admiral Madison now or I'll drive over to your office, and believe me, you don't want me to do that," Rick warned the admiral's secretary on the other end of the line.

"Agent Harden," the woman said, in a long-suffering voice, obviously used to dealing with insistent callers demanding the admiral's attention. "Other than a national emergency, I'm not allowed to interrupt the admiral right now. Please call back later, or leave a message."

"Write this down," Rick bit out, with cold emphasis. "If Nikki Taylor, *my wife*, the admiral's star witness on his panel, dies, please fire your secretary and make sure she'll never get another job with the Pentagon or any branch within the government of the United States. Did you get that?"

There was a pause, and the admiral's secretary replied, "Please hold."

"Let's keep it short and simple, shall we? We know you have downloaded files using Denise's password. Tell us where they are and I'll make sure your husband lives. There's no point in killing him if he doesn't have anything."

Nikki's eyes followed the blade as it weaved in front of her face. She winced when the tape on her mouth was pulled off, then felt the cold steel of the blade against her lips.

"Where's the file that you stole, Nikki?"

Her mind blazed through all the possible culprits. Whoever was behind this had the power to move things around through the directorates. The Directorate of Administration was the entity that supplied all the different task forces, and thus kept track of what went where. It also meant that shady deals could be easily done if there were enough double agents involved. Money laundering. Stolen supplies. State secrets. Anything could be slipped into a delivery and no one would ever know.

The blade dug in a little harder. "I'm delaying this explosion to give you a chance to save one life. One call and your husband dies, so you'd better give me the right answer."

She stared into the cold eyes of the man threatening her life. Death was in his gaze.

Anger stirred inside her at the thought of Rick being used by these people for so many years. Resolve hardened. No one was going to hurt her husband. She was a GEM operative and personally trained by T., one of the best escape artists in the field. It was time to let her other training take over.

"You guys run a crooked post office," she said, tasting the salty tang of her cut lip. "It'd be a shame to have to shut the whole system down."

"The possibility of that happening is pretty low once you're dead," he pointed out.

"You forget Gorman is in jail. He and Denise were the ones who made this list, not I," Nikki reminded. "My telling you where my files are doesn't solve your problem."

The man shrugged. "Gorman isn't my problem. Besides, he's a targeted man. He could easily be taken care of. We've people behind bars."

Nikki arched her brows. "First Denise. Me. Gorman. All these people suddenly wiped out—wouldn't that look suspicious? Who's next? Admiral Madison?"

"You can't talk me out of this. I'm the one who can do you a favor—make this quick and painless." He traced the edge of his knife down the front of her blouse. He drew closer, a sneer of a smile appearing as she tensed up. He deliberately stopped at her crotch for a few seconds before moving slowly down between her clenched thighs. His voice turned into a menacing whisper as he leaned even closer. "But I have a couple of hours to kill while you make up your mind. Now, where is the file with Gorman's list?"

Sweaty stinking men looming over her. Rough grabbing hands, the sour taste of . . . Nikki blinked. She wasn't going to be defeated by dark memories and fear. Not now. Not ever again.

T. always stressed perfect timing. Nikki refused to close her eyes. Endure. Breathe in. Endure. Breathe out.

The man above her, like all those nameless others, fed on fear. She trembled, but she shook from a black rage that rose from those months of abuse. His sneer was confident when she clamped her knees together with all her strength. It wouldn't stop someone his size. She knew it. He knew it. His eyes glinted like a monster's in the garish red emergency lighting.

He dug his blade in between her tightened legs to drive home the point. She choked with the need to scream, but she didn't. Her strangled breathing seemed to amuse him.

"There's no one here. You can scream as loud as you like, Nikki," he mocked.

She shook her head and spat in his face.

His expression changed. "Scream," he ordered.

She shook her head again, squeezing the blade tightly between her knees. He jerked angrily at the handle of his knife to free it. Timing. She suddenly opened her knees, allowing the momentum of his action to distract him, and she screamed as she turned sideways, bringing her knees to her chest. Screamed as she kicked at the groin area just within reach. Her tormentor grunted, one big hand covering his privates, but he was still on his feet.

"Bitch!" His roar of anger echoed in the vault.

She caught the red glint of the raised blade and she screamed as she kicked again, rolling off the table. She landed on her back, the carpeting softening the fall. There was a loud, sickening crash when the knife shattered the spot where she had been.

There was no time to think, no time to figure out what to

do next. All she had left was the instinct from training and the will to survive. She had one advantage, and that was her size. She rolled under the workstation, among the electrical cords and small metal file cabinets.

"Fucking bitch!"

Nikki looked up. She was right under where she had been lying before. Same position, same predicament. Sweat trickled down her neck as she caught sight of the ugly serrated blade buried so deeply into the table. That thing would have driven clear through her chest. She stared up for a moment—a quick prayer—then used her hands and feet to scramble painfully on her backside. He was going to go for his gun now. Time was running out.

She saw the rollers under the file cabinets. She scooted back further under the table, squeezing behind and nudging them forward to make room. She could see him on his haunches, crawling in after her. Desperation lent strength as she slammed all her weight against each cabinet, gambling on the hope that they weren't full. They moved forward, the rollers gliding easily. One cabinet went smashing to the left when he pushed it out of his way, looking for a view of her. She heard his big body lumbering under the table, knocking each cabinet aside like a toy. Her heart in her mouth, she watched with grim determination as she stared at her last defense. This was it. She had maneuvered him as close as she could.

She knew she had the advantage for an instant—his big size would be a tight fit under the table. With one hand holding his weapon, and the other shoving the cabinet, he would be slightly off-balance. The exact moment he tossed the metal obstruction to one side, instead of moving back, she twisted and rolled forward into his line of fire, close to where he was half kneeling. He had to bend his head low. In the semidarkness, their eyes met.

Nikki wouldn't allow herself to have second thoughts. She lifted up her knees and smashed her feet into his throat. His body jerked back and up in surprise. A loud hiss escaped his open mouth as his head smashed into the protruding blade of the knife he had used. There was a series of loud pops above her head when he squeezed the trigger on his semiautomatic, the silencer muffling the bullets.

One large hand reached down for her, his nails raking her cheek. Nikki screamed and kicked harder, sobbing loudly as she shoved his head deeper into the knife, aiming for his Adam's apple over and over. He never closed his eyes, his death-rattling breaths followed by black liquid pouring from the back of his neck. His hand clutched at her in one final desperate move, and stopped.

There was silence as Nikki stared up into those open eyes. Death was still in them. She fiercely shook her head free of that heavy hand, hot tears wetting her cheeks, mingling with her sweat. Then she realized his blood was dripping on her. She choked back a cry as she rolled and twisted out of the way. Hysteria threatened to take over. She gagged.

Fear. It was happening all over again. That sickly helpless feeling that spread with its icy fingers, slowly eating up all faith and hope. He had gone through it before—the despair that followed, how everything was questioned over and over in the hours when he was alone.

Nikki. She was out there, possibly injured. This time she wasn't unreachable. He could do something. He must do something.

"Don't go there." Jed was on the line now. He was with the admiral, dashing Rick's hope that Nikki might be with him.

"Don't fucking tell me what to do or not to do." The instructions on the note were standard hostage fare. Go to Point A. Alone. Unarmed. Except, instead of money, they wanted his list.

"It's a trap, Harden, surely you know that. They aren't going to let you live if they know you have the files. Files can be duplicated. You, however, are useless if you're dead."

"I didn't call to get permission. I wanted to make sure that Nikki wasn't with Admiral Madison. And since you're with him, you saved me a call."

"So you're just going to walk in there and give up everything you've worked to find out, and for what? Would that save Nikki?"

"Look, I don't have the time to argue. I want Nikki back safe and sound, McNeil. This is all I've got to follow up on."

"Harden, think—"

Rick cut Jed off. "They fucking cut off her hair, McNeil. I have her hair here in a box." He was shocked to hear a tremor in his voice. "You tell me how I'm going to sit here and wait for you to fucking come up with some extraction plan while they're chopping her up and sending me pieces of her."

There was a moment's pause. "I'll drive over. We'll go together."

"They said alone."

"Fine. Go alone. But you won't be alone," Jed told him calmly. "We're going to get her back alive, Harden, trust me."

"If anything happens to me, you *will* get her back for me," Rick stated, just as calmly. He trusted Jed to save Nikki, if he failed.

"You'd better get her yourself, Harden. I'm tired of being your substitute."

"Fuck you."

"No time. Keep calling her cell. If she's conscious and it's close by, Nikki will find a way to get to it. That woman's a survivor. Good luck, I'll be watching you. Oh, and Harden? Don't give me a chance to show off."

Jed rang off before Rick could say anything. He shook his head. How did he do it? With a few sentences, Jed had returned a measure of control. His assurance that Nikki was a survivor helped. He didn't know why, but hearing it from Jed's lips made everything possible.

Rick jabbed at his cell again. No answer from Nikki. He then called Cam. His voice mail came on. Of course Cam wouldn't be answering his phone. He was probably with Patty Ostler in the evenings. Putting his laptop into his briefcase and the box with the braid under his arm, Rick looked around at his office. It might be the last time he'd see the place. He nodded to nothing in particular and walked out, leaving the door open.

Blood. Nikki hated the taste of blood. The smell of it. She could hear someone sobbing. She told herself to ignore her. Concentrate on the job.

She couldn't stand up without help. She didn't want to touch the dead body, but she had to. Someone was sobbing, but there wasn't time to pay attention to her right now. She had to get free. Bracing her forehead against the slumped chest, she managed to get up without toppling over. Something soaked through her hair. It smelled and tasted of blood. Oh God.

Nikki's breath hitched. She swayed as she swallowed down the nausea. She looked down to see the body half-hidden under the workstation. Pressing her middle against the edge of the table, she dug her knees into the back of the dead man, pushing her whole weight downward. That far-off sobbing resonated louder inside her head, and she shook it off fiercely. Concentrate on the job. Tears and blood blinded her, and she rubbed her face on one shoulder.

She could do this. She pushed down again with all her strength, trying to shift the dead body but it stubbornly remained wedged to the blade. Her small size was now a disadvantage, and, unable to pound her frustration out, she hit her forehead against the table.

She yelled at the crying woman to shut up and heard choking noises escaping from her lips. It was only then that she realized that she was the one causing that racket.

Taking in deep breaths, Nikki closed her eyes. She had to get over this black terror and think . . . Rick's face floated in her mind, that tough determined look in his green eyes. He had told her he loved her and she had held back. If she got out of this alive . . .

Her eyes flew open. *She could do this.* Climb up. Pull the knife out a few inches. She leaned forward onto the table and used her knees to shake the dead body, ignoring the grinding sounds of bone and blade as the knife slowly dislodged from the man she had killed.

Rick frowned, slowing down the blistering pace of his strides. Strange. Cam's car was still in the half-empty parking lot. Maybe he left with Patty. Then he spotted Nikki's car parked right beside his. *She had been here. Where the hell was she?* He stared blankly for an instant. Something was so wrong but he couldn't place a finger on it.

He walked between their cars. If she was here this afternoon, why didn't she leave a message? Maybe she was nabbed here in the parking lot. He shook the thought off. His mind was running around in circles and he didn't have time to figure out what had happened. When he opened his car door, the dome light flooded the space between the vehicles.

He was about to slide in when something grabbed the leg of his pants. His muscles bunched instantly as he glanced down. It was a blood-stained hand.

Someone whispered from under the car. "Don't drive . . . your car, sir."

The knife was sharp. Cuts on her wrists proved it. But Nikki finally freed herself after agonizing minutes. She hunched forward, the sudden release of the pressure pulling at her arms and shoulders giving its own kind of pain. She gasped as she shrugged tentatively, then pulled her hands onto her lap as if they weren't part of her body. Even in the garish light, she could see the inadvertent cuts on her hands caused by the knife and electrical cords.

She bent forward to untie her ankles, but her fingers were too numb. She tried pulling the knife out of the table, but it was still embedded deeply with the dead man underneath. She didn't want to think about that, didn't want to bounce off his body again. Lifting her legs onto the table, she trapped the knife between her feet, wiggling them up and down against the blade.

* * *

Rick ran with possessed speed, his mind racing over what Agent Jones had told him, even as he willed his body to go faster. He had tossed his jacket over the young operative as he made another call to the admiral to take care of the injured man. He now knew Nikki had gone off with Cam and Patty to the vaults. Erik's account of what happened had made his blood run cold.

"I tried to save Nikki, sir, I really did, but I wasn't . . . prepared for her showing up." Jones's usual confident voice was a cracked whisper, and Rick had to lean down to hear him. The younger man had some kind of a head wound, but he hadn't been able to tell how serious it was. *"This was my first chance at getting evidence against them, sir . . . I showed them how I traced Denise's password to the vault, and since I had a copy of the files, I thought . . . it didn't matter. I wanted to catch them red-handed, get some hard . . . evidence . . ."*

Fire. Rick loosened his tie, tossing it away. He tore at the buttons of his shirt. He had to get there in time. He had to. There was going to be a major fire caused by electrical malfunction. Erik said they had gone to specific vaults where the security was lax and worked on the electrical panels. When the air-conditioning came on during its infrequent rotation, the motor would kick-start a special device, making a fire seemingly caused by faulty wiring.

"You . . . go . . . get her, sir. But don't drive your car or Nikki's. I think John . . . that's one of the men in the vaults . . . I think he had orders to wire them. He was busy . . . didn't notice me escaping from the van. Go get Nikki. I'm okay. Head wound. My Kevlar did its job but he went for . . . I'm still alive, right, sir?"

Erik had started to sound confused at that point, patting his head as if he were looking for a hole there. There was so much dried blood soaked into his hair, he looked as if someone poured a bucket of thick red paste over one side of his head. Head wounds were like that—the slightest cut bled profusely. The young man sounded remarkably steady for someone with a head injury. He appeared to have difficulty breathing, so Rick unbuttoned his shirt, only to discover a bulky Kevlar vest underneath. It looked as if it had saved Erik from a gunshot there, too. After determining that the bullet didn't penetrate, he called Admiral Madison to come to the scene.

Rick had no time to check the extent of Erik's injuries. He didn't have a choice. He couldn't stay till the paramedics arrived. He had to get to Nikki.

Fire. Only Nikki mattered. He must get there in time. But without a vehicle, all he could do was run—something he had trained himself to do for ten years.

Please, let her be alive. His heart rate was going too fast. If he were to make it, he must fall back into his routine rhythm. With single-minded determination, he willed his breathing back under control. He prayed as he sped up, cutting between buildings and across the open space in the gathering dark.

Live for me. I'm coming, darling. Just stay alive.

Fifteen minutes or so later, he heard an approaching car coming up the crest of a slope. Then the beam of the headlights fell along the road as he continued running in the shadows. He had taken as many shortcuts as he could. There weren't many vehicles moving in and out after work hours, and he didn't feel like bumping into security and being forced to stop for explanations.

Nonetheless, the car stopped ten feet away from him, and clicked on its high beam before turning off the lights. Whoever had spotted him wasn't from security for sure. Rick reached for his weapon in his holster.

"It's me." Jed's voice carried softly in the dark. "Unless you want to meet me there."

Rick slowed down, heading for the passenger door. Not bothering to respond, he climbed into the car. Who cared how the man had breezed through security? It was unlikely he had gotten authorization this quickly at this late hour. All he cared about was getting to Nikki.

The man apparently knew the way; he drove on without directions. Rick wiped the sweat from his face on his sleeve. He pulled out a flat plastic case, the size of his palm, from inside his back pocket and handed it over to Jed.

"Here," he said. Jed glanced at it briefly before accepting it. "That's what I've decoded from the encrypted files from the other day. It's not what you think it is. I'm not done with it yet, but in case something happens to me, I want you to get those bastards."

"Do you have a copy?"

"Cam does, but according to Erik Jones, he's in a crate somewhere with Patty Ostler. I don't know whether he's still alive. The Directorate of Administration is rife with double agents, it seems, all underlings to some cadre outside."

"Interesting. Good infiltration network. Administration being in charge of supplying and security, everything done under its guise wouldn't be questioned."

"Money laundering," Rick suggested. He was beginning to like the other man's lightning-fast thought process, jumping from point to conclusion with analytical precision.

"Yes, but let's up the ante to weapons. With a delivery system that uses the best from the USA, weapons make sense." Jed tapped something on his clothing. Rick couldn't make out what it was in the dark. "Did you get that, Center?"

Rick knew he wasn't talking to him. "Do you guys record every fucking thing you say?" he asked, remembering how Nikki had patched a link on him without his knowledge that night Denise had interrupted them.

Jed didn't answer him. Perhaps he never meant to. Rick would never know, since they were pulling into a scene straight out of a TV show. Black hooded teams, flashing lights, armed personnel. Except for one thing. When the men surrounded the car before they could get out, Rick noticed the silence in the air. This was no ordinary team of men. Jed presented an ID.

"This is Rick Harden, Task Force Two operations chief. His wife is in there," Jed told the hooded man standing at the car window.

"Yes, sir. Admiral Madison already filled us in. STAR Force team at your disposal, sir."

Rick opened the car door, studying the quiet efficient men

moving about. These were the admiral's men. There were no bullhorns, no shouting. They were military-trained. STAR Force consisted of the admiral's black ops. SEAL teams, the ones TIARA's Task Force Two was supposed to work with. They relied on TIARA and thus, Rick's men, to get their job done. Their lives were literally in TIARA's hands because any wrong information could get them killed. Because of Gorman's betrayal, the last few years had undermined some of the admiral's operations. Yet here they were, doing their job, knowing full well Ricardo Harden was Gorman's operations chief, with a high probability of having betrayed some of them.

"The fire department should be here any minute." The man stepped in front of Rick. "Sir, you can't go in there."

Rick took another step. The soldier didn't move aside. "I'm going in there," Rick said. "You will have to shoot me to stop me."

"Let him through," Jed said from the other side of the car.

"But sir, I strongly advice against that. We're evacuating the building. The fire is starting from below, so there is no chance of using the elevators. We're still waiting for EYES personnel to give us the codes to countermand the vaults' electronic locks and access wells."

Rick had heard enough. He started running toward the building. The fire had already started. Somewhere down there was Nikki, and she could be one of the first victims.

He heard Jed call out. "Let him go, soldier."

Other operatives rushed forward at the sight of him running straight at them and the building, but Jed and the other man must be right behind him, because they stopped and allowed him to pass. As he ran up the stairs of the building, he passed the few who had worked late hurrying out of the building. A few of them even greeted him, surprise and curiosity on their faces. No Nikki.

"All the electronic gates going down to the vaults need eye scans and codes," the soldier explained to Jed. "We're asking the few who are coming out of the building if any have access."

Rick didn't turn around as he headed toward down the hall. "I do," he told them.

Access was nothing. For ten years he had collected access codes to find out the truth. He had been battling the system on his own, thinking it was better late than never. Better late than never. No. He couldn't be late this time.

Chapter Twenty-seven

There wasn't an explosion. Just the dull hum of the air conditioner coming on, and then several snapping sounds from the direction of the panel. An electrical smell filled the air, becoming stronger as the air conditioner continued to churn for a few minutes before coming to a grinding halt. New crisis.

At least she was freed from her bindings. Smoke burned Nikki's eyes and lungs. She crawled to the back of the large vault, keeping as low to the floor as possible. It didn't matter. She could already feel the temperature in the room rising. The panel was at the far end but it wouldn't be long before the fire became stronger. She was going to die. Without Patty's coded keycard, she had no chance to get out of the place.

It was strange how quiet fire was. Her new enemy didn't crackle or roar; in fact she couldn't see it as it choked and seared her throat. She had to stop several times as violent spasms of coughing took over. She dragged in a lungful of air and coughed again.

The silence. No one to hear her screaming. No warning alarm. Nothing to connect her to something she could hang on to.

The sprinkler system hadn't come on. She was going to die. She looked behind her desperately, trying to gauge how far away the fire was. It was so smoky that the reddish glow of the emergency light cast a hellish fog. Where pockets of air were still untouched by the smoke, the light glinted back like angry red eyes, glaring and mocking.

Nikki turned away from the sight, scurrying toward nowhere in particular. She couldn't outrun this enemy. She was going to die.

She hit something solid—a wall. She curled against its surprisingly cool surface. Resignation filled her, even as she willed herself not to fear what was to come. This was it. She didn't want to die alone, not as she had so many years ago. She thought of Rick, would not forget him this time. Would he hear her if she called him?

She closed her eyes, willed herself to look for her center, for that place called her *chuung*. She saw her beloved husband there and she called to him. "Rick," she said softly, and his name sounded strange in the room. Her heart pounded and she could barely breathe, but she determinedly hung on to his image, with his green, green life-giving eyes. She would say his name with her dying breath. "Rick!"

She thought she heard a wind chime. Its soothing music was loud and clear, and she knew it came from inside her. Maybe she was losing it; maybe her grandmother had come for her. But something kept disturbing her peace, jarring the floating sensation of letting go. Like that magical chime that called her mind back that dark, dark hour long ago, something reached and grabbed her consciousness. It buzzed repeatedly against her thigh. Her eyes flew open. Her cell phone was ringing.

With a shaking hand, she dug into her pocket to retrieve the small phone. She had forgotten about it. It was her lifeline and she had forgotten about it. She punched buttons and held the phone to her ear. She heard the sweetest thing in her life.

"Nikki?"

She burst out laughing.

Rick stared at Jed. "It's Nikki," he stated. His voice came out calm and cool, as if there wasn't an emergency in his life right now.

Jed's silver eyes seemed to catch an inner fire, and then it banked. "And?"

"Nikki?" Rick said into the phone again. He said to Jed, "She's laughing."

"Hysteria?"

"She's alive. That's all that matters. Nikki!" he yelled into the phone.

"I hear you, my love, I hear you," Nikki gasped out her reply. Her face was wet with tears. "I love you, don't ever forget I love you."

Rick swallowed the lump that had suddenly formed in his throat. "Don't you give up on me," he said quietly, grasping his cell phone tightly. "I'm almost there. Move as far away from the fire as you can and wait for me. I'll be there, baby, please don't give up. I know where you are, Nikki, do you hear me? I know where you are this time."

Nikki understood what he was trying to tell her. "I know," she whispered. "I know you won't give up, but just in case . . . just in case you're not here in time, I want you to know that you're the only one I love, will ever love. I'm sorry I forgot about us, so sorry I was afraid to come back to you. I—"

"No! I won't have you giving up on me," Rick interrupted fiercely as he ran. He could care less if the others were following him. He knew instinctively that more than anything else, Nikki needed to hear his voice. "I'm almost there. Where are you in the vault, Nikki?"

"I'm against a wall."

"The far end?"

"I don't . . . know. Rick, I can't see. It's dark. It's getting really dark here." Nikki peered at her surroundings in vain, her eyes slitting in the smoky atmosphere. She tried to remember. "I moved as far away from the panel as possible. That was to the left when we entered. Then I was on a table close to them when they were talking . . . then I killed him . . . and then the fire started . . . I crawled to my right . . . Rick, I must be at the wall to the right of the entrance."

Her jumbled story tore at Rick. She said she had killed someone. He hoped it was the bastard who had cut off her hair. He shook off the images of what had been done to her, what she had gone through. He couldn't afford to worry about her injuries right now.

"All right. Listen to me, Nikki," he told her as he punched in some codes to an electronic door. "There are access wells going out of the vaults instead of stairwells. The elevators are useless. These wells are like air holes. Some of them come out in the grounds outside the building. Others are connected to access tunnels for air conditioner and electrical ducts. Am I making sense?"

"Yes."

Rick frowned worriedly as he heard her coughing on the other end. He lowered his voice. "Regular air-conditioning pulls in air from an intake shaft for circulation. For underground vaults, they'd designed them to pull air through and direct it to the access tunnel. That means, if you can get close to the intake shaft, I can get to you from the tunnel. It's usually a hole covered by a grilled panel."

"Yes. I know what you're talking about. I'll look for it."

"Good girl. And I'm right at the first access entry right now. I'll be there soon."

"Okay."

Rick turned to find Jed right by him. He pointed to the small recessed panel he had opened with a keycard. "The air tunnels are for maintenance work, easier to get to her that way, but if she's injured, it'd be difficult to maneuver through the narrower shafts, with all the ducts and electrical works in the way, to get back up here. I need you to show the outside access entrances to the firefighters. Here are the access codes."

Jed listened to Rick's instructions before asking, "Location?"

"They look like regulation manholes." Rick gave the co-ordinates, then switched his attention back to his cell. "Nikki, are you there?"

Her reply was reedy soft. "Yes. I can't find the intake shaft, Rick."

He could tell that the smoke was affecting her. He took a calming breath and said quietly, "I'm there. Hang on for me, okay? Just stay where you are, little bird."

"Okay. The wall is nice and cool where I am. So nice and cool."

Rick handed the cell phone to Jed. "You talk to her while I get down there. She's passing out." When the other man took the phone from his hand, he added, "Thank you."

Jed merely nodded, waving him to get going. Rick climbed through the small entryway. Before plunging into darkness, he heard Jed speaking behind him, "Nikki, this is Jed."

Nikki hung on to the cell phone like an anchor. Rick was coming to save her. She heard somebody else talking to her as she crawled into the corner where two walls met. She placed her aching head against the cool wall. The other one felt strangely warm when she touched it.

It was Jed murmuring in her ear. She concentrated on what he was saying. "Nikki, don't drift off. That's an order."

She had to smile at that authoritative tone. "I'm not, Jed," she assured him. "Can't you order the smoke to go away?"

"Doing the best I can. How's the oxygen down there?"

"I'm still breathing. Barely, but there's some left."

"Fresh oxygen will make the fire bigger, so we can't open the vaults from inside the building. The people behind this fire didn't really account for the thick walls impeding it from spreading. You would think they would understand that since there aren't any attics, all the usual ductwork had to be accessed from somewhere else. Obviously, our bad guys aren't construction subcontractors."

"Is there a reason why you're giving me a lecture?" she asked.

"Multitasking. Telling you and the men around me who are going to rescue you, love."

She imagined Jed running around, talking to her and giving orders to whoever was with him, coordinating her rescue without screaming out commands. *Love.* "Where is he?"

"Isn't he there yet? Must I do everything?"

Nikki laughed. Then coughed hard.

"You know I only let him come for you this time because you love him more." His voice was low, as if he meant those words for her ears only.

"Yes, Jed, I know."

"And he'd better get there in the next sixty seconds or I'll just have to rappel down from where I am and get you myself."

As if he had heard the ultimatum, Rick's voice suddenly called out from behind the cool wall. "Nikki? Can you hear me?"

"Yes!" Nikki yelled back, jerking her head and bumping it on the hard surface, from being surprised to hear him so close. He sounded . . . like he was on the other side. She banged hard on it. "Rick?"

Rick silently thanked God for giving Erik Jones the strength to escape harm. Without him, he would never have known where Nikki was, or which vault she was locked in. It wasn't as dark in the tunnels as he'd thought it would be. There was enough lighting from the above levels filtering through cracks and vents to help him along. He was sure there was a lighting system somewhere but didn't want to waste any time looking around for light switches.

It had gotten hotter as he went deeper, until his shirt and pants stuck to his body as he fought through chunks of insulation and electrical cords in the narrower spaces.

"Nikki!" he called out. He was pretty sure he had followed the right air-conditioning duct, the long silver tentacle that circulated the air.

"Rick!"

Her reply was so clear it made him jump. Then he heard a sharp rapping close by. "I hear you!" he yelled back, pounding the barrier in return.

Nikki stood up, pressing her ear hard against the wall. This must be why it felt so cool to the touch—the access tunnel was right behind it. "Here!" She kept rapping, trying not to breathe too deeply. The smoke was getting thicker.

Suddenly she heard a series of loud crunching noises. The side of her face against the wall felt the reverberation of each blow but she couldn't tell their origin.

Rick savagely kicked at the aluminum air intake. It was bolted down.

"Come on, you piece of shit! Come on!" He vented his frustration with each kick. The grating crumpled inward at each punishing blow, slowly loosening the small bolts at the corners.

Nikki sat back down. Her eyes were closing on their own, refusing to take any more torture. Her lungs felt like they were going to explode. Her head spun.

"Nikki!" Rick put his head through the opening and was immediately wracked by coughing. He covered his nose and mouth with a hand. "Nikki!"

"Rick . . ."

She was down there somewhere but he couldn't see anything. "Stand up, baby," he said. "Let me see where you are."

"I can't."

"Yes, you can, come on, darling. Stand up for me," he pleaded. He pulled back from the hole and jumped into the vault. The smoke engulfed him and he went down on his knees. He heard Nikki coughing to his left and scrabbled on all fours to get there.

In the corner was his precious bundle, huddled like a lost puppy. He pulled her into his arms and wrapped her in a tight embrace. He had found her. Thank God. He found her and she was alive. She hung on when he lifted her, hiding her face in his chest.

The thick smoke disoriented him for a few precious seconds and he shook his head to clear it. First thing to go was the sense of direction. He backed into the wall and felt its coolness. The access tunnel behind it. The air intake above, to the right.

"Nikki, baby, you'll have to grab while I push you up through the intake, okay?"

She coughed out a yes, lifting her arms free. He braced his knees and held her by the waist while she groped for a firm hold. She pushed off him and slipped through the escape, her legs dangling for a few moments before her body disappeared.

Rick then pulled himself up, ignoring the broken grate as it scraped and cut through his sleeve. He took gasping deep breathfuls of needed air. Musty tunnel essence had never smelled so wonderful. His eyes adjusted to the dark and he reached for Nikki lying on her side.

"Rick . . ." she croaked.

"Yes, it's me. We're almost outside." He lifted her high against his chest. She put her arms around his neck, and her lips felt like heaven against his jaw.

"Are you injured?" he asked. He didn't want to hurt her more than necessary.

"I love you," she told him instead. "I love you, I love you, I love you."

He paused to savor the moment. Had to savor her lips, taste her. Just for a moment. He had waited so long to hear those words, had never thought to hear them from her lips again. He tasted blood in her mouth and was reminded of how close he had been to losing her all over again. There was a cold tightness in his chest, and then a burst of lightness, as if she had squeezed his heart and released it at the same time.

"I love you too," he told her quietly. "I will always love you."

She nuzzled his neck and he could tell she was drifting off in exhaustion. "I know," she replied and lay her head down heavily. "I'm safe now. Take me home, Rick."

She felt cocooned and protected. The strength and tenderness within his arms obliterated what she had endured. There was only Rick. She belonged here near his heart beating so steadily under her ear as he hurried through the darkness. She didn't care where he was taking her—she would go anywhere with him.

She opened her eyes suddenly. "Can you hear it?"

"Hear what, baby?" Rick glanced down at her before continuing to look for the tiny reflector patches that mapped out the tunnel routes.

"A wind chime," she whispered.

"Hmm?"

"A wind chime. Listen, Rick."

"Darling . . ."

"No, stop for just a sec. Listen."

He wanted to move on. The outside access was around the corner and he wanted Nikki out of there, in the open, where he could see her. But for her, anything. He stopped and stood quietly with her in his arms. The semidarkness around them added to the eerie sensation of time standing still. And then he heard it. A very soft, clear melody that resembled a wind chime, its notes far away but resonant in the heart of darkness, floating like a distant dream from nowhere.

"There," Nikki whispered again, shifting a little in his arms.

"I hear it, too," he whispered back.

"That's the center, Rick, perfect harmony. That's what I heard when I was all alone and afraid, and it brought me back."

He placed a soft kiss on her forehead. "Back to me," he told her, just to make sure.

She tucked in under his chin. "At long last," she agreed, closing her eyes again.

Rick reached underneath the outside access easily. Jed and his men had already opened the manhole, shining a long shaft of light through. He stood in its beam and squinted up.

"Yo!" Someone shouted from above. His voice echoed and reverberated. "We're lowering a harness for the fire victim. Then we'll get to you next. Does she have any broken bones? Is she conscious? Over."

"Negative," Rick called back. "She appears to have smoke inhalation problems. Might have some cuts and bruises, I can't tell, but she's conscious and coherent. Over."

"A-OK. The medics will take care of everything once you get her up here. Over."

"Ten-four. Over."

Nikki didn't want to leave him down there. She wanted to stay in his arms, wanted to feel his warmth and strength, but the harness was for one person and she reluctantly let him secure her in place. Her voice was hoarse from too much smoke, and she couldn't speak without her throat aching.

"I'll be up there after you," Rick promised.

The light showed him for the first time her shocking physical appearance. She was covered in blood, so much that he could tell that it hadn't come from her, or she wouldn't be talking right now. There was a dark patch on her forehead. Cut? He couldn't tell. And her hair. He bit down hard on his tongue, hid his fist behind his back as he watched her slowly going up. She looked like a forlorn battered doll, and the need for revenge slammed into him. Someone was going to pay for that. Someone was going to pay for what they had done to her.

"Hurry up," she said, struggling to make the words come out. She didn't like leaving him down there. "I don't want them touching me. I don't want them probing and asking questions without you by my side."

And she started to cry from the aftermath of her ordeal. Her adrenaline had finally petered out as she watched him growing smaller and smaller below her. There was confusion when she reached ground level. People touching her. People yelling questions at her. Shining light. Poking. Touching.

Nikki started to struggle. Someone screamed no. Her head ached as she tried to push away hands and older memories of rougher hands. She shook from the smell of blood and sweat and her eyes squeezed shut as images rained in her mind.

"Rick!" She realized it was she who was screaming his name over and over, her body shaking uncontrollably.

A grim voice penetrated her hysteria. Sharp staccato orders. Suddenly no one was touching or yelling at her anymore. Relieved, she started to cough hard.

"It's me, Jed, Nikki. No one's touching you." She recognized the voice, turned toward it blindly. "No one will bother you till Rick's here. Open your eyes for me, hmm?"

She obeyed. The silver eyes looking down at her glittered like hard gems. "You're angry," she managed to whisper.

"Not at you, little one. I hope you got the one who did that to your hair." His hand combed through her knots. "On second thought, I hope you didn't. The pleasure will be mine."

"Too late," Nikki said tiredly. "His body is down there."

"Then the firefighters will retrieve it so I can return it to his boss," Jed said, and his voice now held that dangerous ruthless edge that Nikki and all her covert teammates recognized. "Do you think I should send him back in pieces?"

"Do you know the boss?" Rick interrupted.

"Rick." Nikki lifted her head eagerly as his familiar outline squatted down by her.

"I've looked at your disk," Jed said as he got up, letting Rick take his place by Nikki. "We'll talk about this later. Both of you to medical. Now."

Jed signaled and a soldier appeared. "I want them guarded, as well as the other man with the admiral. No one questions them, not even Internal Investigations. Do you understand?"

"Yes, sir."

"Any problems, refer them to Admiral Madison."

"Yes, sir."

Rick watched silently as he listened to further instructions on how to secure the scene. One day, when he had the time, he would gather information about Jed McNeil. The man might be wearing torn-up jeans and scruffy boots, but he was no ordinary operative. He had the air of someone used to authority and commanding officers. And it was interesting how he cloaked all that with a casual shrug. As now, when he turned back toward Nikki and him. The military crispness slipped seamlessly back underneath that low-key façade. No ordinary bastard at all.

In his arms again, Nikki had finally drifted off. Jed studied her for a long moment before saying softly, "I don't want to see her like this again."

"I second that motion," Rick agreed.

"I trust these men guarding you. You'll be safe. The admiral and I will handle EYES tonight. Rest up for tomorrow, you two."

"Thank you." Rick followed the medic and the soldier a few feet, then said over his shoulder, "Oh, McNeil?" He waited a beat. "Thanks for the chimes. They calmed her."

Jed's eyes glinted like a cat in the dark. "Chimes?" he asked. "Do I look like a man who owns a wind chime? Better get checked out ASAP."

"My mistake," Rick apologized easily and turned away, satisfied, as he continued on his way to the ambulance. He hadn't said they were wind chimes. He thought he heard a chuckle behind him, but of course, with all the commotion, he could have been mistaken.

Chapter Twenty-eight

Nikki drifted in and out, hearing bits and pieces of conversation.

"Was she . . . ?"

". . . obvious blunt trauma . . . contusion to the forehead . . ."

"Blood on her face and head appear to be arterial."

"Is it from her head wound?" That was Rick's voice, and Nikki felt his hand stroking her forehead. "She's bleeding worse than Erik Jones."

She opened her eyes. "They shot Erik in the head," she told him weakly. "He's dead."

"He's alive, Nikki. Were you shot too? Where did he hurt you?"

"Erik's alive?"

"Yes, he is."

"What about Cam and Patty?"

"We can't find them. But tell the medic where you're hurt, baby."

"It's not my blood," she said, and closed her eyes again, turning her face into Rick's hand. "It's his . . . Clean me up, please."

She floated in a dreamlike world, capturing things people said about her, but too exhausted to respond. Voices. They were talking softly, almost out of range.

"Has she said anything? I heard they scraped some blood

from under her nails. That's the only man Agent Erik Jones couldn't identify. Are her injuries serious?"

"She's still out, admiral. They put her in a hyperbaric chamber for a bit just to make sure her bloodstream is clear of smoke and carbon. Other than that, some cuts and bruises. She's going to have a whopping headache from that goose egg. How about Erik?"

"He's one lucky young man. Shot twice but the Kevlar saved him and the other bullet shaved a few layers off his head. All that blood. I thought he wasn't going to make it but they told me head wounds bleed like the devil, even the cuts. Damn lucky, like I said. A few inches lower, he would have been dead for sure. I've put him under heavy protection. The kid has found out a lot, especially with shipments, and he knows some of the names involved. Here, I retrieved your laptop from the scene and Erik said you told him to hold on to this box."

"Let me show you what's in here, Jake."

There were a few moments of silence, then a softly issued curse from the admiral.

"Admiral, can you do me a personal favor?"

Nikki tried to concentrate but that only made her headache worse. She gave up and allowed herself to drift off again. Rick was with her.

Her grandmother looked taller than she remembered. Her hair was white and long, longer than she remembered. She was smiling.

"When the center and the heart find each other, no more hungry ghosts."

Nikki woke up feeling sore all over. She moved her head carefully to the right and immediately relaxed. Rick was asleep in an armchair by a window, an open file in his lap. He must have heard or felt something because his eyes opened, instantly alert. When he saw that she was awake, he put away the file and crossed the room to her bedside.

"Hey." The rims of his eyes were red, and there were lines of worry around his mouth.

"Hey, yourself." She lifted her hand to touch him and he captured it, bringing it to his lips. "You look terrible."

A faint smile hovered over his lips. "You should see yourself."

"Get me a mirror," she said. She had to know.

That immediately chased away the soft humor on his face. "Are you sure?"

She hesitated and looked at her bandaged wrist. "I couldn't do anything. I knew he would use me to get to you. I didn't want to put you in danger."

He tipped her chin and she met his green eyes. "You were the one in danger," he reminded her softly. "When are you going to stop putting me first? I was so afraid I'd lose you all over again—not knowing where you were, not knowing who to call."

"I knew you were calling me but I couldn't get to the phone in my pocket. It gave me strength, just knowing that you were out there. Every time I felt that I was in an impossible situation, the buzzing gave me hope. I didn't give up this time."

Rick leaned down to kiss her but Nikki shook her head. As he read her silent request, his green eyes darkened, then he scooped her into his arms and carried her to the private bathroom. She stared at her reflection for a few long seconds.

Her forehead had a huge purple and green bruise. It stood out magnificently against the paleness of her skin. She recalled pounding her head on the workstation. There was a long red scratch on one side of her face. She got that from shaking her head ferociously when the brute was hacking off her braid. Her hair—she had been afraid to look at it.

"You're beautiful," Rick told her, his eyes meeting hers in the mirror.

"He was a bad stylist," she joked mildly. She angled her head one way, then the other, gauging the damage. Someone had washed and combed out the shorn locks. The uneven lengths looked strange. Part of her mourned the missing length, the familiar weight, but she tamped it down. She was alive, after all. "I've had worse bad hair days."

She closed her eyes when he dropped a kiss against her hair. There was no point crying about it. She laid her head against his heart as he carried her back into the room, but this time, he sat down in the armchair with her on his lap.

"You took care of the bastard that did this to you," he told her in a low voice, muffled a little by her hair. "Let me take care of the rest. I'll make sure that every one of them is caught and punished for what they did to you."

Not just to her. "I remember you told me Erik is alive. What about Cam and Patty?"

She turned too quickly and saw stars for a few seconds as her head spun. Rick muttered a curse even as he fingered through her hair soothingly.

"Shhhh, take it easy. Are you all right?" He waited till she nodded before continuing, "Nobody knows where Cam and Patty are. We'll find them, Nikki."

She fell silent, worried for the missing couple. She felt responsible. If she hadn't asked for Patty's help, they wouldn't be in danger now, or worse. Rick seemed to sense her pain, folding her fully against him in comfort.

"I decoded the encrypted disks," he told her, changing the subject. "Erik Jones also gave us more files."

"So do we have the name of the double agent?" It was so surreal talking like this, enveloped safely within his arms. Did she really kill a man?

Rick sank deeply into the armchair, his hand caressing her shortened hair absentmindedly. "If I told you who she is, you wouldn't believe it."

His fingers were doing magic things to her headache but she wanted to know everything. "She?" she prompted.

He reached out and retrieved the file from the nearby table. He opened it and leafed through several pages before pointing to a specific one. Nikki quickly read it, then went through it a second time.

"It makes horrible sense," she finally said, "but no one is going to allow this to come out. And it says here that you're the last person to talk to her. Please don't tell me they're going to suspect you like they did with Gorman's case."

"EYES would probably want to lay this at my door. It looks better to have me as a traitor than a blue-haired little old lady," Rick said. "However, even they can't pin this on me since all the shipments and verification of shipments from Gorman go through the Directorate of Administration. The files Jones downloaded had all the dates of armament and monetary deliveries that were approved under the table, gone unchecked for years."

"It's a very clever operation," Nikki agreed, as she thumbed through the file. "All these years, Gorman relates information from Task Force Two's operations through Task Force Two's secretary to the Directorate of Administration. It would look normal to anyone checking up since administration handles delivery of weapons and tools. Meanwhile, Greta—the connection between all the information going back and forth—passes this on to her own handler, playing middleman right under everyone's noses. Who would suspect that she would process the information? Who would guess that she's the one giving orders to two powerful men?"

"Yes, Gorman and the director of administration were in cahoots all these years selling our weapons and using our government warehouses to launder these sales. That's how they make their money on the side while also selling state secrets. Remember I was the one up against Gorman for a promotion? It all started then. They had gone up the system's hierarchy, and in the process, built an entire network for themselves." Rick gave a sigh. "It's not going to go down well when the DOD and Congress find out that our own planes and equipment had been used to finance arms dealers and our enemies, that our secrets could have been leaked for so long."

Nikki frowned. "But how could that happen? Sure, a few signatures can hide caches of money being laundered, but shipments require planes, trucks, and a paper trail."

"Drugs and weapons too, Nikki."

"But how? We can't just drop shipments everywhere without lots of people knowing. There are pilots and other personnel involved."

"Not if the orders were to drop relief shipments for victims of war or weapon relief for freedom fighters," a voice interrupted from the doorway.

Nikki and Rick looked up. Jed moved from the doorway and sauntered into the room with lazy grace. Nikki wondered how long he had been standing there, listening in and watching them. No sound had betrayed his presence until then.

His usually hard and implacable expression softened as his gaze dwelled on her face. Then he gave Rick a nod. "You both look terrible," he remarked casually before taking a seat nearby, stretching out his long legs, "but not as bad as the body they found in the vault." His expression hardened slightly before he added, "As well as the two men who were in there with Agent Erik Jones."

"Where were they?" Rick asked.

"The one who delivered that box didn't even know the whole operation was coming down on his head. He was at home watching the news about the fire when I dropped by." Jed's tone of voice was pleasant, conversational. "The other was still dropping off his deliveries. Put up a little fight. Slightly injured."

"Where are they now?"

"They're in the hospital and will be ready to answer questions soon. We're tracing their drop shipment orders, looking for signs of Agent Candeloro and Patty Ostler. I'm sure those two wouldn't mind volunteering information to assist you."

Nikki marveled at the way the two men spoke their coded messages to each other. Why were men always so protective at the wrong time? "I'm perfectly able to understand what's going on, you know," she remarked. She raised a brow at Jed's quizzical expression. "If you beat the shit out of them, how are they going to testify? And if you let Rick take his turn, how are they going to survive?"

Jed's lips lifted into a ghost of a smile. He said in the same pleasant voice, "They'll survive." He looked past her at Rick. "Ready?"

Rick's hand soothed the back of her neck but his voice had the same ruthless edge.

"Ready. Who's going to guard Nikki while we're gone? The men outside and around are fine, but I'd prefer someone I know here."

"She'll have someone we both know here," Jed replied.

"Good."

Nikki collared Rick with her arms as he stood. "Can the two of you at least tell me·what's happening?" she asked, frustrated.

He settled her into the bed, tucking the sheets. He framed her face with his hands, his thumb rubbing her temples rhythmically. "In your writings, you talked about feeding ghosts. Let me go put away mine. Rest for now. They're waiting to debrief you as soon as you're able."

"Promise me you won't do anything violent." She didn't want him put away. Not now.

His eyes glinted and his jaw tightened. After a moment, he said, "I promise."

She smiled and relaxed into her pillow. "With Jed and you together, I feel bad for those men. You promise to tell me everything when you get back."

"Yes."

She watched as they walked out, the two men who meant so much to her.

"She did that to me, too, you know," she heard Jed say.

"What?"

"Wrapped you around her finger. Made you promise; now you can't hurt those guys."

"You didn't."

"Surrogate fists. I like that."

The door closed. Nikki shook her head helplessly.

Outside the room, Rick found a contingent waiting. Four women and a man crowded the small area among the medical monitors, staff and security guards. He raised an eyebrow in recognition. Steve McMillan, who recently had worked under him at Task Force Two, stood next to Marlena Maxwell. He didn't know the other women but they were all studying him intently as Jed and he approached them.

"What are you doing here, Trouble?" Jed addressed the

youngest of the women, who looked like she should be in school.

She tilted her head, chocolate brown eyes regarding Jed seriously. There was a deep dimple in her chin . . . Rick paused. This was the little girl in the photograph, all grown up. This must be . . .

"I came to see Nikki," the girl answered calmly. "She's injured. You didn't even tell me, Jed."

Rick frowned. She called her father by his name? Jed didn't seem to mind as he put his arm around her shoulder. "Didn't stop you from finding out, did it?" he countered dryly. "Harden, McMillan will be guarding Nikki. You've met Marlena. This is T. And the other two are O. and S."

"Chief," Steve greeted. Rick nodded. They still weren't on the best of terms.

"And I'm G.," Jed's daughter chimed in, amusement etched in her voice. "We're the Alphabet Soup Gang."

"Then you should know how to spell 'trouble,' " Jed said in the same amused tone. "G-R-A-C-E. Now go on in to say hi to Nikki before the others."

Grace didn't argue, just gave her father a knowing smile and sauntered off after a mocking sing-songy, "Yes, Dad-dy."

"Did you have to tell her now?" Jed addressed the woman called T. There was mockery in his voice. "I thought you were on assignment. Where's Diamond? Hasn't he found you yet?"

"I don't appreciate your sending him after me, darling."

"Oh, but I didn't. You two will just have to settle this thing between yourselves."

Rick's eyes narrowed. This was the infamous T., the one who had orchestrated Gorman's capture. She was not quite how he'd imagined her—all golden, with the sinuous glow of a model, slanted tawny eyes with lurking laughter. It didn't fit the image of the hard-assed negotiator on the other end of the phone bargaining Steve McMillan's freedom with a promise that he'd get answers about his past.

"You're Tess Montgomery?" he addressed the woman, just to make sure.

T.'s smile was slow and sultry. "Yes," she answered, then returned her attention to Jed. "I didn't tell Grace. I'm still on vacation, so this is a detour from a shopping expedition."

Jed's eyebrows shot up. "Shopping? You choose shopping over Diamond?"

"Darling, a woman has her prerogatives," T. said. "You should do that sometimes. Shopping is good for the soul. Ask Stash."

Jed and Rick both looked at Steve at the same time. He was looking extremely fit and tan, showing better form and muscle definition since he left his position with Task Force Two to work for these guys, Rick noted, wondering where the navy SEAL had been training. These GEM teams were beginning to intrigue him more and more.

"Well, is that so, McMillan?"

Standing behind Marlena, Steve shrugged. A rueful grin tugged at his mouth. "It all depends whether you like color-coordinated shoes and clothing." He flicked a telling glance at Marlena. "The changing rooms are interesting places."

Marlena, clad in her usual leather outfit, carelessly tossed her hair, took a step back, and bumped up against Steve, causing him to wrap a possessive arm over her front. She didn't say a word, just leaned back and smiled naughtily as she ran a hand down his bare arm.

"I stand corrected. Shopping is really good for the soul," Steve said with a straight face.

"We'll leave you with the ladies, then, McMillan," Jed said. "As liaison, you can report back to the admiral about the debriefing."

"Of course," Steve said.

"Wait a minute," Rick interrupted. "They're here to debrief Nikki? I won't allow it. She's still not up to it."

Tess picked up a small briefcase. "Nikki is GEM. We take care of our own. And besides, she's going to need me to fix her up."

"Fix her up," reiterated Rick, with a frown.

"Just go with Jed," T. said, and started to walk in the direction of Nikki's room. "Trust me, Nikki will look and feel better after we're done with her, and you can talk to me then, Rick Harden. Right now I've no time for you. I have a student to take care of."

"Let them go, Harden. We got an appointment, remember?"

Rick ignored Jed, turning to follow T. and her operatives. He wanted to make sure about Nikki. T. swung around just at the entrance. Her catlike topaz eyes slowly swept over him, like a woman appreciating a man. Rick stiffened.

"Don't try your NOPAIN shit on me, Tess," he warned. "It won't work."

T.'s laugh tinkled like soft rain. Her eyes remained bold, unperturbed, and Rick was suddenly aware of the intelligence lurking in them, looking for weaknesses. She was, after all, Nikki's leader. It didn't take much to see why Alex Diamond had a hard time going after the woman. She exuded an elusiveness that rivaled Jed McNeil's.

Her gaze turned thoughtful. "You trusted me enough to free Steve that one time. Don't you trust me with Nikki?"

His own gaze narrowed. "I didn't trust you. That's why I wired Cam."

"Which proved to be a good idea, since you needed all the evidence you got to trap Gorman," T. said. "Now, why would you worry about Nikki in my hands? She is my operative. Her job is to report to me." Her voice lowered. "I promise she'll be here when you return, Harden, if that's what you're afraid of."

Damn them all. They all knew the heart of his fears, that this was still an assignment for Nikki. He was afraid this would remind her that it was just a job.

"What's the matter?" T. asked, eyes suddenly shrewd. "Don't you think Nikki would know what she wants on her own?"

Rick clenched his jaw but he'd be damned if he let this woman have the last word. "Well, she *is* your student," he pointed out softly, "and I know, from watching Diamond, how good you are at disappearing. I'll hold you personally responsible if she does. And if she isn't here when I get back, I'll find you for Diamond myself."

With that he turned on his heels and stalked past Jed. He heard Jed's short bark of laughter, followed by, "T., Alex's going to get a kick out of hearing about this."

"And I'm going to kick you if you tell him where I am, Jed."

"Tell you what, I'll kickstart the race after I take care of some business. Should be interesting to watch you screaming and kicking when he catches up with you."

Rick didn't hear the rest of the jibes as he left the whole damn room of manipulation experts. Covert tongue twisting. One-upmanship mind games. He didn't need any of them to do what he had in mind. He had a promise to fulfill.

The man, manacled at the wrists and ankles, climbed into the secured van. He sat down where the guard pointed. A look of anger and disdain crossed his face as he watched the guard unlock his chains, then shackle them to the seat, thus impeding any chance of escape. His lips thinned, as if he was having a hard time being silent.

Rick continued studying the man while he waited for the van to start up. There was silence as the engine fired up and the driver pulled out into traffic. The prisoner stared resolutely at nothing as his body swayed to the van's movements.

After a few minutes, Rick tipped up his guard's hat. "You're thinner," he remarked. "The food must not be the same rich diet you're used to."

Gorman raised his head sharply at the sound of Rick's voice and his eyes widened. He looked at the two guards in the van with him. "What's he doing here?" he demanded. When the two guards remained silent, he swerved back to Rick and mocked, "What's the matter, Harden? Breaking the law now? I thought you were all for rules and regulations."

Rick allowed a cold smile. This was Gorman, his nemesis, the man responsible for Leah's disappearance, the man behind his own fall from grace. This was the man who had almost cost him Nikki. It would be so easy to unleash the violent storm of his hate, to go after this piece of garbage. He could imagine killing the man for what he had done. He could even convince himself that it would be worth going to jail for.

"This isn't legal without the presence of my lawyer," Gorman continued, his voice filled with confidence. "Moving me to a high-security prison won't make me talk. Intimidation isn't going to work so you can just tell EYES to stop playing games and take me back."

"If you think this move to a high-security facility is just a trick, then you're dead wrong," Rick informed him. "The DOJ has deemed you a high security risk ever since your sidekick, Johnson, disappeared with *your* boss—remember her?—at the same time. Imagine, the head of the Directorate of Administration and Greta, Task Force Two's secretary. No one left but you, so guess what, Gorman? EYES aren't willing to deal anymore. There's a huge list of questionable shipments dating back for a decade that they want answers for and the main guy in charge is gone, leaving you behind. And there is still the matter of the missing laptop you were caught stealing. They sure as hell aren't going to admit to the public that the government had been duped by a mole disguised as a fifty-something secretary."

Rick paused, allowing the other man to digest what he had revealed. His face had grown pale and tight, making the lines deeper.

"Things don't look good, do they? In a few weeks or so, Admiral Madison is going to commence with his panel on national security and a lot of information is going to come out. Most of it has to do with you—your ten-year rise to power and your misuse of it. No one will even look at me. You know why? Because I made a deal with EYES. I won't bring up their cover-up of Leah's operation ten years ago, won't reveal their leaving behind operatives who were still alive. In return, they will reopen the case and reinstate my wife's status, and they get to blame everything on you. They have evidence now, Gorman, that you leaked the operation's mission."

Rick noted with satisfaction the thin sheen of sweat on Gorman's forehead. His own fury was churning like thunder still but he kept it under control as he continued his verbal assault. "This isn't a threat, Gorman, so technically I'm not breaking any big law here. I'm just informing you as a former underling of all the information in my hands, as I've so often done all these years, to my detriment and to your gain. So use this as you always have. You might even escape the death penalty they give to traitors."

Gorman pursed his lips into a sneer. "I still have friends in high places."

Rick shifted, leaning forward. "You don't understand, do you? Your friends are deserting you, Gorman. They killed Denise. Do you think they're going to give you any chance to wheel and deal? Johnson's disappeared. Who knows whether he's dead? You're moving to a facility with violent men. Who knows whether you're going to last long there?" He sat back, stretching the silence as the van rumbled on. Softly, predatorily, he ground out, "Frankly, I don't give a damn whether they kill you or not, Gorman. What you did to Leah . . . if you were a free man, I'd come after you personally and give you what you deserve. But you're under the protection of the law, and . . . you know what? I think it'll do you good to sit in solitary confinement for a long, long time."

He nodded at Jed, who was sitting close by. Jed rapped on the divider between the front and the back of the van, and the vehicle came to a halt.

The back door opened and Rick stood. Two security guards appeared to take his and Jed's place. They had been ordered to follow the van in another car. Jed got off first.

"All this over a dead woman," derided Gorman bitterly. "I should've had Marlena Maxwell killed off exactly the same way your Leah disappeared. You disappointed me, Harden. You couldn't rise above a dead woman. You'll never do anything but passively mourn for the rest of your life."

Rick pulled Gorman to his feet and slammed him hard against the side of the van. He grabbed the man's throat, squeezing hard enough to cut off air. "Women seem to find a way to defeat you, Gorman. Marlena Maxwell smoked you out from the rat hole. And Leah . . ." He met Gorman's bulging eyes. "My wife's alive. She's alive and will be testifying against you. And no one will mourn for you."

He pushed off, leaving Gorman choking for breath. Out in the open, he stared up into the bright expanse of sky. There wasn't a cloud at all, no hint of the roiling storm raging within him. It was hard to swallow that much hatred for a person who had done him and his so much wrong, but he had to. He wouldn't allow Gorman to haunt his future. If justice was delivered, he needn't worry about that traitor any longer.

"That wasn't bad," Jed remarked from behind. "If they kick you off the agency, give me a call. I like your style, Harden."

Rick gave him a brief glance as they strode toward the waiting car. "Wasn't bad?"

For a second, Jed's silver eyes glinted with humor as their gaze met over the hood. "It'd have been better in my book if you had punched the daylights out of him."

Rick stared back, and then laughed. And just like that, the killing storm inside dissipated into something less dangerous. He climbed into the driver's seat, and canted a brow at the other man. "I thought you were my surrogate fists."

Jed's eyes narrowed for a second. He slammed the door. "You're in the driver's seat today, Harden. There's always tomorrow."

Rick put the car in gear. Jed McNeil, he was discovering, was a man of infinite patience, a quality that he himself had plenty of. He hadn't done anything today out of respect for him, and Rick appreciated that. He suspected that Jed didn't put other people in front of him too often. Whatever he had planned for Gorman, Rick approved. He didn't care any longer. He looked ahead at the traffic.

He had been focused on the past for so long because he had thought he didn't have a future. Now there was only Nikki. Everything else could wait.

Chapter Twenty-nine

Nikki breathed in the sweet scent of the night blossoms drifting in through the picture window. The cool air brushed lightly against her bare skin, lifting her hair. She stepped forward a little more, peering into the darkness to see whether the moon was out.

A long male arm scooped under her breasts and pulled her back possessively and she smiled as she turned without demur into her husband's naked heat. She shivered in delight as his fingers caressed the curve of her spine. He splayed them through her short hair, playing with the tresses as his lips nibbled at her earlobe.

"What are you doing up so late?" he whispered. "Come back to bed."

"It's our last night here," she whispered back. "I just wanted one last look at the garden."

It had been a glorious two weeks. She had missed her sanctuary so much. This was her place and she had needed to be here to recuperate. In light of all the investigations going on, Task Force Two had been suspended indefinitely as Internal Investigations prepared its reports to the Department of Justice.

"Are you ready for tomorrow?" he asked.

Nikki laced her arms around him and lay her head against his chest. Tomorrow they returned to reality. Admiral Madison's panel on national security was scheduled to begin, and she was needed to give her own report on the security holes she had discovered. Not to mention that she was the star witness. Everyone in Washington, according to the admiral, was buzzing about the ten-year-old case of the missing operatives, and how one of them made it back after so many years of having been thought dead.

That was the concession from EYES. Not *abandoned* and labeled as a "broken wing," as she had been, but *missing*. In return, she received the acknowledgment she sought, and the case on the ill-fated operation would be reopened. It all tied in neatly with the man who was being held responsible for leaking information and selling national secrets for ten years—Gorman. Everyone in the higher levels was pleased. They had someone to blame.

Nikki was only happy about one thing, that it wasn't Rick that they were staking, as they had all originally intended. She hugged her husband a little tighter.

Sensing her thoughts, he dropped a kiss on her head. "Nikki?" His finger tipped her chin. "Are you going to be all right when you go in to testify?"

"Yes," she assured him. "I was just thinking about you. If not for certain events, you'd be the one they'd hang because Gorman had so much over them. With the missing director from administration and your secretary, with Erik's files and testimony, and with Admiral Madison's support, the right person is standing trial."

Rick framed her face with his hands and tenderly traced the delicate bone structure. He smiled down and shook his head. She was still protective of him, still thinking about his welfare when tomorrow was *her* moment, *her* day of recognition.

"You forgot the most important thing, little bird," he said.

"What?"

"You." He lifted her into his arms and turned toward the bed. He laid her down on the silk sheets and settled his weight slowly on her welcoming body. She opened her legs and gave a sigh of pleasure. He kissed her briefly before continuing, "You're the most important thing. Without you, I'd still be half alive. Without you, there'd be no future. As long as you're with me, I feel I can do anything. Tomorrow, when we return to Washington, we'll face every challenge together."

"Yes," Nikki murmured, wrapping loving arms around her husband. "So much to do. And there's still Cam and Patty . . ."

"We'll find out what happened to them," Rick promised. "We've already zeroed in on the shipments, so we've got an idea where they might be. It's just a matter of getting more information from those drop-off areas."

"I know." Tomorrow their lives would again be filled with details, bureaucratic rules and red tape. This time, they sat in the driver's seat, in control of their future. But for now, she wanted Rick all to herself one more night. "Kiss me."

He did. And he made such sweet love to her, her body sang like the harmonizing chimes in her garden.

Epilogue

Admiral Jack Madison scowled as he hung up the phone. He had a major problem on his hands. One of his SEAL commanders had been arrested overseas. Interpol would not release him until he had been ID'ed, but none of his men were supposed to be over there. Damn it, he could not afford another scandal while he was still dealing with the one here over Gorman.

He needed outside help and, as luck would have it, Tess Montgomery was in town. Using his secured line, he punched in her number. She picked up almost immediately.

"T., I have a problem."

"It must be big if you're calling me, Jack."

"I need you to help me with an international jurisdiction problem. Here's the number to call my man, Hawk McMillan. He'll give you all the details."

"Oh, Stash's cousin. Interesting. Is he the one in trouble?"

"No, it's another team commander. Jazz was arrested by Interpol. Can you handle it?"

T. didn't hesitate. "Of course. You helped Nikki Taylor. I can do no less with one of your operatives, Jack. I'll get in touch with you soon. By the way, I happen to have something going on there that needs some macho SEALs. It has to do with our 'missing' laptop, by the way. I have a proposition to make—a Joint Mission."

Jack Madison smiled. T. always took advantage of a situation. "Jazz and Hawk are two of my best. You get Jazz out and they're all yours."

"Not me, darling. I have just the right woman to get Jazz out of trouble."